The School Run

HELEN WHITAKER

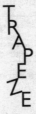

First published in Great Britain in 2019 by Trapeze Books,
an imprint of The Orion Publishing Group Ltd
Carmelite House, 50 Victoria Embankment,
London EC4Y 0DZ

An Hachette UK company

1 3 5 7 9 10 8 6 4 2

A CIP catalogue record for this book is
available from the British Library.

ISBN (mass market paperback) 978 1 4091 8372 3
ISBN (eBook) 978 1 4091 8373 0

Typeset by Born Group

Printed and bound in Great Britain by Clays Ltd, Elcograf S.p.A.

MIX
Paper from
responsible sources
FSC® C104740

www.orionbooks.co.uk

For Mum and Dad

I

5 September 2018, first day of term, 8.40 a.m.

30 places available

Lily

Enid is emitting the kind of piercing sound that makes Celine Dion's highest octave climb seem effortless.

'Baby, why don't you stand there?' I try, leading (read: dragging) her to a wall next to the inside gate of the playground. It's the perfect spot – nice red bricks to set off the bottle-green uniform – and from the line of other three-year-olds being nudged in front of it, the other parents clearly agree. It's the kind of set-up Instagram loses its #nofilter mind for. Enid snatches her hand away. The green of her uniform is currently being offset by the puce of her cheeks. To be fair, the Coco Pops sugar rush isn't helping with the hysteria, but after she lobbed my first attempt at breakfast – the both nutritious and filling scrambled eggs and toast – on the floor approximately four minutes after Joe left her sitting angelically at the table, I did not have the patience to try and reason her into eating something more nourishing. That's today's excuse, anyway.

And right now I don't have the patience to argue over this photo. I have to be at my office, report in hand, in sixty minutes. My conscientious parenting decision to walk the short distance to our first day at St Peter and

Paul's nursery (and thus prove to myself that I am a Good Person who cares about the environment) has buggered up everything. My work commute is forty minutes, and I now have twenty minutes to hustle this tiny bag of tantrum into her first day of preschool, get her settled, and take a cute photo that will procure me enough likes on Facebook to feel like a successful parent (that number, FYI, is 100). One of Enid's pigtails is sagging, she's got a milk stain on her brand-new big school sweatshirt, and now she's doing the cackling sob thing that she normally reserves for the hour before bedtime when we've been on a massive day out. It usually means she's about to go Britney 2007.

'Enid,' I coax, mentally cycling through my list of bribes, but great, now the primary school head teacher has just turned up in the playground. First chance to make a good impression. He looks distinctly speechy, even though he's milling around and not making any moves to start talking. Everyone is ignoring him and taking selfies with their kids. I can see Jusna from church playgroup smoothing Mo's hair down and telling him to drop his head slightly to the left as she blitzes her camera roll, and Yasmine has commandeered the perfect Pantone red wall for Arlo. Of course she has. Yasmine, Jusna and I were in the same NCT group, and she once told me she thought parents who let kids under three eat chocolate should go to enforced nutrition classes. I have never been friends with Yasmine.

Right, this is not a Rihanna gig: someone needs to hustle the main act onto the stage. Until today, at private nursery, I could luxuriate in the 8 a.m. until 6 p.m. hours, and also quickly drop her off and run, but now we've swapped to the preschool attached to St Peter and Paul's – the first step in our 'get Enid into the off-the-scale-Ofsted-good C of E school' strategy – we have to become part of the 'community'. The head is obviously trying to give today some ceremony. 'Mr Brown, did you want to say a few words?' I call over to him. He's about eight thousand years old in a double-breasted grey suit, bald aside from the tufty grey patches that dot each side of his skull. He flinches as though he's heard someone but can't place the voice.

'Everyone! Mr Brown is making a speech,' I say, in my best positive-member-of-the-community voice, while chivvying Enid over in an affectionate headlock. The playground rings with the sound of three- and four-year-olds going 'shhh'. It's very cute. I remind myself that these three- and four-year-olds are still our competition. There are thirty intake places available for next year's reception class, with priority given to children living in the tiny catchment area. Last year they had three applications for every place, and once you've taken into account kids whose older siblings already attend, and the goddiest godly Christians, who are a shoo-in, that means there are actually even fewer spaces than that.

'Good morning, everyone. I'm so pleased to welcome our new nursery intake to St Peter and Paul's infants school. It's traditional for us to open up our preschool a day earlier than the infants to get the new ones settled. I recognise some faces from church –' I crane my head up a bit higher. A year I've already been going to that church and hanging around for the post-mass playgroup. He'd better recognise us. '– And for lots of us this is just the start of your St Peter and Paul's journey. Just a few bits of housekeeping before we line up, and join together in prayer—'

God, always with the bloody prayer. Enid's already embraced it and become part of the prayer police. I wonder how other parents deal with it when their kids remind them to say prayers at bedtime, and you can't decide whether to

3

hypocritically go along with it or explain that Mummy only pretended to believe in God so she'd get into the good school, but we must never tell anyone. It's the first one, clearly – only an idiot would trust a three-year-old with that kind of information – but it doesn't mean I don't feel stomach-clenching guilt on a daily basis about pretending to be nine hundred per cent more goddy than I actually am.

Bore-off Brown is still wittering on. 'As many of you will know from mass on Sunday—'

Which, of course, is the week we missed. Even though we had a legitimate skive. We were visiting my mum and dad in Leeds before term started.

'– Reverend Terry is retiring at the end of the month, and so I'd like to take the opportunity to introduce his replacement, Reverend Will.'

Mr Brown gestures to the tiny Victorian-era doorway of the main infants school building. A six-foot-tall man in his mid-forties appears. He has matinee idol-style swept-back salt-and-pepper hair, and black jeans and a jumper on. We all wait patiently for the hot dad to move and let the new reveren out. And then I clock the dog collar. This is no God-like dad, this is a *man of God*. *He* is Reverend Will. Realisation hits us all simultaneously and a humming undercurrent of breathy nervous chatter ripples across the playground. Because he's not just church-hot, like the bloke who plays the guitar at St Mary's on Sunday, and everyone (me) has developed a crush on because he's male, under retirement age and it makes church less boring if you fancy someone. He's *properly* handsome. He strides over to where Mr Brown is standing and gives the crowd a small wave in greeting. I swear I see Ava's mum swoon as he smiles and gives her a look of recognition. He's basically the Ryan Gosling of clergymen.

4

Mr Brown is deep in his inspirational first-day speech but has lost all the remaining parents who were pretending to listen, male or female. We're all too busy ogling Reverend Will. 'As we start another school year, I'd just like to encourage you all to take the time to reflect,' he says. 'To pause and think about the moment we're in, and not just as something to record through your phone. At this point, let me take the opportunity for a gentle reminder that there is to be no photography inside the school premises, which includes the playground.' Ninety-nine per cent of the parents shove their phones into a pocket or bag.

I check my watch. I now have fourteen minutes until I need to leave for work. I hope he's wrapping this up.

'We spend so much time rushing around and thinking about the next thing, the replacement, the upgrade, buying into the idea that new is better and change needs to be instant, that we don't often reflect on what is happening *now*.'

I look down at Enid, who is now hanging onto my right-hand side, chubby little cheek pressed against my thigh, and give her a squeeze. She seems to have calmed down, at least. Maybe this dreary speech is lulling her into calmness the way the white noise machine used to when she was losing it at naptime as a baby. I should record this speech to play back tonight before bed.

'It's important to remember that not everything has to keep changing. Consistency can be reassuring, and some things improve over time, the longer they are simmered. Like stew,' he says, chuckling at his own joke. 'Or love.'

I snort, and the mum next to me looks over. I think I recognise her from the maternity leave circuit too. Baby sign language or baby sensory or baby show tunes. One of them. They've all blurred into one long circle of singing.

'Love stew,' I whisper. 'Sounds a bit spunky.'

Her face crinkles into what I think is going to be a smile, until I clock the look of distaste around her mouth. Luckily a round of applause punctures the moment. Mr Brown has finally finished.

'So welcome to preschool, children and parents!'

I give Enid a squeeze and then release her. 'Off you go then, Enid.'

'I DON'T WANT TO!' she screams.

Fuck. Nine minutes. I need Mr Brown and his dulcet voice over here now. I thousand-yard stare into the distance, pretending to ignore her. Previous experience has proved that trying to reason with her in this state only makes it worse, and what we need is a distraction, preferably the hot rev, but he's disappeared. Instead I'm surrounded by other parents silently judging me for ignoring my feral daughter as she thrashes like a badger in a trap. A couple, including Bex who lives a few doors down from me, shoot me a sympathetic look, but once Enid realises that she has an audience she takes it up to eleven, throwing in some pretend crying for good measure. I'm about to pull out an emergency bag of Buttons when I catch sight of Yasmine crinkling her nose in my direction, as though her kid has never had a public meltdown before.

I see a flash of red hair coming in through the gate. At least someone's arrived later than us. Plus, their arrival pulls Yasmine's judgy face away from us and angles it in their direction. Oh my God, it's Imogen! I thought I'd seen on Facebook that she was moving here from south London, but on the rare occasions she pops up on my feed, I tend to scroll over her statuses without taking much notice. Weird how quickly you can go from having intimate and real-life daily knowledge of exactly what

6

(and who) a person has in their body, to a social media algorithm fading their existence out of your Facebook page entirely. I had no idea Imogen was even pregnant, until a load of old mutual friends liked Imogen's birth announcement, six months after I had Enid. And that was nearly four years ago.

'Lil!' she shouts over the thrum, seeing me – or, more likely, seeing Enid going nuts. She seems unaware that Mr Brown is at the front about to launch into a Hail Mary, and that she's getting pointed looks from all the other parents to shut up, because despite her middle-class mum uniform of rolled-up boyfriend jeans and Selfish Mother 'MAMA' sweatshirt, she looks as harassed as I feel. Thank. God. Her face is splodgy where it looks like she's been either shouting or crying, and her little girl, Winnie – her total mini-me with light red hair and freckly nose – looks the same. My heart lifts. Maybe we can join forces and get out of here within the remaining five minutes I have left. I give a warning nod in his direction and she realises that she's interrupted the whole welcome assembly, bowing her head in exaggerated piety for the prayer. She gives me an embarrassed smile once we get to 'amen'.

'Whoops. Not a great start,' she says, mouthing 'sorry' to other parents in the vicinity, but now that Mr Brown has broken off into some one-on-one chats and isn't surveying the crowd eagle-eyed, they look much less bothered about her tardiness. Funny, that.

'I can't believe it's you,' I say. 'How *are* you? And did you have the same nightmare as us getting out of the house this morning?'

Imogen folds me into a hug. She still smells of the same Marc Jacobs Daisy perfume she used to. 'It's not been the best, no.'

'Tell me about it. Madam lost her shit at breakfast and I've been trying to bring us back from the brink ever since. Then I managed to offend one of the rabid Organics over there with a joke about the headmaster. Thank God I didn't tell her that the only thing that will get me out of here before she reaches Armageddon-level meltdown is the promise that we'll go to McDonald's for tea after big girl school.'

Imogen smiles, kind of. But is looking at me the way Louis Theroux might look at a white supremacist in one of his documentaries, all stoic sympathy and controlled non-judgement. The puff of joy I felt at seeing her deflates a little. I don't think she's going to stand here with me laughing at the more frustrating aspects of parenthood, or acknowledge that this whole church preschool thing is part of the game we're all playing to get into the primary school – even though it is.

'Everything took longer because I was just so upset at the idea of leaving her here,' she says eventually. 'The idea that it's every day now.'

'Well, you don't *have* to,' I say. 'There's a whole year before it's a legal requirement. And to be honest, it's a total ball-ache swapping from her previous nursery to this one as it's only open term time and school hours. But if you want to get them to start in reception next September, you've got to do it, haven't you? They've been praised for focusing on each child as an individual, their self-confidence, individual strengths and interests, and not just pushing them through the production line of ever more government tests. But saying that, they *really* get them through the government tests. The SAT scores are consistently excellent and it's the only primary school in the borough with a solid legacy of eleven-year-olds getting accepted to the nearest grammar school.'

Imogen's eyes narrow a shade. She knows exactly what I'm talking about. We've all memorised the same Ofsted report.

'It doesn't mean it's easy, though,' she sniffs. 'And then once I started, it set you off, didn't it, Win?' Winnie's big blue eyes well up, mirroring her mum's, but before I can roll mine, Enid reaches across me for Winnie's hand and smiles shyly. God bless my lovely empathetic child. I have no idea where she gets it from. Winnie grins back and the two girls stand there holding hands, looking completely winsome.

I whip out my phone, one eye out for Mr Brown and his live-in-the-moment no-phone policy (yes, I know there are very good reasons why you don't want adults taking pictures of kids all over the school, but still). It's a definite hundred-liker, only I don't know if Imogen will object to me sticking up a photo of Winnie.

'And now one of just you, Enid,' I chance while she's still smiling, getting a solo pic I know I can use. She gives me a toothy grin and then even lets me cuddle her. 'Is Winnie in St Gabriel room or St Michael?' I ask Imogen over her head.

'Gabriel,' she replies, looking like a fresh round of tears isn't far away.

'Well then,' I say, 'they'll be together. Do you and Winnie want to go and line up, Enid?'

They trot off, looking suddenly very tiny as they're absorbed into the swarm of green-clad pupils in the playground. Imogen is on the verge of losing it, I can tell. Three minutes. I need another distraction, this time for her.

'When did you move here? Don't tell me we were on maternity leave together at the same time in the same place and didn't even know.'

'We only arrived three weeks ago and everything's still a tip. We've moved onto Palmerston Road. It's not ideal, but we're renting until we find a place to buy. Nearer here. It's been a bit of a nightmare, actually – they get snapped up the second they come on the market.'

Of course they do. Prime catchment. Trying to buy a house in the five streets that surround this tiny Victorian building is like trying to get tickets to Glastonbury. Only three thousand times more expensive. I think of our house, bought because it was the only place I could afford, before the phrase 'catchment area' even crossed my mind, and Walthamstow was simply suffixed by strangers with 'What? The *end* of the Victoria line?' rather than 'a few good schools around there'. Somehow, completely by accident I've hit the catchment area jackpot. Just. Ours is the last house in the current zone. We should be in. But only if we can prove that our faith and Christian values are more compatible with the school's ethos than the other applicants, who all live in the catchment area too, and closer.

'I'm feeling really nervous about the move,' Imogen is saying, 'as all my mum-friends are back in Bermondsey. You're so lucky. You must know all the other parents already.'

'Some.' I push away the memory of my maternity leave, twelve interminable months of trying to find ways to fill up the days and wondering where all the people like me were. I couldn't wait to go back to work.

'You'll have to introduce me to some of them.' She nods her head at Yasmine, who is standing with a couple of others. 'Who's that?'

'That's Yasmine, and Kim. They will let your kid play-date with theirs as long as you don't bring contraband into their houses. And by contraband, I mean anything that contains refined sugar.'

'Oh. Are they nice?'

'Sure. If you're obsessed with organic food and think a kid's birthday party should be policed by Cruella de Vil disguised as Deliciously Ella.' I don't tell her Enid's not been invited to one of their birthday parties since 'the yard of Maltesers incident' when they all turned two. It's been pretty awkward since I've started to run into them in church over the last few months. Although of course Yasmine had been going there for over a year by that point, so I was the outsider. As always. And she was able to make a snide comment about me being new to the Christian faith, as though we weren't all there with exactly the same intention.

We're all shushed again for a quick Lord's Prayer. The children are chanting it as loud as they can, so no one notices me miming the words. Then they start to file in, Enid and Winnie waving as they're led through the tiny door.

Imogen sniffs loudly as they disappear, and then looks over at Livvy's's mum and her clan, or as I think of them from playgroup, The Basics. 'What about them?'

'Yeah, they're fine,' I say in what is hopefully a neutral voice, and steer her towards the gate. Imogen's eyes flick back to me, suspicious. Oh, bollocks to it. This is Imogen, my old friend Imogen, who once rejected a man because rosé was his favourite wine.

I drop my voice to a conspiratorial whisper. 'They just have no personality outside of their children, and every conversation I've ever had with them circles back to the kids. I *think* some of them have jobs, but if they do they never talk about them, and they seem to post a Facebook photo album every single day. And then they write things underneath like #soblessed and "my world" with no trace of irony.'

Imogen does that inscrutable Theroux face again. She used to do the same thing after I'd explained to her in great detail why I was going to meet the useless bloke I was seeing at a bar at 11 p.m., even though the only time he ever texted me was around that time on a Friday night.

I point at the group in front of us who are all in super-skinny jeans and UGGs, and are completely fresh-faced, probably because their ovaries are at least ten years too young to hear the clarion call (labour-induced howl) of a birthing suite.

'That lot are all au pairs. Which isn't to say they're not nice, but it's a rotating roadshow. They'll probably be replaced in a couple of months when the current one is overworked or goes backpacking around Europe. If you ever meet the kids' actual parents, it will take them twelve seconds to tell you why they have no time to talk because they have to get to their BIG JOB.' I stop, remembering how dedicated Imogen used to be to her PR job. She was out at launches every night and spent weekends until all hours putting together campaigns. She could well be one of them. 'How's life at the PR coalface?' I ask. We're almost out of the playground.

'I'm freelance now,' she shrugs, throwing a final look back to the closed door, behind which our kids are now ensconced. 'And I do a blog. Part-time. Ish. I just couldn't imagine going back full-time once Winnie was here. It changes everything, doesn't it?' Her face is earnest as she adds, 'But I wouldn't have it any other way.'

She means it. Every word. And all I can think about are the dozens of component parts in that statement that I disagree with. And that I know I have to throw myself into preschool life. And church life. And becoming part of it all. My daughter's future depends on it.

But I'm on minus four minutes. Instead I shout that I'll text her and run to the tube.

2

Imogen

I watch Lily's suit-clad back retreating and let out a breath I didn't know I was holding. Even when she's commuting she moves like the distance runner she's always been, hustling with the same controlled movements that always kept her tall, muscular body pounding 10Ks and half-marathons.

I feel like I've had an unexpected run-in with an ex. *The* ex. One where I've moved on, but somehow it's still very important to *prove* that I've moved on. Of course, with an actual ex, Winnie's mere presence would have been proof enough, illustrating as it does that I've had sex at least once since last seeing them. But it's not about sex with friend exes (frexes? Side note: if I wrote a blog on friend exes, would that portmanteau be snappy enough to make it go viral?) because the break-up really is about ideological differences rather than wanting to shag someone else. Five years ago, Lily dropped me, ideologically, and the weird vibe that came off her when I said how hard it was to have Win start preschool was probably only further evidence as to why she made the right decision.

A wave of something – rejection, or maybe just resig- nation – pulses through me, and fresh tears spring to my eyes. Dropping Winnie off, moving, Lily – it's been a lot. I've been like a bag of leaking emotions ever since I had

13

Winnie, and I think my skin got thinner when my belly stretched.

My phone beeps with a voicemail. 'Imogen, Jay here. Just an update to tell you that the two-bed on Holman Road has gone for thirty over the asking price. Be in touch if anything else comes up.'

Great. I speak to 'Jay' from Stow Place Like Home, the estate agency, more than my own mother these days. We need to find a new place to live. Like, now. That was the other reason we were late this morning. Another long phone call about a potential flat in the area, where I reminded him, again, that if any sales fall through we're ready to step in at short notice and already have a mortgage agreement in place. Because this school is the whole reason we uprooted our life in Bermondsey and moved to a completely average rented flat in Walthamstow. It's the Venn diagram intersect between what area we could feasibly afford and my exhaustive Ofsted research. Last year, St Peter and Paul's received almost a hundred applications, and we're still not quite in the catchment area, so if we don't find one before the application deadline in December, we're at a massive disadvantage. So, we have to be the perfect applicants. I banked some historic godliness with regular churchgoing in Bermondsey, but a letter from the old vicar and going to church every week here isn't going to make us stand out. I need to convince the school, the governors – even the other mums, if it comes to making an appeal on our behalf – that Winnie, and we, are right for St Peter and Paul's.

I turn left out of the school gates and start to trudge home, exhaust fumes from the line of cars and buses on Blackhorse Road mingling with the early autumn warmth and stinging my raw eyes. There's a snotty sniff audible even above the traffic and when I turn to see who it's coming from, I see one of the other playground mums has caught up with me.

'It's been awful, hasn't it?' she says, with an embarrassed smile. She swipes her face with a tissue, sticks it into the pocket of her leather jacket and holds her hand out to me. 'Yasmine.'

It's the one Lily just compared to a Disney villain, but she seems nice enough to me. She's maybe a couple of years younger than me, early thirties, all glossy 'bronde' Jennifer Aniston hair and a boho-style billowy printed dress.

'Imogen,' I reply. 'And yes. I knew it would be hard, but I thought at least I'd be able to hold it together. Turns out I'm the one with separation anxiety.'

'Is she your first?'

I nod.

'Arlo's mine too. Even when I was enrolling him, I felt like it wasn't really going to happen, but here they are. It's too quick!'

'Next stop university,' I crack back, and she laughs.

A revving motorbike with a backfiring engine flies down the street, weaving into the cycle lane outside the school to overtake the queue of traffic, only inches from the painted line that separates it from the pavement. He's going so fast it only takes a couple of seconds for him to disappear around the corner, towards the tube station.

'Did you see that?' I shout before I can stop myself. 'Prick. There's a bloody pedestrian crossing there.'

'Tell me about it,' says Yasmine. 'I pass this way at least a couple of times a day, and even when Arlo was in the buggy, nine times out of ten someone would just drive over without even looking. I've been emailing the council for three years to say they need to put traffic lights in.'

'We've only just moved here. Is the school run traffic always this bad?'

'Yep. Did you see that article about the air pollution? On some days, the air quality is worse in Walthamstow than in Beijing. That's my other pet project.' She grins while she's saying it, and it makes me like her.

'I'd love to get involved,' I say, feeling suddenly shy. 'And it's nice to meet a local mum, seeing as I'm – we're – new to the area.' I try and sound less desperate than I feel. 'How do you even make new friends in your thirties?'

Yasmine laughs and gives my arm a squeeze. 'When I gave up work after Arlo, I drifted away from loads of my old friends. I tried to keep in touch at first, but it just became so obvious that all we had in common was proximity, especially the ones that didn't have kids. They just don't get it, do they?'

'Hmmm,' I murmur, making a non-committal noise that doesn't directly agree, but doesn't contradict her either, and hating myself a bit. Who really cares if your colleagues are proximity friends or not, if you can still have a drink and a good bitch with them after work? Plus, I've always hated that 'you don't know real feelings or responsibility until you have children' rhetoric. Probably not the moment to mention it.

'I actually ran into an old friend of mine at the school, so that made it a bit easier,' I say. 'Lily Walker. Enid's mum.'

'Oh,' says Yasmine, stopping so abruptly I almost bang into her. 'Do you know her?' Her voice is neutral. Almost too neutral.

The day we moved into the new flat I spent two hours trawling through Lily's Facebook page while sitting in the half-darkness of Winnie's bedroom, waiting for her to drop off. Every time I thought she'd fallen asleep, I'd get up to leave, before her eyes flew open to check I was still there and hadn't abandoned her in the strange new place. I'd sit back down, in the chair I used to breastfeed her in, and swipe back onto Lil's feed.

There was frustratingly little to disseminate. Enough photos to see where she was in her life (married, still a criminal investigations officer, daughter the same age as mine), but barely any captions, opinion-y status updates or other people tagged in pictures. For the last few years there was hardly even any mention of Joe, who had been the centre of her world before she moved out of the flat with me and bought a place with him six years ago. I couldn't find anything to confirm why I should hate her, not even the phrase 'echo chamber', which fuelled my last FB cull, post-Brexit.

And then seeing her today, she was the same. Spiky, funny Lil. Spotting me across all the commotion and bringing me into her fold. Before being desperate to ditch me. Again.

'I used to know her. It's been years since we've seen each other.'

Yasmine smiles, and starts walking again, as though this is the right answer. 'Well, I'm sure I'll be spamming your inbox about all the projects we have on the go soon enough. Unless you fancy coming for a post-drop-off coffee?' Yasmine pulls out an eco coffee cup from the big, slouchy, acid-yellow leather bag she has hanging off one shoulder and nods to a café with a vintage-style, green and white awning at the junction of Blackhorse Road, where the new student flats face the tube station. The complementary candy colours and old-fashioned fronts of the shops suggest quirky, artisan small businesses, but they house a newsagent, a dry cleaner and an off-licence. The café at the end, though, might as well have a neon 'gentrification' sign where it actually has an organic vegan menu written on a chalkboard outside, along with the promise of free tea for breastfeeding mums and kundalini yoga classes in the back room on a Tuesday night. Two of the other mums from the playground are sitting at the table in the window, the one that offers a prime view of what they're trying to package as 'Blackhorse Village' (a view of the bus stop in one direction and the Costa in the other). I feel a pang of regret that all that's waiting for me at home is some urgent but very boring work.

'That's so nice, but I can't today,' I say. 'The one positive of Winnie starting preschool was getting full days to work and not having to cram it into evenings when she's asleep, but now it's arrived I feel like my attention will be elsewhere anyway.'

Having given up my account manager job at a beauty PR agency after Winnie, I've been freelance, working on smaller ad hoc projects without ever really getting my teeth into something long-term. I've been putting off brainstorming ideas for the launch of an 'avo-toast generation' beauty delivery box until my first official 'work' day, but now it just feels like I'll be going back to an empty flat, while I wait until three o'clock to pick her up. Danny wanted to take the day off and come too, but I told him it would stress Winnie out too much if we crowded her. He accepted it, but has been texting me constantly to check she's OK and now I wish I'd told him to come, not least because I feel guilty for excluding him, and especially having seen Lily. I'm getting a friendlier vibe from this stranger than from my former flatmate. Maybe it's not a bad thing that she and Lily aren't friends.

'But count me in for anything I can do to help with the pollution campaign,' I say. 'I work in PR and actually have my own blog with a bit of a cult following –' by 'cult', I mean 'small to non-existent' but Yasmine doesn't have to know that '– so I'll definitely write something about it on there and try to rustle up some support.'

'Oh, well done.' An impressed look flashes across her face. I get a little kick out of being responsible for it. 'I've been dying to start a blog, but I just never have the time.'

Everyone always says that, but I stay quiet.

'Maybe you can inspire me to get my arse into gear,' she says. 'What's yours about?'

'Being a mum – what else?' I say with a faux-embarrassed shrug, to hide the fact that I am a bit embarrassed. If you'd told me before I had a baby that I'd be interested in being a mummy blogger, I'd have laughed in your face, whereas the post-baby me squealed when Mother Pukka followed me back on Instagram. 'It's called "Manager Turned Mumager". Because of my old job. Although it's still my job, but . . . less so.' I trail off. I'm not really sure what I mean.

'Ooh, I'll look it up. And in that case, I'll email you about the *other* campaign we're starting, at the school. I don't know if you're aware, but the food there is atrocious. I'm dropping off Arlo's lunches every day until they do something about it, and it's the same for Mo and Thea. That's Jusna and Kim's kids.' She gestures at the café again. I'm guessing Kim and Jusna are the women in the window.

'What?' Now I am shocked. 'At the open day they told us that the meals were made onsite, within budget, and lunches were things like home-made stews and spag bol. They were really proud of it. Not a Jamie Oliver-horrifying, reconstituted chicken nugget in sight.'

Yasmine rolls her eyes. 'As though they should be given a medal for doing the absolute bare nutritional minimum. And what about the massive, unhealthy puddings that come with every meal – treacle tart and custard, ice cream. And there's worse.'

The look on her face is so earnest that I dig deep to think of what might constitute worse than a delicious home-made treacle pudding.

'Like?' I prompt.

'Baked beans.'

Right. I wasn't expecting that.

'From a tin.'

I say nothing.

'Do you know how much sugar is in a tin of baked beans?'

I don't. I also don't want to know, seeing as beans on toast is a household staple and one of the few meals I know Winnie will always eat. Yasmine's too nice for me to laugh, but as I look at her solemn face, the effort of *not* laughing makes my eye twitch.

'Well, send me the details,' I manage, fiddling with my phone in my hand. 'My Instagram handle is @manager-turnedmumager, so you can find my email address there. Or I'll be there at pick-up this afternoon if you want to chat more then.'

Yasmine holds out a hand. 'I'll put my number into your phone.'

I pass it to her and she taps away her details before passing it back, saying 'cute' about my screensaver of Winnie. 'If you're sure you can't pop along now and meet some of the others?' She obviously hasn't noticed my lack of enthusiasm over the school dinners and marked me down as an ally, as thankfully the warm smile is still in place. Its beam makes me feel chosen. This is exactly what I was hoping for when we moved. Aside from the beans thing. A friendly mum gang to have pre-pick-up coffee with while putting the world to rights. 'When we're not talking about the handsome new vicar – er, *hello*!' She pulls a face that's meant to look like a teenager crying at a One Direction gig as I laugh and nod in agreement. 'I heard,' she says conspiratorially, 'that he was "asked to leave" his previous parish.'

'No! Why?'

'Apparently he was a little *too* welcoming to one of the *married* congregants.'

We both start snickering like teenagers, and then Yasmine gets a teary look on her face again. 'We'll probably spend all morning wondering how they're all getting on,' she says.

My heart flutters. 'Winnie was so nervous. I'm really worried about her. It's almost worse now they aren't babies any more because you can't control everything they do. It makes me long for the early days when I could keep her safe with me.'

'I'm the same. Hopefully they're making friends with each other!'

A lorry rumbles past us, displacing the claggy air and wafting the fabric of Yasmine's maxi dress tight across her body, away from the road. There's an outline of a small but unmistakable bump on her stomach. She strokes the material gently back, her hand lingering on her belly. I did that all the time when I was pregnant with Win, even before I had a bump to prove that she really was on her way. Yasmine catches me looking and I stuff my clenched fists tight into my jeans pockets.

'You know what they say when you're sad that they're not your baby any more?' she says.

'What's that?' I whisper. The busy road suddenly seems to have gone quiet. It's as though everything other than Yasmine's voice has dropped to a muffle, so I can *really* hear what she's going to say next. Even though I know what that's going to be. I'm so sure that my reflexive rictus smile starts spreading across my face before she starts talking, belying the thump of my heart and the knot of dread that rises whenever this topic comes up. And when you're female and have a three-year-old child it comes up all the fucking time.

'It means it's time to have another baby.'

She grins, in what I'm sure for her is another conspiratorial moment. Half my Bermondsey NCT lot are on to their second now. All mums together, and we must be crazy to go in for round two, but we're going to do it anyway, hey? Except Danny and I haven't even talked about it.

I wish I could flee as fast as Lily did.

3

1 p.m.

Lily

'They found four hundred thousand litres of booze in the warehouse, worth over five hundred Gs in duty. It'll be on the front page of the *Yorkshire Post*, the Sheffield *Star* and the Donny *Mercury*, not to mention the six o'clock news.' John is sitting on the edge of my desk and waving around an email printout from his counterpart in the Sheffield office. Aside from the fact that he's in his fifties so has been here forever, you wouldn't think he was the bureau chief. I think he's had the same three ill-fitting suits on rotation since the eighties, and they're all foul. This one looks like it could once have been charcoal in colour, or dark blue or slate grey, but now it's just some random muddy tone with shiny patches on the elbows.

'That's a brilliant result. Well done Yorkshire.' I'm always weirdly pleased when my home region does well, even if I haven't lived in Leeds for fifteen years.

'Yep. They're looking at seven years at least for the bloke at the top. *If* they can get a conviction.'

I nod. A raid to impound the contra is one thing. The court case to make it stick is another, involving endless paperwork, and covering their arses to make sure the loop is fully closed.

At our HMRC office in a squat, strip-lit government building in Vauxhall, we deal with duty evasion, diversion fraud and many other high-volume scams that involve people bringing fags and booze into the country without paying tax on it. Duty evasion is probably the least sexy-sounding crime ever, but we all get a buzz out of the surveillance, meticulous case-building and raids that sometimes (OK, once) involved me dragging a suspect out of a car window in the exact way they taught us to during our training. Especially when it leads to a big haul that then leads us to a guy (and yeah, it's always a he) who considers himself a Mr Big in the fraud game. While we're pleased for Sheffield, we're also excited to get intel that their case is part of a bigger framework, and that the network is operating out of our patch, in Greater London.

'I need that second address checking ASAP, Lil.' John says ASAP as one word. Just like he says Gees instead of pounds when he's talking about money, and 'binos' instead of binoculars. It's a weird hybrid language of *The Wire* and *The Bill* and I'd take the piss out of it regularly if I didn't also do it myself, especially when I'm fired up about a big case like he is now.

'I'm on it.'

Somewhere under John's left bum cheek, my phone vibrates with a text.

''Scuse me, John,' I say, nudging him to one side to pick it up, and ignoring how warm it feels to the touch.

It's Joe.

The toilet wasn't flushing when I left. Think we'll need to get the plumber back.

'We' presumably means me, seeing as the fact that he's telling me means he obviously hasn't done it, and as he's now on his way to Heathrow to catch a flight to Detroit for work, he isn't going to. Unless he thinks Enid and I can last until he's back on Friday without using it.

A pang of worry pulses through me. I hope Enid's OK. What if she needs the toilet there? Will she feel comfortable asking to go? We barely squeaked in with accomplishing the mandatory toilet training before she started. Is she making friends? Would they call me if she was upset but wasn't ill? I have no idea. I distract myself by being annoyed at Joe instead.

OK, I tap back.

Did you take that lasagne out of the freezer to defrost before you left?

. . .

Sorry, forgot. Give E a big kiss from me when you pick her up.

If he'd told work he couldn't go on this trip then he could have given her a first-day kiss in person. But God forbid.

'Lily?' John is glaring at me, and now Eddie and Sanj are standing beside him. 'Sorry if we're interrupting your social life,' he says.

'Fuck off,' I fire back, with a smile. He doesn't bat an eyelid, just runs his hand through his thick dark hair – he's very proud of the fact that he's neither started greying nor thinning – and fiddles with his tie, a skinny zigzag number that doesn't work at all with his suit. I'm guessing one of his kids bought it for him.

'Can we work out who's going on the recce this afternoon?' he says, looking at the three of us in turn. We're all dressed in near-identical navy suits. Even though there's just a vague 'office wear' dress code in our typical government office building – slightly too airless, painted an apparently well-wearing but slightly depressing institutional shade of cream, with handmade posters everywhere informing people not to leave unwanted printouts to pile up in the trays – there seems to be an unspoken agreement in my team – me, Eddie, Sanj – that we interpret the dress code as smart. The men, both tall, dark and at an age where they sign up for weekend triathlons, carry a suit well, so that's probably why they're so keen on it, while I've always been rubbish at clothes shopping and working out what suits me versus what gets me taken seriously. Back when I first started, I was twice mistaken for a PA at meetings while wearing some variation of a dress and a cardigan, and since then have been one of those people who stocks up on multiple identical trouser suits in the Next Christmas sale.

'Not me,' I say. 'I've got a half-day in lieu, so I can't. I'm going at two.'

'Any chance you can swap it for tomorrow?'

'No.'

John holds my gaze but I keep it steady. He turns to Eddie.

'In that case, mate, you're up.'

Eddie looks pissed off, but I don't offer an explanation. I've found that the best way to deal with anything child-care-related here is not to, just to give a hard no when I have no other choice, and make sure it doesn't happen too often. The whole concept that I can't just drop everything for work would be alien to John anyway. He's got four boys aged between eight and eighteen, but he's also got a stay-at-home wife who deals with the logistics of pick-ups and drop-offs and feeding and clothing everyone and, well, everything. Whether she's happy with that arrangement I've no idea because I only see it from his side, but it seems to work absolutely fucking brilliantly for him.

And Eddie hasn't got any kids. Despite the fact that he's good-looking, intelligent, capable of holding down a job and owns a flat, he's been single for most of the time I've known him, which, as we started at the same time in our mid-twenties, is ten years. Depending on how much he's had to drink, he's either totally fine that he hasn't been 'shackled' by 'some demanding woman' or thinks he's in love with *me*, because I am neither demanding nor interested in shackling him. Sometimes I'm barely interested in talking to him and I'm definitely not interested in shagging him, so you can see what level of emotional intelligence he's at, and the real reason he never has a girlfriend.

Meanwhile, Sanj is about five years younger than us and may or may not have a girlfriend, depending on whether it's on or off with Mia at the moment. She wants to get married, he doesn't. She breaks up with him, he ends up talking her round. Then the cycle starts again. I'm convinced she'll waste her late twenties on him, in the way so many of my mates did with some feckless bloke, and then Sanj will meet someone else during one of their fallow periods and marry her within about a year. He's not a bad bloke, just a commitment-phobe – until he meets someone he wants to commit to.

'I'm too senior to go out on these recces now, chief,' says Eddie, pulling a face. His mockney accent (he's from Chiswick) always gets stronger when he's trying to convince our boss to take his side.

'If that's your way of trying to say I should do it, how many times do I have to say it: we started here at the same time.' It still irks me that Eddie is further up the hierarchy than I am, not because he's not good at his job – he is – but because I haven't also been recognised for being equally good, if not better, at mine. Because I had the audacity to go on maternity leave, I missed my chance to get promoted, and instead have to wait for some arbitrary moment to come around for another shot. Also, it means that Sanj and I are on the same level, and I am definitely better at my job than he is.

'But you're criminal investigations officer and I'm senior crim—'

'God, *this* again. We literally do the same job. You're senior in *title alone*, because I wasn't here during the last round of promotions – three years ago.' I see John sidling away to avoid having to get involved in the ongoing mystery of why I haven't been promoted yet.

'Which means I have a year's more experience,' says Eddie. 'That's what happens when you take a year off.'

I sidestep the phrase 'year off', in case I actually kill him, and take a breath.

'If we end up raiding a warehouse as stuffed with loot as the Yorkshire one, you'll be gagging to claim the case as your own, so pipe down and do the recce. And then if you end up having to stay there on surveillance I'll come and relieve you tomorrow morning.'

He smirks and opens his mouth to talk but I put a hand in front of his face.

'If you were going to make a joke about me relieving you, don't.'

He and Sanj both laugh. 'Ooh, sorry Lil, have you caught a touch of the #MeToos?' he says in a faux-whiny voice.

'Good to see that a global movement to clear scumbags out of the workplace has been boiled down to a sarky comment in here.'

'Don't be so stroppy. It's all bants, isn't it, Sanj? God, we don't even know what we can and can't do any more.'

I'm about to launch into a long and reasoned explanation about why flippant comments like that from self-professed 'good guys' are part of the problem, but I've got too much to do and they're just being deliberate dicks. Instead I say, 'How about you use this as a handy guide: if you ever feel like a comment you're going to make needs to be followed up with "I was only having a laugh", then just don't fucking say it.'

I turn back to my computer screen to dismiss them, hearing them both lightly grumbling as they go back to their respective desks. Seconds later, a calendar invite pops up from the team assistant. It's for an 8.30 a.m. meeting tomorrow morning, and it makes my nerves jangle and my heart plummet simultaneously. I'll never make it from drop-off in time, but I don't want to have to make my excuses for another appointment so soon. In a couple of weeks, I'll get a childminder to help with the pick-ups and drop-offs – 'wraparound care' as it's known, or 'being able to go to work', as I think of it – but I have to let Enid settle in first.

From: lily.walker@hmrc.gov.uk
DECLINE (WITH COMMENTS)
Please reschedule for 9 a.m. or later.

It's only a few moments before John's response drops into my inbox.

We'll go ahead without you. You can catch up later.

Because, of course. I mean, if we did the meeting at 9.15 it might interrupt John's tea and Sky Sports News break. Meanwhile, to make my dead-on 5 p.m. exits above reproach (although they're still sometimes commented on), I have to ensure I'm never seen doing anything non-work-related in the office, barely take a lunch break and save all my admin and social media scrolling for when I briefly nip out for a sandwich to eat at my desk. Even now, when my half-day off officially started half an hour ago, I'll stay until it's time to go and pick up Enid. Pre-baby, I slacked off as much as anybody. Daytime Facebook posts, gossipy group email chains, birthday lunches that went on way longer than an hour and 3 p.m. Pret coffee runs followed by a chat with someone at their desk. I didn't keep track of the days when I arrived a bit early (or late) or hung about once the clock hit 5.30 (even if the reason I was doing it was because I was meeting someone for a drink), and neither did anyone else. But as soon as you have a hard out, everyone starts keeping a tally of any other time you might be shaving off the system. Or maybe it just feels like it does. I've seen John roll his eyes enough times when asking after staff members only to discover that their flexitime hours mean they've gone home. And the only people who work flexitime here are women. Mothers.

I'm too pissed off to abide by my own rules today and, fuming, I log on to Facebook (fifty likes for the photo so far) while digging my M&S Ploughman's out of my bag. Imogen has also posted a photo from this morning, one of both the girls, complete with heart eyes emoji.

It's really cute. I hit like (she already has ninety-four, despite posting hers an hour after mine), and then fill the comment bubble with a row of broken heart emojis. I wish I'd been less rushed and stressed this morning and had time to hang around for a proper chat with Imogen, one where we got beyond our standard mum chat. It's not like I can vent to anyone here about the juggle or the guilt, or how

30

when I'm not at work and worrying about being shit at my job, I'm at home and worrying about whether my parenting choices will mean Enid grows up to need therapy or become a murderer (but *not* a serial killer. Having a girl means it's statistically less likely, so at least there's that).

We were always able to talk to each other, even the dark thoughts we'd be ashamed to admit to anyone else, like when she told me she genuinely wished her dad had died rather than left her mum when he did. The picture links to her Instagram so I end up on @managerturned-mumager. Terrible name. But there's Imogen beaming out from the profile photo with Winnie. There's a website link too, and the click hole takes me to a blog with joined-up, purple cursive along the top spelling out 'Manager Turned Mumager', and her bio underneath.

I'm Imogen, former PR manager and mum-in-training. Three years in, I'm pretty sure I've done at least 10,000 hours of parenting, but WTF, I'm still nowhere near expert level!

A blog for apprentice parents.

I try not to pull a face. It's not as cringy as some of them, I suppose. She's already updated it today.

---

5 September 2018

PLAYGROUND BADDIES OR BUDDIES?

Sweaty palms, nerves about whether I can handle the classwork and anxiety about making friends . . . it must be the first day of preschool!

And the person feeling all of the above? Well, that'll be *me*.

Why is it when you're trying to stick to a schedule, you end up more disorganised than ever? It took forever to get out of the flat, we were almost late, and I was on. the. verge. by the time we made it. But then she instantly bonded with another kid (hooray for an old friend who materialised with her daughter at exactly the right time!). Meanwhile I'm still sitting here, putting off work and trying to process what the hell just happened.

The last place I want to make an appearance is on a mediocre mummy blog, but I can't help but smile at my cameo. I'll see if she and Winnie want to come over for a playdate at the weekend, and pull up the contacts list in my phone while scanning the rest of the post. I wonder if Imogen is still on the same number.

Thankfully, the second I stepped out of the school gates, I was taken under the wing of another mum who was as raw as I was about 'big school' starting.

We swapped tearful stories about our 'babies' and she told me where I can find her gang if I need some solidarity or support. New school, new flat, new area . . . I was overwhelmed by the new this morning, but you know what *has* made me feel a bit more optimistic? The prospect of new friends.

Oh. So, Imogen has already found some new friends to talk everything over with. While old friends are relegated to a passing mention. I close the browser and find the number I'm looking for.

I'll text the plumber. Get it out of the way.

4

Imogen

The mums along the pavement at the gate have been jockeying for position since three o'clock and the stale mid-afternoon air is trapped between all the bodies, making it even muggier. We're flapping ineffectual hands in front of our faces, while taking small swigs from eco water bottles (apparently everyone got the anti-plastic memo). The mothers around me are all trying to manoeuvre their way into the elusive spot where you can see the door and therefore be the first person to see it open, the equivalent of front and centre in the standing pen at a Beyoncé gig. Yasmine is there and isn't budging. For a slight, and also pregnant woman, she's strong, and she leveraged her Baby On Board badge to get to the front and then pulled me and the two other mums I saw her with earlier, Jusna and Kim, via her slipstream. As there's a big sign on the gate saying we're categorically not allowed in the playground unless expressly invited in by a member of staff, and even then, MUST go through the entrance next to the school office, this is as close as we're going to get.

Lily's just arrived and is further along the road, looking sweaty and out of breath in her office suit. I give her a wave. She smiles back, a bit distracted, half pulls a plastic bottle of Pret water to the top of her bag and takes a furtive sip before pushing it back down again, hoping no one has noticed. She then frowns and pulls her phone out of her jacket pocket.

'Here they come!' Yasmine calls and the gate opens, letting us stream in to pick up our charges. I get into the building and look over the stable gate door into the 'big room' as we're told everyone refers to it, and see Winnie sitting with Enid, examining a pile of Duplo, their faces etched with concentration, as though they're working on an intricate restoration plan for a listed building. My heart swells: there's something particularly cute about watching her when she doesn't know she's being watched. Along with watching her while she's asleep, it's the time I can barely believe that I created a living, breathing person, one that now has sentient thoughts and an inner life. Usually she punctuates these moments of me marvelling silently at her with a declaration like 'I need a poo', which reminds me that children are also masters of timing.

'One day of nursery and they've started their own architecture practice,' says Lily, coming up beside me into the peg-lined corridor that opens up to the pick-up zone at the door. She's got a clammy film all over her face, her hair frizzing out of her ponytail from the humidity. I remember the summer tube sweats well, and do not miss them. 'Do you think they've been playing together all day?'

'I hope so. Look at us with our children who are friends.'

'I don't think it would ever have crossed our minds back in the days when our night bus route home to Shoreditch at two o'clock in the morning was our biggest concern.'

'That took up *a lot* of brain power when we were drunk, had no money and neither Uber nor the twenty-four-hour tube had been invented yet.'

She bursts out laughing. 'The record was five different buses, wasn't it, and it took two and a half hours. God forbid we got a cab.'

'Who could afford *that* in 2005?'

Lily's phone, in her hand, shrieks again and she looks at it and sighs, throwing me an apologetic smile before ramming her finger hard on the 'accept' button.

'Eddie, for fu— *eff's* sake, what now? I told you I can't get that data, I'm not in the office at my machine. I left twenty minutes after you did. Ring Sanj. He was doing a deep dive into the SMS situation.' She wanders back out of the front door to deal with the call, and Yasmine appears beside me holding Arlo by the hand. His chubby little arms are criss-crossed with green paint and his brown hair is sticking up at all angles. All the kids coming out look a bit like this. Sweaty, exhausted, covered in arts and crafts, happy.

'A few of us are going back to mine for a play in the garden. Do you and Winnie fancy coming?' Yasmine asks. 'I've made a few first-day treats, and it could be nice for you to meet some of the other mums. We might even open a bottle of fizz and have some bubbles while they tire themselves out in the garden.'

'That sounds brilliant. I'll nip into Tesco on the way and get some prosecco.'

She waves my offer away. 'Don't worry, we've got loads in, left over from a barbecue we had a few weeks ago.'

'Mummy!' The nursery staff member has pointed me out to Winnie and she runs towards the gate, Enid in tow, as an irate-looking Lily comes back inside.

'Hello, baby, did you have a nice day?' she calls, catching my eye and grimacing. 'For a bunch of people who earn a living from collecting and acting on intelligence, you'd

35

think they'd be able to retain the information that I'd booked a half-day. Muppets.' She spots Yasmine and subtly rearranges her face. It looks more try-hard somehow, but closed off. 'Hi, Yasmine. Hiya, Arlo. Don't they all look cute in these polo shirts?'

'Gorgeous,' says Yasmine, mouth smiling, eyes doing the opposite. Her voice is chummy but there's a trace of acid beneath.

'This is my peg, Mummy,' Enid says, one lopsided brown pigtail waggling, pulling Lily over to the row. Their names are printed on card next to a photo of them, only two feet from the floor. There's a note stuck behind each peg.

'There's a charity cake sale next week,' says Lily, unfolding it. 'Fancy making some fridge cake this weekend, E?'

'Yeah! Smarties!'

'What's in fridge cake?' I ask.

'Everything,' Lily says cheerfully. 'You basically melt all the chocolate, biscuits and sweets in your house into a pan, then stick it in a cake tin in the fridge. It's the best thing ever.'

'Can we do fridge cake?' asks Arlo. He's got a little piping voice. So cute.

'I'm not sure that's the kind of thing they're looking for,' Yasmine, who has been watching us, interjects.

'Why's that then?' The tone of Lily's voice matches her expression. Crisp.

Yasmine is trying to look anywhere except at Lily. She seems flustered that she's being challenged. 'Well, if they need donations in advance, it can't be something that has to be kept in the fridge, can it?'

'Hmmm. Yes, I guess it'll have to be a lovely indulgent flapjack or something, then.' Lily's voice isn't so much sarcastic as openly hostile. 'So decadent.'

'Have you checked in about nut allergies, babe?' Yasmine says with a passive-aggressive smile. 'I think I'll do that before I bake anything.' I'm sensing this isn't about cakes. What is this weird beef between them? 'There was a story on Facebook about a woman who died after someone opened a bag of trail mix on an aeroplane.'

'Good point. I'll make hash brownies instead,' replies Lily, turning away and towards me, effectively dismissing her. 'It's so nice to see you, Im. I was wondering if you fancied catching up? We could take the girls to the park on the way home.'

Shit. From the corner of my eye, I can see Yasmine is giving Lily a hard, cold look. She's clearly fuming. I pick some – what is that, rice? – from Winnie's forehead to buy myself some time before I answer.

'Oh, that's so nice,' I say slowly. 'Only Yasmine just asked us over to hers this afternoon.'

It punctures Lily's smile. An awkward second passes. And then another. Yasmine doesn't say anything. The moment simmers between them and I realise Yasmine isn't going to invite her. A flutter of guilt butterflies against my chest. What do I do? It's not my place to invite her. It's also *really* obvious that Yasmine doesn't want her to come.

'Well, that will be lovely,' Lily says in the end. 'You must come to us another time. See the house. We're only a few streets away.'

'Although at opposite ends,' says Yasmine.

'Opposite ends of what?' I ask. *The parenting spectrum*, I think.

'The St Peter and Paul's school district,' says Lily. 'That's a slight exaggeration. If you look at the map online, Yasmine's place is well within the catchment area on her side, but we're right at the edge. It cuts off halfway down my street and ours is the last house in it.'

'Lucky you, though, making it in.'

'Unless they re-zone, but so far so good. There's a house directly opposite us – well, the upstairs flat, actually – that I swear is empty, but according to the estate agent is constantly occupied.'

That rings a bell. 'It's not 200 Morris Road, is it?'

'Yes! That's it.'

'We looked at that one. They were asking for a fortune in rent, even though it's an absolute dump inside. When we rang up to see if there was any chance of improvements being made to it before we considered it, the estate agent said it had already been taken off the market.'

'Sounds about right. It's only a one-bedroom place, so you couldn't fit a family in it anyway, and the old lady who lives in the downstairs flat has been there for thirty years. She's the only person I ever see coming in or out. It's got to be someone renting a second property, just so they have an address in the catchment area, but not actually living in it. Phantom tenants. Whoever's signed the latest lease is probably in this room.' She looks around as though expecting them to materialise in the vicinity.

'I think it's outrageous, fraudulently renting a property like that,' says Yasmine. 'The school is all about community – how can you be part of it when you don't intend to live nearby?'

Easy for her to say. I've read all the tabloid stories about parents renting catchment area properties to use as their school application address, while living far away in a better house, but a worse school district. I've judged them for lying, for denying someone else who really does live closer a place, and for not either moving properly or going to a school in the area they *do* live in. And then I became a parent who couldn't find a decent place to live in the catchment area and reassessed my stance. Bottom line: a fraudulent rental is still cheaper than private school.

Yasmine and Arlo go to retrieve his stuff from his peg, clearing the way for other parents to arrive, and a little boy with a mass of tight black curls barrels through us, making train noises, before heading towards a tall, black woman who has just rushed in, looking even more stressed out than Lily did when she arrived.

'Hello, Jeb,' Lily says to him. 'Hi Clara. Clara and Jeb,' she says, gesturing to them. 'They live down the road from us.'

'Made it. Just,' Clara says, raising a sheepish eyebrow and swiping the film of sweat from her top lip. 'I had to run from Blackhorse Road with all this.' She's in a fitted black suit and block-heeled boots and is pulling one of those briefcases on wheels.

'Any luck dropping some hours?' Lily asks.

'Nope. And my nanny has just told me she's going back to university to do a master's. If someone wants a nanny share I'm in the market. Although I don't have time to actually recruit one right now, so what I mean is, if you need me to share your nanny, count me in.'

'Clara's a lawyer,' Lily explains. 'So is her husband, Mike. We're all usually running to the tube at the same time in the morning.'

'And have an agreement not to talk to each other when we get on so that we can have twenty minutes to ourselves on the way to work.'

'You have no idea how grateful I am that you have as little interest in making conversation at 8 a.m. as I do. It's one of my favourite things about you.' They grin at each other, and their back-and-forth gives me a little pang of envy. It sounds like they barely see each other but still have an easy intimacy that Lily and I haven't shared for years.

'Same. Right, gotta go,' says Clara. 'I've got to go to my mum's in Enfield to speak to the care team.'

'How is she?'

A sad look crosses her face. 'The same, you know.' She nods in my direction and calls 'nice to meet you' before grabbing a scooter from the hallway and propelling Jeb out.

'Her mum has dementia,' Lily says in a low voice. 'It's really tough. She's got a lot of plates spinning.'

'We're off, Imogen, are you coming?' Yasmine calls from outside the door. There's a group of them gathered there, waiting with their kids.

'Come on, Winnie,' I say, realising at the same time as Lily that she and Enid are picking at bits of 'artwork' displayed on the walls and dropping them onto the floor. We both spring at them at the same time, and pull them away.

I give Lily a little wave, but I'm too embarrassed to look at her as I follow Yasmine into the street.

Yasmine's house is beautiful. Semi-detached, wrought-iron gate, art deco mosaic tile path, restored front door with cast-iron letter plate – and that's before you even get inside. As soon as she lets us in, I realise I've actually already seen it, because I spent two hours working today, an hour blogging and the rest of the day on Zoopla stalking houses that have been sold in the area in the last decade. It cost £260k when they bought it in 2007 and as an estimate it's worth at least three times that now – far, far removed from the dumps listed in this area that Danny and I can afford, even though Danny is convinced that my part-time situation is the only thing holding us back from owner-occupier smuggery. He wants to move further out, but I can't face it. I didn't leave a small town outside Leicester and come to London only to end up back in a town on the fringes of a city. There are many different types of wanker I aspire to be – Insta-perfect parent, person who makes her own granola, smug yoga show-off – but not the kind of wanker who moves to a commuter-belt town and then moans about how you can't get decent sushi delivered outside London. I'd settle for a Warner flat – on the right road, that is – one of the Victorian red-brick terraces dotted around Walthamstow and Leyton, but even the smallest two-beds get snapped up straight away. I keep reading in the *Metro* that the property market is 'slowing down'. Ha. There's no more depressing phrase in London than 'closed bids'.

Aside from me, there's Jusna and her son Mo, Kim and her daughter Thea and a couple of others I've only spoken to briefly. They all head straight to the back of the house where huge glass doors at the end of the kitchen recede into the wall and open up into a landscaped garden. Winnie hangs back with me a bit shyly, looking around, while the other kids barrel out into the garden where there's a paddling pool set up, plus a play area that rivals the local park. A couple of minutes later, Arlo runs back in and says, 'Come on, Winnie,' coaxing her into the garden. Jusna, who I discovered on the walk here is thirty, and a part-time copywriter, settles herself into a retro wicker chair on the outside deck, while Kim – Pilates teacher at the local hipster studio – drags the paddling pool a bit closer, before sitting down, pulling her Birkenstocks off and sticking her feet into it. Jusna laughs and does the same. The whole thing is infused with the kind of familiarity that makes it obvious they've been here loads of times before.

I circle back into the house to have a proper look, and the inside is even more impressive than the exterior. All the original Victorian features are restored and gleaming: curlicued ceiling, picture rails, cast-iron fireplace, exposed wooden floorboards. The living room and kitchen have been knocked into one big open-plan living space downstairs, with navy-blue walls, bookshelves arranged by colour and pendant light fittings overhanging a kitchen island that also features a dedicated wine fridge. Plus, as Yasmine mentioned, it's an absolute lock catchment-wise.

Her 'few bits' of a spread is also basically an aisle at Whole Foods, but from our conversation earlier I know she made it herself. Vegan, gluten-free, no-nut brownies that should taste of superiority but are delicious, and a load of savoury party food that the children are already running in to grab as though they're sweets but are in fact secretly laced with their five-a-day. Winnie would be horrified if she knew.

Yasmine's rummaging in a kitchen cupboard to find beakers for the children, so I go over to help, catching sight of her clashing patterned splashback tiles. I almost gasp with envy, and have to stuff a sugar-free brownie into my mouth to stop myself.

'Your place is amazing, Yasmine. How long have you been here?' I ask, chewing, even though I already know.

'Oh, ages. Ten years. You should have seen the place when we moved in. The previous owners had been here since the war and when we tore the carpet up the floor was lined with newspapers from the fifties. It was a real project. But –' she gives a little self-deprecating shrug and points out a tiny smudge of something on the wall next to a copper shelf filled with gleaming matching crockery and succulents '– I've let it all go since having Arlo and being pregnant again. No time for the upkeep.' When we moved into our rented flat, it took Danny and me a week to remember to buy a new bulb for the ancient living room light, and two goes to get a voltage that didn't make the room look more sepia-toned than the off-white walls already did. 'When things are back on track I'm going to project-manage a loft conversion, as otherwise we won't have a spare room when number two turns up and moves into her own. It's getting so poky, but we can't move house. Not until Arlo's safely enrolled.'

I look around her 'poky' kitchen, at the double oven and the double-width, limited edition teal Smeg fridge, and a searing dart of jealousy cuts through me. She pulls a bottle of prosecco out of the wine fridge. 'Come on, ladies, we made it. Let's have a drink to take the edge off our nerves.' She pops the cork and starts pouring it into some glasses.

The sound of the front door opening and shutting reverberates and an expensive-suited man walks into the kitchen, handsome in a crumpled, been-up-all-night kind of way. He's either smouldering or bad-tempered-looking, depending on whether you're attracted to that sort of look or not. He has city finance written all over him. 'After-school club, is it?' He smiles, but it's more of a sneer. Definitely a moody Joaquin Phoenix type.

'You made it!' Yasmine says, opening the cupboard to grab another champagne flute. I admire the soft-close function as she pushes it shut. She goes over to kiss him. 'This is my husband, Tom.'

Tom shakes his head as she goes to pour him some prosecco. 'Only popping by to see how today went. I'm going upstairs to get back to it. I'll have a drink later.'

Yasmine pulls a pouty face at him and makes a big show of sighing in our direction in a 'what is he like' sort of way. 'It was fine. No, it was great. No tears from Arlo. We're having a drink. Now we're all officially slaves to school term dates and our holidays will cost the earth, we have to have our fun where we can.'

Tom glances at her bump with a small but noticeable expression of disapproval. 'I thought we'd decided not to drink during your pregnancy.'

His 'we' has me gritting my teeth, not least because he obviously hasn't given up for the duration, and the tinkly laugh that comes from Yasmine doesn't ring quite true. 'Oh God, not me! Elderflower pressé all the way here. I just wanted to drink it from a glass I didn't feel like a toddler toasting with.' She was definitely about to have a glass of prosecco before Tom arrived, but I'm not going to grass her up.

'Have a glass of the proper stuff, Yas,' Jusna calls as she comes in from the garden. She fans at her face and pulls her heavy black hair from around her neck and into a ponytail. 'One in nine months won't hurt.'

'One!' I say, without thinking. 'I used to prescribe myself a glass a week when I was pregnant. I'd plan meticulously what I wanted and then be counting down the minutes to my drink at the weekend.'

'Me too.' Jusna clinks her glass to mine. 'Near the end I *may* have occasionally had more than one.'

'Well,' says Tom, with a tight smile in her direction, 'we just don't think it's worth the risk.'

Yasmine's smile is extra bright to counterbalance it. 'It'll make that first post-breastfeeding drink taste all the better.'

'In that case, 2021 wants to watch out,' Jusna says with a polite laugh, and we awkwardly look at each other until Tom says 'well' again and disappears out of the room.

'He works in the city,' Yasmine explains, as though it wasn't obvious. 'He'll probably have to head back to the office in a couple of hours and end up sleeping there again.'

'Sounds tough,' I say, knowing how knackering a job can be if you're working in an industry that expects you to be on call constantly.

I think of my last office job, as Senior PR Manager for a range of beauty and skincare products that boasted the most diverse range of skin tone shades at a high street price point. You Little Beauty had exploded in the US, and we were responsible for managing its entrance into the UK. The pressure to get each concealer and foundation into the hands of the right influencers and beauty editors – in their exact skin tone match – was exhausting.

Because they came in fifty-one shades (the extra one was added when E. L. James' lawyer kicked off about copyright infringement) for each product, we had to get fifty-one of the right people (read: social media following of over 10,000) to mention the brand and what shade they were wearing. And it had to be 'organic' rather than paid-for content (because there was no budget to pay them). I learned *a lot* about how much influencers earn for a post.

'I don't know how I used to plan campaigns, organise events, *go* to events and then get up and go to work again the next morning,' I say, trying to think of something sympathetic to offer. 'It must be hard for Tom. I loved my job, but there would have been no way to balance my previous role with getting home for bath time more than once a week, if that.'

Even when I made it home, You Little Beauty's founder – a self-made woman who had remortgaged her house in the States to come up with the idea – would be firing emails at me from America, and expect me to respond, whatever the time difference. It was only the adrenaline from that, and the buzz of seeing her products sell out once they hit Boots, that kept me from total collapse. It was around that time I got pregnant with Winnie, which was even more unexpected considering Danny and I only saw each other a handful of times during that two-month period. 'I couldn't sustain it with Winnie, and I know Dan hates it when he has to go away for work now,' I continue. 'He's managed to cut it right down, but he still always claims she's changed in the few days he's been away.'

'Lucky you,' Yasmine says with a definite edge. 'When Arlo was in the bath the other week and Tom was miraculously home, I shouted to him to grab a new pair of pyjamas. When he still hadn't brought them five minutes later I found him in Arlo's bedroom examining it as though it was an undiscovered planet. He didn't know where they were kept.'

She gives another weird laugh.

'That must get quite lonely at times,' I say, thinking of mornings in our flat, with Danny getting Win dressed and then dancing around the living room with her while I get showered. Most of the time she likes the outfits he puts her in more than the ones I choose; Daddy is cooler than me, apparently.

Yasmine gives me a smile that doesn't quite make it to her eyes. 'You're joking. It's actually less annoying when he has to sleep in the office, because it doesn't piss me off as much when I have to get up in the night with Arlo.'

She tips some more prosecco into my glass as we move through to the garden. Kim jumps up to give her a seat and I plonk myself in a shady patch next to Jusna, checking to see how Winnie's getting on. She's climbing up the slide, which I'm going to shout at her about until I realise that they're all doing it, piling on top of each other as they slide back down.

She said 'when', not 'if'. I pull a sympathetic face. 'Is he not a good sleeper? We have phases of that. When Winnie's ill we take it in turns to sleep in her room so the other one can be on some semblance of parenting form the next day.'

'He hasn't started sleeping through yet, and I don't believe in forcing it. But Tom refuses to do any of the night stuff.'

I choke on a mouthful of my drink. 'What, *ever*?' There's nothing worse than the judgy tone of someone whose family operates in a totally different way to yours, but WTF. Who 'doesn't do' night stuff, except, like, a raging misogynist? And hang on, Arlo still doesn't sleep through the night?

'How often does he wake up?'

'A couple of times usually.'

'You've been up at least twice a night for the last FOUR YEARS?' I find myself asking.

'It's really stressful to leave a child to cry – research has shown that it raises cortisol and results in lowered intelligence and stunted emotional development,' Jusna chips in. The lightning speed with which she recalls that information makes me sense that it's something she's heard before. I panic-googled the same kinds of articles at least twice a week for the first year of Winnie's life, when she woke up every three hours for nine whole months, before Danny decided enough was enough and we started the 'gradual retreat' sleep training method. I sense that this is not a safe space to say the words 'sleep training'. I'm inwardly chanting *don't judge, don't judge, don't judge*, but the scorched earth look Yasmine is giving me tells me my face is failing to stay on message.

47

'You must be superwoman, considering you're pregnant again,' I tell her. 'I fell asleep on the Jubilee line home every evening when I was pregnant, and I didn't have to look after another kid when I got home then. I'd go to bed as soon as I was free of work emails and sleep right through to seven the next morning. I thought I was exhausted, but then she was born and I reassessed where I actually was on the tiredness scale.'

Every mum in the garden is listening and has a faraway, almost hungry look on their face, as though they're remembering a really amazing sexual experience they once had, but I know, like me, they're actually fetishising the amount of sleep they used to get.

Yasmine snaps back first, any trace of previous vulnerability gone. Jusna goes to pour some prosecco into her glass. 'I'm not drinking,' she says, batting her away. 'I've been thinking about all your PR experience, actually, Imogen. And I thought we could definitely use someone with your knowledge to help with events and campaigns. It would be a good way to become part of the St Peter and Paul's community too.'

This is safer ground. Fundraising for new computers and ways to raise interest and engagement – that I can do. And it's the perfect way to make me known to the school as a joiner-inner. I'll contribute to the school community by PRing their cake sales as though they're a waist-trainer on a Kardashian's Insta feed, and prove our worth as enrolees.

I watch Winnie going up and down the slide set in the play area of the garden. There's a little white picket fence around it and a droopy-looking sunflower against the back trellis that clearly formed the backbone of a family summer project. When will *we* have somewhere we know we'll be long enough to plant flowers?

'Tell me what you need,' I say brightly. 'I've started thinking about what we can do to raise awareness of the speeding cars on the main road. We could go in hard to the council, use the idea from that Oscar-winning film about billboards and murders to make a point about child road deaths and send the pictures out on social, using shareable stats. You know, parents leading the charge on creating safer spaces for their children, a campaign that has *Daily Mail* potential.' It would be good to get my teeth into something big again.

'That sounds . . . interesting,' says Yasmine. It's a bloody good idea. I was expecting at least a bit of enthusiasm. She drops her voice. 'Kim's husband works at the council, though, so it might be a little *aggressive*. Maybe we can focus on that later and start with something more rooted in the school itself. Something that has a real day-to-day impact on our children's health, and we can register an easy win – build up a reputation.'

'Oh. OK.' I don't tell her I was researching stats earlier or mocked up a design. A project is a project, after all.

'I had a think today and I've even got a slogan for you.'

I try not to groan. Non-PR people always think it's easy. And I've realised what campaign she's talking about.

She puts the healthy snacks down and actually does jazz hands. 'Ban the Beans.'

5

19 places available (eleven children with older siblings at St P&P's — and therefore an automatic place — identified)

Lily

I'm so sorry to do this again, but could you collect E along with W? I'll be at yours by 5, 5.30 at the absolute latest. New childminder has a family emergency. I owe you. x

The reply bubbles appear.

. . .

I hold my breath.

Sure x

Relief. One thing that's sorted. Imogen to the rescue once again. Now Joe.

Can you pick E up from Imogen's at 5? I'm on a recce and can't leave now.

. . .

Presentation prep has gone to shit. Everyone here is calling their childminders because it's going to be a late one. Sorry!

Fucking sorry! As though I've asked him for a favour, and it's a terrible shame but he can't help me out this time.

My hands are vibrating with annoyance, which is a good job because otherwise I'd be typing *SHE'S YOUR DAUGHTER, DICKHEAD*. Or throwing my phone out of the car window. But not only would that make Eddie look up from the stinking bag of extra-cheesy Doritos he's chomping his way through, but, knowing my luck, that's exactly when the suspect will come home and clock the two bored-looking, desperate-for-a-wee people sitting in a car outside it.

I just look at my phone instead, hoping it will provide me with the answer to my latest childcare crisis. Even if I left now I wouldn't make it to Imogen's for 5.30, and I'm clearly not leaving now. I'm sitting in Eddie's car outside a smart flat in Kingston that we think is owned by part of our smuggling ring. We've been sitting here since 10 a.m. waiting for someone to arrive, so we can confirm his identity and address, and so far he hasn't, so we have to stay until he does. This has always been the dullest part of the job, the laborious on-the-ground confirming to double-check something we already know, but these days, with childcare commitments to consider, the boredom is undercut with an extra layer of stress, ticking down to when I need to be able to go. You'd think you could hack into a computer or email system to get this sort of information, but if – when – the case goes to court, HMRC needs to be able to confirm that a couple of plods – us – gathered the intelligence in real time, on the ground, and can testify to that effect.

So I end up spending a lot of time in a car with Eddie, where we're dependent on each other to stay alert and for entertainment, and I'm quietly and constantly revolted by the bodily aromas that he emits after six hours in a compact space. He probably feels the same about me. Every toilet break, every coffee burp, every time we sweat through a T-shirt on a hot day, it's a weird intimacy. We've always been competitive – we have an annual bet on who can bring in the most arrests, and who can recover the most revenue for the department – and over the past decade we've developed detailed knowledge of the things that really piss each other off. The Doritos directly contravene one of my rules, but aside from that, Eddie's straightforward to work with. On recces, we can't get away from each other, and we have to keep talking. Constant communication is the key to getting the intel on a job, so nothing ever festers.

Joe and I could probably learn something from it. With us, it's all unsaid. Passive-aggressive texts and simmering resentments. It never used to be like that: it started the year after Enid was born. No real rows, but small actions, or small inactions, and me finding it harder and harder to say when I needed help or he wasn't pulling his weight. He had this rotating stock of quiet phrases, meaningless on their own, but that turned into a constant drizzle of judgements and accusations.

'I'm leaving now.' 'I don't know why you let things bother you.' 'You're being emotional.' Tiny lies and denials that made me feel as though I was the problem, I couldn't cope and that I was being unreasonable when I felt trapped and lonely at home with the baby, or resentful of him not clocking off on time to come home and help. The worst was, 'You wanted to have a baby.' As though he hadn't also wanted her. As though we hadn't tried for eighteen months to have her.

'Incoming, Lil,' says Eddie. There's a bloke walking in our direction down the street. 'Look like we're coming back from a date.'

I give him a once-over. Floppy brown hair, smart-casual shirt, stray bit of orange Dorito dust around his mouth.

'It's gone brilliantly if we're sharing a grab bag of crisps in the car. Can't you just pretend you're dropping me off? Why does there have to be a whole narrative?'

'In case he taps on the window.'

'And asks what two people are doing in a car together? And the only reason we'd ever be doing that is if we were on a date, is it? Chill out, Mike Pence.' I watch the man keep going down the road. 'Anyway, it's irrelevant: he's gone. Now you've got time to come up with a better backstory for this whole suspicious "being in a car" thing we're doing.'

'Good one. Does Joe know he lives with a comedian?'

I snort. 'Believe it or not, Ed, you are the most appreciative audience for my jokes.'

The whole time we'd talked about having a baby, I'd assumed it would all be equal. Why wouldn't it be? Joe did his share of the cooking, and it wouldn't cross his mind that I should give up work to be a full-time housewife and mother. Which is why I was shocked into silence when, five months into maternity leave, he made a comment about the state of the house that ended with 'because you're at home all day'. It *was* a tip, but as I looked at the piles of washing-up, the overflowing bin and a laundry basket that was constantly full of reflux-drenched onesies, I realised: he thinks this is *my* problem now. I was too tired to row, so instead just started putting more washes on, incorporating supermarket runs into the walks I did to get Enid to sleep, and making a mental note of when we ran out of things because I knew how many nappies and wipes we were getting through. When Joe eventually came home from work every night, I'd empty the bins and do the washing-up because it meant I could spend fifteen precious minutes on my own, without the baby. By the time I went back to work, 'running the household' was something I did, so I carried on doing it, just on top of a full-time job. Every time I tried to make him share the responsibility we'd run out of nappies, or the washing would sit in the machine for three days while I waited for him to notice. And then when I lost my temper he'd say it was my fault for not reminding him. Which everyone knows is the same amount of mental work as doing it yourself. So I just did it myself.

I suspect Joe would be appalled to discover that he isn't the gold standard dad, because men are so used to being patted on the back by society for doing the absolute bare minimum. 'Giving you some me-time, is he?' the hairdresser said to me when I handed Enid to Joe at the door and went in to have my hair cut and highlighted for the first time in a year. I don't recall Joe skipping one of his bi-monthly trims during the same period, or anyone referring to this basic part of his maintenance routine as 'me-time'.

'Lob me a bag of those crisps, Eddie.'

He snags another from the multipack he's got stuffed in the footwell. His car might stink of stale junk food, but I've never been on a stakeout with Eddie where we've gone hungry, even if we stand a good chance of developing diabetes by the end of it. Luckily he's as obsessed with the gym as he is with sugar, although we've both moaned recently about 'reaching that age' where it all starts to catch up with you. He's absorbed in his phone and looking as dejected as I feel. I glance at the screen. He's on Tinder. Swiping furiously.

'What about her?' I say, as I see a pretty brunette sailing to the left.

'She says she's looking for a partner in crime.'

'And that's bad because you've got enough on your plate with trying to track down the Kingston Kingpin?'

He pulls a 'kill me now' face. 'It's just the kind of shit cliché you read on every other dating profile. Boring.'

'Everyone's a cliché, Eddie. What does yours say? I bet there's a 007 reference on there, or something about being a spy.'

'I'm not showing you,' he says, all flustered. That means there is.

'Come on. I'm not some easily shocked spinster. I did loads of internet dating before I met Joe.'

'You call it internet dating. Pre-app. That proves how long ago it was.'

He's right. It was. It also made trying to meet someone into a full-time job. Working out which site people signed up for if they wanted a girlfriend, rather than a shag, then working out the various sub-genres of people on there. By the time I'd swapped a couple of messages and made a date, I'd filtered out all the obvious loons and all the obvious misogynists, but seemed to be left with the kind of people I might sit next to at a wedding, make small talk with for three hours during the meal and then forget ever existed the second the DJ started playing. Nice, but bland. Weeknights drinking more than I'd want to just to take the edge off my nerves or the tedium. On the rare occasion I liked them, they either ghosted me afterwards or said there was 'no spark'. It was alternately self-esteem-crushing and boring. After a year, I decided to sack it off and put the time I'd spent dealing with the message admin into getting fit again and entering the ballot for the London Marathon. I joined a running club and six weeks later I met Joe. It was that easy.

He still goes to that running club. I don't have time.
My phone buzzes.

You have been added to the WhatsApp group 'St P&P'

. . .

There are at least fifteen phone numbers on this partici-
pants' list but Imogen is the only one that comes up as a
name. That means I'm currently in no individual contact
with anyone else in this group.

Unknown number
Hi P&P Peeps! Thought it might be easier to start a
group so we can easily discuss business and events and
swap information, especially with all the fundraisers
coming up, and the babysitters' group we were talking
about the other day.

Babysitting group? Now I'm interested.

Lily is typing . . .
Sounds great! Thanks for the add.

The grammatically offensive floodgates open.

Who's this?
Who this
Dnt recns dis no
Lily Walker. Maybe everyone should text their name, so I
can save them all into my phone. A few I don't recognise
here either!☺
Gd idea!
Grt!

Lol!

Is some of the business we're going to discuss the hot vicar?

OMG 🔥

💔

Srsly, where did he COME from?

Word is, he's been in Burkina Faso building a school over there. Wonder if he did the actual building 💪💪💪💪💪

WHAT'S UNDERNEATH THE CASSOCK? 🍆🍑

I heard he was 'encouraged' to leave his last parish because he got too close to one of the MARRIED parishioners.

I heard she was a celebrity.

I've thought of one way to pass the time in this car.

Lily: You do know the vicar's number is on the chat list, right?

I put the phone on the dashboard and watch it light up with hastily retrieved messages. I mean, he could be, how would I know? But I'll give it five minutes before I tell them.

The following afternoon and I wish I was back in the car with Eddie, even though we ended up putting in a ten-hour day and I only made it to Imogen's at 7.30 p.m., when she was on the brink of putting Enid in the bath with Winnie because she'd started her bedtime routine. I was firing apologetic texts to her every fifteen minutes from 6 p.m., and she was understandably pretty short with me when I finally turned up. The memory of it makes me burn with shame. But not as much as I'm burning with anger right now. Joe and I have become masters of the blazing row conducted in very low voices, lest Enid hears us arguing over whose turn it is to be responsible for her welfare at a given moment.

'You said you'd go to this one,' I say to Joe in a tight voice. I cannot believe he has announced this now, ten minutes *after* he's supposed to have set off to Mo's fourth birthday party with Enid. Jusna invited us – although to be fair she invited the whole class – and Joe actually volunteered to go.

'That was before this pitch started dragging on,' he says now. 'I'm back in Detroit tomorrow and it has to be sorted today. It'll probably be an all-nighter.' He runs a hand over his stubble. 'I need to check I've got a razor and some spare clothes in my bag.'

My paperwork from yesterday's surveillance also needs to be dotted-I perfect for first thing Monday and my vision of working on it this afternoon, in an empty house, while Enid has some dad-time, is rapidly diminishing. It's replaced by the vision of me impatiently trying to hustle Enid into bed tonight so I can spend the evening cranking it out, and getting pissed off if she dares to not stay in her room.

And also the vision of spending the afternoon at Mo's birthday party, which means facing a group of women who strong-armed me on WhatsApp into 'chipping in' for a tablet for Mo rather than choose my own, price-appropriate four-year-old's birthday present. Instead, Mo now has a better iPad than I do. I suspect Jusna only invited the whole class so that she could rinse as many people as possible for a contribution.

Joe's expensive trainers thud across the stripped floor-boards as he gathers up his laptop and rucksack, decision clearly already made. He always was single-minded. It's one of the things I always loved about him: always doing, always moving, and when you're the object of his focus, it's dazzling. I used to find it sexy. But that's because *I* was his focus. 'These things tend to be mum-centric anyway, don't they?' he says. 'I'd just be the odd one out.'

'How would you know that? How many of "these things" have you ever been to? Loads of dads go.' I think. Maybe.

'Yeah, but you know them all.'

'That's really not a compelling case for me to be the designated representative.' I think of the Organics, who'll be there en masse. And then I think of how delighted they'd be to have Joe turn up instead of me. He'd turn on his charismatic Marketing Man persona and they'd all be really nice, and then he'd come back and tell me how lovely and welcoming everyone was and why was I always moaning about it, because it's just constant coffees and gossip on the parent circuit, isn't it?

'Fine,' I snap. 'I'll go.' Even though it's not a choice at all. 'ENID!' I bellow up the stairs, while pulling on my Converse. If I'd known I was leaving the house I would have made more of an effort than leggings and wet hair stuffed into a topknot. The effect is less Gigi Hadid on a California coffee run, and more sad C-list celebrity being mocked by *Closer* for 'letting herself go'.

Enid barrels down the stairs, in her sparkly leggings (much better than mine) and a fluffy panda sweatshirt party outfit, tangled brown hair flying up at all angles. She races to the door. 'Come on, Daddy!'

'Change of plan, E. Mummy's coming – yay! I didn't want to miss the birthday cake.' Will there even be birthday cake? Yasmine's lot are so anti-sugar that I imagine the 'cake' will be like the fake concoctions they used to make for the pets' birthdays on *Blue Peter*.

Joe gives Enid a big hug. 'Have a great time. Daddy has to go away for work, so I'll see you on Thursday, darling.'

'Buh-bye.' She hugs him back and then runs out of the door, used to Daddy being on a plane, and oblivious to the smash-and-grab that has been exacted on my free time.

'Have a good trip!' I call, following her. And then as Enid goes out of earshot I hiss, 'You *owe* me for this.'

By the time we've made it to the church hall, which is an ugly seventies stuck-on addition to the school, we're a full twenty minutes late, and the inside looks like a hurricane has violently spewed out the cast of *Frozen*. Needless to say, Enid is delighted, but during the first four steps I take into the room from the front door, I manage to accumulate about three tubes of glitter on my ratty black leggings. I wipe uselessly at them, only succeeding in smearing it all over my palms.

'I thought glitter was supposed to be bad for the environment,' I mutter.

'It's actually this great brand call Global Glitz,' Jusna says from behind a trestle table to my left, where she's laying out kraft paper party bags with personalised labels. 'It's a bit pricy but completely biodegradable.' She points to a shrieking mass of three- and four-year-olds. 'We've just started the games, so if Enid pops over there she can join in with musical statues.'

She races off, leaving me alone without my security blanket and wondering who I should talk to. I'm all nervy, the misfit at the school disco, as everyone seems to be in their own little parent groups already. My eyes flit across the shabby church hall. At one end, in front of a hatch that opens up into the kitchen, Mr Brown is having a cup of tea, surrounded by a bevvy of smiling parents.

On the other side of the room, sipping a beer from a small can and looking at the notices on the church hall message board, is sexy Reverend Will in his jeans and black jumper combo. I stifle a laugh thinking about the mums who genuinely thought he'd seen their WhatsApp messages last night. Of *course* Jusna would think of inviting the headmaster and the vicar, along with both of the nursery classes. It proves how inclusive and welcoming (and therefore Christian) she is. All the school governors are probably here too. There are a couple of dads manning a table of grown-up drinks nearby. The vicar catches my eye and waves, and there's a little shock of connection before I instinctively look behind me, because why would someone as hot as him be waving at me? Behind me is Imogen, and she waves back. She's got on a slouchy pair of dungarees and Vans trainers and looks casual but cool, exactly how I wish I looked right now. She was always much better at fashion than me.

'Oh, hi,' I say. 'Listen, I'm so sorry about last night. I can't thank you enough for keeping Enid for her tea. Work's been mental, and this week in particular was a disaster—'

'It's OK, Lily, I told you last night,' she says, with a smile a bit too brittle for me to believe her. 'These things happen.'

'That doesn't mean I should keep burdening you, though. I'll make it up to you, I promise. Let me know when you need a babysitter, and count me in.'

Her expression softens. 'I will. Thank you. Look – the vicar's waving at us. Shall we go and get a drink?'

No, I think, but let her propel me towards him. 'Have you met Will, Lily?'

'Only fleetingly,' I say, just as Will says, 'I don't think so.' Every time I've seen him at the school or church playgroup

I've bolted. I've seen all the other mums flock around him, including Imogen, but there's something about him – not just the way he looks but the way he looks *at* you – that makes me think he'll be able to see right through my faux Christianity. His sermons are so much more tuned in to real-world issues than the last vicar. Every time something terrible happens in the world – which is all the time – he doesn't just offer up platitudes like an American senator after a mass shooting; he actually tries to mobilise people. After a gang stabbing on the high street the other week, he's been going out to try and talk to some of the teenage victim's friends at the shrine. God knows what they think of him, but at least he's trying. I should be making an effort to charm him, but I'd rather he thought I was shy or aloof than a massive hypocrite who's only here for the reception place *Hunger Games*.

'Would you like a drink?' he asks, gesturing towards the table, and the three of us awkwardly wander over to the selection, where Jusna's husband Ajay is enthusiastically tapping a keg of artisan ale. It's all microbrewery brands and organic wine that you can only get from the posh shop in Walthamstow Village. No last-minute supermarket panic-buy for Jusna.

'I always like a beer before I attempt the hokey-cokey,' I joke, picking up one of the cans.

There's a scream from across the room and Imogen's head snaps up. Winnie is disputing her elimination from musical statues. She runs off, calling, 'Can you get me a white wine?' over her shoulder, leaving me and the vicar alone.

I rack my brain for small talk. I can't bolt now, so this is the moment I should be trying to charm him. 'Do you come to many kids' parties?' I ask, and then go bright red. It sounds like an accusation.

There's a strained silence, and I don't know where to look or what to do with my body. It's like I've forgotten how to stand. After a thousand years, Reverend Will gives me a kind smile. 'It's OK, you know.'

'What is?' *The fact that I don't appear to have any friends here, my useless small talk, the overall state of me?* He could be referring to anything.

'People often feel uncomfortable or a bit tongue-tied around me to start off with. They don't want to offend the vicar,' he says. 'And also because' – *you're really fit*, I think, just as he says – 'I'm not a pensioner. They don't seem to have any context for me.'

I laugh, relaxing maybe 0.5 per cent of an iota, even though he's basically just told me what hard work I'm making of this conversation. 'The only points of reference I have for the clergy are *The Vicar of Dibley* or *Father Ted*,' I say.

'*Father Ted* is an old favourite of mine,' he replies with a smile.

'And the only others you hear about are, like, the ones that make the news . . .' It's everything I can do to stop myself clamping my hand over my mouth. That makes two cloaked paedophile references in five minutes. Well done me.

'Sorry,' I burst out. 'I'm not very good at this. Mixing, that is. I always say the wrong thing. I think I'm seen as a disruptive influence.'

'Sometimes being disruptive is exactly the right thing,' he says, giving me a conspiratorial look.

'Like Jesus with the money lenders?' I'm pretty chuffed I remember that one.

He nods and has a swig of his drink. 'I was thinking more of the people I met on the anti-Trump protest last year. I'm not sure it did any good, but at least it pissed him off.'

I laugh. 'I was there too!' I took the afternoon off work and picked Enid up early from her old nursery, so I could take her with me. Joe was livid.

'Where's your accent from?' I ask. His vowels aren't quite as flat as mine, but I can tell he's not from London originally.

'Wakefield,' he says. 'But my family tells me I've gone posh. What about you?'

I laugh. 'Leeds. And I get told that too. It's part of my "London ways", apparently, along with sometimes going to Itsu for lunch – according to my dad nobody really likes sushi, it's just an affectation.'

'My mum has the same sort of disapproval for fizzy water.'

We exchange a smile. I point at Mr Brown; his fan club keeps growing and they're looking adoringly at him. 'It's like he's Taylor Swift at a post-gig meet-and-greet with fans,' I say.

'He's always the most popular person in a room,' Will says, still smiling, but his eyes have a hint of understanding about them. He *can't* be unaware of all the preschool parents that suck up to him, right up until the places are announced in April – not when you never see the unsuccessful applicants in church again.

'I'm sure he is. Absolutely everything to do with his scintillating chat, and not at all to do with parents trying to make an impression that will further their school place application, eh?'

'Lil!' Imogen chimes in, coming back over and picking up her wine, but the vicar laughs, which is satisfying.

I don't know why I'm pretending that I'm exempt from this; I should be doing exactly the same thing. It's half the reason I wanted Joe to come instead of me, so he could smile and deceitfully ingratiate us with anyone here who holds power over our daughter's future education. Every time I come along to a churchy social event I vow to make an effort and then I get here and ruin it. Only this time, instead of lurking at the sidelines, I'm trying to impress the vicar with my school place insouciance rather than thinking of what's best for Enid.

'It's true, though, isn't it? Who are the only people in this room *not* trying to get a special moment with Mr Brown?' I gesture at a group of five mums who have commandeered two bottles of wine and are sitting on the church hall stage, swigging it from plastic beakers. They look relaxed and like they're genuinely having a good time. 'Them. I don't know any of their names, but one thing I do know about them is that they all have multiple children – *older siblings* – who go to St Peter and Paul's primary school. AKA The Golden Ticket.' I extend a finger in Reverend Will's direction. 'Mr Brown's entourage will be over to sweet-talk you next.'

Right on cue, Yasmine comes over. 'Will, can I have a word with you about a little campaign we're launching? We've got a PR expert on board and everything.' The vicar nods – is it me, or does he look a bit resigned?

'See you both later,' he says, as Yasmine leads him towards the kitchenette, giving an almost imperceptible wink to Imogen. I wonder what that's about.

I look over to where our kids are running around the hall, strangely awkward now it's just the two of us, without the buffer of our children or the structure of pick-ups and drop-offs. I try to remember the last time we saw each other before that first day at school. A year or so after Joe and I got married, I'm guessing. That's when I started having the miscarriages, and I couldn't face seeing anyone. I didn't even know how to start talking about it. But we'd already been drifting apart before I moved here. She was single, and I was with Joe; she was consumed by her job and I worked long hours too.

I pick up an empty Thomas the Tank Engine piñata from the table next to the drinks stand. 'Do you think this needs filling up with –' I look at the selection of 'sweet' packets nearby and try not to pull a face '– organic fruit and vegetable treats?'

Kim pops her head up from below, where she's rummaging around with some 'craft sodas', whatever the fuck they are. 'Yes, it does. Thanks.' I can't identify the look she gives me, but it's neither grateful nor friendly.

Imogen and I put our drinks down and start dutifully emptying the bags into Thomas's bum end, then find two A2 sheets of various Tank Engine character masks that haven't been cut out yet underneath the empty treat packets. I top up Imogen's wine, grab another tiny but very strong beer and we flop into a couple of chairs with scissors and a few metres of elastic that needs stringing through the holes.

'How are you settling in to the 'Stow?' I say, trying to cut some eyeholes in a Percy.

'Yeah, OK.' Seeing me about to take out Percy's entire face with the scissors, she grabs the mask off me. 'You do the outlines and I'll do the eyes and punch the holes for the elastic. The flat is . . . well, it's not great, to be honest. It's fine, but it's not *ours* and it feels like such a massive job to get it the way we want it when we could end up moving at any time.' She sighs. 'Danny didn't want to move from Bermondsey until we found somewhere to buy. He said it was stupid to waste money moving into a rental place only to move again, but I convinced him we

66

needed to be on the ground to find a permanent place, because we keep getting gazumped. He's happy to move –' and at this Imogen, who used to think spending time outside Zone 1 was 'pointless', cringes '– further out. Says there's more space and a better selection of schools. But I want to be here. St Peter and Paul's is a great school. We just need to get her *in*. Which means I need to be nearer where you are.' We get into a groove, me cutting the masks out using big, not particularly exact slices, and handing them to her, where she makes tiny, neat snips in the eyes. Craft stuff is another thing she's better at than me. She made some bunting for our shared living room once, which I was convinced was going to be some terribly executed Cath Kidston knock-off, but it actually looked cool once she'd finished it.

'It's not like I'm some property mogul,' I say, swigging my drink. They're far too small and lethal. I can almost feel my inhibitions loosen as I swallow. 'Remember when I told you we were buying it, and you said, "But it's in Zone 3. I'll never see you again"?'

We both laugh, but it's undercut with the fact that we know that turned out to be true.

'That's when I thought nothing fun ever happened further north than Old Street. Now you've got a three-bedroom house in the best school district in Walthamstow. You and Joe are all set. You're so lucky!'

My mouth makes a noise, and then suddenly I find myself on the brink of tears. I'm mortified. Imogen's blue eyes go all wide and she pulls me up by the arm, turning me round so my back is facing the room. It's the kind of reflexive gesture born of years of knowing when the other is about to get tired and emotional, and her knowing it makes me feel worse. My mouth collapses into a sob.

'Tell me,' she says quietly.

I take another swig of my too-strong ale to buy me a couple of seconds.

'Recently, it's just been . . .' I can hear my voice shaking. 'Hard. And maybe not just recently.' Now I've said it, the words are threatening to come out in a rush. They're all piled up, pushing to squeeze themselves out. 'It just doesn't feel like we're doing it together – me and Joe.'

'You did say you had some work you needed to do today. I thought you said Joe was coming here so you could get it finished.'

I swipe at my eyes, hoping the vicar – or, God forbid, Yasmine – doesn't come back. 'It's not just today. Today I feel like an idiot for expecting to get some time at the weekend to do my own thing. Not even my own thing. Work. I wanted to be able to leave today in Joe's hands, without having to project-manage it.' The laugh that comes out is bitter. 'Like, he gets to think of himself and his stuff, and then separately there's me and Enid, and he joins in when he chooses. But there's no separate me. Do you know what I mean? Before you have kids, you see all those idiotic memes on Facebook from women moaning about "the husband not putting the bins out" and "wine o'clock", and the next thing you know, you *relate* to them, and you wonder how you not only became entrenched in some bullshit binary gender role, but that somehow your husband also gets to label you as a nag when you ask him to do anything. And you always have to ask. What do they call it? Mental load. Urgh.'

I can see from Imogen's face that she thinks I'm ranting. I *am* ranting. I can also see that while there's sympathy in her face, there's no understanding. This is obviously not how it works in her house.

I sniff, trying to pull myself together. I'm embarrassed. I've always prided myself on being someone who can cope. 'Would Danny have come today if you'd asked him?'

'Yes,' she says simply. 'I told him not to bother, as I thought it would give me an opportunity to make friends. I don't want everyone to just think of us as a pair. I want us to make our own friends in the area. He's gone to some talk at the William Morris Gallery.'

'Do you do stuff like that too, then?'

'I'm not really into historical stuff. Oh right, you mean, more generally. Well, it depends. I sometimes do cinema matinees with the NCT girls from Bermondsey. It just depends what each of us has on.' She looks at her glass and realises she's out again, and reaches for a top-up. 'Organic wine isn't meant to give you a hangover, right?'

I can't even imagine. Time. To go and see a film. That doesn't come with a U rating and a wriggling three-year-old.

'You sound like brilliant co-parents.'

'We are.' Somehow Imogen now looks as glum as I feel. Not like she's living the equality dream. She chews her lip, seeming to be on the verge of saying something. 'It's all very amiable, very respectful.'

'So why do you look bloody miserable?'

'We haven't had sex for eighteen months,' she blurts. 'We're like two long-term flatmates who get on really well and take great care to take each other into account. We split the housework and the childcare and Danny has never expected me to do more cleaning because I work less, because I'm present more for the parenting side.' I can't help it; a strangled jealous noise comes out of me but she doesn't notice. 'We come home and we watch Netflix together and would never carry on with the next episode of something if the other one was out, but we just never—'

'Shag,' I finish.

'No,' she wails. 'And I don't even think he wants to. Shit.' She turns so she's got her back to the room too. Now we're both sniffing. But while it felt good to unload, it feels even better to know I'm not the only one struggling and that Imogen and I are starting to reconnect like we used to. She's different around all the other mums; maybe what we needed was some one-on-one time. Well, one-on-one in a room of fifty other people, including the clergy.

'Do *you* want to have sex?' I've seen pictures of Danny. He's good-looking. Clean-cut, very Imogen, and in all the photos she posts of him, he looks like he's completely in love with Winnie. He's like a living Athena poster, but in a crisp white button-down shirt.

'Yes. Sometimes, anyway. Less often since Win, but I definitely don't want to be in some asexual companion-ship situation at thirty-five. It's like you were saying, all those clichés that happen when you have a kid. We don't have sex any more. But some couples *must* be shagging.' She flings an arm out in the vague direction of Yasmine and her bump.

'They were probably only having sex to try for another baby,' I suggest.

'Hopefully,' says Imogen gloomily. 'Do *you*?'

'Want to have another baby? No.' I suppress the urge to say, *I can't even cope with my life as it is*, because we're talking about Imogen's thing now. Hopefully this is the first of more candid chats between us. Because I've got *a lot* more to say about my relationship.

'No. Have sex, I mean.'

I squirm. 'Erm. Not much. Way less often than when we used to live together.' When Joe and I first got together, Imogen and I analysed everything about him. Every text, every gesture, every sex move. Although when it came to the sex moves, she probably didn't have to ask. Our two-bedroom flat was originally only a one-bedroom flat, and the false plasterboard internal walls provided no sound insulation at all. I could practically hear her putting her tights on if she hadn't shaved her legs, so chances are she heard *everything* going on in my room. But it's been a long time since my boyfriends were anecdote fodder for Imogen. Or for anyone. I can't remember the last time I vented. Clara and I talk about work stuff when we have time for a catch-up, but I know next to nothing about the state of her and Mike's marriage. Just that there is one.

'Put it this way,' I say now, 'I'd rather go to a historical talk at the William Morris Gallery than have the occasional resentful quickie.'

Jusna claps to get everyone's attention and 'resentful quickie' echoes around the church hall in the ensuing silence. Reverend Will stares straight at me. I quickly look away, but not before I catch the tiny, amused look on his face.

Jusna clears her throat. 'Cake, everyone!'

I roll my eyes at Imogen. 'Tell me, is it a vegan, gluten-free, sugar-free, nut-free, taste-free *Blue Peter* dog cake?'

I turn round to see Yasmine has crossed the room and is standing silently behind me. 'Imogen, can I fill you in on Will's thoughts about the campaign?'

'I'll just find Enid,' I say to avoid having to talk to her, and next thing I know I'm in charge of spinning children for pin the tail on the donkey. It's a relief to have a task to concentrate on. At least it stops me having another public emotional breakdown in the corner.

By 4 p.m. Enid is completely wrecked. She has home-made hummus all down her front and is missing one of

71

the shoes she arrived in. The mums on the stage are drunk and doing the 'Single Ladies' dance, and even though no one is making a move to go, Jusna and Ajay are calling 'thanks for coming' in an attempt to get rid of us, so they can tidy up, congratulate themselves on a successful party and collapse on their sofa at home.

'Enid!' I shout. 'I'm going to find your shoe and then we're going. Do you remember when you last had it?'

She's twirling in circles with Winnie and Arlo. They seem to have gravitated towards each other. I'm pleased about her and Winnie. Less pleased about Arlo, but that's not the poor kid's fault. 'Outside,' she says, pausing to think. I know this because she has her thinking face on. She seems incapable of pondering anything without screwing her mouth into a cat's bum shape. 'On the slide.'

'Right,' I huff, going outside to the playground, picking up various stray cardigans, hairbands and caps on my way over to the slide, where I can see Enid's sandal lying underneath. There's a trainer at the top of the steps, so I climb up to grab that too, before taking the whole pile back in.

'Jusna,' I call across. She's tipping approximately twenty quid's worth of eco glitter into a non-biodegradable bin bag that Ajay is holding. 'If anyone's missing something, tell them to check in the kitchen. I'll stick all the lost property in there.' I walk in and dump it all on the counter, before stooping to retrieve some plastic balls that have made their way in from the ball pool in the main hall.

I hear Yasmine's voice drifting through the hatch.

'I see Lily deigned to give Jus a hand with the party games.'

'Not like her to join in with anything.' That's Kim, Yasmine's henchman. I freeze on the spot, captivated. I don't want to hear them slagging me off, but I also do. It's one of those.

'I don't know who she thinks she is, always taking the piss and acting like she's better than us all.'

I knew she'd heard the cake comment. I don't know what it is about Yasmine that makes me act like a teenager. She's just so annoying and sanctimonious. Who are 'us all'? I creep up and sneak a look over the counter through the hatch. There's three of them. Yasmine, Kim – and Imogen. I tense. Seeing her there with them makes my heart plummet.

'Although the biggest piss-take is how often she gets you to pick her daughter up from school,' Yasmine says with a toss of her chin in Imogen's direction. 'Doesn't see you for years and then uses you as an unofficial after-school club when it suits her.'

The fucking cheek.

I wait for Imogen to defend me. To tell her I've been stressed out or say 'she's always been all right with me', which everyone knows is the way you defend someone who is an arsehole to other people but *you* like them. A friend who just cried on your shoulder about how shitty everything is. And who you unloaded onto right back.

I wait.

She doesn't.

6

14 places available (five genuine Christians within the catchment area have been identified)

Imogen

The queue stretches twenty metres down the street and there are at least ten people in front of us and another twenty behind. Mostly couples. Well, the ones directly in front of Winnie and me are, seeing as they're kissing – make that *snogging* – while they wait. A full-on PDA at nine o'clock in the morning. We've been waiting half an hour already, under grey cloud cover, in the type of cold that seems bearable at first but then seeps into your bones. I stamp my feet to warm them up.

Winnie has been misled into thinking this is a diversion on the way to the park, instead of a forty-five-minute wait to do a walk-through of what I'm predicting will be a grossly overpriced and ultimately disappointing two-bedroom terraced house. So far, she seems happy on her scooter, a blur flying up and down the strip of pavement not occupied by our competition. It's always pairs at these viewings. Because who can afford to buy on their own? Plus, what single person in their right mind would want to blow everything they can scrabble together on a place whose biggest boast is being able to hear the shrieking from the primary school playground?

A couple in their late twenties, both dressed in unhemmed jeans and black Converse, walk from the house clutching the estate agent's printout. I'm not fooled by the unassuming uniform of the casual hipster. If they're looking at this place they either have family money or at least one highly paid job between them. I squint at the A4 to see if I can make out an 'offers in the range of' section or any interior pictures, but the only visible shot is the exterior we're queuing outside. It's a red-brick terrace with the original front door, a chipped paint job and cracked path slabs. The price could be anything, especially as it didn't even make it on to the estate agent's website. I got a phone call last night from Jay, with a time and an address for a one-time-only group viewing this morning. That's what it's come to. Like a mundane version of a tip-off about an illegal rave. Although from previous experience of these hastily called viewings, this is probably being held in a dingier property than any squat party I went to in the early noughties. Oh, please let it be decent. And *please* let us be able to afford it. Five hundred metres. That's all we need to gain. There are other schools around here, and they're . . . good, according to Ofsted (well, two are; one 'requires improvement'). But we didn't move here for 'good'. The schools were good in Bermondsey, where we also had a lovely new-build flat and loads of friends within playdate distance. We moved to future-proof Winnie's schooling, so we could transition from the safe-bet primary school, via the eleven plus, to the grammar. We moved for *outstanding*.

The queue shuffles a few feet nearer to the house. The other houses on the road either have well-manicured, gravel-filled front gardens and tastefully arranged pots of rosemary and lavender, or grotty untended concrete yards fenced by scraggy hedgerows with discarded energy drink cans stuffed into them. There's the dim echo of a siren coming from the direction of Blackhorse Lane, and when I stand very still, the distant vibration of the tube every few minutes beneath our feet.

'Stay where I can see you, Win,' I shout. She goes right to the edge of the pavement, where it meets the road, and looks back, testing me. I've stopped having a heart attack every time she does it. Now it's more like every other time.

I'm the exception to the couples rule. Danny refused to come this morning, said it was too last-minute because he'd booked the car in for its MOT. He also said it would be a waste of time because they're always shitholes. He's right. Plus, I've been saying I'll MOT the car for weeks and haven't got around to it, which he didn't even remind me about, just said the car was non-negotiable because it was on the brink of being illegal. He's always been better at sorting out household admin than me. He has reminders in his phone for everything – the car, the flat, energy bills – and just gets on with dealing with them because he knows I hate it and can't be arsed. He's the only person I've ever met who starts shopping around for home insurance weeks before it needs renewing and doesn't just let it roll over to whatever premium they've put it up to this year.

Meanwhile, Operation Walthamstow House is my area. And one day one of these places won't be terrible and we need to be ready. If we don't turn up to these things, Jay will stop calling us, and then we won't be on the viewers' list for the perfect non- (or at least only semi-) shithole. But between weekend house viewings and church on a Sunday, we've basically cut our weekend time in half, and we *have* to find a place soon. The school application deadline is creeping closer and everyone has exactly the same strategy. Turn up at church, and afterwards ingratiate themselves with the vicar and the head. The other day, Kim mentioned the 1920s-themed drinks party she threw for Mr Brown's birthday in June. She's been laying the groundwork for ages – we're newcomers, we can't compete with that! And that's just Kim. Who knows how the other parents have been sucking up to him before we arrived. I can't wait around for opportunities to prove our school spirit and hope for the best. We have to be a geographical *and* a spiritual lock. Oh God, please let this house be decent.

I idly check my blog figures. There's been a bit of a jump in hits since last month, most likely from Yasmine and Co. all having a nosy. That's what I would do if any of them had a blog. Have a root through to find out about them. I've been very careful to seem positive and enthusiastic about Walthamstow and the people, but I wonder what she thinks of it. Is she genuinely interested, or hate-reading it? Or has she had a look but isn't really bothered enough to have an opinion? All the blogs that get shared and go viral are by mums who hate on being a mum; where they treat their baby like an annoying flatmate and go on about how much gin they drink to get through it all. Then there's the perfect-mum bloggers who dress their daughters in matching outfits that they obviously got given for free, or even better, were paid to wear by a brand, and appear on Instagram doing activities and crafts every day of the week. Half their readers are obsessed with it, and the rest troll them for painting an unrealistic picture of parenthood, but either way they have massive follower numbers. At least if you're being trolled it means someone has noticed you. I know mine's too meh to be anything. Some good days, some bad days. No scathing takedown of my child's fussy eating habits, but no mini-me outfits either. I'm just another mum. Except that's the name of a really famous blogger, so I'm not even that.

I've just remembered I muted the WhatsApp conversation from the St P&P's group last night, so I pull it up to see what I've missed.

Thirty-two notifications. Not as many as I was expecting. I scroll back up the conversation trying to make sense of it.

Jusna: Hi all, so the word is not to dress up for Halloween at preschool – it's on a Wednesday – this year.

Lily: LOL. E will probably be dressed as Spider-Man all week.

Clara: Jeb wants a Spider-Man costume too. Better make sure we check which kid is under the mask and don't pick up the wrong one.

Lily: 😂😂😂😂

Rachael: Why don't we make them ALL Spider-Man? Too cute right.

Vickie: 🕷🕷🕷🕷🕷🕷

Hannah: OMG where did you get the Spider-Man outfit from? All out in big Tesco and big Sainsbury's.

Lily: Amazon

Rachael: Amazon

Jusna: No Spider-Men (or other outfits) for 31st at St P&P though everyone. They're NOT doing Halloween.

Lily: It's nursery. Uniform is only the sweatshirt and polo and even that's not compulsory.

Yasmine: Guys, this comes from Mr Brown. Church is uncomfortable with the message of Halloween. They're rolling out a dress-up ban for the rest of the school and he's asked nursery to support. We've said of course, but it has to be unanimous. We can't have some kids dressed up and others not as it would cause ructions.

Lily: What does God have against Halloween? 😛

Clara: 😝

Yasmine: God might not care, but he's not overseeing the school admissions. Mr Brown is.

Lily is typing . . .

Lily: OK

My phone buzzes again. Lily to me directly. I'm surprised to hear from her, as I've heard nothing since Mo's birthday party the other week, when she upped and left without saying goodbye. We were getting on really well, and even had a moment when we started telling each other how life had *really* been for the last couple of years, and then she just shut down. Maybe she felt guilty for all the times she's asked me to help her with preschool pick-ups recently so decided to put some conversational legwork in, but it felt like more than that. For me, it was the first real conversation I'd had with a mum since moving here. But opening up before clamming shut again is pretty typical of Lily. She always was hard to read. She hates relying on people emotionally.

Lily: Do you want to have a mini-Halloween party for the girls and maybe a couple of others? After pick-up? We'll keep it on social media lockdown, like Kylie Jenner's pregnancy, and get everyone to sign NDAs to protect against snitches.

Imogen: Of course. Got to get some use out of the Elsa costume before she grows out of it.

Lily: Great! I'll dress as a crone. By which I mean I'll bring my usual face.

I smile and walk the gap where the queue has moved up again. It looks like it's going to rain. Imminently. I haven't got a brolly or Win's waterproof jacket.

'Look, Mummy, it's Ava.' She scoots down the pavement to where Ava from school and her mum are coming across the road. I've seen her mum at church a couple of times and outside the playground, but she's not really someone I've spoken to much so far. The two little girls say hello to each other, one of those increasingly frequent moments when it hits me that she has this whole part of her life that's now separate from her life with Danny and me. Ava's mum – whose name I cannot for the life of me remember – is pushing a Bugaboo with a tiny sleeping baby in it. Her brown hair is scraped back into a ponytail, and she's wearing the kind of easy-access breast-feeding top that always ends up sagging open, usually when you're in public, to reveal an equally unattractive but functional nursing bra. The baby can't be any more than six weeks old, though, so I imagine she's still at the stage where she's too exhausted to care if her tits flop out in Costa.

She gives me a cheerful wave. 'I'm so sorry, but I can't remember your name,' she says. 'Ava helpfully told me you're Winnie's mummy and I haven't got the energy or adult brain function at the moment to pretend I can remember. I'm Bex,' she supplies helpfully.

'I'm Imogen, but don't worry, "Winnie's mum" is fine. I don't have the excuse of a newborn and I was racking my brain for yours too. I was just thinking how weird it is that they know each other, but it isn't through us.'

'Ava's the one that spotted you guys from right down the street.'

'Are you having to walk to get the baby to nap? I remember those days. I had to have Winnie strapped to my front almost constantly for the first four months or she'd wake up after twenty minutes.'

It's started to drizzle, but Bex tucks in and stands along-side me to make room for Ava, now scooting relays with Winnie. 'Compared to Ava, he, Grey, is actually pretty good. He'll nap anywhere. Touch wood. It was more that I thought Ava could do with getting out of the house, so we were going to go to the park after going to the church to talk about Grey's christening in a few weeks. He slept through the whole thing. I managed to drink an entire hot coffee and everything.'

'I wish I could sleep through church,' I say. 'Needs must, though. And great idea to christen him so young. We faffed about until Winnie was two, but this makes you look serious from the start.'

She gives me a puzzled look. 'Ava was twelve weeks when we christened her, too.'

'God, you *are* organised. I only wish we'd got our act together earlier. We've got a letter from our old vicar in Bermondsey saying that we were regular churchgoers, but it still gives a better impression if you get in with them from the off, doesn't it?'

Bex laughs politely, and the penny drops. She isn't pretending to be religious. She *is* religious.

'I mean, when I say get our act together, I mean that we were always very *spiritual* people, but it just took a while for us to find our religious centre.' I'm gabbling. 'Now we can't remember a time before it. Well, we can. But it wasn't as good.' I'm talking too much and too fast. 'It's just so peaceful at St Mary's on a Sunday, isn't it?'

Sometimes, in the quiet, when Winnie stops fidgeting, it *is* peaceful. My mind stops buzzing and it gives me a chance to think. It feels almost meditative. At those times I sit on the hard bench and think, *Is this what spirituality is? Maybe I've cracked it*. But I can never be sure if God would count the mental clarity to recall *exactly* what you need in the Tesco order later as a higher state of being.

'I'm not sure peaceful is the word when the kids won't stop kicking off,' she says, 'but I've always liked the ritual of it and the routine. And the fact that it's a break from the rushing around of the rest of the week. Plus, the new vicar is a lot better at speaking to the congregation than Reverend Terry was. Those sermons he used to give were so irrelevant. It feels like the new one has at least *lived* in the modern world.'

Oh God, we're going to have to talk about the Bible. I only know the parable about the mustard seed, or is it a camel and the eye of a needle? Or there's Joseph and his Dreamcoat – but is that Old Testament? I only actually know it from Andrew Lloyd Webber.

'The new vicar could probably read out the back of a cereal box and we'd all be interested, though.' She laughs the way we all laugh when we talk about Reverend Will. Like a bunch of tittering mums who fancy him. But at least she's nice-goddy and not judgy-goddy.

She peers to the front of the line at the house. 'Are you viewing this place? We've been trying to move since before I got pregnant for the second time, but it's not happening. We can't afford anything with three bedrooms.'

'Where are you at the minute?'

'Morris Road.'

'That's Lily's street!'

'Yes, we live a couple of doors down.'

'I think she's had a loft conversion. Maybe you could do the same? It's cheaper than moving around here.'

'Yeah, that's our back-up plan. But we want to move. Somewhere like this. If only we could afford it.' She suddenly looks a bit shifty.

'Which side?'

'What?'

'Which side neighbour are you from Lily?'

'We're number eighty-seven.'

'Ah,' I say, and she gives me a what-can-you-do look.

No wonder she wants to move. She's on the wrong side of the catchment area. By a whisker. Surely her genuine faith will count for something, though. She'll inherit the earth. Or in this case, the school place. Or is that the meek? I *have* to start listening in church.

'Anyway, I'll let you go in.' We're at the end of the path. There's a greying, sagging mattress in the front yard, two empty vodka bottles and a few rusting Castrol oil containers.

'Let me know how it is. Whenever an estate agent says "auction" I just hear "forget it".'

'Winnie! In here!' We shuffle in, Winnie sliding herself along the narrow, dim hallway wall as the previous viewers pass us to leave. They're also younger than me, under thirty, but they don't look like they've found their dream house; their brows are furrowed and they're murmuring something about how they could maybe make it work if they knocked through.

It's only when the hall opens up to a (tiny) living room and there's more light that I realise the entire place – including the wall Winnie has been slithering against – is speckled with dark, black mould.

'Come away,' I hiss. Mould spores can kill you if they get into your lungs, can't they? How do you stop that happening? Are they already in?

Jay is standing in the middle of the spore-ridden hovel, holding his iPad. He's running his other hand through his floppy brown hair, bicep straining at a muscle-fit white shirt. The best way to describe his look is *Geordie Shore* by way of Hampshire.

'Imogen Roberts,' I say, to pre-empt the fact that he never has any idea who I am, despite fielding increasingly plaintive emails from me, as well as regularly seeing me on the viewings circuit.

'Imogen. Of course.' He ticks me off a list he's pulled up on the screen. They *do* keep a note of who turns up. I can smugly report that back to Danny later. If there's the equivalent of a Nando's Black Card for the Stow Place Like Home estate agency, I *will* get it.

'As you can see, it's a period property,' he begins in a monotone voice. He's not even trying to sex up the patter that he's obviously wheeled out loads of times this morning already. 'This is the front reception room, which leads through to –' he wastes no time describing the front reception room, because what is there to say, other than, "it looks and smells like mouldy bread", and instead starts walking down a couple of steps '– the kitchen, which has ample potential for renovating to a high spec.'

Winnie takes off running and I trot after her. Of course, 'ample potential for renovating' translates as 'you need to tear it out and start again'. Through the doorway is a kitchen – if you can call the ramshackle collection of grubby MDF units and warped lino a kitchen – and it smells of cigarettes. At the back, there's a flimsy, flaking wooden door that reveals an overgrown back garden through the dirty glass. Looking more closely, it's the kind of garden that would be great once you've cleared away the detritus (another mattress, a rusting bike) that's been lobbed out there, and re-educated the local cats about where they can and cannot shit.

'If you want to go upstairs, there are two good-sized double bedrooms, both with exposed floors, and a period bathroom.'

I make my way to the first of the bedrooms, realising why Jay didn't say exposed *wood* floors. You can see chunks of crumbling underlay between patches of thread-bare carpet. It *is* a good size, though, despite the graffiti on the wall. Sadly, it's not the hip street mural-style graffiti that has popped up all over Walthamstow since its regeneration; this is bus stop graffiti: a giant spray-painted cock and balls.

'What that?' asks Winnie, pointing to it.

'Someone's done some colouring,' I say, thrusting her hastily along the corridor to the next bedroom.

It's marginally better in that there's no penis drawn over the hideous shiny floral wallpaper. But there is a hole in the floor. And two in the wall. The holes in the door have been patched up with some random bits of wood. All the holes have a distinctly 'made by a sledgehammer' look about them. There are also some red stains on the door, near the holes. I try not to think about what that might be. We cross the landing. The 'period' bathroom is a salmon-pink seventies number with a cracked corner bath. Actually it's not a full bathroom, as there's no sink. Still, it's the least offensive room in the building.

'It's mad how these properties are just standing here vacant when people are desperate for places,' I say to Jay, who is coming up the stairs, holding his arms in such a way that I can tell he doesn't want to touch anything. 'How long has it been empty?'

'It wasn't empty,' he says, his face blank. 'Not until the owner died a few weeks ago.'

My eye catches another staircase, twisting around from behind the bathroom door, which for some reason opens outwards. 'Oh! There's a loft conversion. You didn't mention that on the phone. I thought it was only two bedrooms.'

Jay's eyebrows arch a shade. 'That's, er, not officially a room.'

'Is it just boarded out? Weird to have an exposed staircase with no door.' Winnie scrambles up the stairs and I go after her. A converted loft means it might actually be worth bidding for. It would give us *loads* of extra space. Even enough room for if we—

'You do that at your own risk!' Jay barks, scaring us both into freezing on the spot. The lip of the top step is obscuring a clear view into the room, but I can see an expanse of lurid patterned carpet that seems to sag where it meets the walls. One of the Velux windows is boarded up. And, like the kitchen, the smell of cigarettes wafts from it.

'The owners didn't get planning permission for the loft conversion, so it can't be classed as a "room",' he says, making bunny ears around the word 'room'. You could apply the same inverted commas to this entire 'home'. 'The good news, though, is that it gives you a good idea of how much space there is to convert if you wanted to do it.'

'Presumably as this "space" didn't pass its building regulations and is "illegal", you'd have to rip the whole thing out, apply for planning permission and then rebuild the "room" from scratch.' Now I'm doing the bunny ears at him.

'Yes. That's correct.'

'Gotcha.'

Jay surreptitiously presses the home button on his iPad and glances down. We've clearly outstayed our allotted five-minutes. His arm bulges through his shirtsleeve as he gestures back down the non-illegal section of stairs. I reach for Winnie's hand. The first couple of steps seem to buckle when you step onto them.

'It smells, Mummy,' Winnie announces. Anywhere else I'd be mortified, but Jay knows that if this was a tent perched on a toxic waste dump he'd still be looking at the equivalent of a hefty deposit on an Audi TT in commission.

'Yes, Win. It does.' I remember to yank her into the protective aura of my parka as we renavigate Spore Alley. The faces of the next viewers are looming ominously in the glass of the front door, no doubt panicking that their turn has been nixed because of us making a big on-the-spot offer.

Jay pushes a piece of paper into my hand, the one the others all had, with the property's vitals on there. In the interior photos, the graffiti has been photoshopped out of the shot.

'So how much are we talking?' I blurt as we get to the door, panic rising. This place is awful. *Awful.* And yet. I mean, if we bought it, we wouldn't need to live here until it's been made habitable. I'll ignore the question of exactly where we *would* live for now, because it would be ages before it was safe to move in. But basically, as long as we can change the address on our council tax it doesn't matter. Five hundred metres. That's all we need.

'It's going to auction.' Of course it is. It's the same with every dump that comes on the market.

'What's the estimate or reserve?'

Jay openly laughs as though the word 'estimate' is meaningless.

'It needs loads of work doing to it before it's anywhere near fit to live in,' I say. 'You wouldn't be able to stay on the premises for months.'

'A similar one down the road went for six hundred the other day.'

'Did it have rampant mould and an illegal room that will cost more to remove than it cost to put in?'

Jay looks at Winnie and shrugs. 'It's in a great school catchment area.'

'I KNOW!' I shout. 'Why do you think I'm even considering moving my child into a total hellhole? We *have* to get within fifty metres of St Peter and Paul's school. We *need* this, Jay.' My voice is getting higher and higher, and Jay's eyes are widening. 'No one else out there needs that school yet. They're all young and childless. All they want is a grown-up pad decorated in the same grey palette that everyone on Instagram uses. Pineapple-shaped lamps, Jay, that's all they care about. Vintage cocktail cabinets!' I look down and I'm grasping his arm, but he needs to know our desperation. 'We need *education*.' He looks a bit scared. He can't be any more than twenty-six. I dial it back and try to sound reasonable, accommodating, *warm*. 'What can we do? *Tell me*. I've been on your books for eighteen months now.'

'Well,' he starts. 'There is one thing that could help.' He scratches his carefully tended stubble. It has very definite edges to it; he must have spent a long time deciding the exact parameters of his facial hair.

I give the rest of him the once-over. He's wearing tight tapered-leg trousers along with his tight shirt. I can imagine him getting changed into a similar version of the same thing to go to the pub tonight. It's a definite look, the kind of bloke that likes everyone to notice how crisp his shirt is, or what make of trainers he's wearing. Like an off-duty footballer. It's never been my type but he *is* good-looking. Ish. So . . . would I? If that's what he's getting at? I mean, not with Winnie here, and not in the cock-and-balls room, but . . . I definitely slept with worse people before I met Danny. Like Advertising Sleaze Guy, and I wasn't even drunk for that. And what am I, ten years older than him? I look quite good today, though. I put make-up on and curled my hair before we came out and have got on a pair of nice skinny jeans. Although he wouldn't know that as I'm swaddled in my mega mum-coat. And acting like a wild-eyed crazy person.

'The best way to guarantee an offer acceptance—' he says.

'Yes.' I'm leaning in to him as though he's either going to kiss me or reveal the meaning of life.

'And push a sale through in the shortest amount of time—'

'*Yes,*' I whisper. More leaning – I'm very close to him now. Right in his personal space.

'Is to be a cash buyer. Is there any way you can free up some capital?'

I drop his arm. 'Goodbye, Jay. Call me if anything else comes up. Under five hundred grand. ANYTHING.'

I yank the door open and push past the twosome that are waiting, taking no care not to knock them with Winnie's scooter, and we hustle past the rest of the queue still lining up patiently down the street. I can no longer distinguish between their individual faces; it's just a blur of advantageous mortgage-to-deposit ratios and hefty cash injections from the bank of Mum and Dad.

'It's got mould *and* Japanese knotweed,' I say loudly as we pass them. It's worth a try.

7

27 October 2018

Lily

From: Yasmine Swift
Subject: Dark Arts

Nothing too dramatic then.

I inhale before clicking to open it, willing 'Dark Arts' to be the name of a new pop-up bar and Yasmine suggesting 'mum drinks' or something similarly lame. Nope.

Hi P&Pers
There seems to be some confusion about Halloween in the WhatsApp group so I thought an email would be the easiest way to clear things up. St P&P's ISN'T celebrating Halloween this year – or in the future. Mr Brown has been trying to phase it out for some years now as he feels that the original Halloween message is tied to the Dark Arts and not in keeping with the core Christian values of St P&P's. So please be mindful of the fact that there will be no dressing up on 31st.

The jovial tone she uses on email is so annoying. Best buds with Mr Brown. And who made her chief spokes-mum? Or Mr Brown's enforcer? Although it *is* possible that there was a vote on that front during one of the twelve thousand meet-ups that I can never go to because of work.

The last line, however, reads as the threat it is.

Anyone contravening this directive will be asked to pick their child up, and a note made in their record.

Who says 'directive'?

I message Imogen. I started avoiding her after Mo's birthday, but she carried on being as friendly as ever at drop off, and to keep being pissed off I'd have to confess that I'd been listening in to their conversation. Plus, she's helped me massively with pick-ups over these last couple of weeks, when I've twice ended up stuck in an over-running meeting, and once at the mercy of a tube strike nightmare.

We better make sure our children don't get a record – otherwise they'll never be eligible to take the bar.

Satisfyingly, she sends a slap face emoji right back.

Imogen: Thing is, I DAREN'T break the rules, because we all know it means OUR record – the dossier of who's in and out.
Lily: Of COURSE we have to abide by the rules. Officially. I just need someone to reassure me that this is NOT NORMAL.
Imogen: Oh yeah, it's totally weird.
Lily: We're still on for our clandestine Halloween party though right? NDAs distributed at the door. Social media super-injunction.
Imogen is typing . . .

Imogen: I completely forgot. I told the Bermondsey NCT lot ages ago that I'd go to their Halloween do. Sorry!

I feel a little inner tilt. The edge of a memory nudging at me. Of Imogen being more popular. She always had loads of different friendship groups and was a natural in PR because she didn't consider all the tedious schmoozing tedious or schmoozy. She genuinely enjoyed it, becoming friends with loads of the journalists and beauty execs she worked with. Meanwhile, whenever she coaxed me along to a launch, with the promise of free champagne and a goodie bag, I regretted it the second I arrived, realising that the pay-off was having to make small talk with strangers that I couldn't really be arsed to speak to for the next three hours. Imogen was always full of sympathy for the parts of my job that involved having to sit in silence in my car for hours on end, but for me, spying on people as they go about their lives, without actually engaging with any of them, is far preferable to fake chat with people at press events.

I much preferred evenings when it was just us two in a pub, or better still, at home. After a while I started making excuses not to go to her events, and eventually she stopped asking me, instead propping a goodie bag outside my bedroom door when she came home.

Lily: No probs! Enid and I will be dressed as witches and dancing to 'Monster Mash' in our kitchen. Think Clara will pop in so planning an all-nighter (until 7.30 p.m.). See you at school!

The replies to Yasmine's email have been rolling in, everyone lightning-quick to agree with her about how we should opt out of Halloween. The school place blacklist is the main reason, but no one would dare argue with Yasmine either. Including me. She's the Meghan Markle of St P&P's: whatever she endorses is an instant sellout.

Fine by me.

My response sounds as forced as it is but at least they can't accuse me of being a dissident.

For Halloween, the atmosphere is, ironically, dead when I rush into school to pick up Enid that Wednesday. But that's my fault because I'm eight minutes late and she's the only child left. The look of abandonment on her face as she sits there, alone, is even worse than the ten-quid late pick-up fine that is being added to our monthly invoice even as I pepper the air in front of me with apologies.

'This is the third time in six weeks,' Charlotte, Enid's twenty-one-year-old key worker, grumbles at me.

'I know. I'm sorry. I was stuck on the tube and couldn't get the signal to call.'

'Winnie's mummy didn't take me with her,' Enid says dolefully, as I hustle her into the hallway.

'Winnie's mummy doesn't *always* take you home,' I fire back, a bit too snippily for someone whose kid was just thinking that she wasn't coming, but the guilt makes me defensive. I had to walk out of a pointless 'strategy' meeting that had degenerated into a debate about who should drive to Sheffield next week for a forty-five-minute in-person briefing with the Yorkshire lot, only to then drive straight back again afterwards. My absence guarantees it will be me, because I'm not there to argue otherwise, but I'll deal with how I'm going to fit it into the school day later. Right now,

I need to up my parenting game, stat. But as Enid doesn't know about the Halloween shenanigans that await at home, it's going to be hard for her to forgive me any time soon.

'They all went together,' she says, as she pulls on her coat, angrily stabbing her hands through the little elasticated cuffs. Her eyes are brimming with tears that she must have been holding in since she was left behind.

'They didn't go together,' I say gently, 'they must have all arrived for pick-up at the same time, so it just felt like everyone was leaving together. And I was late. I'm so sorry. It must have been frightening.'

I quickly pull the door open. 'Winnie's going to see some of her mummy's friends from where they used to live,' I say quietly. 'We'll do our own Halloween thing when we get home.' I look around to see if any of the nursery staff heard the mention of the H-word, but the few staff members that are left are tidying up, or hurrying to go home themselves.

The ten-pound fine – if not the lingering memory of Enid's miserable face – is worth it when she sees the cobwebs I've sprayed all over the front gate, and screams with delight. And I'm properly forgiven when she spots the rest of the pound-shop tat I've strewn around the living room: pumpkin bunting, fake spiders, plastic skull buckets filled with Haribo and a giant cardboard skeleton Blu-Tacked to the wall.

'Right,' I say, pulling out a full-size witch's hat from behind the settee and putting it on. 'Do you want your Spider-Man costume or a spooky one?' I hold up a matching mini-witch number, which she grabs from me before immediately taking off all of her clothes.

'Not your knickers, E, you can leave them on. Here, let me help you.' I bunch one leg of the orange and black

94

stripy tights up so she can step into them, and hit play on the Halloween playlist I made at lunchtime. 'Ghost Town' by The Specials drifts out from the speakers.

There's a rap on the door. 'Ooh, that will be Clara and Jeb,' I say to Enid, who is absorbed in stuffing gummy bears into her mouth. 'Don't you want to see his costume?'

She prises herself past my legs to the door, tights already falling down and bunching up around her skinny little ankles. She yanks it open.

'Trick or treat!' shouts Ava from within a unicorn onesie. Bex, who only lives a few doors away, but I only really know from church, is standing behind her wearing black jeans, a black jumper and some cat ears. She's got Grey strapped to her front in a BabyBjörn and I can see from his dangling leg that he's in some skeleton pyjamas. Bex is the last person I expected to be out doing the rounds, seeing as she's so tight with the church lot. I glance out of the door and to each side. What if this is a trap?

'You're trick-or-treating.' It's a statement, not a question. If she's bugged, we're going down together.

'We had to do *something*,' she replies with an eye roll. 'I went along with the whole "Halloween is cancelled" email, from what's-her-name again, Yasmine, and I know Mr Brown is completely evangelical about trying to ban it, but it's all a bit OTT, isn't it? I think Christianity has a lot more to be preoccupied with than whether my kids wear fancy dress. I figured we'd be safe knocking on your door.'

My eyes narrow a shade. 'Why's that?'

'You've got Halloween branding on your front gate.' The glow-in-the-dark pumpkin glints at us.

'Right, yes.'

'And I figured you might feel the same way as I do about it.'

'Which is?'

'That the last thing we need is to teach our kids that religion sucks the fun out of everything. The new vicar made that point at the church meeting about it – which I completely agree with – but Mr Brown was having none of it.' She shrugs. 'You can't go against the grain, can you? Especially not this year. Oh Ava, honey, no.' Bex pulls an apologetic face as a snatching fight breaks out over a bag of Starmix. 'I'm not sure she was offering to let you put the whole lot in your pumpkin.'

I'm not sure Enid was going to let her put *any* of her Starmix in her pumpkin. 'Enid, can we share?' I say, trying to prise the bag out of her grasp. 'We've got more upstairs. Let Ava have some. No, let her.' She won't let go and the bag starts to rip as we tussle over it.

'Well, this is embarrassing,' I say, but Bex barks out a laugh. 'Don't worry. She just had a meltdown when some people across the road said she could choose two Celebrations from their tub. *Only* two, imagine. *So deprived.*'

'Do you want to come in?' I ask, deciding I like her. I wish I'd known earlier that there was someone at church I might feasibly be friends with. 'I wasn't going to take Enid out trick-or-treating but we're having a little Halloween do.'

Twenty minutes later Clara rushes in with Jeb, and about half an hour after that, Enid, Ava and Jeb are hopped up on chocolate and going berserk to 'Gangnam Style', having rejected my playlist of spooky classics. We're all sitting on the sofa trying to coax them to drink water at two-minute intervals because they're all clammy and look like they're in serious danger of overheating in their cheap poly material outfits. Between swigs of tea, Clara is alternating between checking her watch and then her emails on her phone. She's still in her work suit.

'If you need to work,' I tell her, picking another fizzy cherry from one of the Halloween bowls, 'I can drop him back round at yours in an hour.'

'No, no, it's fine.' She glances at her phone and frowns, a muscle in her neck clenching as she taps away.

'Clara, honestly, *go*. I can see that you're stressing, and if you try and get Jeb to leave now your life isn't going to be worth living.' It feels good to be the one offering to help for once. I'm usually the Clara in this situation, navigating between crushing guilt and the gut-gnawing panic of knowing I'm going to be up until all hours getting some work finished, even if I make a start on it now.

'If you're sure.' She's already halfway to the door, an apologetic but relieved look on her face. 'This party was supposed to be a proper bit of time for us together but then a load of briefs landed on my desk at three and the trial starts next week.' She stops to kiss him on his sweaty little head. 'Mummy's got to nip home, Jebby, but you can stay here and play.' He ignores her. 'Not even bothered. He's so used to me having to go. I could leave him with the dog and he'd be fine. Except we can't get a dog because then we'd have to get a dog walker because no one else has any time to do it.'

'I wish I could leave this one for a bit,' says Bex, gesturing at her boob, where Grey has been latched on since she arrived. 'But I'm deep in cluster-feeding hell right now. I'm not sure what I would have done if we had carried on trick-or-treating rather than come in here. I'd have had to hang a muslin over his head with some eyes drawn on so that when people answered the door they were confronted by a miniature ghost rather than my bare boob.'

'Yeah, but when you leave them you feel terrible,' says Clara.

'And when you can't leave them you feel trapped. Then you feel guilty for feeling trapped,' says Bex.

'All roads lead to guilt in the end,' I say. 'Huzzah for being a modern woman.' I hold the bowl of fizzy sweets out to Bex and she grabs a handful. 'Clara, GO. He'll be fine.'

'Thank you, thank you. Bye, Jebby,' she shouts, banging the door behind her. Once she's gone and the kids are occupied, there's an awkward moment. Even though Clara's attention was elsewhere, her presence relieved the pressure of only having Bex to talk to. I've only really chatted to her at the church playgroup a few times. She was always involved in serving teas and coffees, and because I knew she was well in with the God squad I've always steered clear. I always think I'm going to accidentally commit some conversational offence.

I stick to my safe topics. 'Do you want a glass of water or another tea? What is it you do for work again? Are you still on maternity leave at the minute?'

'I'd love a water actually, thanks,' she says, and I hop up to get her a glass. 'I forgot how dehydrated you get from breastfeeding.'

I put a pint glass down where she can reach it, and she takes a couple of thirsty gulps before putting it down, picking up her tea and doing the same with that. 'Thank you. I'm an account manager for a digital marketing agency. We work mainly with chain restaurants.'

'Have you thought about going back to work yet, or is it a bit early for all that?'

'I'm trying *not* to think about it, to be honest,' she says, her face twisting into a grimace. 'When I went back after Ava, they kept on the guy who covered my maternity leave, gave him the same job title as me and he kept most of the accounts that were originally mine, so I was effectively demoted. As this is my second maternity leave in four years, I can only imagine what'll happen this time. I want to go back part-time, but the last woman who did that never got to be the lead on any of the accounts and ended up being a sort of glorified admin assistant. So depressing.' She shrugs. 'And there's such a presentee attitude. As soon as you're not completely flexible for client meetings you're made to feel like you're letting everyone down.'

'I hear you. At work I spend a lot of time pretending I don't have a kid. It just seems easier to ignore it.'

The kids start warbling along to 'Sexy and I Know It' by LMFAO, completely unaware what the lyrics are or what they mean. Bex and I look at each other and burst out laughing. 'How is this always on kids' party playlists? I'm skipping this one,' I call, to everyone's dismay, moving the music on to something with only very ambiguous sexual references. 'Are there many mums at your work?' I say to Bex.

'Not really. Hardly any women return to work after having children at my company, and it's definitely not because they all want to be stay-at-home mums. The part-timer left in the end too. It's just so hard to make it work. No one ever dares ask for flexible working because it's top-heavy with men who are stuck in a 1950s mentality. Then I look at how much my nursery will cost, and if I go back to work part-time, I'll clear about six pounds a day. But if I don't go back, I take myself completely out of the game. I mean –' she gesticulates with her mug and almost sloshes tea onto Grey's now sleeping head '– I went on holiday for two weeks in 2011 and someone invented Snapchat! If I stay at home until this one goes to school, everything I know will be obsolete. Plus, I'll be bored out of my mind. I *like* my job.'

I nod along, without the words to say anything to make her feel more positive. Luckily Enid picks that moment to bang her head on the bookshelf while shimmying too vigorously to Pharrell, which creates a distraction while I kiss and rub the spot.

'Let's get a picture,' says Bex, carefully lowering Grey onto the settee to ensure he stays asleep, before pulling her bra up, her top down and her phone from her back pocket in one fluid manoeuvre. 'Come on, kids.'

They line up in front of the giant skeleton, a tearful witch, a beaming unicorn and a Spider-Man, striking poses that I have no idea they knew existed, a weird mixture of rap hands and duck face. It's far more terrifying than their outfits.

'What's your number? And do you have Clara's? I'll send some to you both.'

'Yes, hang on. Do I not have yours saved already?' I reach for my phone. The home screen is full of WhatsApp image notifications from Jusna. 'God, we've been spammed by the St P&P group.'

'What St P&P group?'

'The WhatsApp group. The school one. Aren't you in it?'

Bex shrugs. 'Don't think so.' She swipes at her phone. 'No.'

'I thought everyone was in it. Jusna started it but Yasmine seems to be the powerhouse behind it all.'

'Maybe I was to start with and I left.' I'd be gutted about the snub, but Bex doesn't seem bothered either way. 'The email group is enough to keep up with, especially considering it's not even anything officially to do with the school. Smile, Ava,' she says, breaking away to take some more pictures. 'She's a funny one, Yasmine, isn't she?' she adds.

It's a throwaway comment, but I cling to it. I'm interpreting 'funny one' as good Christian shorthand for 'cow', but opt for non-committal. I still can't be one hundred per cent certain she's not informing for the school.

'Right, are you ready for my number?' I ask and then read it out.

Notifications from Bex start to pop up, and I swipe on them to have a look. All fifteen from Jusna's message have automatically saved to my camera roll. Annoying. I need to change my settings to stop that; I'm constantly deleting images from it to free up memory. I tag the first few to trash before catching sight of some dressed-up children in Yasmine's perfectly decorated living room and getting nosy. Interesting. It looks like goody-two-shoes Yasmine is having a party of her own. I wonder if she authorised Jusna sending these pictures out to the public group – anyone could forward them on to Mr Brown. I enlarge a shot at random. From the decorations, I can tell she's gone all out, even if her spooky Halloween lights – that I strongly suspect didn't come from the pound shop – look tasteful, strung as they are around her restored Victorian fireplace and complemented by the navy-blue walls and overhead pendant lights. Arlo and Mo are dressed as little wizards, and Kim's daughter Thea is Moana. A spear of guilt pierces through me. It's been a fun group at our house, but if I were on better terms with Yasmine, Enid would have been invited to this party. She's always mentioning Arlo. I push away the thought that my daughter is being punished for my unpopularity and focus instead on a small yellow velvet cocktail chair in Yasmine's living room. I've seen one like it on made.com but have no space for it in our house. You need an extension like hers for attractive but ultimately pointless furniture that most likely no one will sit on. I zoom in to see what else she has. Side tables and a big steamer chest as a coffee table – loads of stuff that people would refer to as 'pieces' rather than furniture, by the looks of things. There's a second chair in the same yellowy colour, a sort of mid-century retro thing with wooden arms. This one looks more comfortable. You could feasibly sit in it. I know this because someone is. I zoom in closer on the picture just to make sure. Yep, it's Imogen.

8

13 places available (According to Kim, Mr Brown told her an army family are moving to Walthamstow. Parent in the armed forces = automatic place. Too late for Danny to 'enlist'? Look into what proof is needed.)

Imogen

'How was Halloween in Bermondsey?'

My heart starts battering against my chest. I've always been a terrible liar. Lily has waited in the playground to catch me after drop-off, for once not seeming to be in a panic about legging it to the tube, and now I can only assume I've been caught out in my deception.

'Yes, fine,' I say vaguely. 'Sweets, games, a couple of tantrums. You know, the usual.' I shrug. It's about as convincing a performance as a soap character picking up 'heavy' suitcases in their big leaving episode.

'What did Winnie dress up as?'

What is this, an interrogation, I'm about to snap, but it's a perfectly normal line of questioning about the kids' party I was *supposed* to be at yesterday.

'She was a princess zombie.' At least that's not a lie. She was in a ballerina costume and tiara, until I started dabbing my face with fake blood and she wanted in on the action.

'Cute. Let's see a picture.'

'*What?*'

Lily is looking at me weirdly. Or maybe it's my face that looks weird and she's just reacting to that.

'A picture,' she repeats. 'Of Winnie in her outfit.' She swipes at her phone. 'Look, here's a few from ours. It was slightly random, but Bex – do you know her? – and Ava ended up coming to ours too. I haven't really spoken to her much before but she's nice.' She holds up the screen, smiling. 'Look at them. Clara said Jeb was sick when he got home, and it was made up entirely of Percy Pigs. Gross.'

I finger the camera app on my phone, directing the screen away so she can't see me scrolling through the eight billion pictures I took at Yasmine's yesterday: unmistakable evidence that I wasn't in Bermondsey. For the millionth time, I wonder why I lied about it. Actually, I don't. I lied because I was invited and Lily wasn't because Yasmine doesn't like her, and I know Lily would be upset at me going. But why should I be loyal to Lily? We haven't seen each other for years. And Yasmine's right. I only hear from Lily when she wants something. Which at the moment is about three times a week, due to some work emergency or other meaning she can't pick Enid up from school. I haven't even seen Joe yet. The only reason I haven't been more openly annoyed with Lily is because he seems so useless as to be practically non-existent when it comes to the childcare heavy lifting. I hear from Yasmine because she likes me. And I like her. Mostly. Plus, Yasmine's lot are *far* more useful to my social climbing mission at the school, especially as we're getting nowhere with the house-hunting. That shitty house the other day – and I say shitty as a fact, from the mouse droppings spread liberally around the place – went for six hundred and fifty grand. Danny told me again to consider going back to work full-time. I asked him as what, Arianna Huffington?

Lily's still looking at me, waiting to see a picture, so I settle on a shot of Winnie, on her own, in the corner of Yasmine's living room. She's pulling her scariest face while waggling her magic wand into the camera.

'Amazing.' She laughs. 'I love that she's ninety per cent covered in fake blood. No "less is more" mantra for Winnie. Ooh, nice chair,' she adds, zooming in on the background. 'I've been stalking one just like that. Where's it from?'

'Not sure,' I say weakly. It's vintage and upcycled. Yasmine took great pains to tell me that after I wrongly identified it as made.com.

'Well, your friend has great taste,' is all Lily says. 'What was her name again?'

'Er, Sheara.' Shit. What if she looks on Facebook and sees that I've liked Sheara's post about having a cheeky autumn week away in the Canary Islands?

It doesn't help that I'm behaving hyper-suspiciously. Should I just confess? Jusna sent a load of pictures out to the P&P WhatsApp group, and the barrage was punctuated with a stark 'Lily has left the conversation'. But did she do that before or after the pictures were sent? Is she waiting for me to tell her? She's being too nice for someone who knows I lied. Unless she's *trying* to catch me out. Jesus, how do people have actual affairs?

'Anyway,' she starts carefully. 'I wanted to talk to you about something.' An awkward look crosses her face.

She *does* know. How can I tell her that she's just not part of the group, without sounding like an eight-year-old?

'The Bonfire Night fair is coming up and I thought I could take the girls to it.'

'What?' My voice sounds as though she's asked me and Danny for a threesome. Would Danny be interested in a threesome?

'Seriously, Im, are you OK? Bonfire Night. The fire brigade run a firework display every year. I thought I could take the girls.'

'Yes, I know about the bonfire. Danny and I were planning on taking Win.'

'I thought I could take both Winnie and Enid. You've helped me out so much lately with after-school pick-ups –'

And before school drop-offs, and the odd 'hour' at weekends, I add mentally. At least she's acknowledging it. Finally. She's forever banging on about a childminder that keeps letting her down, but it happens so often that I'm starting to wonder if she even exists.

'– I wanted to return the favour. I thought you and Danny could have a date night.' She gives me a meaningful look and I try not to squirm with embarrassment.

A few weeks ago, at Mo's birthday party, it felt like Lily and I were picking up our old friendship. But we had that one honest chat and the next thing I knew she was throwing a goodbye over her shoulder and stomping out with Enid as though we hadn't spoken. Since then I've barely seen her. We swap friendly texts and she asks me to help with Enid, but whatever intimacy it ignited has fizzled out. It bothers me that she knows things about my relationship that I haven't told anyone else.

'They can have their tea at ours and then I'll take them to the bonfire,' she's saying. 'Winnie can even stay over if she wants.'

Lily's face is eager, as though she's waiting for me to agree. Open, vulnerable. Like she was before she told me Joe was useless and burst into tears. She's always been like this. One of those people who would rather be seen as spiky and glib than confess her true feelings, but then every so often there's an unexpected outpouring of emotion.

Not long before she met Joe, she drunkenly told me she was frightened she'd never meet someone. The next day she pretended it never happened and just gave me a cold look when I asked how she was. That was when we were younger, when I had time to prod and cajole her feelings out of her, and it was exhausting. *She* can be exhausting.

But she *does* owe me one. More than one. Danny and I have enough babysitting credits with Lily for a three-week holiday in the Maldives. Maybe this is Lily making an effort, properly this time. With her it's best to take your chances where you can.

So, a date. Together. Out of the flat. Lily's right, even if she's been cack-handed about saying it. Everyone I know is trying for a second baby and I haven't even seen Danny naked in weeks. Months.

'Thank you, yes.'

Maybe I'll book a hotel. Get out of the crap rented place that we still haven't done up properly. We were always shagging in posh boutique hotels when we started going out. If I hadn't accidentally got pregnant with Winnie seven months in – conceived in a junior suite at the Hoxton Hotel – we probably would have done a lot more of it. And it's been gnawing at me. When was the last time I even tried to initiate sex? When was the last time *he* did? Danny's not like Joe, selfish and spoiled. He makes me feel respected and valued. But it's been a long time since I felt desired. We *do* need this.

'And yes, it would be great if Winnie could stay over,' I say.

Four days later I'm reminded how gut-searing it feels to put yourself out there and to be let down. Small and nothingy, like your needs are inferior. The humiliating burn of rejection.

Gah, nightmare day. I'm not going to make it back from work in time. Can you take the kids to the bonfire instead?

It's an announcement, not even a proper apology. So like Lily. I start to cry as I reread the text for the billionth time, just as Danny opens the door with Winnie and Enid in tow, fresh from picking them up.

'What's wrong, Mummy?' Winnie runs over, confusion and worry etched across her face. A twinge of anger directed at Lily fires through me. I hate that she's made me like this in front of Winnie; it frightens her when I'm upset. Enid is hanging back, not knowing how to react to the sight of Winnie's mummy sobbing on the sofa.

'Oh, nothing,' I say, swiping my eyes and forcing a smile that I don't feel onto my face. 'I was watching a video of a tiger befriending a goat and it was just too sweet.'

'Show me!' shouts Winnie, laughing with delight. I open the app, praying that YouTube can deliver on this particular configuration of unlikely animal friendships.

'In a minute, girls,' Danny calls, shooting me a worried look. 'Let's have some fish fingers before we go to the bonfire.' He steers them into the kitchen, squeezing my shoulder as he goes past. This small, kind gesture threatens to set me off again. 'Don't worry. We'll go out another time. Some of the nursery staff do babysitting on the side. We'll pay someone, that way we're not relying on someone's goodwill.'

'It's not goodwill if they're returning the three thousand favours you've already done for them. Plus, that's not the point. She shouldn't have let us down like this.'

'I know. It's shit. But these things happen.' He doesn't even know about the hotel room. That was going to be a surprise. A boozy meal – nothing too heavy so we'd just want to sleep – followed by a night in a hotel. Like the old days. But in the old days, the hotel room was usually a perk of one of our jobs, whereas I've just wasted a hundred and fifty quid that we don't have on a hotel room we're not going to stay in.

My resentment is still simmering when we get to the former industrial estate that's being used as the site of this year's bonfire. The girls are so excited, but all I can think is: we shouldn't be here. This is my night off. My *one* night off. I try to get into the spirit of it, but I'm short-tempered, snapping *no* when the girls ask if they can have a sparkler for the twentieth time while we're standing in the queue to get in.

Lily's text, saying '*Ubering back. I'll meet you there*' doesn't help. I've fallen for that one before. She usually sends a message like that when she's thinking about leaving work in about forty-five minutes' time.

Like everywhere in Walthamstow, the area we're queuing outside is earmarked to have flats built on it, but the developers have bought favour with the council by lending them the razed land for the annual community bonfire, supervised by the fire service. They've already lit it when we finally get in, the air thick with the smell of smoke, and firefighters are manning the barriers that keep the public away, handing out stickers and glow sticks. Two engines flank one end of the site, which at least makes the metal fences that run around the whole thing look less depressing, and they're letting children take turns at switching on the lights. At the other end there are fairground rides, ice cream vans and hot dog trucks, so Danny runs to get some lollies before we look for a decent spot to see the twenty-minute firework display. It's packed, and within half an hour they've stopped letting people in; the queue that circles the metal perimeter barriers stretches all the way down the street. He hands me a bag of bonfire toffee. 'Thought you could chew this. It'll give your mouth something to do other than pout.' He nudges me gently with his hip to show he's joking.

'Ha ha. Sorry. I'm just fed up.'

'I know. But look –' he points to a group of people waving outlines with their sparklers in front of a stall selling them '– we can finally cave about the sparklers and then spend the whole time panicking they're going to burn their hands on the hot end.'

I laugh properly this time. 'Let's try and hold them off a bit longer. This way, guys.' We squeeze through a gap in the crowd, to get to the funfair games at the periphery, and I spot Yasmine, Kim and Jusna with their kids and some of their husbands huddled around the hook-a-duck.

'What are you doing here?' Yas shouts over. Humiliation rises again. I'd made a big show of telling her we were having a night away. Fucking Lily. Everything is *always* about her. She didn't even say sorry. I give Yasmine a wave, in what I hope is a casual manner, and direct everyone away again.

'It's a bit busy at the minute. We'll come back to the games in a bit,' I say. The last thing I want to do here is start crying again. I grab for Danny's hand and he drops his phone on the ground, where it bounces on the uneven concrete. We both dive to grab it.

'Shit!' He picks it up, turning it over to check the screen. 'It's OK, it's not cracked.'

'Right, girls, it's a bit less crowded over there. Let's go.' I look down at Winnie. 'Where's Enid?'

She just looks at me, and instantly my blood starts to rush. Everywhere I look there are swarms of people, and none of them is Enid.

'Danny, stay with Winnie,' I shout. 'ENID!'

I push through the people looming towards me. My breath is all little gasps, panic hurtling through my body. The smells of the bonfire, candyfloss and chip vans mingle together. I think I'm going to be sick.

She can't have gone far. Fuck, fuck, fuck.

Away from the light of the bonfire it's really dark.

'ENID!' I'm sweating and shoving people out of the way, not caring what they think, and working my way back to Yasmine. I grab her arm. 'Have you seen Enid? She's wandered off. She was right there two minutes ago and now I can't find her.' My voice is shaking, and Yasmine's eyes widen with alarm, before she jumps into gear.

'We'll find her.' She turns to the group, radiating efficiency. 'We've got a lost child, people,' she shouts. 'Jus, you stay here with the kids, and Kim and I will split up and look.' She points to the left. 'Kim, you go that way. Tell the person on the front gate what she looks like and give her your number. I'll go that way, and Imogen –' she gives me a little nod '– you retrace the way you came. Get Danny to tell one of the firefighters and they can put a call out on the radio to all the others. What's she wearing?'

My mind blanks. My insides clench as I reach for the outfit she arrived at our house in and tears start spilling down my face. 'I can't remember. A Gruffalo jumper.'

Yasmine puts her hands on my shoulders, holding me steady.

'Breathe, Imogen. She's here, we'll find her. Just focus: what's she wearing? Coat, trousers, any hat or scarf?'

'Erm, erm.' I force myself to inhale. 'Red coat, blue jeans and brown furry boots. A green bobble hat.'

'Good.' She gives me a reassuring look. 'EVERYONE! WE HAVE A LOST CHILD. THREE-YEAR-OLD GIRL. RED COAT. BLUE JEANS. GREEN HAT.' People around us start murmuring and looking, spreading the description like a ripple. Kim takes off running, shouting to call her with any update. 'Imogen,' Yasmine says, 'do you remember which direction you're covering?'

'Yes,' I say. 'I'm going over there.' As I turn, I see Enid standing in front of the carousel, not even ten metres away, staring at it, entranced, as it whizzes round.

'ENID, GET OVER HERE RIGHT NOW!' I scream.

She's in her own world and the terror in my voice cuts through, causing her to burst into tears. I run over and grab her, probably a little too hard. I'm shaking all over.

'Oh my God, you frightened me so much. DON'T walk off like that, I didn't know where you'd gone.'

Adrenaline pumps through my system as my mind starts feeding me snapshots of how bad it could have been. Of her being burnt by the bonfire. Of someone taking her. I can't stop crying either.

'We're all in a flap here, Enid, because we didn't know where you'd gone,' says Yasmine in a soothing voice. It's as helpful for me as it is for Enid. I feel my breath returning to somewhere near normal, the queasiness dissipating. 'But we've found you now, darling, so we're all relieved. We were just very worried.'

'I came to look at the horses,' she sobs.

'It's OK, it's OK.' I wipe my face, pulling myself together. 'Come and hold my hand. I'm sorry I shouted. You won't wander off on your own again, though, will you? You need to make sure you stay with me and Danny.'

Danny. I need to tell him where we are. He must be freaking out.

'Yasmine, thank you so much for your help. Will you tell Jusna and Kim that the panic is over and we've found her?'

'Of course. I'll text them now. But I'll stay here with you until Danny gets here. It'll give us all a chance to calm down.' I can tell it's because she doesn't want to leave me with Enid in the state I'm in, but I'm grateful all the same.

I pull out my phone. It trembles in my hand. It's been four minutes. The longest four minutes of my life. I dial him one-handed, so I don't have to let Enid go for a second.

'Dan, I've found her. Thank God. I'm coming back over now.' As I hang up, it rings again. I answer without looking.

'WHERE ARE YOU?' Lily screams. 'I GOT TO THE GATE AND KIM WAS TELLING THE WOMAN ON THE DOOR THAT THERE WAS A LOST KID WEARING THE SAME CLOTHES AS ENID.'

'It's all right, I've got her. She's here. We're next to the trucks at the back, where all the games are. She's all right.' I stand stock-still with Enid, my hand trembling. 'Your mummy's on her way, Enid,' I manage to croak out. 'We'll just wait here for a minute.' Yasmine pulls a packet of tissues out of her pocket and starts cleaning up Enid's face, murmuring about the fireworks starting soon, and how fun that Mummy will be here to see them after all.

Minutes later, Lily tears through the crowd, face pale, and grabs Enid on sight.

'What happened?' she barks at me without waiting for a reply, and then shouts, 'Are you OK?' at Enid. 'It's OK, baby, I'm here,' she says in a gentler voice, pulling her hard into a hug. She gives me a furious look over Enid's shoulder. 'It's rammed,' she says, her voice jagged. 'How could you take your eyes off her?'

I jerk as though she has slapped me. 'It was a split second,' I say, tears threatening to come again. 'She wandered off and I went straight after her. I feel terrible about it.'

'It's so easily done,' Yasmine chips in, throwing a sympathetic look in my direction. She might as well have thrown petrol onto the bonfire.

'Is it, Yasmine?' she snaps, pointing an accusatory finger at her. 'So have you lost your kid too?'

Yasmine stiffens, but Lily's spite cuts through my shock. 'Yasmine was *helping* me look for her, Lily. Everyone was.'

Lily reaches down to stroke Enid's head as if to check she's still there. 'How did she slip out of your sight to start with?'

'I don't know. There's so many people here, we were trying to get through the crowd, and then Danny dropped his phone.' My voice catches. 'We looked up and she'd gone. I didn't do it on purpose, I'm so sorry. But she's here, she's safe.'

Lily lets out a long, shaky breath. 'I nearly had a heart attack. I've been queuing up for ages to get in, and then I got to the front and all I could hear from the security guard's radio was that a child had gone missing. I kept thinking, "who would take their eyes off a child in this crowd", and then I realised they were talking about Enid. They wouldn't let me in to start with. It was Kim turning up that convinced them.'

She's right, it must have been horrific. But it sounds like an accusation. I take a step towards her. 'I'm sure you would have done a much better job if you'd been here,' I say, my voice dripping with sarcasm. 'Like you were *supposed* to be. And if you had been, I wouldn't have been responsible for your child. *Again*. Maybe you could think about that instead of having a go at me.'

Being challenged startles her, and Lily's face, which was so self-righteous a second ago, collapses. 'You're right. I'm sorry. I was stuck at work, and I couldn't get away. You've helped me out lately and I'm really grateful.'

'Yes, I bloody well have.' I'm on a roll now. 'Try at least twice a week. You've been taking the piss, Lily. Tonight you didn't even apologise. Just assumed I'd pick up the slack.'

'Didn't I? We were in the middle of a raid briefing. I barely had time to message. I'm so sorry, Imogen, though, I really am.' Her voice is humble now, and she seems to shrink, pulling Enid into her, but it feels like something has loosened inside me. Memories are hitting me like missiles.

'You always did take the piss, though, didn't you?' I say, gesticulating madly. 'Good old Imogen. No need to make an effort with any of her friends because you think they're all shallow. Move your boyfriend into her flat but don't bother getting him to pay any rent, she won't mind. Ghost her as soon as you find the bloke you want to settle down with.' Every time she has ever wronged me is fizzing out. I tick them off on my fingers and then look at her, inviting her to tell me I'm wrong. Yasmine is looking down at the floor, deliberately not making eye contact with either of us, probably in case she gets dragged back into it. I clock that she's still staying there to listen in, though.

Lily returns my glare, jaw tensed. 'What are you talking about? Ghost you? You came to our wedding. You didn't even invite me to yours.'

'WE'RE NOT MARRIED!' I shout. Even over the din of the fairground rides and the chatter, people around us have started to stare at the two women having a public barney. I'd be mortified if I wasn't so fucking livid. 'You'd know that if we'd actually spoken to each other in the

115

last five years.' Even as I'm saying it, I wish I hadn't. I was keeping our marital status on the down-low from the church. I race on. 'But now I'm just someone you use for childcare while you get on with your important career, and God forbid you actually return the favour. I'm more than a hundred quid out of pocket for the date Danny and I should be on tonight, when instead you're accusing me of being negligent to your daughter.'

'I'm not. It was just a shock. It's been a hell of a day.' I shoot her another death glare for daring to circle the conversation back around to herself. 'You can still go, I'm here now.'

I stuff my clenched fists in my pockets and a bitter laugh comes out. 'I don't think I could be *less* in the mood for a night out than I am at this moment.'

'Winnie could come to us if you like,' Yasmine says tentatively. She takes a small step towards me, nodding gently, as though she's negotiating a hostage situation.

Lily shoots her a dirty look and Yasmine recoils again. 'I've just *said* I can have her, Yasmine.'

She holds her hands up in surrender. 'Sure, fine. I just thought I'd offer.'

'Well, no need to insert yourself into this. I'm sure you can have a good bitch about me later. But a quick tip – it's probably best not to do it in a public place if you don't want to be overheard.'

Embarrassment clouds Yasmine's face, and she makes as though to go. What the hell is Lily on about now? How has she managed to turn this around on us?

'Don't have a go at her, Lily,' I snap. 'And she's not inserting herself into anything. She's trying to help, which is more than you've done for me in the last five years, never mind in the last five weeks. All you've been since

I arrived is an extra complication.' It's true. She's been using me. My resolve hardens and I feel myself standing straighter. I say what I should have said to her weeks ago. 'Winnie and Enid have become friends, and that's lovely, but it seems stupid to keep pretending that it makes us friends too.'

The sound of my voice is snatched away by the shriek of the first fireworks exploding. But I hold Lily's defeated look for a long second, before turning away to find my boyfriend and daughter in the crowd.

9

10 places available (three parents vocalising 'medium-term house moves' — further into the catchment area — due to 'major renovations')

Lily

Trials, Tribulations and Experiments

Motherhood, eh? A constant rollercoaster of emotions. Am I doing everything I can to protect my daughter's future? Am I being overprotective? How much do I intervene in the ever-evolving friendship politics? I know snatching toys = bad, but do I just leave her to figure the rest out on her own? I mean, we've all watched *The Secret Life of 4-Year-Olds*, but this isn't a social experiment, it's my kid!

Full disclosure: she's not the only one dealing with 'evolving friendships' right now. It's funny how after becoming a parent some parts of your life fall away and others are thrown into sharp relief. Maybe they need to make a *Secret Life of 34-year-olds*! I wrestled with whether to go here, but *deep breath* not all my friendships have survived motherhood. One friendship, with someone I thought I'd be friends with forever, disintegrated before either of us even became parents, and I'm sure (hoping!) anyone who's been friend-dumped will be able to relate. Your lives were different, moving in different directions, but you had a shared history that bonded you together. Didn't you? Until it didn't. That person recently came back into my life, and even though we're in similar places – in life stage and geographically – now, the distance is too much to bridge.

I fidget in the car seat, adjusting my stab vest, which always digs into my hip when I'm sitting down, then pull the other end down where it's pinching the crease in my underarm. Imogen's blog is about me; and I can't stop reading.

Another bit of TMI: I got pregnant by accident. Regular readers (hi, Mum!) will know how much I love being a mum, but four years ago you might not have predicted it, and no one's been more surprised than me. D and I? Well, we were sort of a seven-month-stand. We both had jobs that took us around London's champagne and canapé circuit, with terrible salaries but excellent perks – business credit cards, hotel rooms, corporate accounts at Fresh and Wild, and LOTS of parties. We didn't so much date as end up at the same events before falling into bed together. Yeah, one of those. It was probably never supposed to be serious, and then it got really serious, really quick. And now it makes my heart break and sing at the same time when I see Winnie with her dad. She adores him. And so do I. He's my rock, my therapist, my love, my everything.

So what I'm saying is, some friendships might not last, but if you're lucky you can end up with your best friend – plus crazy stupid sex too – result!

I snort out loud. I've been stalking her archive for the past twenty minutes but the latest one has got to be the worst offender yet. What a load of bollocks. Unless they've been at it since Mo's birthday party, they haven't even *had* any of that sex she's bragging about. Although how would I know? She wouldn't confide in me, she made that abundantly clear at the Bonfire Night event. My face goes hot with shame. Thank God I haven't had to face her. A new childminder who so far hasn't fallen through, followed by a life-saving visit from my mum, has afforded me almost two weeks of avoiding the school run. Not to mention some space to breathe. Whenever Mum comes down I fantasise about what it would be like to move back home to Leeds, with parental help on tap. Mum does school pick-ups for Pearl twice a week, plus babysitting. My sister's entire childcare set-up takes Mum's ongoing support into account – as I well know from the aggy texts she's been sending me this week about what a 'nightmare' it is having Mum away for seven whole days.

My radio crackles and Sanj's voice cuts through the silence. 'We're approximately three miles from the location.'

Eddie then springs into action, from where he's been taking his turn at keeping lookout from the driver's seat next to me.

'Look lively, breaktime's over,' he says, jutting his chin at the windscreen. I put my phone away, adrenaline surging through my body. He keeps passing the warrant he's holding from hand to hand: a nervous tic to make sure it's still there. Two men are approaching the self-storage building in east London whose car park we're in, and although it's still too shadowy to make a proper ID, we're confident that somewhere around here is Raymond Stamp, the Mr Big we've been building a case against for the past two months. We've been staking out this desolate industrial estate for three hours, and now I offer up a silent thank you to my mum for facilitating this all-nighter and letting me concentrate on the job in hand. In two hours, she'll get Enid up, dressed and fed and then deposit her at St Peter and Paul's, before collecting her again this afternoon if need be. For once I don't have to worry about it, or rush back.

The two men are lurking outside the dark entrance of the building, which is exactly where we want them to be. John and Sanj have been tailing another member of the gang following a tip-off about a consignment of 'plywood' that was driven off a ferry in Dover, and if all our intel is correct it will end up at this lock-up, where our mark will be waiting to unload it into a unit that sniffer dogs would disagree contains only timber. At that point, we'll swarm the place in co-ordinated simultaneous dawn raids, or 'knocks' as we refer to them. Following the collaboration with Yorkshire, this is what we've been working towards.

More of our squad is dotted in and around the container yard, and more still are sitting outside Stamp's house, poised to produce another warrant when we give the signal, before turning over his home for money and contra.

A brand-new BMW transit pulls in, and a few seconds later I see the dim glare of John's dipped headlights as he stops down the road. From our spot concealed halfway behind an outbuilding I see a third man – and *yes*, it's Stamp – walk out of the unit's front door and gesture for the driver to pull in closer to the building. He does, and then the driver – Ashley Towndrow, a known suspect – along with two male passengers in their early twenties, jumps out of the van and they all start unloading crates from the back.

From there it all happens at once. Eddie coils up, cuffs in one hand, warrant in the other, and shouts 'GO' into his headset. He jacks his car door and simultaneously I tear mine open. Then I'm out and heading to where the men are moving the stash, while the other teams surround them from all sides. Stamp clocks us and runs back into the building, and Eddie follows, with Sanj running through the front gate to join him. John, like me, is moving towards the van. It's exactly as we choreographed.

'HMRC, we've got warrants to search,' shouts John as we close in. Towndrow freezes, his body language showing he's resigned to the catch. He drops the crate he's holding and stands limp with his arms hanging next to his sides. One of the other guys turns and instantly I can tell. Most of the time, people go quietly, but occasionally – like now – you see the fight-or-flight reflex kick in. I shake my head at him, but no, he bolts, heading for the front gate, his baggy jeans and skinhead blurring as he shoves past John and knocks him over.

'I'm on him, Chief,' I call, taking off after him. I pull a sharp left at the gate, and see him disappearing up the road, into where the warehouse buildings give way to a housing estate crammed with concrete tower blocks. He's quick, but I know I've got it in me to accelerate so I do, even as my lungs start to burn. Then he gets to a junction and stops abruptly. I'm seconds away from him. My next thought is to brace inside my body armour, but at the pavement's edge he starts bouncing on the spot and looking around wildly, and I realise he has no other plan than 'escape'.

As I reach him, I grab and then twist his arm behind his back to restrain him, the way we've been taught in our six-monthly officer safety training sessions, and it gives me a firm enough hold to get the cuffs on. Whatever instinct was driving him has dissipated and, stock-still, he meets my eye with apprehension. Early twenties was an overestimate. Close up, he looks around eighteen. My guess is that he's just a hired grunt, paid to unload, which could work in our favour, because when you arrest a whole crew in one swoop, there's a good chance you can persuade some of them to inform. My kid here is a good bet.

I finish reading him his rights while he gasps for breath.

'You're fast,' he pants, once I've told him of his right to legal representation and to consult the codes of conduct.

'I know,' I reply cheerfully, guiding him back up the street. I'm not even tired, just pumped. My legs are aching in a pleasing, purposeful way. 'I used to run for Yorkshire as a teenager. If my boss had chased you, you'd probably be halfway to Essex by now. Unlucky.'

He's silent after that, but the entire yard is buzzing with activity when we come back through the front gate. I deposit him next to John's car, where Towndrow is standing in handcuffs, having not moved an inch since we've been gone. Officers are meticulously photographing and cataloguing the crates, or directing and carrying what seems like an endless parade of them through the storage unit doors. Overseeing it all, and making sure due process is being followed, is John.

'Well done,' he mouths, giving me an approving nod. I beam, prickling with pride, and look around to see where Stamp and the others might be sequestered. On the other side of the lot is another huddle of men in handcuffs, including Stamp, with Eddie, Sanj and a couple of others supervising them.

'Nice one, Paula Radcliffe,' says Eddie, spotting me and coming over to slap me on the back. He grins, flips his hair – another Eddie affectation when he's feeling pleased with himself – and gestures to the containers. 'First estimate is, there's a million mixed-brand cigarettes among this lot.'

'I'd put money on him testifying against the others too,' I say, pointing over to where my teenager is standing.

'Even better. Plus, Zed team hit the jackpot at the house. Meticulous "sales records" dating back to 2010, and a shit-ton of cash. I bet John's already practising his Senior Officer voice for the press turning up.'

'This is going to piss all over the Yorkshire lot's haul,' I say, trying to hold in the urge to offer Eddie a high five.

'It's not a competition,' John chips in while walking over, and looking very much like someone who's just won a competition. 'We wouldn't have been able to do any of this without their input and hard work.'

'Yeah, yeah. No need to be magnanimous. The press aren't here yet, Chief,' Eddie grins. 'Team breakfast after this to celebrate?'

'Tradition demands it,' confirms John. 'So, let's get all this processed, please.'

'I'm guessing you won't be able to make it,' says Eddie to me mildly. He doesn't mean anything by it, but it stings all the same. They're used to me ducking out of things by now.

I look at my watch. Five a.m. In three hours, after we've started the paperwork, my mum will already have taken Enid to preschool. And no matter how boring the paperwork is, there's no way I'll be able to go home and sleep. I let my mind linger on the job we've just carried out, the success it's been and my part in making it happen. Months of work paying off, even if there's still plenty of work ahead to make a conviction stick when it gets to court in a few months' time. I'm too wound up and energised to switch into mum mode. Plus, while my mum will congratulate me, she won't be interested in or understand the details. I want to relive the whole thing with people who are as buzzed about it as I am.

'Count me in for the team breakfast,' I say. 'But I veto the usual greasy spoon. Let's go somewhere good.'

IO

5 places available (five families in catchment-lock streets identified, who all display appropriate churchgoing, God-fearing behaviour)

Imogen

'It's just not . . .' Yasmine pauses as she flicks her eyes over the PowerPoint slides I'm scrolling through and searches for the right word. 'As *strong* as I was hoping for.'

I force my face into a neutral expression. Inside my head I'm screaming, *I'm sorry I haven't managed to come up with the baked-beans-banning equivalent of This Girl sodding Can.*

'I just think that it's a bit pie-charty and dry,' she's saying, swiping past all the infographics I spent ages designing and even longer researching. She flaps a hand in front of one. 'What are all the other elements on there? It's confusing. And there are loads of statistics. I was thinking of something with a bit more . . .' Another pause for the right word as she smooths her Jennifer Aniston hair. 'Pizzazz.'

Strictly Come Dancing has pizzazz. That's why it's Saturday-night prime time TV. Beans and their perceived dangers do not have pizzazz. I repress the image of Lily calling Yasmine and her gang 'the Organics'. Why couldn't she have got obsessed with road safety like I suggested? It would have been easy to convince the other parents of its importance, and it wouldn't also involve directly having a go at the school, which is why this is making me so uncomfortable. Do I really want to stick my head above the parapet to criticise the way they do things while trying to get a school place? No. But I can't say that to Yasmine. I need to be delicate.

'The thing is, Yas,' I start carefully, 'is that it's just not really a campaign.'

Ice. Her look is ice. And her voice is flat. 'And why's that.'

Because I've worked on about seventy billion campaigns, and this isn't one, I think, but don't say.

'Because I feel like there's only one obstacle and one goal, that would be just as well achieved by asking the other parents to sign a joint letter or by speaking to Mr Brown and providing a cost-effective alternative. There's just not much –' and here I falter because the ice is still emanating from her eyes '– meat.' I try and follow up with a joke. 'Especially because they use free-range meat, so we can't even throw that in as part of the issue.'

'I see.'

Yasmine has her chin propped up on one elbow at my kitchen table, and every time she looks away from the screen I feel like she's looking around our dingy flat in judgement. I hate it when she 'pops over' to our place, but don't want her to think I always expect her to host gatherings and make coffee, so always have to invite her in.

I ramp up my verbal jazz hands. The peppy tone everyone at my agency used with clients when we were struggling to come up with ideas that they liked. The brands that were determined to try and sell pink beer to 'women', that famously one-type demographic. There's only so many ways you can say that people – even women – who like beer will drink it regardless of what colour it is, and those that don't will just drink something else. But at least with the pink beer brigade we cynically knew that a sexist campaign would at least get them publicity, and therefore a platform: the beans don't even have a whiff of controversy. We just want to swap beans for no beans. Or home-made beans. End of.

Back to the voice. 'The charts are to show what other everyday foods contain hidden sugar, because there are loads. We need a hook to get everyone's attention, so I thought we could root it there.'

Yasmine pouts. '*Surely* everyone knows about hidden sugar by now. Jamie Oliver's been banging on about it for years.' She says the last bit as though Jamie Oliver stole the idea from her.

'Yes. He has.' Which is what I said to her when she brought up the beans to start off with. 'He's also brought hidden sugar to the masses, been prepared to have a go at the government and influence policy, and has a massive platform from which to talk about the bigger picture. So far, we have one product and one school, so it might be worth invoking Jamie to harness some sort of larger awareness campaign and make it about more than this. Piggyback on some new research or figures.'

'I just don't think it's what we discussed. You're over-complicating it. I think we need to strip it back.'

I physically hold in a truculent sigh. I was offered some work this week and said no, because Yasmine was so determined to present our anti-beans campaign at the next school governors' meeting that she gave me a two-day deadline to get all this work done. And now I have to start again.

The conversation hangs there like a vague threat. 'How's the house hunt going?' she asks. It could be her attempt to lighten my increasingly dour mood, but only serves to remind me that she's in a catchment-lock and I'm not.

'It's not. The latest house of doom ended up going for seven hundred grand.' Jay isn't even returning my calls. I'm toying with the idea of leafleting the streets surrounding the school to see if anyone is thinking about selling or renting. Although Lily once told me she gets a couple of those type of leaflets stuck through her door every month.

I haven't heard a word from her since Bonfire Night, when she sent a text a couple of hours after our argument.

Sorry. Thank you for your help. And I appreciate everything you've done for me and Enid. I hope it won't be awkward on the school run.

I didn't reply. If I'd acknowledged her, she'd probably have fired one straight back asking me to watch Enid in two Thursdays' time or something. I know what she's like. Plus, I've been busy. Yasmine has been bombarding me with deadlines for this campaign, even though she's yet to tell me when the governors' meeting actually is.

'Something will come up,' I continue. 'How are you feeling?' I nod at her bump and try to change the subject.

'I've definitely popped a lot earlier than I did with Arlo,' she groans. 'I'm the same size at five months that I was at full term last time, and I spend about forty-five minutes every day applying E45 cream. I'm SO itchy. It's like I've got fleas.'

'Well, you look great.' She does. 'The epitome of glowing.'

'That's contouring, babe, but you're sweet. I'm worried about how Arlo's going to handle the new baby, though. He's so used to getting all my attention. Between a new sister and starting school, it's a lot of change.'

'It is,' I agree. I suppress my jealousy. I wish that was a problem I had. I force a light, jovial note into my voice. 'He'll adapt, though. They all do. And aside from anything, one day he'll appreciate sharing the burden of deciding which old people's home to shove you and Tom in when the time comes. That's what siblings are for, right?'

Yasmine smiles politely. Lily would have laughed at that joke.

'You're right, it's best not to be an only child,' she says, before quickly adding, 'if you can help it, I mean.'

I've alluded before that we're having trouble conceiving number two. I haven't told her that the trouble is that the last time I could feasibly have missed a period was before the Brexit vote. There's an awkward silence where I just nod.

'Have you and Danny thought about getting married?' she says next. Another pivot. Her voice is light, but I sense the edge of unsolicited advice bubbling beneath the froth. I wish again that I'd never blurted out my unmarried status at the bonfire.

'We've talked about it a few times over the years.'

At one point, when I was pregnant, Danny proposed to me on average once a week. Sometimes he was joking, a couple of times he was romantic and earnest, and once he'd thought it through enough to screengrab a photo of a ring he thought I'd like but didn't want to buy in case I hated it. Or in case I said no again. Because I said no every single time. Not because I was dead against it, necessarily – although marriage didn't work out brilliantly for my parents, who have five marriages between them – but because his proposals felt like a reaction to me being pregnant, and deep down I suspected he wouldn't be contemplating marriage to me if I wasn't up the duff. Two months after we found out I was pregnant, I moved out of my poky rented flat and into his sleek new-build flat in a trendy part of Bermondsey. I barely even had enough savings to subsidise my statutory maternity allowance, while he at least owned his place, and while it was the best financial decision, I quickly felt dependent on him, financially and emotionally. But even as I was freaking out about the idea of being a single parent, I wanted to keep back one part of myself – one big decision – for when it felt like I'd be choosing to do it, rather than a kneejerk to finding myself unexpectedly, terrifyingly pregnant by a man whose middle name I'd only recently learned. After Winnie – like, immediately after Winnie, when I was still soaked in birth fluids – he proposed again and, drugged off my tits, I said yes. But not yet.

'I mean, technically we're engaged,' I say to Yasmine now. If she has to know about my marital status, she can at least think there's a statement of intent.

Danny used to bring up planning the 'wedding' occasionally when Winnie was tiny, and I'd tell him that we'd look into it when things settled down, not realising that things would never really settle down. But also, however much I tried I just couldn't be arsed to decide if I was more of a marquee or an urban registry office kind of a person (answer: neither. My parents have both had both, plus one barefoot beach do, and they're all equally lame, IMO). Plus, weddings cost a fortune and I want a house *way* more than I want a chocolate fountain.

'If you've already started planning, that's great!' Her face transforms at the prospect of a project. 'Any date in mind? If you need any help just let me know. I went Pinterest crazy when I planned mine. It was in a marquee at my parents' place in Surrey.'

'Mmmm.'

'Also –' I register the conspiratorial tone as the one she uses whenever she's about to say anything 'helpful' '– you might want to consider doing it sooner rather than later. It would look good with the school if you did it at St Mary's.'

'Good idea,' I say, just to stop her talking. Why does she care so much? *Is* it weird that we're not married? Would it really make a difference to our school place? Only if the head knows we're not already.

Yasmine swallows the last of her herbal tea and pulls herself up on the table. 'Anyway, I'd better get to yoga. The breathing techniques were so helpful last time round that I didn't even need any drugs. Did you ever try it?'

'Breathing techniques, yes. And then I quickly moved on to drugs.' I force out a laugh and she joins in, both of us desperate not to look like we think our choice was the best one (although Christ, who doesn't want the drugs?).

I stand up too and walk her to the door. 'I'll have another think about the whole campaign thing,' I say, forcing my tone to be enthusiastic, even though the thought of picking over all those slides again makes me want to throw my iPad out of the window.

'Good idea,' she beams. 'I know you said you've been out of the game for a while, so maybe you just need a bit more time to brainstorm.' Anger fizzes in my stomach. *What the actual?* I've presented multiplatform campaigns to MDs. I once spoke up at a meeting to a CEO who kept rejecting our ideas for vitamin supplements in favour of his own 'genius' one, oblivious to the fact that his press blitz called anyone – including the journalists we were sending the mailshot out to – over a size twelve, fat. He ignored me. The eventual ad campaign was withdrawn after thirty-six hours because of a public outcry. So why am I just standing here watching her go down my front path with a tense smile on my face and not telling her where to shove it?

She turns just as she gets to the pavement. 'Remind me to let you know when we've settled on a date for the autumn drinks night, so you have plenty of time to get a babysitter. It's just going to be a few people – some parents, Mr Brown and his wife, the vicar – you know, the gang.'

That, right there, is why. 'Enjoy yoga,' I say weakly.

'See you at pick-up,' she calls.

I'm sitting back down at the table, leafing through all the articles I printed out as research and trying not to despair, when Danny strides into the house and the kitchen, his laptop bag slung over one shoulder.

'Hello!' I say, glad of a distraction. 'What are you doing home so early?'

He puts his bag down on a chair and groans. 'I've got loads of stuff to do and I couldn't concentrate in the office.' Like me, Danny's background is in PR. 'We've been lent a Watson-enabled robot concierge by a client to create some clips with, and it was basically chaos. When I left, the social team were getting it to mix cocktails and serve them at their desks.' If I think beauty PR is sometimes ridiculous, Danny's tech stuff makes me feel better. He started as a press officer for an electronics company, but as the world has Apple-fied he's moved into content creation and social media. At thirty-nine, he's one of the oldest and most senior people in his office, and while he still nerds out about all the new tech he gets to play with before everyone else, he leaves the socialising to the younger ones in favour of getting home for Winnie's bedtime. Usually when there's team drinks he'll stay for the first round and then withdraw so the juniors can get drunk without their boss there. He seems to know where he is in the professional ecosystem – there to join in but not to cringily attempt to be the last man standing, which means they like and respect him. He's started dressing more smartly since I first knew him, and has settled into a sort of debonair preppy style, with swoopy Don Draper hair and a collection of chinos in neutral shades. Alex, his young, directional-hairstyled assistant in the office, once called him 'normcore' as a compliment, which we thought was hilarious because his 'look' is more 'almost forty'.

'You didn't fancy it?' I ask him.

'I'm expecting a call from a client, and I needed some quiet. Plus, I thought you might be able to help me with some of it.' He gestures to the rejected printouts that are spread on the table. 'Except I can see that you're in the middle of something. Did a freelance job come in?'

'It's not exactly new,' I say, defensive. Danny doesn't quite know how much time I've been dedicating to Yasmine's thing, mainly because he rolled his eyes and said 'Jesus wept' when I told him about it.

'Is it some more stuff from the avo-toast beauty people?' Back in the day we used to bounce ideas off each other all the time, but it's been ages since I've had anything to get my teeth into.

I don't want to get into this now, plus that whole thing with Yasmine – the 'brainstorm' where she shat on my work and made me feel like I need her to get in with the school, even if I do – has made me feel weird. Disorientated. She might be winning with the big house and the second baby and having a school place in the palm of her hand, but I was supposed to be the one with professional expertise. And now Danny's asking what I'm working on and I have nothing to tell him. I don't even need to do the school run for another couple of hours. And, it occurs to me, the house is empty.

'Don't worry about that now, Dan. You do realise we're at home, alone, together. When does *that* ever happen?'

'There was that afternoon when we moved out of the old flat and Winnie was at your mum's. I think there was fifteen minutes between the movers packing up the van and us setting off up here in the car.'

'Exactly.' I go over and put my arm around him, pulling him in for a hug. Without Winnie here turning it into a group hug situation, it feels off, like trying to stroke against the grain of a cat. I kiss him, tentatively, on the lips. I was hoping it would feel charged, but it somehow feels wrong.

Why does it feel like I need to be drunk to try and get off with my own boyfriend? At one point in our relationship we had sex in one of those posh hotel rainforest showers and there wasn't even a shelf to hoik my leg onto for a decent angle. And now I can't remember how to kiss? I persevere, and I want to say that he stiffens, which he does, but not in a sexy way. What actually happens is that his entire body tenses up. But he does slowly trace his knuckles down the line of my back, and start kissing my neck, which takes the pressure off us having to try and make our mouths work in unison, and also reminds me how much I like having my neck kissed. He hasn't been anywhere, but I get the sensation that I've missed him. I start to relax, pulling him closer, and feel him do the same.

But then Danny's phone starts buzzing in his pocket, and the vibration of it against my thigh makes me laugh. I move closer to him.

'It'll be that work call,' he says, pulling clear of me. Putting distance between us. He gets his phone out of his pocket, looks at it and then puts it away.

'Aren't you going to answer it, then?' You can hear the sulk in my voice, but I don't care. We were having a moment. The first one for a long, *long* time. And he's going to answer his phone?

'It's a random number. Probably PPI.'

'You don't know that.' Something's niggling me. Wasn't he dicking about with his phone the night we lost Enid too? That's why he dropped it. Could there be someone he doesn't want me to see calling or texting him? 'It could be a client. It's not like you have every single number of every single work contact saved in your phone.'

'It's a Manchester area code. All the junk calls I get are from there. There must be a call centre.' He sounds touchy. Is he touchy? It's still ringing.

'Answer it.'

He makes an irritated noise and yanks the phone back out of his pocket. 'Hello, Danny Graham speaking.' A pause. 'No, I haven't been involved in a car accident that wasn't my fault. Thank you, bye.' He hangs up and shoots me a look that says *happy now?*

I half-heartedly stroke his arm, trying to muster up some of the heat that was between us a few seconds ago, but the spark was already tiny and now it's impossible to revive. There's tension between us; it's just not sexual. We're like two people who have missed the same train and are now trapped on the platform, bound only by our shared awkward experience.

'I really should do this work and prep for the call,' he says, giving me what is best described as a fond squeeze on the shoulder. 'Do you mind if I move some of this over?'

Our place is so small that Winnie's bedroom is barely big enough for a single bed, her wardrobe and a chair. As a result, most of her toys are in crates in the living room, and it resembles a playroom rather than a grown-up living space. The table in the kitchen is the only place we can do any work, and even that is constantly covered in house detritus – paintings Winnie's brought home from nursery, leaflets for Pilates classes that I keep meaning to go to, taxi cards that get shoved through the door but never seem to make it to the recycling bin.

Danny starts piling my stuff up neatly at one end to split the table into duel workspaces, presumably so we can work side by side. Like colleagues. Sexy. Halfway through he stops, holding one of my pie chart-populated pages in mid-air. He squints at it.

'Is this that bloody beans thing?'

I snatch it out of his hand, embarrassed. 'It's just a few bits of research I've been messing about with.'

'A few bits . . .' He rifles through the sheets of paper. 'This is like a dissertation. Actually it's probably *better* than my dissertation was. Is this what you've been doing?' He sounds properly pissed off. 'Did Mags from the eco start-up not get in touch?'

That'll be the work I turned down. Her fledgling business, Earth Mother, is one of those fancy beauty companies selling high-end but all-natural and eco-friendly skin products for mums and babies – body wash, shampoo, pillow mists, all that stuff. She vaguely knows Danny from one of his previous jobs and emailed him on LinkedIn for advice because she doesn't have enough money or work to pay an agency yet, but thought he might have some ideas. He did: me. And he told her my 'boutique PR approach' (his words) could help both her and me out.

'I wasn't sure if I could do it in time for the deadline she gave,' I say, knowing how lame it sounds. 'I didn't want to do a crap or rushed job, otherwise she wouldn't think of me again.'

Danny looks perplexed. 'She told me she just needed a consultant in the first instance to talk through ideas. And you have time now Win's at preschool five days a week.' I've always valued Danny's opinion on work stuff, but I'm pretty sick of people telling me today what I should be doing with my time and energy.

'I don't have *all* this time, Danny,' I snap. 'I have other stuff on.'

'Other paid work?' he says, curious. I look away and he groans. 'Or bullshit school projects?'

'Don't make me feel guilty,' I fire at him. 'I need to get us in with the governors and head, and Yasmine is my way in. Getting Winnie into St Peter and Paul's is worth more than a few thousand quid in the long run.'

He sighs. 'It's not the *only* school, though, is it? We don't *have* to stay in Walthamstow.'

'Who looked into the schools? Who did the research? If you think you can find an affordable area that's a lock for a good primary and secondary *and* isn't a commute from hell into London, then be my guest. But you're going to have to do it in the next six weeks, because that's when the application deadline is. But maybe you don't even care if our daughter ends up at a decent school. I'm the only one of us still looking for houses. I'm the one doing everything I can to ingratiate myself with the right people.'

'Don't I bloody know it,' Danny mutters.

'What's that supposed to mean?'

'The way you're sidelining your career to suck up to a bunch of school mums—'

'I'm not sidelining my career.' My back is well and truly

up now. 'And don't say it like that. *School mums.* As though liking a bunch of mums would be pathetic.'

Danny rubs his hand across his stubbly chin and looks like he's trying to think of the best way to formulate his words. 'What happened to all the other things that used to get you fired up? The old you would have been desperate to manage Mags's project. Or to sink your teeth into pro bono work that means something. Not the dangers of desserts at a middle-class nursery.'

I think guiltily of the stuff I used to do with a literacy organisation in Bermondsey. I haven't been in touch with them for ages. 'I do still care about all that stuff. It's just that this – Winnie – is more important right now. Once she's in—'

'It feels like that's all you've been talking about for months, and now these – what did your friend Lily call them – the Stepford Organics? What, after you've ingratiated yourself with them, *then* you'll be ready to step back into your career? I just never thought you'd become one of *those mums.*'

'Well I'm SORRY, Danny.' I'm shouting now, and shaking, tears bubbling at the edge of my vision. If that's how he sees me, no wonder he's not interested in sex any more. I know at the minute I'm 'just' a mum. I'm even prepared to be *just a mum* until Winnie gets into the school. But until this moment, I didn't think there was anything wrong with that.

11

Lily

'She told me she was having marital problems,' comes the hushed voice as I approach the preschool stable gate. My heart sinks. From the back I can see there's one be-skinny-jeaned one and one in leggings, a figure-hugging running-type top and a bodywarmer. Yasmine and Kim. It's Yasmine speaking, of course.

I brace myself. It's the first time I've done the drop-off for two and a half weeks. Am I really going to immediately stumble into another hissed slating of my personal failings? Yasmine and Kim have already let Arlo and Thea run in and are now just chatting.

'Off you go, E,' I say with loud false cheer, to make sure they know I'm there.

Yasmine doesn't even flinch and gives me a steady look. I hold her gaze, even though I can feel myself going bright red. Has Imogen told her about me and Joe?

'Hi Lily,' she says, all chirpy. 'We're just talking about Jusna.'

So, not me then. Instead she's spreading gossip about one of her so-called BFFs to me.

'Right,' I say, going to put Enid's coat, hat and gloves on her peg. Somehow, we've lost a glove since we came in the door. I start rooting through my bag while Yasmine carries on talking as if I'm not there. I'm listening in but she's speaking so loudly I don't even really have to try.

'She told me that she and Ajay have been having some problems recently, poor thing. They're going to have a –' she does that thing people do when they ostensibly lower their voice and mouth something, but it's somehow louder than their original voice '– trial separation.'

'No!' Kim's hand flies to her mouth. 'I thought those two were rock solid. They're so well matched, and they always behave like the other is the most hilarious person they've ever met. Out of every couple I know, they're the ones who seem to like each other the most.'

Yasmine shoots her a pointed look. 'Apart from you and Tom,' Kim adds quickly. She gestures at her bump. 'I mean, you guys are always all over each other.' I've met Tom a couple of times. He really doesn't come across as an all-over-you kind of person. Unless you're in the service industry and have disappointed him. Then, I imagine he's all over you, but in a different kind of way.

'I know,' Yasmine says with a sigh. 'It's really sad. She says things just got really bad really quickly.'

For once I have to agree. That is sad. Jusna and Ajay always seemed like the most normal of her cronies. When she was separated from the pack, Jusna was always the most fun of the NCT crowd.

'I'll drop her a text,' says Kim. 'They seemed completely fine when I was round there the other week. God, there isn't anyone else, is there?'

'No! Nothing like that. She says they need some space and are going to get some counselling. He's rented a place, so he can be close to Mo, and they will both stay there half the week. It's in the new development on Dante Road.'

'That's fast work,' I blurt, interrupting, and revealing that I've found the glove and am now just earwigging. 'They only finished building it a couple of weeks ago. I thought most of them had been sold off plan.' There was a local protest when those flats were announced because the developers claimed to have included a certain number of affordable units, but from the prices it seemed like they were only affordable if you worked for a hedge fund.

'All the two- and three-bedrooms were, but there's some rentals apparently – they're tiny but at a push you can make the one-beds into a two-bed by converting the study-utility room that they all come with. Super-close to the school too, so he's still nearby.' She looks at me, and then to all Enid's paraphernalia that I'm holding.

'Is that the coat you've brought for Enid?' she asks.

'Yes,' I reply wearily. Too much to expect that we might have a normal conversation. Back to questioning my parenting choices. 'She grows so quickly, Yasmine, I can't justify spending insane amounts of money on clothes. I'm sorry it's not organic and sustainable, but I usually have to grab a coat while I'm doing the big shop because it's the only place I go clothes shopping these days.'

She flashes me a sarcastic smile. 'I didn't mean that, babe. And the big supermarkets can be very good these days when it comes to sustainability. You just have to make the effort to look. No, they asked them to wear waterproof coats and bring wellies today because they're going to the farm.'

Shit, they are as well. The winter school trip to the city farm, where they'll be outside all afternoon. Enid's already got her wellies on, because she insisted this morning, but she's wearing her duffel coat. I look out of the windowpane in the door. It looks like it's about to start pissing it down.

'God, you're right. I'll have to run home and fetch her puffa. What time are they leaving?'

'Not until nine thirty,' Kim says, 'you have time.'

'OK, good.' Although now I'm definitely going to be late for work and will no doubt get caught in the rain myself.

'She just needs a waterproof over the top of that one, I'd say,' says Yasmine.

Thanks for pointing it out, Yasmine, I want to say, but instead say, 'Yep, but we left that at Grandma's a while ago. I'll have to fetch her other coat, otherwise she'll be cold.'

'I think I've got Arlo's pac-a-mac in my bag. Do you want to borrow that?' she says, fishing around in her massive designer tote bag. She hands a little grey pouch to me. 'It'll save you going all the way home. I'm sure you've got to get to work.'

The pointed tone is unmistakable, but an offer's an offer, and it's one that's going to save me a twenty-minute round trip.

'If you're sure. Doesn't Arlo need it?' Enid will probably immediately fall in a cowpat, or lose it, and then it'll turn out to be from Gucci or something, but I'll deal with that later.

She shrugs. 'I always have a spare in here. The day I don't is the day Arlo will find a giant puddle and launch himself into it before I can stop him.'

'OK.' I brave a smile. 'Thanks. I'll wash it afterwards and get it back to you tomorrow morning.'

'No problem.'

'And I hope Jusna is all right. You know, with her marriage. It isn't easy going through a break-up at any time, but especially when there are kids involved. Must be rough.'

'It's just a trial separation,' Yasmine says, a touch of her usual ice back. 'I think having kids either brings you closer together as a couple or exposes your flaws, doesn't it? But

I'm sure they will be strong enough to work through it. Not everyone is.'

Is she still talking about Jusna? 'You're probably right,' I say. 'Thanks for the jacket.'

'Boardroom, meeting, now,' John says to me the second I walk in the door.

Shit. That's where they take you when you're going to be disciplined or fired. I look at my watch. I'm not late, so it can't be that. And then I look to see if Heather, the HR manager, whose existence I only ever register on annual pay increase day or when redundancies are being made, is in the vicinity.

I drop my bag on my chair as I pass and follow him, carrying my Pret coffee and croissant. Everyone else is doing the same, which calms me down a bit. Unless they're closing the entire office, it can't be job losses. I meet Sanj at the threshold of the boardroom door and he looks as nervous as I feel.

The boardroom is packed. All thirty of our section are in there and the seats are long gone. I spot a spare bit of wall to lean against at the back of the room.

'What's going on, Chief?' I hear as I make my way there. It's Eddie, who is sitting front and centre, and sounding much more than usual like the public school boy he is. Which means he's anxious too, and he's obviously been here a while to get pole position, so must have been stewing in curiosity. 'Nothing to do with the raid the other week, is it?'

'Sort of,' John says, and the room explodes with noise.

'Typical head office having a pop after the fact,' snaps Eddie. 'They're not the ones pulling fourteen-hour shifts to get the job done, though, are they?'

'That was a watertight knock, Chief. Textbook. How could anyone have a problem with it?' Sanj is shouting. 'And Lily went over our team's paperwork, so it's perfect.'

I'm weirdly proud about the unexpected compliment, although if it turns out I have missed something, I've no doubt that he'll be the first to turn on me.

'Simmer down,' John's saying while flapping his hands in front of him. The noise reduces to a loud grumble. 'Everyone here? Good. The knock went off like a dream, no one is questioning that. And the work was meticulous.' John catches my eye as he says this. 'In fact, it went so well that we've now got additional intel from the perps that indicates it's a much bigger operation than we, or Yorkshire, thought. *Much*.'

'How much?' Eddie again, back in full mockney flow.

'If we're right – and I think we are – we're talking one of the biggest hauls ever. Conservative estimate says, what is it –' he looks to the front row '– ten mill?'

A middle-aged woman who I've never seen before says, 'Intelligence points to more like fifteen, as there's a whole new network that has been—'

'What new network?' Eddie cuts her off and looks at John. 'Aren't we supposed to get a heads-up before they send the intel for general circulation?'

John glares at him. 'Yes, Eddie. That's what this is.' John's look is pure *shut up* and Eddie does. 'Head office has allocated extra resources so we can follow the chain to the top. We're talking international.'

There's a collective intake of breath and we look around at each other. This is big.

'The very welcome extra resources,' John is saying, 'include our Deputy Director of Fraud Investigation Services, who's going to say a few words.'

Eddie visibly blanches, as he realises someone from the head office he's just been slagging off is in the room, and we all look around for who it could be. The middle-aged woman sitting next to him stands up, and while we're all surprised, Eddie can't contain the shocked look on his face. She doesn't give him a second glance as she takes her place at the front and John stands back respectfully.

'Hi everyone, thanks for coming this morning,' she says. 'I'm Amanda Herriot, and the reason we're able to continue with this already highly successful operation is because of the hard work and perseverance of everyone in this room.' Amanda's voice is deep and low, and it makes us all take notice of her. I'd estimate she's in her late forties or early fifties. Her dark hair is shot through with grey and pulled back from her face in a neat chignon, and her smart navy trouser suit is a world away from John's sludge-coloured one. 'We're confident that we can get an even bigger result through intelligence gleaned from arrests already made, and our own ongoing investigation. Slow and steady. There's a whole web of information that's filtering through from port impounds, and our sources are building up a network of contacts, here and in Europe. I'll be here in a supervisory role for a few months, so I can connect the dots and see what additional resources your teams need to second from other regions.'

She's making it sound as though we're going to bring down the mafia (knock-off booze branch) through surveillance and submitting reports. I can't help being thrilled by her mere presence. She's the only woman I've ever heard of in that senior a role. At our branch there are quite a few at my level, all a bit younger than I am now, if I'm honest, and I assume it's the same in other regions, but above a certain level in head office, it's just white middle-aged men. Or so I thought.

'I've been impressed by the case work I've seen from several members of the team here.' At this John gives me a visible nod. I know it's visible because Eddie follows his gaze and I can see the spark of competition in his eyes. 'And I'm confident we can pull this one off. There are also going to be a number of new roles opening up, both temporary and permanent, so I'll filter down that information as and when.'

The briefing lasts another ten minutes or so, while she covers the logistics of where the seconded staff will sit and how John will put together teams, and then we all file out. My head is humming at the thought of our job feeding into an even bigger investigation. As I walk back down the corridor towards my desk, I realise that Amanda has fallen into step beside me.

'It's Lily, isn't it?' she says, fixing me with a focused look.

'That's right.' I hold my hand out and try to sound more confident than I feel. How does she know who I am? 'Nice to meet you. I'm really looking forward to working with you on this.'

'Likewise.' Her voice is just as slow and assured one-on-one as it is when she's presenting. She's tall, even taller than me, and carries herself confidently: straight posture, chin up, as though she's surveying the scene, which, as she's the biggest boss in the building, she probably is. I notice she's wearing clompy boots with her suit, which means she also sounds like she means business as we pass through the open-plan office back to where my team are filing back to their desks. I can tell everyone we pass is intimidated by the way their eyes flick in our direction and then quickly back to their computer screens, as though they're checking they have something work-appropriate on their monitor. 'From the catch-up I had with John,' she says, 'I hear you're going to be a real asset to the operation.'

'Thanks.' I go bright red. Professional. But I'm delighted. 'Whatever I can do to help.'

'Amanda!' John calls from somewhere behind us. I beam at him, grateful that he has bigged me up to her. He squints back at me as though I'm crazy but stops short of making a sarky comment in front of his superior. 'Can I borrow you?' he says, addressing her, and gesturing to me with his eyes to bugger off.

'Another meeting, I'm afraid,' she says to me, flashing me a smile. 'Nice to meet you, Lily.'

I'm still floating when I go to pick up Enid from the childminder's, despite clocking the stains she's managed to get on Arlo's mac in one day, including one that looks like permanent marker. 'The goats were cold, so they were all wearing jackets,' she informs me on the walk home. 'And the ducks are going to have babies but not until spring time.'

'That's right. What was your favourite animal?'

'The abacca,' she says. 'It was really fluffy.'

'The alpaca?'

'Yes. Abacca. And I'm going to be in the Nativity play,' she adds. 'Charlotte said I'm Mary.'

'Are you? That's brilliant.' The closest I ever got to the lead was as one of the angels standing in Mary's aura. I never even got to say a line. But maybe they all get a go as Mary. I keep seeing headlines about 'non-competitive sports days' where there's no winning, only taking part – as someone who excelled at running and loved nothing more than winning, I cannot get on board with this, especially as I was never in with a chance in drama – but maybe

148

they're branching out into other areas of competition. Like who gets to be the lead in the school play.

'Is everyone getting a turn to be Mary or Joseph?'

'No!' She looks outraged, my own competitive tendencies writ exaggeratedly large across her face. 'Just me, because I was the best at remembering the words. I don't want to do it, though,' she says airily. 'I want to swap.'

'Well, I'm sure that won't be a problem.' Loads of other girls will be dying to be Mary. 'But why don't you want to do it? I know it can be a bit scary being on stage in front of lots of people and talking, but we can practise and see how you feel.'

'I'm not *scared*.' The withering tone gives me a terrifying glimpse of how she's probably going to speak to me all the time in ten years. 'There's just another part I want more, and I've already asked to swap, and they've said it's OK.'

'Which part is it?'

'Joseph. I want a beard.'

I laugh. 'Well, OK. If the other person doesn't mind, that sounds like it should be all right.'

My phone beeps. It's Yasmine. A friendly reminder about the cagoule, I'm sure.

Wrong. All she says is:

We need to talk about the Nativity.

12

6 December 2018

4 places available (one marriage breakdown, facilitating a second address nearer the school)

Imogen

Yasmine looks like she's about to die of outrage.

'I just didn't take you for someone who was so intent on reinforcing binary gender norms,' Lily says to her lightly. Even though we're not speaking, and I'm ostensibly sitting at this school play summit in support of Yasmine, I have to suppress the urge to clap. Lily has completely out-gamed her on this one.

Around us, in the church hall, the Christmas decorations are half up. We had to abandon the job halfway through in order to have an 'informal' chat that Yasmine insisted on having, here and now. So now Yasmine, Lily, Mr Brown, the vicar, and somehow me, are sitting on chairs that have been arranged democratically in a semi-circle, while around us the others Blu-Tack snowflakes to the walls. As the wall nearest our group has *a lot* more snowflakes stuck to it than the rest, it's safe to assume they're riveted by the unfolding drama.

I'm surprised Lily has turned up tonight at all. Aside from Yasmine, the other eight or nine parents here, including Bex and me, are in catchment Siberia, and we all jumped at the opportunity to help with the annual decoration evening. Geographically, Lily doesn't really need to be here, so I can only imagine she thinks she needs to curry some favour on the Christian spirit front. This 'dialogue' (Yasmine's words) will definitely get her on Mr Brown's radar anyway, but perhaps not in the way she wanted.

'If we enforce this now,' Lily is saying, with the ghost of a smile as she delivers a killer blow, 'then who knows what it will do to our children's development.'

At the other side of the semi-circle Mr Brown just looks confused, and the vicar, who so far hasn't said anything, looks like he's trying not to laugh.

'Can you explain again what the problem is?' Mr Brown asks Yasmine. 'It's not really my place to get involved in a casting dispute about the Nativity.'

'The problem, Alan –' it's a subtle power play by Yasmine, proving she's the only one of the group that's on first-name terms with the head '– is that my Arlo is supposed to be Joseph, but Lily's daughter has convinced him to swap with her. And I'm just not sure there hasn't been some *coercion* –' nice, she won't actually say 'bullying' but we all know that's what she's implying '– involved.'

'COERCION!' Lily shouts, and Yasmine purses her lips as though Lily's being unreasonable by losing her temper. 'Enid says Arlo told her he wanted to wear a blue dress and hold the doll and she wanted to have a beard and hold a lamb. There's no coercion. It's win-win.' Lily flicks her attention to Mr Brown.

I know this voice. When she got her job at HMRC, she was terrified before her first court case. Not only had the defendants defrauded the government of about two hundred grand in tax, but during the raid, Lily's team had found a group of migrants locked inside a windowless storage container. They were being forced to roll the dodgy tobacco into cigarettes, and Lily was shaken for weeks afterwards. They'd done weeks of court case role-play during her training, but this was going to be her first real time on the stand, testifying. 'I can't fuck it up, Im,' she'd told me. 'If I waver, the defence will seize on it and they'll walk.' I practised with her the whole week before, and the head of the gang got seven years. That's the voice she's using now.

Mr Brown looks at me. 'What do you think?'

Four pairs of eyes laser in on me, as though I'm the deciding vote in their children's fates. Yasmine's gaze feels the heaviest, as though the whole thing is a test, while Lily looks away, an expression of defeat on her face. She's expecting me to side with Yasmine. Yasmine is expecting me to side with Yasmine. But I just can't bring myself to do it.

'If the children have decided this between them and are happy to swap,' I say carefully, 'then perhaps that's the most important thing.' Yasmine is very in favour of self-determination when it comes to Arlo's needs. Surely she can't argue with that.

Yes she can. She stares at me open-mouthed, and her look lets me know I have failed her. An uneasy feeling comes over me: it was the wrong decision.

Lily uses the silence to hammer her point home. 'Well, exactly. I'm not sure what there is to gain by us getting involved.'

'Getting involved!' Yasmine's almost jumping out of her seat, which is no mean feat considering how pregnant she is. 'We're their parents. Getting involved is what we do. Sorry if my style isn't so hands-off as yours, Lily.'

Lily doesn't rise to it this time. Just sits there calmly with her hands in her lap and looks at her. Exactly like she does in court. 'In this instance, I'm choosing to step back,' she says. 'Sense of self, and especially how it relates to gender identity, is very complicated – I'm learning all the time, and maybe I haven't read as many child-rearing books as you, Yasmine, but my instinct is telling me that I don't want to force something on Enid *or Arlo* that might lead to feelings of insecurity or shame. Why shouldn't Arlo be Mary? Why shouldn't Enid be Joseph? If that's who they feel they are right now, then that's who they should be, don't you agree?'

Yasmine might, but Tom wouldn't. Apparently, he went mad when he heard Arlo wanted to be Mary. And I'm pretty sure Lily's identity politics are less important than getting one over on Yasmine, but I am appreciating her performance all the same.

'I think,' the vicar jumps in, though he still looks like he's struggling to take this seriously, 'that this is very straightforward.'

'Yes,' says Mr Brown. 'The boys will play boys and the girls will play girls.'

Yasmine looks triumphant until Will interrupts again.

'No, I didn't mean that, Alan. Sorry.' Mr Brown now looks completely befuddled and turns to him for an explanation. 'The children are happy with their new roles, and I – we, the church, that is – am supportive of the children having some autonomy over their Nativity play. Plus, if there *are* deeper gender issues to explore –' Yasmine shoots him a look of pure poison '– on either side, or indeed with any of the other pupils at St Peter and Paul's or the wider congregation, then we are supportive of each person's individual journey. The school is a safe space, as is the church. I think the main thing in this situation is that the parents get on board with the new casting and don't react in a negative way.'

Lily is smiling earnestly and gives the vicar an admiring glance. 'Exactly,' she says.

This has not gone Yasmine's way at all. Mr Brown doesn't look entirely happy about the situation but can't undermine the vicar in front of us – how could he after that glowing monologue about being supportive of non-binary inclusion? He doesn't say anything else, just gives Yasmine an apologetic shrug.

She seems to have regressed into a surly teenager before our eyes. Her shoulders are slumped, and she's refusing to lift her gaze from a fixed spot on the floor, as though we'll all disappear if she ignores us for long enough.

'Do you agree, Yasmine?' Will presses. His voice is gentle but firm. He's going to force a response out of her.

'Yes.' She hisses the 's' but still won't look up.

'Lily?' She's in the seat next to him, and his tone is definitely warmer than when he was addressing Yasmine. I'm not surprised. Even vicars must lose patience with ridiculous congregants.

'Of course,' she replies primly, but the twinkle in her eye now belies the courtroom tone.

The group lapses into silence and Yasmine pulls out her phone while the rest of us sit there not knowing what to do next. Mr Brown says 'Well,' and stands up, drifting back over to the snowflake display, and the vicar nods at us all in turn before muttering, 'I ought to go and put up the Christmas lights,' and going over to a nearby box. The pressure of the atmosphere weighs down on me, and I jump up, hoping it's safe for me to speak. I feel like I should apologise to Yasmine, even though I don't actually think I have anything to apologise for.

'Shall I do a tea round? I brought some herbal ones,' I say, directing that bit to her, and hoping we can have a drink and a chat. She must know it makes sense, deep down.

'I can't stay, actually,' she says, her voice sounding emotionless. 'Tom's texted to say Arlo's a bit under the weather, and has been asking for me, so I'll head back. You know how kids just really need their mummy when they're out of sorts.' It's another barb aimed at Lily. I lean over as though to help her up but she ignores me.

'I'm sorry that didn't go your way. I hope Tom won't be annoyed about the outcome tonight,' I say to her quietly.

'He'll be fine,' she snaps, glowering at me. 'But it's not like you helped.' Brilliant. I'm getting the blame, even though all I did was contribute one wishy-washy non-opinion.

'Sorry,' I backtrack as she pulls her coat on. 'I just started thinking about what you told me the other day. About the new baby making Arlo feel like things are out of his control. And then I thought that maybe this was a way for him to regain it.' I'm gabbling, but it must make some sort of sense, because she hesitates. But maybe that's because she can't have a go at me for deploying her own logic. I try and get the conversation back onto safer territory. 'Let me know when the governors' meeting is locked in for the beans campaign.' I emailed version five over to her two days ago and am desperately hoping that's the last one. At least that feels like one argument she can win.

Is that a smile? 'Don't worry about it, babe. I ran into Lesley – one of the governors – yesterday and told her about it. She agreed there and then to tell the school to stop serving tinned beans. They're going to put a notice up in the nursery.'

I try to say *What?* but the noise that comes out is more of a squeak. I take a breath and try again. 'Did she look at all the stuff I prepared?'

'I didn't go into all that. I didn't have any of it on me. But a good result, isn't it?' I wait for her to thank me, or at least acknowledge the work I did. She doesn't. Instead she says airily, 'See you at drop-off.' With one final arctic glare to the others, she leaves.

What the actual fuck? I stand there awkwardly, wishing I had someone to share this moment of total disbelief with. I look at Lily, who is still sitting in her seat, looking less pleased with herself now Yasmine has gone. I smile at her and she smiles back, giving me a small wave, but doesn't make any move to come closer. Probably because the last time I saw her, I told her never to speak to me again.

'Fucking shitty fucking things,' the vicar seethes under his breath, holding one giant mass of tangled-up lights in his hands. Lily and I look at each other and snort with laughter. I move a bit closer to her. I want to tell her why I didn't support her more strongly during that dispute, but don't know how to, so for some reason instead I blurt, 'Who's with Enid tonight?'

Her face immediately calcifies. 'Joe,' she says. 'I have to get back.' Next thing, she's gone too.

The scene with Lily niggles at me and two days later I start to text her, writing and rewriting before giving up when I can't think of any other opening than 'How are you?' It sits in the speech bubble, reflecting my banality back at me. My finger hovers over the send button, but I can't take the next step, and idly flip into my emails instead. More properties in E17 have come on to the market. I click on one. It's lovely *and* affordable. Three bedrooms, manicured garden . . . and about four streets too far away to be any use to me. I delete it, just as my phone rings. My heart leaps. Jay! Any thought of Lily evaporates.

'Hello?'

'Imogen, Jay here. It's about your offer.'

It takes me a second to catch up. 'Offer?'

'Willow Road.'

Oh, *that* offer. The two-bedroom downstairs Victorian flat that we could actually move into straight away, as long as I don't mind the granny-fied decor and three-million-year-old kitchen and bathroom (nope). There are no holes in the floor, no mould and no chain (RIP beloved widowed grandmother), and it's even within the realms of affordable at four hundred and fifty thousand pounds. However, the reason it's affordable is that the leasehold for the land the building stands on – and owned by some landed gentry who own the land in half of London – is only 79 years, which means we'd have to pay *a lot* to extend it back up to 120. Danny was subdued when I made him go and look around, and said it didn't give him a great vibe. Then when he heard about the lease, he said we'd be crazy to put in an offer. So I didn't tell him before I put in an offer.

'The vendors have said if you can go higher than the other bidder, it's yours.'

My whole body starts tingling. Finally. *Finally.* I can't remember a time when I didn't feel stressed. Our mortgage offer is on the brink of expiring, and school applications are due next week, but this could be it.

'What's their offer?'

'Four sixty,' Jay fires back immediately.

That was our limit.

'Could we say four six one?' I say cautiously.

Jay snorts. 'They're looking for a more meaningful increase. I'd suggest at least five to ten on top of that to make sure they know you're serious.'

I can hear Danny's voice in my head saying, 'We don't have it, Im, even before factoring in the hundred grand the lease will likely cost us.' But we can't lose it. We *can't*. We're so close. Even if the offer is accepted now, there's no way it will be our official address by next week, but by God all the relevant parties will know it's in the pipeline: I can screenshot the confirmation email from Jay (as proof – I know everyone will try the 'we're moving' ruse; I've read the tabloids), and send it to the school secretary, along with an enquiry about how to change Winnie's home address halfway through the application process.

And we can deal with the lease situation later. We only need this place for eight years, until Winnie's on the grammar school track. Once it's ours Danny will come round, he has to. It will be good for us all to have a permanent base. We can relax, make it ours and focus on other things. On us. Maybe, *maybe* we can even talk about having another baby. The thought of me waddling to drop Winnie off at the school, bump straining at the maternity jeans that are vacuum-packed in storage, along with all of her newborn clothes, almost makes me gasp out loud. I am serious and the vendors need to know it.

'Go for it,' I hear myself saying to Jay. 'Offer four seventy.'

13

14 December 2018, 3 p.m.

Lily

Of *course* the first people I see on the day of the Nativity are Yasmine and Tom. I'm hovering in the church hall vestibule entrance and looking into the room while I anxiously wait for Joe — who is 'on his way', apparently, as the parents arrive in pairs and start taking their seats. Thankfully I only see Yasmine from a distance, as she and Tom have already bagsied the best seats in the house by the time I get there. I stare at them for a moment, eyes narrowed, and then duck below the hymnbook case when she looks around to see who else has arrived. I've seen her a couple of times since Nativity-gate, and both times she's blanked me. Which is a bit rich considering the stupid fuss she made about Enid and Arlo swapping roles, but especially because from the way that Enid talks about Arlo, they're obviously friends. From what I can gather, all her BFFs at school are the bloody second-generation Organics, so it's going to be interesting to see what they do when I invite them all to Enid's birthday party in February. If I can be civil, why can't she?

Despite the frankly sinister selection of baubles that are best described as 'festive babies' — think Anne Geddes posters meet creepy Victorian doll — the explosion of tinsel, the lights that the vicar finally untangled and the glitter-bombed paintings that the kids have been doing all month, the church hall actually looks respectably festive. I mean, it's a shrine to bad taste, but that's what Christmas is all about. I'm surprised Mr Brown allowed it.

It's impossible not to check out the parents together, and how they look as couples who existed before their kid did. I'm not used to seeing them in the same place at the same time, together. Kim and Steve arrive next. Kim allows herself to give me a terse nod in greeting, seeing as she's not with Yasmine. You'd never put them together at all, him in a suit, loafers and glasses, with a sunless sort of complexion, and her looking like she's on her way to or from a Bikram class in her Lululemon yoga gear. When I first met her – through Yasmine – we went to a couple of buggy-fit classes together during maternity leave. She once told me that before Steve, her 'type' was fitness buffs, but it never worked out because they were so competitive about exercise. 'Separate hobbies, that's the key in my opinion. I don't want my husband muscling in – literally. I like spinning, Steve likes video games. It's the best relationship I've ever had.'

I see Jusna and Ajay settling down next to each other a few rows back from Yasmine and Tom, and relations don't look anywhere near as strained as Yasmine was saying, or they're at least putting on a united front for Mo's benefit. They're chatting away and Ajay laughs when Jusna points out the creepy baby baubles to him.

The heavy double doors swing open again, and Joe arrives, bringing with him a blast of frigid air. His hair springs up as he pulls off his woolly hat, and his nose and cheeks are all red from the cold.

'Made it,' he says, taking out his headphones and stuffing them into a pocket. It takes all my energy not to reply with a sarcastic 'congratulations', because he clearly expects a medal for simply showing up. But he is here, and I could do without any more drama where this play is concerned.

'Where do you want to sit?' I ask instead, and we make our way further into the room to find a spot.

'I think angels stand on God's right-hand side,' a man's voice says, coming up behind me. Another couple of stragglers – Imogen and Danny. They make a good couple, both sort of hipster preppy types, but they're talking to each other in clipped, ultra-polite voices, as if they don't know each other very well.

'Do they?' Imogen says. 'Well remembered. But is it the same if it's Jesus and not God? Or are they the same thing?'

Danny looks doubtful. 'I actually might be thinking of the Holy Spirit.'

'The Angel Gabriel?'

'No, he's just an angel,' interjects Joe, turning round. 'Hi, Imogen. Long time no see. Lily told me you'd moved to the area.' He smiles at her, and I realise that the only impression of Joe Imogen has had in the last six years is my rant about him at Mo's party. I wonder if she is looking at us together and judging whether or not we fit. I smile at her nervously. It felt like she was on my side the other night, albeit not very emphatically, but then she couldn't resist making some crack, asking who was looking after Enid. She's obviously still annoyed about the times she looked after her, but I didn't want to have to apologise *again*, so I left without thanking her.

I wonder if she'll get her own back by dropping me in it with Joe. But she just says hi as though nothing is wrong and then introduces him to Danny, who I've only met myself a handful of times, back when I was picking Enid up from their place a couple of nights a week. It feels awkward to me, but Joe – who I haven't told about any of it – doesn't pick up on anything.

'We're trying to work out where we should sit to get the best view of Winnie's angel appearance.'

'And is she Gabriel?' Joe asks.

Imogen smiles. 'No, she's just a bog-standard angel. Unnamed. Only Gabriel gets that honour in the Bible, I think.'

'There's actually one more,' says Joe. 'I didn't do seven years of –' he drops his voice to a stage whisper and looks around as though he's going to get in trouble '– Catholic school for nothing.' I like Joe like this. Funny, engaged, playful. In two minutes, he's managed to get us all united into a group, and any awkwardness between Imogen and me has dissipated as he takes the pressure off us to make conversation.

'Go on then, who is it?' says Danny in the end.

'Michael the archangel. Top dog angel,' he replies immediately. I'm impressed with his recall. Not least because in the last eighteen months Joe has only come to church with Enid and me a few times. He should have been in charge of this stuff all along.

'Isn't he a saint?' Danny is asking.

'Yes,' Joe grins, 'patron saint of Marks and Spencer, I think.' They both laugh. 'Shall we find some seats? It's filling up in here and we'll be stuck in the restricted view seats if we're not careful.' A rush of last-minute arrivals have appeared behind us and are flowing around our group.

'Do make your way in when you're ready,' says Reverend Will, who has appeared among them and is nudging past.

'That's the polite way of saying "stop blocking the aisle",' Joe cracks. 'Sorry, vicar.'

'Ah, hi Lily, and Imogen. And it's Danny, isn't it?' says Will. He turns to Joe and holds a hand out. 'I don't think we've met.' He's in his usual uniform of black jeans and jumper, but with the added accessory of a giant sparkly star badge that says 'The Rev' in bubble writing.

'This is Joe, Enid's dad,' I say, before quickly clarifying, 'My husband.' I see Imogen shoot me a side eye and I try not to laugh.

'Great to meet you, Joe. Good we got all the character stuff sorted out before the big night, wasn't it? Lily made some excellent points during the meet-up.' Joe shoots me a quizzical look, but Will is still speaking. 'I've got to go and introduce the show, but I hope you can all hang around for a drink afterwards. I convinced Mr Brown to let us have a late licence on the church hall for an impromptu Christmas mixer.' He nods. 'Enjoy!'

'What was that about?' Joe asks. 'What meet-up?'

I don't want to get into it with him. He'll just think it's typical of me to cause a fuss or tell me it's no wonder I'm not in with all the mums if I argue the toss with them over stuff like this. We're supposed to be going for pizza with Enid afterwards and I don't want the atmosphere to sour. 'Er, I'll fill you in later.'

'And is *that* the vicar?' he asks. 'No wonder you're so keen to go to church these days.' He and Danny both laugh but I swallow another retort. Keen to go to church. As though it's something I'd rather do than go for the long runs that used to punctuate my Sundays.

As though she can read my thoughts, Imogen jumps in. 'I like this,' she says, pointing to my dress. It's a swooshy black maxi dress with gold spots on it.

'Oh, thanks. Zara sale. We're going out afterwards, so I thought I'd dress up.'

'Well, you look great.' It feels like the first warm moment between us for a long time, and I smile at her gratefully.

'Four seats, there,' Danny shouts, racing away. It's only when he's already insinuated his way into the row that I realise they're right next to Yasmine and Tom. I pray that she's going to tell him they're taken, but she sees Danny and Imogen a good half-second before she notices they're with me so moves her bag to let them sit down, and I find myself three seats away from her.

'Hi, Yasmine,' I say wearily.

'Hi,' she replies, looking away as Danny exchanges oblivious hellos and handshakes with her and Tom.

'Well, this is a lovely end to the week, isn't it,' Imogen says, her voice bright and false. She's bravely trying to make this less like a temporary ceasefire and more like the magical evening of memory-making we're all supposed to be here for. There's a silence. 'Did I tell you we just bought a place?' she tries next.

'Have you? That's great.' It is. She's been looking for months, and I know she hates the flat they're in now.

'It's not gone through yet,' Danny says across her in a flat voice, and Imogen shoots him a look. He sets his jaw. 'It's not definite.' Now it feels like there's more than one bad atmosphere on this row.

'There's no reason why it shouldn't be straightforward,' Imogen adds hastily. 'It's a two-bedroom flat, and *well* within the catchment area. No chain. It only came up last week, so we swooped in.'

On hearing this, Yasmine can't keep up her disinterested act. I can see her straining to listen.

'Where is it?' I say quietly, so that she will have to either actively join the conversation or ask me to repeat what I said. Instead she pulls out her phone and pretends to send a text. God forbid she just has a normal, civil conversation that includes me.

'Really near you, but even closer to the school,' Imogen says. 'Willow Road. God, I can't wait to move.' Danny doesn't look like he feels the same way.

'Let me know if you need any help with Winnie when you move,' I start to say, but the lights dim and the vicar strides onto the stage. The audience bursts into the kind of applause that would be more appropriate for George Clooney heading on stage to pick up an Oscar, rather than a vicar appearing to kick off a Nativity with a blessing and a quick prayer. Someone whistles. I think it's Jusna's husband.

'Thank you,' Will says, batting his hands to try and quieten down the crowd.

'We're all very much looking forward to this year's pre-school Nativity, which, like all the best movies, has had its fair share of pre-production drama.' I snort with laughter and try and turn it into a cough. I was surprised by how enthusiastically the vicar took my side the other day, which only enraged Yasmine more. I can't believe he's bringing it up in front of *everyone*. Sure enough, I can see her shooting me daggers in my peripheral vision.

'Do stay on afterwards for a festive drink, where I'll be serving behind the bar,' Will continues. 'As a student I worked part-time as a mixologist –' audible murmurs from the crowd at this. I'm guessing that, like me, they're all nurturing a visual of an early-twenties Rev Will as Tom Cruise in *Cocktail* '– so I'll be dusting off my skills tonight in aid of our chosen charities. I'm planning on travelling to Syria next year with the Red Cross, and proceeds will be split between that and our appeal for Morris House, the homeless shelter here in Walthamstow. I'm also kicking off an appeal this evening for the women's shelter in east

London, which is on the brink of closure due to government cuts.' There's a definite tension to his voice when he says the word 'government', as though he's really having to force himself to be impartial. 'And I'm looking for cash donations as well as collecting women's and children's toiletries for the residents.'

I see Danny nudge Imogen. 'Are these the other school issues you've been working on?' he whispers.

Her face is in shadow, but I can still see how sheepish it looks. 'No,' she whispers back. I'm surprised. I thought she was well involved. I'd have taken more of an interest in the church's causes myself if I'd realised it was this sort of thing they were doing – actual real-world problems – rather than the nonsense that Yasmine's always sending emails about.

'You should speak to Mags about it,' he whispers.

'I'll talk to the vicar about it afterwards,' she says, just as Yasmine shushes them. I see Danny pressing his lips together and looking at Joe and me as if to say 'oooh'. I try not to laugh, glad for once not to be the one in trouble.

'So without further ado,' says Will, 'it's the St Peter and Paul's preschool Christmas story.'

We all burst into applause again, and Joe actually gives my hand a squeeze as Enid, replete with false beard and her carpentry tools, and Mary – Arlo, prematurely clutching the Baby Jesus doll by one arm, until Charlotte from the nursery rushes over to snatch it out of his hand – wander onto the stage. Mr Brown is stalking up and down the aisles, telling parents to stop filming, as though he's an anti-piracy security guard at the cinema, but Ajay manages to surreptitiously hold his phone at an angle that captures Mo's Angel Gabriel telling Mary she's going to have a baby and has to travel to Bethlehem. We all laugh when he declares that this baby will be the 'ham of God that takes away the sins of the world'.

Joe's face is full of pride as Enid's lines start and I feel myself welling up as she stutters through asking all the innkeepers if they will take them in. We keep looking at each other in a soppy 'we made her' kind of way that makes me doubly glad we didn't start bickering earlier on. We hardly ever do things as a family, together. We shouldn't wait until there's a ticketed event to do it again. I sneak a look at Yasmine and Tom, and thankfully even they seem to be enjoying it. The whole play is hilarious. The children keep talking over each other and range from delivering their lines so quietly that they're basically just mouthing the words to shouting them at a Brian Blessed-level volume. When the children dressed as the stable animals appear, they look too cute for words. I spot Bex's Ava dressed up as a donkey and licking a lollipop, which I've learned is Bex's preferred bribe, along with Jeb as an ox, although I haven't seen Clara in the audience so far. Arlo announces that Baby Jesus is born, and then quickly dumps him unceremoniously into the manger, as the various visitors – wise men, shepherds, angels – all troop in, some waving at their parents or talking among themselves.

It's at this point that I see Enid look out to the audience and freeze. It's as though she's just realised how many people are out in the crowd, and I see a look of fright work its way across her face. Slowly, she starts to sit down and then curl herself into a ball until she's mostly hidden behind a row of angels. Her face is crumpled with tears. It feels like my heart has stopped. She looks completely overwhelmed.

'Joe, look.' I poke him, but he's already watching her, the expression on his face as stricken as I feel.

'What do we do?' I hiss, but he's already up out of his chair.

'I'll go and get her,' he whispers, forcing Yasmine and Tom to stand up so he can get past to the middle aisle, which is the most direct route to the stage. Five quick strides and he's there, up on the stage, moving through the kids and gently picking Enid up. A collective 'awwww' goes up from the crowd as Enid holds onto her dad like a baby chimp and he carries her off stage left, smoothing down her hair and talking quietly to her so as not to disturb the wise men, who are now presenting their gifts to the Baby Jesus (lobbing them into the manger). I edge my way out of the row in the opposite direction, so I can intercept Joe and Enid as they come down the side gangway.

In her dad's arms, Enid seems to have recovered from her stage fright.

'She's all right,' he says, giving me a reassuring smile, and I kiss the top of her head. She wipes her nose across his shoulder and peers over the other one, so she can see what's happening on the stage, and we stand as a group of three at the back to watch the rest of the show. Enid keeps looking from her dad's face to mine, clearly pleased to have us both here with her at the same time, and I idly lean my head next to hers, on Joe's shoulder.

Mo's little piping voices declares, 'And that's the story of Christmas,' before the whole hall bursts into noisy applause. The standing ovation goes on for a good ten minutes until the vicar comes back on stage and asks for volunteers to help put the chairs away, so the mixer can begin. The children file down from the stage and the room is buzzing, with everyone chatting at full volume. It's as though a pressure valve has been released and we can all relax.

When I look up at Joe's face, his eyes are shining with tears. 'That was lovely,' he says, looking around the room

168

as though he's been imbued with the Christmas spirit. 'And so nice to meet up with Imogen and her fella. We should invite them round or something, along with their little girl – Winnie, is it? I should try and get to know them all a bit more.'

'That would be great. I'll mention it to Imogen,' I say to him. Imogen and I seemed to get on OK tonight, so maybe I actually will. A little group of us, hanging out with our kids: I hardly want to admit how much I would like that. 'I'll go and help with the chairs. You stay with E. Then we can go for pizza.'

I go back to our row and start stacking the chairs up, finding myself next to Danny and Kim, who are working the same row. 'Is Enid all right?' he asks with a sympathetic smile.

'Yeah, she's fine. I'm guessing we can rule out theatre as a career for now though.'

He laughs and points over to where Imogen is at the side of the stage with Winnie. They look like they're deep in negotiations. 'Winnie is refusing to take her costume off, so maybe it's us that have a future as pushy stage parents. He looked like he enjoyed it too,' he says, gesturing in Yasmine's direction. She and Tom are still sitting in their chairs as we clear the space around them. Arlo is in her lap, scrolling through her phone and looking at the pictures she was taking throughout. 'Look, Mummy, it's me!' he keeps saying, holding them up for her to see, but she's only got half an eye on him as she keeps looking at me. I move to another spot to collect chairs, but I see her gaze following me, accompanied by a smacked-bum expression. I hope the spirit of Christmas doesn't wear off Joe quite so quickly. I try and ignore her but can feel her eyes boring into my back. It's as though she's trying to intimidate me off her turf. No. Not having it.

'Everything OK?' I say, hoping that by acknowledging it head on, she'll back down in embarrassment.

But that's obviously not Yasmine's style.

'Enid didn't seem to want the Joseph role that much in the end anyway, did she?' is all she says.

Her implication that Enid has done something wrong makes my temper flare, but I try to push it down. We've had such a nice afternoon so far. 'These things happen,' I say as jovially as I can muster, while simultaneously wanting to smack her smug face.

'It's just strange, isn't it, seeing as drama seems to follow your Enid around. You'd think she'd like being the centre of attention.'

That flare instantly ignites. Is she genuinely having a pop at my kid?

'For God's sake, she's three!' I explode. 'I'm sorry she didn't bring the stage presence of Meryl Streep to the role, but what is your problem? Why does it matter who played who? They're just made-up people in a made-up story!'

At that second, the talking stops dead, as does Mr Brown, who is standing stony-faced right in front of me. He's flanked by the vicar, and they're both carrying plastic crates full of bottles of spirits. Mr Brown's expression evolves into a glower and I go bright red. Every single person in the room is looking in my direction, and I can feel the glee radiating from Yasmine.

'The story of Jesus's birth is the culmination of our advent festival and an important cornerstone of the whole Christian belief system,' he says in a grave tone, as the parents around me silently nod in hypocritical agreement. I want to slap the sanctimonious smile off Yasmine's face. I feel like I'm being told off. I *am* being told off. 'The fundamental message that Jesus was born unto Mary and became man is why we're all here.'

I bow my head, shame-faced at being taken to task so publicly, and I'm murmuring apologies under my breath.

'I'd also kindly remind you that all of the children here are at the beginning of their Christian education and the spreading of conflicting messages, when we've been teaching them about the Nativity for the past few weeks, is incredibly detrimental,' he continues. 'There's enough fake news out there as it is.' Is he invoking . . . Donald Trump? I look from him to the vicar, who looks as stunned as I feel about the last comment. Even so, I can't ask him to clarify. I'm most definitely in the doghouse.

'Sorry, Mr Brown,' I repeat. 'That's not what I meant. I'm just frustrated about the ongoing *situation* over the play.' I try and bring it back round to Yasmine being in the wrong, but it backfires.

'ENOUGH,' roars Mr Brown. 'I think we've had quite enough debate about the play.' Yasmine raises a triumphant eyebrow. 'I suggest you spend the coming days deciding where your beliefs lie with regard to the school,' he says.

Fuck, fuck, fuck. That has to be a threat about school places. Have we been blacklisted before our application is even in? 'I'm so sorry,' I say again. 'It was just a stupid thing that I said in the heat of the moment.' Mr Brown adjusts his grip on his box, and the vicar gives me a sympathetic look. It reminds me of the one the whole country saw Gary Lineker give on TV when Gazza got yellow-carded against Italy in the World Cup, meaning he'd miss the next match. Yes, it says, you've sabotaged yourself, but I feel for you all the same.

Cheeks flaming, I rush back over to Joe and Enid. The look on Joe's face is very different. He's not looking sympathetic at all, more annoyed, but I can't handle him telling me how I've messed up, especially in front of everyone.

The room is still hushed but a few people have started to murmur to each other, and the sound of tables being dragged around masks the horrible silence.

'Don't,' I say, not giving him a chance to say anything. 'Let's just get out of here. Enid, let's get your coat on.' My voice is all shaky and I can feel my mouth wobbling. Joe must sense I'm on the verge of losing it, because he doesn't say anything, just lets me guide them both to the edge of the room, where we're out of the way. There's a dull ache behind my eyes, and as I absorb what I've just done, I feel sick. I feel like there's an invisible contamination zone around us that no one wants to breach, in case our pariahdom is contagious. I turn my back to the room and hold in hot tears while I pull on my coat.

'Excuse me.' I jump. It's Danny behind me, holding a stack of chairs and wanting to push them up against the part of the wall we're blocking.

'Sorry, sorry.' I pull Enid out of the way.

'Are you all right?' he asks. I just press my lips together, not trusting myself to reply.

'Would you like a cocktail?' Next, Winnie appears holding a lurid yellow drink with an umbrella sticking out of it. She still hasn't taken off her halo or angel costume.

I take it from her and sniff it. 'Where did you get that, sweetheart?'

'From the vicar,' she says. 'It's for you.' In the middle of the room, Will is behind the tables that have now been arranged into a makeshift bar set-up. He's spinning a bottle of Blue Curaao in his hand and looking in our direction. He gives me a nod. His kindness is almost worse than the telling-off for making me want to cry. I grab the drink from Winnie and take a big gulp. Sadly, it's just fruit juice. 'Thank you, Winnie.'

I see Imogen approaching, her face cloudy with anger. 'It's just a soft drink and I didn't ask Winnie to bring it to me,' I say, pre-empting her. The last thing I need is her accusing me of getting her daughter to serve alcoholic drinks. But she tears straight past me to where Danny is still absorbed in piling up chairs.

'The flat, Dan,' she says, livid. 'Some fucker has gazumped us.'

14

4.30 p.m.

Imogen

'Imogen,' Danny hisses, clumping down a pile of chairs. Everyone was looking at Lily until I dropped the F-bomb, and Danny doesn't look happy about the fact that I've become the entertainment. But I can't stop myself. Our house and school dream have just been ripped away from us.

'It's a joke, Danny. And they didn't even have the courtesy to call me.'

'What did they say?' he says quietly. He's using a deliberately calm voice, which turns my insides into a seething, simmering mass of snakes.

'They said – IN AN EMAIL – that after careful consideration, the vendors have decided to go with another offer.'

He twists his mouth into a 'what can you do' formation and nods. 'I'm guessing that means they just used our higher offer to get an even higher offer from someone else,' he says wryly.

Why is he not pissed off about this? He's just standing there, arms by his sides, looking like he's trying to work out the best way to contain all the swear words I might be about to unleash. Spoiler alert: he can't.

'Yes, I'm guessing so, Dan,' I snap. 'He – Jay –' I spit out the word. God, I *hate* him '– says he'll let me know if anything else comes up.'

'It will,' Danny says simply.

'Well, I'm glad you're so confident about it.'

'Hey.' Anger flares behind his eyes. 'Don't take it out on me. This is a setback, but we'll find something else.'

'Don't you get it? Gone. Our catchment-lock is gone.'

'I know that. But maybe . . .' He pauses. I can tell he's weighing up whether or not he should carry on. He takes a deep breath. 'Maybe it's for the best. We can keep looking and find something that we *both* love. And isn't so expensive for what it is.'

'Will something come up by Wednesday?' I say in a tight voice, eyes narrowed at him. I know he didn't want this place. When I told him that I'd made an offer on it, all he said was, 'Are you sure this is the place you want?' He hasn't wanted to talk about it, and has gone all quiet every time I've mentioned it, even though he knows that location-wise it's perfect. 'Wednesday is the school application deadline. In case you've forgotten.'

'Of course I haven't forgotten,' he bursts out. He's stopped trying to keep my voice down and now his is rising to meet mine. I notice Lily, Joe and Enid using the moment to make a discreet exit. 'Will you STOP implying that I don't care, or don't remember any of this stuff? I just don't think there's anything we can do about it, so we need to explore other options. You're so obsessed with this *one* plan, and whenever I try and have a discussion about it, you shut me down. But there are other areas. There are other schools. We could probably afford to send her private for a bit if you went back to work full-time.'

My stomach lurches. I know there's truth in what he's saying, which is what makes it worse, but this has never come up before. 'What?'

175

'But . . .' The sinking feeling keeps on sinking. One set of school fees would be manageable, but two definitely wouldn't. And we couldn't do one thing for one child and not for the other. Which means Danny isn't thinking about another.

'Oh, thanks, Winnie,' Danny says absently. She sloshes one of the lurid drinks she just handed to Lily in his direction and he takes it off her.

'I'll get one for you, Mummy,' she says, beaming and running off again.

'Can anyone explain why my daughter is being used as a cocktail waitress?' I shout into the room. 'Is this even legal?'

The room seems to tilt. It's getting hotter and hotter from the overexcited children running around, and Mariah Carey's 'All I Want for Christmas Is You' is being piped through some speakers, which sound like they're malfunctioning. It keeps getting louder, then quieter, then louder again. The whole time, Danny and I are just staring at each other. We can't have the second-child conversation here, now. It's tangled up with too many other things. I just need to think what we can do. How we can still get her in, prime-location flat or otherwise. And then it hits me. 'We need to get married,' I say. 'The sooner the better.'

'What?' Danny splutters through a mouthful of his drink. 'Where the hell has that come from?'

'No, listen. The flat falling through is a setback. A massive setback. So we need to be completely above criticism in the rest of our application. And getting married would look good, like we're serious.'

'About what? Our relationship, or about how far we'll go to get our daughter into a Christian school?' His voice is level, but there's something, some catch behind it. 'Do I get a say in this?'

'We always meant to get married. It's just we never got around to it.'

'You kept saying no,' he says. I can't read the look on his face. 'I assumed that marriage just wasn't for you.'

'I thought you wanted to get married,' I say, deflecting.

'Not like this.' It's not lost on me that he hasn't flat out agreed. 'It's been so long since we even discussed it. It feels like we'd be doing it for the wrong reasons. Shit, it *would* be for the wrong reasons.' He takes another pull on his drink. 'I can't do this, Imogen. I've gone along with everything so far. I've moved to a new house, I've started going to church, I was even prepared to move to this flat if it's what you wanted. But I'm not having a fake wedding. I just can't.'

'It's not fake if we were going to do it at some point anyway.'

Danny doesn't say anything, just stares across the room to where Yasmine has exacerbated the speaker problem by starting a game of musical statues with all the children. Now the volume is going up and down, as well as the music turning abruptly on and off. His face is expressionless.

'Someone needs to sort the stereo out,' he says eventually. 'I'll do it.' He walks off, leaving me standing there. No flat, no wedding, no second baby. The phrase *just a mum* flashes through my memory again. It's as though everything is disintegrating. I watch the kids dancing for a few minutes, as Danny fiddles with the stereo and studiously avoids looking in my direction.

The room seems too loud and too bright. I want to bolt but it'll only draw more attention to us if I run away now, so instead I decide I need a drink. Everyone else in the room seems to be gently steaming on whatever concoctions the vicar is putting together, so maybe it will blur the edges and take my mind off the fact that everything we've done has been for nothing. And what that conversation means for Danny and me. He doesn't want to get married like this? Or he doesn't want to get married full stop? He never answered the question.

I pitch up in front of the vicar. 'I'd like the world's strongest margarita, please.'

'Coming up,' he says, nodding. 'I even have ice.' He faffs about tipping some table salt onto a paper plate, and roots through his plastic crate until he settles on a bottle of Patrón.

'How are you, Imogen?' he asks, concentrating on the task, but talking to me. 'I couldn't help but notice something going on.'

'That's a very polite way of putting it.'

'It's a stressful time of year.' He splits a lime that he's produced from somewhere and skims its flesh around the rim of the plastic cup, before dipping it in the salt on the plate.

'You weren't lying about your cocktail skills,' I say, raising an eyebrow.

'Three years at Steinbeck's.'

'The members club? I worked in a pub in Leicester during university holidays, but the most exotic thing I mixed was a Campari and soda.' Steinbeck's has been legendary since the nineties. My agency boss was only granted membership there after five years of trying. We always knew when someone was going to get promoted because she'd take them there for lunch.

'I quoted Bible passages with every drink I served.' He sees the horrified look on my face and laughs. 'I'm only joking.'

'So how did you make the leap?' I'm deliberately trying not to talk about me. If he knows I'm doing it, he doesn't say anything. He picks up a cocktail shaker and pours in the tequila and Cointreau, before putting on the lid and starting to shake it.

'It's a bit of a cliché, the troubled soul that finds God, isn't it?' He expertly dribbles the liquid into the cup and looks like he's about to carry on talking, but at that moment Kim's husband turns up next to me.

'Two of those, please,' he says, pointing at my cup.

I smile at Will gratefully and rummage in my bag for some money. 'Thank you for this,' I say, pulling out a ten-pound note.

'Blimey, they're not that expensive, are they?' says Steve.

'It's for charity! Besides, I'm hoping that this buys me a couple in the tap too, so I can come back later.'

Will nods. 'Just ask me for your usual.'

'Oh, and I'd like to talk to you later about the women's refuge appeal,' I add. 'I know someone who may be able to help.'

'Brilliant. Yes, please do.'

I step away, drink in hand. 'Steve, did you know Will used to work at Steinbeck's?'

I leave them to it, finding a seat around the edge of the room where I can watch the kids playing and be part of things, without actually being part of things. I wave at Winnie, who is dancing, and sip the margarita. The tang of the lime hits the back of my throat. It's good. Also strong. I take another mouthful, too quickly, but like the way its boozy warmth is making me feel. I can see Danny chatting with Ajay, the thankfully now fixed stereo the centrepiece between them. By the way they keep gesturing at it I can only assume they're deep in discussion about its prognosis and what sound system the church would be wise to invest in next. Electronics are Danny's favourite subject. He sees me looking and it takes me a couple of beats to look away, which is when I know I'm already a bit pissed.

'Are you ready to make a move?' Danny says, coming over. 'Winnie's hungry, and I said we could get fish and chips on the way home.' His voice is completely normal, as though he hasn't just told me that marriage and more babies are off the agenda. I drain the rest of my drink and look into the bottom of the plastic cup. It might be empty but it hasn't done much for my personal humiliation levels.

It's still only five thirty. I envisage how the rest of the evening will play out. We'll go home for fish and chips, pretend everything's fine in front of Winnie, and then when she's gone to bed we'll sit in our crappy rented living room while I look at all the same places on Rightmove that have been hanging around forever. No thanks. 'You go,' I say. 'I said I'd talk to the vicar about that charity stuff, so I'll follow you later.' My gaze drifts back to the bar. There's an enormous queue now. Will might have to rethink how meticulously he's making the cocktails if he wants to keep people moving.

'Is that to benefit Winnie's chances, or are you genuinely interested in helping?' The mildness in Danny's voice stings more than his previous scorn. I bite down my indignation. I'm too worn out to have this conversation again. Why is trying to get into the school the bit that's wrong? Why isn't *he* wrong for not trying as hard as me?

'FISH AND CHIPS,' Winnie bellows, legging it over to us, her halo now skew-whiff. She hurls herself over my knees. 'Daddy said we're having fish and chips.'

I hesitate, wanting to go with her, but also not wanting to go with Danny.

'I've got to stay here and help with the tidying up, darling, so I'm going to have some later. Why don't you go with Daddy and save me some?' I search Danny's face for a sign to make me change my mind, but his smile is wan.

'Did Jesus like fish and chips?' she asks, as I button her up into her coat.

'Only on special occasions. Like Christmas,' Danny quips. The daftness of it tugs me somewhere inside, and again when Winnie nods solemnly, taking her daddy's word for granted.

I watch them go, my anger at Danny giving way to a more general feeling of guilt. The one thing I needed to do was secure us a place in the catchment area, and I've let Winnie down. But somehow, I've also let Danny down, just in a less specific, nebulous way. I sigh and carry my empty cup back over to the makeshift bar.

'Ready for another one?' Will calls over the queue of heads. His voice is cheerful but from the sheen of sweat on his forehead, his matinee quiff flopping onto his face and his pushed-up jumper sleeves, I get the feeling he's more harassed than he sounds. There are at least ten people in line, with expressions of barely concealed impatience on their faces. Commuter faces. I sense that they would be much more vocal about their wait time if it wasn't the vicar serving the drinks.

'I only want a soda water,' I hear Yasmine complain from a few places in front of me.

I make my way up to the table and say, 'You look like you could do with a hand. I've no idea how to make anything complicated, but I can handle a few gin and tonics or a house party-quality Cosmo.'

Will is in the process of holding a flame underneath a lump of brown sugar for some sort of rum cocktail and he shoots me a grateful look.

'Two Negronis, please,' says Jusna from her spot at the front.

'Errr, what's in that?'

'Gin, vermouth, Campari, orange peel.'

I rummage through the crate of spirits. 'Would you accept a Campari and soda?' I haggle.

'I'd accept petrol fumes if it got me served any quicker,' someone huffs behind her. I think it's Mr Brown's wife.

'OK, new system,' I call. 'If you want a bog-standard drink, please queue up in front of me. Or if you want the full cocktail experience, please queue up in front of the vicar.' I see Jusna smirking at me and shoot her a look. 'Cocktail, Jusna. I said cock*tail*. And first things first –' I pour soda water into a cup and give it to Jusna '– can you pass that to Yasmine.' The drink makes its way back, and Yasmine mouths 'thank you' before moving away. Most people are happy with some variation of a spirit and a mixer, so I quickly find myself getting into a groove, tipping liberal measures into the plastic cups in return for generous donations into the charity box, leaving Will free to painstakingly create Manhattans and Bloody Marys.

For the next hour and a half, I serve drinks non-stop. Then there's a lull and we find ourselves alone, and slightly shell-shocked, behind the table.

'Wow. Preschool parents know how to drink,' I say. I look out into the darkened hall. The children have taken over the dance floor while the parents stand in loose groups around the edge, swigging their drinks. The atmosphere is like being at a wedding. Everyone dangerously but acceptably tipsy a bit too early in the evening and keeping a benevolent eye on the congregated children. Arlo and Thea are currently taking run-ups and then skidding across the room on their knees.

Will plonks a margarita onto the table in front of me. It's littered with squeezed citrus segments and booze spills, but the cash box is heaving with money. 'The usual,' he says with a smile. 'And thank you for the help.' I sip it. It's even more lethal than the first one. 'I think the punters were about to revolt.'

I perch on the edge of the flimsy table/bar to take the weight off my feet but it immediately starts to tip, so I leap back up. 'They all seem pretty happy now.'

'It might be a good time to close, though, as otherwise we'll never get rid of them. I told Mr Brown we'd have everyone out by 8 p.m.'

'You're right. A few more like this and they'll be chanting for a lock-in. Let me at least make you a drink first, though. You've been flat out.'

Will pulls out a couple of bottles of Peroni from under the table and opens one. 'They're warm, but one of these will do. I don't do spirits. Not any more.'

'A mixologist who doesn't drink spirits? That's even more unusual than going from barman to man of God.' Now we're on our own, I was expecting to feel a bit awkward, but Will is friendly and chatty and nowhere near as earnest as I was expecting a vicar to be.

He picks up a half-empty bottle of vodka and searches the table for a matching lid. 'They're all interconnected.'

I'm dying to know, but also don't want to seem nosy, so to occupy myself I start brushing lemon and lime segments from the counter into a plastic bag, and then wiping it down, handing him the bottles as I clean, hoping he'll carry on of his own accord.

'The bar job got the better of me in the end. Nothing official that I sought help for but back in the day, we'd all drink while on shift and then go out afterwards.' He holds a dark green bottle of Jägermeister up to the light to see if there's any liquid left inside, and then plonks it to one side. 'After a while I was pretty much at a constant level of drunkenness. Just topping up as the day went on. And it meant I made all the decisions being in that state entailed. One-night stands –' I blush as he says this, but the vicar seems oblivious '– hanging around with people who just wanted me to get them into the bar. I quickly started falling behind on my university course but couldn't seem to stop, even when it went way beyond being any fun.' He picks up a lid and looks for the bottle it goes with. I find a bottle of Malibu behind me and hand it to him. 'Thanks. One day I was kicking around the street near my student flat. I didn't want to go home because no one was in and I'd got really bad at being on my own, and I ducked into a community centre where there was a talk happening. A few people a bit older than me, talking about volunteering abroad.' He gives a cynical smile. 'At that point I didn't realise they were a Christian group, but what they were saying struck a chord, and I ended up signing up, assisting in refugee camps in Somalia that summer and gradually getting more involved. It definitely helped me find more meaning in my life.'

'Gosh.' I don't really know what to say. One of the things I've been dreading since we became regular, God-fearing churchgoers was the idea that I'd have to confess my worst thoughts while being judged by a priest, who had never struggled with the same real-world problems as the rest of us. But Will doesn't seem like this. He *is* the rest of us.

I start separating the rest of the bottles while I organise my thoughts, moving empties to one side of the table to take to the recycling, and handing the others to Will to put back in the crates.

'I'm not sure I'd ever given the meaning of my life that much thought before I had Winnie,' I admit, hoping I'm not about to get hit with a load of well-meaning spiritual guidance. 'Even now I don't really dwell on anything deeper than "she needs me", so I have to get on with things even when I'm having a bad day.'

Will finishes on the crate and starts filling a recycling bag with soft drinks bottles and plastic cups. I collect some strays and he holds the bag open for me to put them in. 'What is meaning if it's not deeds rather than words,' he says absently. It's these sorts of cryptic phrases that remind me why religion gets on my nerves.

'I think a lot of my deeds are quite selfish, though.' I go red. My only current vocation is how best to get Winnie into the school.

He twists the top of the recycling bag into a knot. 'I think the human condition is to be selfish.'

'*Do* you? But what about genuinely good people, like you? Giving over your entire lives to serve God?'

Will gives what seems like a cynical laugh. 'Believe me, it's not just one decision you make that then sticks for the rest of your life. It's something I struggle with every day.'

'But at least you know you're in the right ball park.' The margaritas have loosened me up and I decide to spill out the situation with Danny, even if I'm not going to tell Will that we've been disagreeing over the school. 'When it comes to Winnie, it feels like decisions are clear-cut, but it's been causing . . . friction in my relationship.' I keep stopping and starting. 'We've been . . . disagreeing on what the right thing for her is, and it's making me wonder if things between us are wrong.'

Will is nodding as though he knows what I mean. 'There's no rule book on how you navigate relationships, especially once children come into the equation.' I wonder idly if he has a girlfriend. Or a boyfriend. How the hell do you navigate dating if you're a vicar? 'It's an ever-changing landscape of needs,' he's saying. 'The best you can do is try and see the other person's side in any given situation.'

It's not that I expect the church's guide on how I should live to be as black and white as the two sides of an escalating argument on Twitter, but some clear-cut rules would help. Surely the church is *all about* telling us how to navigate this stuff?

Will picks up one of the crates. Waving away his offer of help, I pick up the other one and follow him as he makes his way out of the church hall via the back corridor to the small dark car park at the back, where a few cars are scattered. It's off a narrow private road at the rear of the school and church hall, and there are no lights, but a rusty blue Mondeo parked a few metres from the door illuminates as the vicar presses a key fob. He clicks the boot open and we carry the crates over to it.

It suddenly strikes me as a bit bizarre that a person who was almost certainly some sort of alcoholic has such a vast collection of booze. 'Does it not feel a bit like tempting fate to have all these bottles in your house?' I ask as I load mine in. Will pauses, seeming to think better of going back in, and leans against the open boot of the car. I find myself mirroring him on the other side.

'Probably, but these aren't mine. I borrowed them from my friends Alexander and Claire. They're one of those couples who have a drinks trolley in their house. They told me half of the obscure ones never get used so I could take what I needed. I'm dropping what's left back at their house.'

It's odd to think of the vicar as someone who exists outside the church environment. My head is spinning from all the new information I'm processing. Should he even be drinking beer? What about the communion wine? But talking to him has made me feel better. Even if I don't really feel any clearer about what I should actually do.

'You were talking before,' I blurt, 'about how to know if you're doing the right thing. Or even if you're with the right person?'

He sighs, an exhalation with weight behind it. His answer takes me by surprise. 'It's normal to have doubts about whether you're doing the right thing.' He stops. And then speaks again. 'Or even about whether you're living the right life.' He says the last part softly, as though it's not just for my benefit.

The door swings open again, and Yasmine walks out into the lot, moving as fast as she can with her protruding belly. Tom is walking slightly behind her and carrying a drowsy Arlo. Their house isn't far, but their BMW is parked at the opposite side of the car park. Tom must have come straight from work.

'I told them we'd call back this evening to confirm,' Yasmine is saying. 'We have to move quickly.'

'We'll be home in five minutes, I'll do it then,' Tom replies, exasperation in his voice.

'Make sure you do, otherwise they're going back to the other—' She passes the end of Will's car and looks across, seeing us there.

'Oh, hi Imogen, hi Will,' she says, stopping dead. 'You can't separate the two of you this evening, can you?' Her voice is light, but her glance says something different.

It makes me somehow feel like we've been caught out.

15

*Applications submitted and under review. Still time to
make an impression.*

Lily

When I cram myself onto the Victoria line on the first
work day after New Year, it feels like Christmas never
happened. A fortnight of proper holiday gets relegated to
the memory layer of my cortex with the first tut I hear
from a fellow commuter.

Between the bank holidays, work's Christmas policy
and my last stray days of annual leave, I managed almost
two weeks off. The good thing about working for the
government is that we – and all our affiliated lawyers and
bureaucrats – shut down completely for the Christmas
break. And with John so militant about his own time off
– the Boxing Day expedition to watch Chelsea with his
boys is non-negotiable – no one would dare plan a knock
for a week each side of it, lest it interferes.

For the first time in a long time, it felt like we actually
switched off. We spent half of our time in Leeds with
my parents, including Christmas Day itself, and with
my sister and her kids buzzing around, and Enid that
little bit older, it felt like she was a lot more capable of
entertaining herself. With my parents on hand, Joe and
I even managed an evening at the pub round the corner

once she'd gone to bed, and we got quite pissed, creeping into the house and then the bedroom where Enid was asleep on an airbed on the floor. Aside from the snoring toddler, it reminded me of the Sundays before we got married when one of us would say 'let's go for an afternoon drink' and it would blur into a boozy evening and then a hungover Monday at work. We talked about going on holiday this year, both with Enid and maybe even a night away together, and made plans to invite some of the other parents over. I made a pact with myself to try and make sure it becomes more than just pub talk. Not just the stuff with Joe, but to make more of an effort with the school mums too. Fresh year, fresh start. If – fingers crossed – Enid gets a school place, we're going to be in each other's lives for at least another seven years. I don't need to be their BFF; I just need not to be a pariah so that my kid can have a social life with the children she seems to like.

The train doors shut, and I'm wedged up against them, but we're held in the platform for a couple of minutes before they spring open again and the driver announces severe delays due to multiple signal failures in the King's Cross area.

'Ticket prices still went up on January the first, though, didn't they?' a suited-up bloke mutters. At least he has a seat during this delay, which is more than can be said for most of us.

We start to get restless, everyone in that antsy decision-making process of whether to take a more complicated alternative route that will end up taking longer if the train moves soon, and what that route should be. I'm wrestling with the same decision. How many buses do I need to make it to a non-Victoria line interchange? I step off the train while I decide. The air on the platform isn't fresh but at least it's moving, which is more than can be said for the hot, stagnant and stale booze-saturated environment of the carriage. All that Christmas and New Year alcohol being sweated out.

As I flit between three equally hellish TFL Journey Planner suggestions, someone brushes past me. I look up to see a woman's back in a slate-grey suit retreating to the exit with a wheel-along briefcase clipping after her.

'Clara!' I shout, and her spine stiffens as she hears me. She turns round and I have to keep the shock from my face. Her skin is grey and waxy, and she looks exhausted. Not the 'my life is so busy, and I've got so many balls in the air' exhausted that we're perpetually claiming to be; she looks shattered down to her marrow. I work out how long it's been since I last saw her, remembering that she and Michael weren't at the Christmas play, and I didn't see her at church in the run-up to us going away. I know she'd found a new nanny, but beyond that I didn't give it much thought, I was so preoccupied with trying to avoid the school gate mums. And now I think about it, Clara never replied to the generic Merry Christmas text that I sent out to everyone in my address book because I couldn't be arsed to send cards.

'Happy New Year,' I say now, and she gives me a weak smile. Maybe she's pregnant and in the phase where you feel like you're about to puke, pass out and then die, in that order, but have been socially conditioned into keeping it a secret until the twelve-week mark.

'It's been an absolute stinker so far,' she says, frowning. 'And now it looks like the trains are fucked too. I'm going back outside to see if I can get an Uber, although no doubt it'll be surging its balls off right now.'

She doesn't look particularly keen to talk, but today I decide not to stand by our no-chat-in-the-morning rule. I haven't seen her for ages and she doesn't look well. If I've vowed to make an effort with the school mums I should definitely start with Clara, one of the ones I actually like.

'Neither of us is getting to work on time today, so do you fancy grabbing a coffee from that new place over the road?'

She nods and turns, so I follow her up the escalators while tapping out a text to the rest of the team at work. My message crosses over with ones from Eddie and Sanj, who are both experiencing the same tube nightmare from other quarters of the network. We make it back into the open air. It's sharp and cold, and the entrance to the station is full of people whingeing about how typical it is for this to happen on the first working day of the year. The bus stop outside has a giant crowd around it, and the two double-deckers standing at it are full to bursting, yet people are still passive-aggressively shouting, 'Can you move down a bit, please,' as they try to shove themselves inside. I don't want to ask Clara anything before we're safely away from it all, and we don't say a word to each other until we've ordered flat whites from the café-come-ceramics workshop across the road. It's tiny and the only place to sit is along a thin wooden bench bordering the window, which looks out into the street we just came from. We pull up two tall stools, made of what looks like reclaimed wood, and I angle myself towards her.

'How are things?' I ask, taking a sip of my coffee. It's too hot, and bitter in my mouth, but distracts me from how trite the question is. She really doesn't look OK.

'I've been diagnosed with breast cancer,' she says, looking straight at me. Then she pulls her coffee cup up to her mouth and keeps it there, like a shield to hold in what she might say next.

My hand flies up to my own mouth. 'Fuck, Clara. No.' I do that thing where I keep saying no, and she keeps having to confirm it. As though the way she looks and the fact that she's telling me isn't enough for me to accept it. She's only thirty-nine. It's so unfair. Poor Clara. Poor Michael and Jeb. I force myself to focus on not saying useless idiotic things.

'When did you find out?'

'Mid-December,' she says shakily. 'I went to the doctor's about a lump, thinking I was being super-efficient in getting it checked the minute I found it, and that it would be a cyst.' She breathes out heavily and it makes a whooshing sound against her coffee cup. 'It sounds stupid, but it never even occurred to me it could be anything worse. I get an annual health MOT through work, I've never put off a smear test, there's no history of cancer in my family. To be honest, I've always been more worried about my mind prematurely packing in – like Mum's – than I have about my body. But they called me back straight away and since then it's been appointment after appointment.' She moves her cup and the expression on her face is one of shell shock. 'The short version is I'm due to have an operation to remove the tumour in two days, and then there will most likely be some radiotherapy.' A few tears spill out of her eyes and she brushes them away with the back of her hand. 'Sorry. I haven't got used to saying it out loud yet. I haven't really told anyone because it all happened so quickly and then it was Christmas. Also, I don't even know how to do it. I emailed work as soon as I knew what was happening and was just on my way in to do a handover. I'm completely dreading it.'

'I'm so sorry, Clara.' I reach for her hand, horrified to find myself on the verge of tears. The last thing she needs right now is to have to manage my outpouring of emotion. 'Have they talked about what stage it is?'

'Early, they think. One B, the doctor said, but they will know more after the lumpectomy. I'm veering between trying not to think about it and thinking that it's going to end up being even worse than she said. I keep thinking that I jinxed myself by not considering the worst-case scenario before.'

'That definitely isn't the case. It's just really fucking bad luck.'

'When I'm not doing that, I'm googling articles on the internet about how to tell a four-year-old his mummy has cancer.'

She stops swiping at her eyes and lets the tears run freely down her face. I do the same. It's easier to talk when I'm not choking on badly suppressed sobs. The multi-pierced guy behind the counter is looking everywhere except at the crying women being the worst possible shop front for his café.

'Jeb doesn't know yet?'

'I wanted to give him a decent Christmas. He knows I've got to go to hospital for an operation, but that's it. I'm sorry I haven't told you, but I didn't know what to say.'

'Oh, Clara. I can't even imagine what it's been like trying to hold it together for him. It sounds like the doctors are acting quickly, though, and that can only be a good thing.' I rack my brain for something I can do. 'What do you need? No, sorry, that's a stupid thing to say. That's me putting pressure on you to find a way for me to help you.'

She gives a snotty laugh. 'I knew I could rely on you not to dole out the usual platitudes. We went to Michael's parents for Christmas and everyone behaved as though I was dying. Every time his mum looked at me, she'd then stare meaningfully at Jebby and dab her eyes, as though envisioning his entire life without me. I had to keep going for walks to get away from them, and then they kept texting to find out where I was. Plus –' her expression darkens '– she keeps sending me positive affirmations and referring to it as my "cancer battle". That can fuck off.'

'Platitudes and affirmations can fuck right off,' I agree. I rummage in my bag for a packet of tissues and offer her one. They're Enid's PAW Patrol ones, and it gives us both a small laugh. 'So your operation is Friday.'

'Yes. And then depending on what they find when they're in there, I'll start radiotherapy soon after.' She tugs on her closely cropped hair. 'At least I don't have much hair to lose,' she says. And then she starts to cry again.

I pull her in for a hug. We're not really huggers, so it's a bit awkward. 'You have a really good-shaped head,' I say, just so I'm saying something, and she laughs a bit. 'I know you don't know yet how you'll react to the treatment or feel, but if you need me to pick up Jeb or give him his tea, just text.'

'That would actually be really helpful,' she says, nodding as though she's thinking it through. 'We've got a new nanny, but I'm worried about him being looked after by someone he doesn't know that well while it's all going on. Weirdly, I think me being at home for the next couple of months is going to freak him out, because it's so unusual. I'd rather he was seeing friends and not coming home to whatever state I might be in that day.'

'Done. He can come to ours one night a week. We'll have a regular playdate, which Enid will love anyway. And the rest you can play by ear.' I think of the mums at school.

'Are you planning on telling anyone else?' I ask gently. 'Like Jeb's key worker, or the other parents? Just because Jeb might say something, and you know how everything gets mangled by the kids and then blown out of proportion by the parents.' To this day, there's a persistent rumour that Kim's bum collapsed, how or why we don't know, and I'm guessing it's not what *actually* happened – although it was apparently during childbirth, so maybe. I originally heard it from Enid. Who knows the true state of Kim's bum? I can hardly ask her.

Clara presses her lips together. 'God, I've been trying to think how best to deal with it and I just don't know.' She stares out of the window, where the tube entrance now has metal barriers pulled across to stop people going in. Clusters of people keep walking up to them to read the handwritten sign that is displayed behind and then turning away.

'I haven't even sent off Jeb's school application yet. Can you believe that I completely forgot and now I've missed the deadline?'

'You've had bigger things on your mind. I'm sure there's something you can do. These are extenuating circumstances. They'll understand.'

'But that means telling them.'

'I know.'

She looks completely overwhelmed.

'I could tell the school if you don't want to. Mr Brown, or maybe the vicar? He was the most reasonable one about that whole school play gender thing.' I have no idea if this is an appropriate offer.

She pulls herself a bit taller on her stool. 'God, these chairs are uncomfortable. Would it kill them to provide a chair with a back? No, you're right. I should tell them. It matters more than ever now that Jeb goes somewhere with people he knows. In case the worst happens . . . But as for telling the mums, I can't bear the thought of sending out a message on that WhatsApp group.'

'It would probably get lost in the chat about the cheese and wine evening and exactly what types of cheese and wine everyone is going to bring. But –' I hold up a hand and remember that twenty minutes ago I decided to make more of an effort myself, for Enid's sake '– while some of them are truly awful—'

'Oh, hi Yasmine,' Clara says in the direction of the door, and I swing round in panic, seeing no one while Clara bursts out laughing.

'Don't *do* that,' I say, lightly punching her on the arm. 'While *some* of them are awful . . . some of the others aren't. Bex, and –' my heart thumps a bit as I say it, but it's true '– Imogen, for example. They might be able to help with Jeb if you need them to. Plus, have you ever had one of Bex's red velvet muffins? She made them for the cake sale. You definitely need to hit her up for a medicinal batch.' A tense smile flickers at her mouth but she's obviously worn out from worry. Her brown eyes are flat and there are dark circles underneath them. I've never seen her not look polished and in control, even during our brief crossover period on maternity leave. When Enid was a few weeks and I was looking and feeling as though I'd been hit by a truck, Jeb was almost six months. Clara had been back at work part-time for two months and was preparing to go back full-time. She'd somehow mastered wearing clothes that were both clean and matched – although to be fair she had both a cleaner and a nanny by then. Now she looks as sleepless and wrung out as I was during the full-on newborn onslaught.

'Sorry,' I say. 'I know I'm being flippant.'

'I'd actually rather have a bit of dark humour. Michael is being great, but he's gone into total practical man mode, as though he can fix it all just by having a positive mental attitude and making me disgusting green smoothies. Tell Bex I want those cakes, stat.' She glances down at her phone. 'My PA has organised me an Addison Lee. She says it will be here in ten minutes.' I see her hesitate. 'I just wish my mum could step in,' she says softly. 'But those days are long gone. Day to day, I just get on with it. I know that loads of people don't have parental help with their kids for all sorts of different reasons. I try and remember that at least sometimes she recognises me, and Jeb, and she got to meet him. But something like this . . .' She trails off. 'Right now, I just *really* want my mum. And the idea that she'll either have no idea where I've disappeared to while I have treatment, or she'll have a moment of lucidity and feel completely impotent to help, breaks my heart.'

'It's shit,' I say automatically, before realising I should be trying to be positive for both of us. 'She's being looked after, though, Clara, and that's the only thing you can control at the moment. Michael can take Jeb to see her, and you will come out the other side. You *will*. It's just the horrible, not-knowing, in-between part right now.'

'No platitudes, remember. And no predictions. The only person I want to hear outcomes from is the consultant. It would be a help if you told a few of the other mums, and maybe the vicar. Just promise me one thing,' she says, one eyebrow raised.

'Whatever you need.'

'Don't let anyone include me in their thoughts and bloody prayers.'

16

Imogen

'Look, it's had twelve thousand likes.' I pass my phone to Will and he squints at it.

'But isn't that just because all these followers like anything that this —' he pulls the phone in for a closer look '— @fluffymummydoodah does? What does it mean?'

'With some influencers, it means nothing, but the ones we've been working with have high engagement with their followers — which is what we're after. So Fluffy Mummy — I know, just get past the name — has included it on her Insta stories and you can swipe up to buy it.' I swipe through and land on Earth Mother's website, where the hygiene basics eco pouch is priced at £30. I show Will and he nods, still looking uncertain.

After the Christmas play I spoke to Mags, and Danny was right. Not only was she keen for me to consult for her, but she loved the idea of partnering with a community charity — specifically the women's domestic violence refuge that Will did the call-out for — and so did a load of east London-based mum-fluencers that I contacted in the run-up to Christmas. Quoting the spike in domestic violence incidences over the holiday period was enough to get everyone from the aforementioned Fluffy Mummy (follower count: 100k) to @hiptwinsinhackney (250k) to pledge their support, and more importantly, pose with pictures of the eco pouch on their feeds. From Mags's end, every time someone buys one, Earth Mother donates another to the women's charity, so that women in need have toiletries – like Toms Shoes, but for shampoo and deodorant.

'Mags says she's seen an incredible uptick in sales, so much so that I think we should get in touch with some other boroughs to expand the scheme.'

'That's brilliant,' he says, and the praise gives me a little buzz. 'Thanks so much for helping with this, Imogen. I was planning on emailing the school parents and congregation to ask for donations of any unwanted Christmas presents, but somehow you've managed to build an entire infrastructure that doesn't even involve me having to collect all the stuff.'

'We should definitely do that too,' I say. 'Because it all helps. And I don't mind picking the donations up from people's houses. I'm just glad to be able to help out. Since we launched, the Earth Mother Facebook page is being inundated with people's personal stories. It's really driving it home how much we need the shelters, and that the ones we have need more funding.'

The vicar – or Will, as I've started to think of him over the course of our three meet-ups – nods and sits down at the vicarage's kitchen table, where we've been talking about the 'We Are Her' project, as Earth Mother has deemed it.

'There's not much we can do about government cuts, but I'm glad we're able to be of some practical help. So, next steps?'

'I think we need to find out if there's a central office we can speak to, so that perhaps they can allocate resources across the borough, and then hopefully across the country, where they're needed most.'

'I'll do that,' he says, scribbling it down on a pad.

'And I'm going to get in touch with some web editors and newspaper features desks to see if I can get Mags on their sites talking about it. These days social media is our best word of mouth, but if I can get her on breakfast telly or into a broadsheet, that will have extra reach with the older generations too.'

'I won't pretend to know anything about that, that's your domain, so I'll leave it to you.' He waggles a mug at me. 'Another coffee?'

I nod. He goes over to a cluttered kitchen worktop, on which sits a shiny new Nespresso machine nestled among the ramshackle collection of pasta containers and assorted papers. It jars with the very clean but very eighties-looking kitchen – magnolia splashbacks, dark faux-wood units and speckly beige lino on the floor – but I know that the coffee machine is the only thing in the room that he didn't inherit from the previous vicar. Mainly because Yasmine instructed us all to contribute towards it for the vicar's Christmas present.

'How's everything else?' he asks, opening a cupboard to reach for some pods. There are dozens in there. The congregants – me included – have been trying to curry additional favour by topping up Yasmine's gift with some supplementary presents. I wish I'd bought him a tin of biscuits now, knowing I was going to benefit.

Our meet-ups have fallen into a pattern. We have a coffee, discuss the appeal and work out a strategy and to-do list, and then we have another coffee and talk about life. He's gone from being the vicar to someone I've started to think of as a friend, and I've ended up telling him a bit about my frustrations with moving to a new area, and how conflicted I feel about working versus staying at home for Winnie. He mostly just listens or points out that staying at home with a child is work.

'Yeah, OK,' I say, even while thinking *pretty crap* and working up to telling him some, but probably not all, of what our Christmas break was like. Danny and I are on OK terms. Like two flatmates going out of their way to be polite to each other. Our time alone was vastly diluted by the rounds of visiting family over Christmas, which made it easier to ignore the atmosphere between us. But since school starting again, the effort of all the exaggerated courtesy has been as obvious as the Christmas lights. I just wish we could put it away in a box along with the decorations.

I haven't even told him that I've been meeting up with the vicar about this project. Not that it's a secret, more that he'd think I was doing it to get in with the school, which I'm not, but I don't have the energy to justify myself to him. The first time I came I thought it would be a one-off, but it's turned into once a week, and now it seems weird that I didn't say anything to start off with. But he doesn't even ask what I'm doing all day any more, and I don't tell him either. And if I'm honest, I'm glad to have something that's mine, and that I can work on without being made to feel guilty about my motivations. The vicar doesn't think I'm just a mum, or a mum on the make for a school place. He respects my opinion about the project and listens when I say what we should do.

My phone buzzes in my hand.

Lily has added you to the group: Hi

I stare at it, waiting to see what happens next. It's not that I haven't spoken to Lily in recent weeks – our daughters really are besties, which means that we often end up sitting in the same row at church on a Sunday – but we haven't had any communication that hasn't happened via our children. Unless you count one generic 'Merry Christmas' text that she must have sent to her entire address book. Which I don't. And now this, a group chat, which only seems to have me, Lily and Bex in it.

Lily: Will you both be at church on Sunday?

My first thought is: uh-oh. What favour does she want now?

. . .

Bex: Yep!
Imogen: Yes

. . .

Lily: If you're able to hang around afterwards, it would be great to have a chat. Sorry to be cryptic, but I'd rather explain in person.
Bex: Sure! Hope everything's OK.

I can't help rolling my eyes. Cryptic and wholly opaque, as though we're still on the same terms we always were. It's probably a childcare crisis that she wants to tackle in person. A wave of guilt hits me. Unless she and Joe have broken up, and she really is having a childcare crisis.

And then: If they've broken up, I wonder if that means they need to sell their house. Could we afford it?

The following Sunday, with our respective daughters sent over to the playgroup in the church hall with Danny and Bex's husband Jerome, the three of us loiter in the pews of St Mary's after the service has finished. Despite the mystery of this meeting, I'm glad to delay going to the hall, because all I can think about is the last time I was there, during the Christmas play, and that stupid argument I had with Danny.

Lily seems to be waiting for everyone to file out before she tells us, but thinking about my own mess of a relationship, and maybe hoping I'm not the only one, I blurt, 'Is everything OK with you and Joe?'

Surprise clouds her face. 'Er, yes. I suppose. I mean . . .' She glances at Bex, who has been patiently standing there, and clearly has no clue what either of us are talking about.

'Anyway. No. This is about Clara. I saw her the other day and she told me she was diagnosed with breast cancer just before Christmas.'

I gasp and Bex's brown eyes widen in shock. 'Oh no, poor Clara,' she says. 'Do you know what stage? My mum was treated for stage two a few years ago and touch wood she's still doing OK.'

'She said it was one B,' Lily says. 'I looked it up. Breast cancer-wise, that's on the more positive end. She had a lumpectomy on Friday where they would be able to check they got it all – I texted to see if she's OK, but I haven't heard back yet – and then she's going to be having radiotherapy, I think. But she's reeling. Obviously. And as she's not that close with many of the parents –' I can't miss the quick squint Lily gives me when she says this '– she didn't really know who to tell or how. But I think she's going to need some help and support.' Lily's agitated and talking very fast now. I can't keep up with the stream of information, but I try to follow what she's saying. She sounds like she's binge-read the Cancer Research site, though, and knowing how Lily thrives in an information-gathering environment, I can only imagine she's been reading every thread she can find since Clara told her.

'She really wants to keep things as stable as she can for Jeb, so I've offered to have him once a week after pre-school for a playdate. If Winnie and Ava want to come too, they're more than welcome –' her eyes flick up to mine again as she says this '– and I thought maybe a couple of others could come too, like Arlo, as I know all of our kids are friends with him.' To Lily's credit, she manages not to grimace, just states it as a fact, even though I can see her jaw clenching up. 'What do you think, Imogen?'

'Sure,' I stutter. The fact is, I haven't heard much from Yasmine since before Christmas either. A few swapped hellos and round robin emails about school stuff that I've been shoving to the bottom of my to-do list. The last one she sent was about the pedestrian crossing, but I've been too busy to do anything about it. The worst thing about that argument with Danny – well, not the *worst* worst thing; that would be the bit where my entire world crumbled – was knowing that he was right about us being able to afford a place if I took on more work. So, along with the consulting for Mags and the charity work with the vicar, I've been in touch with some of my old colleagues at the agency to hustle for more projects.

All three of us stand there silently. We all trooped here in the frigid January gloom because church attendance is monitored, and we can't skip more than the odd Sunday, even if it's that depressing point in the year when it never really seems to get light and we'd rather be inhaling the arse end of a selection box right now. The church is always freezing cold too: we're bundled up in thick jumpers, coats and boots, but right now the temperature seems even colder by degrees. All I can think is *what if it were me?* The idea that I could leave Winnie without a mum, that the treatment might not work – or that it might work this time, but the shadow of cancer would always be there, looming, and threatening to come back.

'I can't even—' I start to say.

'I know.' Lily cuts me off briskly. 'Clara was very clear that she doesn't want a fuss. That's why I thought you two would be the best people to talk to.'

She pauses to let us mull it over. I glance quickly at Bex and she looks like she's trying to hold the tears in too. We're both nodding vigorously, though, to give our faces something else to do other than cry.

'Basically,' Lily says, 'if anyone says something like "you're so brave", tells her that someone they know had breast cancer and cured it by eating clean, or implies it might be part of "God's plan", I think she might knock them out. If she doesn't, I will.'

'Morning, ladies, how are you?' The vestry door next to the altar swings open and we all jump as Will calls out through it, his face smiling and open. He's got a chunky cable-knit jumper on – black, of course – and looks as at ease as we do suspicious, huddled around the end of the pew, like teenagers sneaking an illicit fag. Or an illicit vape. Or Xanax. Whatever it is that teenagers do these days. Oh God, what if I died of cancer and Winnie got into Xanax, and then ended up in the newspapers as a cautionary tale? Lily's stern face stops me spiralling into that thought.

'Everything OK?' asks Will. He had been walking towards us, but falters. I'm not surprised. We're not exactly emanating a welcoming vibe.

'Yes. Fine,' Lily says, visibly prickling.

Bex has a nervous smile plastered to her face. I can see she's torn between lying to the vicar and the promise she made just this second not to draw attention to Clara's situation.

'Actually, Will, we've just had some bad news,' I say. I can feel Lily's eyes boring into me, frown lines etched into her forehead, but I plough on regardless.

'Clara Ihoner, Jeb's mum, has had a breast cancer diagnosis,' I say.

The smile drops from Will's face and is replaced with a worried look. 'I'm so sorry. Has she started treatment yet?'

Lily nods her head at him. 'She's had an operation, but we're waiting to hear the outcome.' She presses her lips together in a straight line and then seems to decide better of it and speaks again. 'I'm not sure she's informed the school yet, so it isn't common knowledge.'

'I see.' Bex and I are both looking at Will as though he's going to say all the wise, comforting words that we didn't. 'It's hard not to spiral when you have no idea what you're dealing with and all you can do is wait. It's a truly horrible situation,' he says. We're all giving him wobbly-chinned looks. 'And something like this can stir up a lot of our own feelings too,' he adds.

I shift uneasily, guilty of projecting Clara's real-life situation onto my own imagined one.

'I don't know Mrs Ihoner that well, but the things that seem to help when there's a serious illness in the family are the practical day-to-day things, like home-cooked meals, doing laundry or helping out with the school run.' I can see Lily's expression softening as she realises he's not going to bring up God. That's what I've been most surprised by during our meetings about the refuge. Away from the pulpit, he hardly ever mentions God at all. 'Parents want to make sure their children feel as secure as possible, and helping with their routines can be a weight off their mind.'

'That's what I wanted to talk about,' Lily says, her tone getting audibly warmer. 'How to support her family without being intrusive. Those are all really good ideas.' Her eyes glisten with tears. 'In your job you must come into contact with a lot of people who are . . . ill,' she says.

A thin smile flicks across Will's face. 'Quite a lot. Often, it's elderly people, but of course not always. Every illness is different, though,' he says gently. 'And every cancer is different. The only thing you can do is support your friend and hope for the best.'

'I know,' she replies huskily. Just as Bex and I are welling up again, she clears her throat and seems to shake herself out of it.

'Shall we work out a rota,' she says, 'and we can go from there?'

We nod, pulling up the calendars on our phones.

'Has she told you to keep it private?' says Will, sounding a bit unsure of himself. 'Or is it OK if I get in touch?'

'She's asked me to tell a few people as and when, but not spread it about, if that makes sense.' Lily goes a bit pink. 'She'd, er, rather not be remembered publicly in church, but it's not a secret.'

He flashes a wry sort of smile and a moment of understanding seems to pass between them. 'Whatever she prefers,' he says.

'Because it came so out of the blue before Christmas, it meant she sent Jeb's school application late,' she says in a rush. 'I think one thing that would give her peace of mind is to know he wasn't going to get penalised for that.' She hesitates for a second, as though weighing something up, and then starts speaking again. 'Are you able to write a letter or make a recommendation?'

He nods solemnly. 'I'll see what I can do.' We all stand there quietly, waiting for Lily to take the lead and start divvying up tasks, but she seems to be finished talking for now. She's got a thoughtful, but impenetrable, look on her face.

'You're right about helping as much as possible with the children,' she says, almost to herself. She starts tapping something into her phone, which leaves the rest of us glancing a bit uneasily at each other and wondering what to do next. Will seems to read the moment.

'I'll check in on her, but if Clara – or her family – need anything else, please do let me know,' he says. 'Or if any of you would like to talk to me, then don't hesitate. There are bound to be good days and bad days, and the treatment affects everyone differently, but the one thing all cancers have in common is that it's an absolute fucker.'

He tactfully withdraws towards Jasper, the almost good-looking bloke who plays the guitar during church, who has popped his head around the main church door, looking for him. So much of being a vicar must be knowing when to make an exit, as well as knowing when to step in. It's like some elaborate upper-class dinner party etiquette but with added spirituality. Lily is staring after him, eyes wide, her phone momentarily forgotten, and I can't help but laugh. Bex follows my look and starts sniggering too.

'I can't believe you of all people are shocked that the vicar has just sworn,' I tell her.

'I can't believe that you two aren't. That was like when an old person in a film drops the C-bomb. Totally out of the blue.'

Bex smiles. 'I *told* you the new vicar isn't like the old one. He's less judgement and hellfire and more like that Canadian prime minister everyone's obsessed with.'

'He *is* a bit like him, isn't he?' I say. 'That's exactly who he reminds me of.'

'Is it? When did you get to know him so well?' Lily asks, looking at me curiously.

Now it's my turn to blush. 'I don't, really. But I'm doing some charity work with one of the brands I work with and we've talked a bit. Like Bex says, he's a lot less vicar-y than you'd expect. I get the impression he's sometimes frustrated with the church. He acts as though it's an interfering boss that prioritises protocol over application. I got here the other day and there was an old lady chewing his ear off about how it's outrageous that Ireland has repealed the Eighth and that everything should be done to stop Northern Ireland going the same way. I could tell by the look on his face that he was indulging her. He was doing the same nod that I do with Winnie when she won't stop whining, the one that looks like you're listening when you're actually tuning them out. I bet you any money he's pro-choice, even if he could never admit it.'

'Admit what?' Yasmine's voice pipes up from the back of the church. She's holding her phone in her hand.

'Here we go,' mutters Lily.

'I was only in the other room, Lily, you could have come to me,' Yasmine says, lowering herself onto the pew next to us and clutching her bump, presumably from the exertion of coming all of twenty metres to see us. I'm surprised Lily has texted her, though, and more surprised Yasmine has come. It must have been a hell of a teaser to spike her curiosity.

Lily half rolls her eyes, then seems to realise what she's doing and stops. 'There's less chance of the children overhearing in here,' she says, her voice clipped. Then she summarises Clara's situation, even more briefly than she did with us. She doesn't even pause for breath until she's finished.

'Clara has cancer. She's just had an operation but will be undergoing treatment, and we're working out how best to help with Jeb and some stuff around her house. Me, Bex and Imogen –' she flashes us a brief, inclusive smile '– are

209

going to work out a rota, and it would be great if you wanted to be involved, because all our children are good friends, and it's important for Clara to know Jeb will be seeing them when she might not be up to looking after him.'

Yasmine listens, looking as shocked as the rest of us. 'Of course. *Whatever* I can do. I can drive her to appointments if she needs me to. I'm around during the day.' She dabs her eyes a bit.

'That's really kind, Yasmine,' says Lily, relaxing her body language. 'I'll mention that to her.'

'Oh, she's *so* brave,' says Yasmine. 'But if anyone can beat it, Clara can. She's so strong. Has she cut out sugar? You know, an alkaline diet can really impact the spread of cancerous cells. I also have the number of a great homeopath.'

Lily tenses up again, and starts tapping at her phone, a fixed expression on her face. I wonder who she's summoning next but am not altogether surprised when my own phone buzzes.

Lily: We need to keep Yasmine away from Clara. Otherwise, she's first 🎤

17

Lily

In, Lily. Now out.

I feel as though my lungs are being squeezed, and my throat is a narrow tube that's contracting, getting thinner and thinner until the only way I can take in air is by using a tiny gulping motion.

I'm supposed to be at my desk, prepping for a briefing with Amanda, and after that I need to study a file for the court case that starts next week. Instead I'm sitting on a closed toilet, staring at the dirty grouting of the grey tiled floor and freaking out that I've forgotten how to breathe.

This isn't the first time I've fled to the toilets at work for a secret cry, but it's the first time that instead of spending fifteen minutes in here, silently shoulder-shaking with tears, I don't have enough breath in my body to do it.

A bubble of fear rushes through me, forcing me to bend over and put my head between my legs. I can't decide if I'm going to be sick. I drop onto the floor, thumping my knees on the tiles in the process, and open the toilet lid, saliva rising. I desperately try to push some air in and out. Sweat is running down my face and drips into the loo from my chin.

In. Out. In. Out.

This must be a panic attack, I tell myself, *you're not dying.* But giving it a name doesn't stop me shaking or dilate my airway. I push out a breath and a noise gurgles from me that sits somewhere between a throat clearance and a cry for help.

There's a soft tap on the door.

'Are you OK in there?'

Amanda. Fuck. *Fuck.* They might be painted the grubbiest institutional shade of beige known to man, but at least we have fully enclosed cubicles and she can't see me hunched on the floor. Although I feel like my heart is hammering so loudly that she'll be able to hear it from behind the wood.

'Mmmggg,' I try, before sucking in enough of a breath to let me croak out a response. 'Feeling bit unwell.'

'OK.' I can hear the concern in her voice and berate myself. So far, she's seemed impressed with how on it I am, and I've become her go-to person for information or research. The last thing I want is to be seen as some pathetic weakling who can't cope. 'Let me know if you need anything.'

'Uh-huh.'

I hear her clumpy boots retreat and the main toilet door open and close. If I could sigh with relief I would. I sit there, forcing myself to concentrate on the dirty streaks that line the toilet walls where hundreds of bags have scraped them, and trying not to think about how many bums have sat on the seat that is now right next to my face.

I don't know how long it takes before my heart begins to slow down, but gradually I manage one longish breath, and then another. After a while I'm still vibrating with anxiety but it feels on a par with the jittery feeling of drinking too much coffee, rather than the sensation that I'm about to combust at any moment. I get up slowly, trembling, and unlock the door. At the sink I look at myself in the mirror. Whole clumps of my hair are drenched with sweat, so I push it behind my ears to try and disguise it. All it achieves is revealing that the skin around my temples is sticky and my face is waxy and white, as though I haven't had more than a few hours' sleep a night for the last few weeks. Mainly because I haven't. Since we started the rota to help Clara out, it feels like there's a permanent pressure on my chest. I wanted to help her – I still do – but all the other pressures are still there too. How did I ever think I'd be able to get more involved in the school and give Enid's application one last push, when I'm also trying to make my mark with Amanda? That's probably the thing I should step back from, but I can't. It's been so inspiring to have her here, and the jobs she mentioned in that briefing include some permanent roles, including a Higher Officer position that is possibly a little bit beyond me, but maybe not if I can impress her. And impress her more than Eddie, who I *know* has his eye on it too.

But so far I just feel like I'm trying to do everything – and failing.

I cleared it with John that I could leave early three times a week for the foreseeable future – although I did lie and say it was to help a family member with cancer, rather than a friend – and he readily agreed, no questions asked, when I assured him that I'd catch up on my missed working hours in the evenings. Which I've been doing once Enid and Jeb are both fed, Jeb is dropped off to his dad and Enid is in bed. So far, I've managed to get everything done, with Joe pitching in a bit with the kids when he's there. But then after I've finished working, at ten or eleven at night, I've been lying in bed for two, three, sometimes four more hours, not able to sleep, and getting more and more wound up about what kind of state I'll be in the next day through lack of sleep. And the guilt that I'm irritated by a lack of sleep, which is nothing compared to what Clara is going through.

It was as suspected – a small tumour – and the lumpectomy caught it all. But she has daily radiotherapy for the next five weeks, and it's leaving her tired and drained. The rota is working well, but at night I can't stop turning it all over in my head. The rota, the worry about Clara, the court case I have coming up next week – not the big one that Amanda is here for, but another one that has been in the pipeline for over a year – and all the usual stuff on top of that: Enid, the vague sensation that Joe and I have stopped arguing, but that maybe it means we've just stopped caring altogether.

And ridiculously, that's what I was thinking about at my desk, right before I had to hurl myself into the ladies'. Joe. Instead of the dozens of things that are stressing me out, it was the thought of how he's been different since the Nativity, and my brain whispering the words 'it's not enough' that yanked my breath from me. I should be *happy* that he's been more attentive, more interested, made space in his diary to contribute to the odd pick-up while Clara is ill, but instead it's making me feel uneasy. Another curl of dread unfolds from somewhere in my stomach and I force out a long, shaky breath to try and clear my mind. I need to run, I think, while simultaneously thinking that I could easily spend the rest of the day sitting on the loo floor.

I wipe my face quickly with a damp paper towel. Applying an armour of make-up isn't an option; I so rarely wear it for work that I don't carry around any of the relevant products to camouflage how rough I look. Besides, it would be so unusual that it would only draw more attention to me. Instead I yank open the door with the intention of bolting back to my desk and hiding behind my monitor with my nose in some case notes until I feel somewhere near normal.

'Lily!' Amanda calls just as I step through the doorway, and my breath is whipped out of me, this time because she's made me jump.

'Is our meeting now? I thought it was at twelve.' I look at my watch. I've been in there twenty minutes. I have ten more before I'm late.

'It is,' she confirms. 'But I thought we could take it out of the office. Have an early lunch.'

'Er.' I'm pretty sure the confidential nature of our cases means that's impossible, but she's the boss. Maybe it's a test.

She clocks my stricken expression. 'What I mean is, let's have an early lunch and then come back for the meeting. Carluccio's OK?'

Two minutes later we're making awkward small talk as we ride the lift down two floors to the entrance. I *never* usually take the lift, both so I don't have to make small talk with people and also because I'm too impatient to wait, but Amanda pressed the button, so I followed her lead. We emerge into the street, the crisp winter morning searing into us, and make the short walk to the restaurant. It's so cold my face aches. I rarely venture any further than the nearest Pret or the M&S food hall a couple of streets away, and it doesn't feel like the right time to start taking advantage of the mid-range chains dotted around the area, not least because of the mountain of work I have to do, but also because my stomach is still churning from my freak-out. As we walk along, I'm aware that I should be taking some initiative when it comes to talking to Amanda, but I can't seem to find my voice. I'm too busy pep-talking myself inside my head.

Luckily, Amanda is a fast walker, and we pelt along past the decrepit offices, high street shops and glass-fronted new-builds that make up the area. At one point I have to trot to keep up, which is a positive in my book. I'm always in a rush to and from work; I cannot stand people who meander.

'Where do you come into the office from, Amanda?' I manage once we get into a walking rhythm. A safe topic. Most people can't help but whinge about their commute, regardless of whether they're a PA or a CEO.

'Surrey.'

Of course.

'I'm not a fan,' she continues, hunching a little as a frigid wind batters us from the front. 'But it's where I was before I broke up with my ex-husband, and my daughter was at school there, so I never moved. Now she's left home – well, just about: these days I don't think anyone in their twenties can actually afford to move out, can they? – I could go anywhere, but I can't seem to make a decision about where.' She reaches the glass door to the restaurant just before me and pulls the door open. 'Two, please,' she says to the server, who whisks us straight to a table. Being barely noon, it's practically empty, but I get the impression that Amanda would have got us seated quickly regardless of how busy it was. We've barely sat down opposite each other when she orders a risotto and a sparkling water. I sense that decisiveness is something she values, so am desperate not to seem like a ditherer. I panic-order the first thing I see on the menu, a giant plate of pasta.

'Thank you,' I say to the waitress as she takes the menus away, and rack my brains for something to talk about, but there's no need because Amanda trains her dark eyes on me and says, 'I wanted to speak to you away from the office because it's obvious something was going on in the toilets.'

My stomach lurches as though I've been caught. The few times I've returned to my desk red-eyed – when Enid first went to nursery or because of some argy-bargy on text with Joe – Eddie, Sanj and John have either not noticed, or deliberately ignored it. John absolutely does not want to get involved in anything emotional, and I think I'd go down several notches in Eddie's estimation if he thought I had any feelings in the workplace other than frustration when a case isn't going our way, depression when we can't make a case stick and anger when we lose a case in court.

Amanda is looking at me as though I'm supposed to say something back – not impatiently, but also as though she's expecting me to tell the truth. I think of all the courtroom training I've had, and how much more that means she's had. But does she really want me to tell her, or is she just prodding to see what my vulnerabilities are? I look at her for a moment, trying to weigh up how much I should say.

'I know that the job can be a boys' club at times,' she starts, leaning forward and crossing her arms at the wrist on the table. 'I've been out in the field as well as based in the office, so I know what sort of "locker room talk" can go on. But if there's ever anything inappropriate being said – or even implied – I want to know immediately. It wasn't acceptable when I started in 1985, and it's certainly not acceptable now. The difference is, I'm now in a position to do something about it.'

Horror rises as I realise what she thinks is going on. 'God, *no*,' I spit out, while emphatically shaking my head. 'Nothing like that.' Sanj and Eddie might be dicks, but as Eddie once bore the full force of a car door opening into his crotch to protect me from an aggressive perp, I can't let her think my bathroom breakdown was because of any office-based misconduct. 'Honestly, I've never felt threatened in any way by my colleagues.' I am, however, careful not to phrase it as though they've never said anything that couldn't be construed as offensive by *anyone*. It briefly occurs to me that all it would take to get Eddie out of the running for that job would be to let her think otherwise, but I couldn't do that to him. Besides, I want to beat him properly and get it on merit.

Amanda nods, as though she's satisfied with my answer. She leans back slightly but maintains eye contact with me. 'So, what's going on, Lily? Talk to me. I told you I was impressed by your work, and I am, but I want to make sure you don't get burnt out. John says you're working some shorter days at the moment. Has that been advised by a doctor?'

Again, I'm mortified. But my defences go up. This is exactly why I don't talk about my home set-up. Shorter days means 'can't hack it' or that I'm not pulling my weight. 'I don't have a doctor's note, if that's what you're asking. But it's been cleared by John. It's only a temporary measure and I'm making up all the time I'm taking off once I get home.'

Amanda's hands are up in a gesture of reassurance. 'No, no, you misunderstand me. I'm not here to cross-examine you about it. We can save that for court practice back in the office. I want to talk about how we can help. You're a valuable member of the team, Lily, and workplace stress is all too real. Sixteen-hour surveillance shifts are hard enough at the best of times, but throw in any sort of home life . . .' I flinch, wondering if Eddie or Sanj or John have been given the same speech. 'John also mentioned that someone close to you has a serious illness.'

The waitress arrives with our food, mixing up our orders and putting each other's in front of us. Neither of us says anything until she's gone and then we clumsily shuffle them round.

'I'm helping out with her little boy where I can,' I say, nudging a spinach ball with my fork. I don't know how I'm going to force this down. I should have got a salad. I can't bring myself to trot out the family member lie; Amanda's kindness is unnerving me more than when I thought she was implying I was skiving. I stuff a forkful of pasta into my mouth so I don't have to tell her anything else.

'And you have a young child of your own too?' She takes a bite of her mushroom risotto, puts her fork down, seasons it and takes another mouthful.

'Yes. Enid's going to be four in a few weeks.'

'So you already have a lot on your plate.' It's a statement, not a question. 'And today was what – emotional moment, stress cry, panic attack, or just needing five goddamn minutes to yourself?'

I feel myself getting redder and redder. 'Erm.'

She gives me the faint outline of a smile. She has one of those faces that's a bit grizzled, in a good way. She's not wearing any make-up either and she pulls it off, like she's too important to give a shit. 'Believe me, I've done all of them in many grotty toilets in government buildings over the last three decades. I guess what I'm trying to find out is if you feel overwhelmed, and if so, what by. Work, personal life, or a combination of the two.'

'It was nothing. I'm fine, honestly.'

Amanda has carried on eating but raises her eyebrow. 'You didn't seem all right. You know we can look at your workload if it's getting on top of you.'

'It's not my workload,' I say quickly. There's no way I want her to think that. 'Work has always been my salvation, to be honest. No matter what else is going on, there's some sort of order to what we do here. Rules. Best practice.'

'Which is more than can be said for everything else, I gather.'

I'm still not sure if I should, but something about the way she says it makes me want to tell her. Holding it in is making me feel a bit like I did just before that panic attack. What if it happens again, here?

'There's just not enough time, and I'm constantly rushing, and then feeling like I'm doing everything badly. Hustling Enid to school and feeling like a rubbish mum when I see the mums who aren't racing off to work. They all know each other, so are always chatting and making plans, and I feel like I'm not part of it, and then when I get here – don't get me wrong, I work really hard – but I worry about what will happen if a meeting gets put in for a time I can't do, or something comes up that will throw my childcare out of whack.' I don't want her to think I'm complaining. 'I can make it work if that happens, though. I always do. You can ask John.'

Her look is unblinking. 'I don't need to ask John. I've seen for myself how committed you are. I take it your husband isn't supportive.'

'Joe is . . .' What is Joe? 'Joe does what he can.'

More eyebrows.

'Joe just doesn't seem to feel the same pressure or guilt as me. He tells me to increase the childminder's hours if I need to work late and he can't get home.' I don't know why I add the last bit. I don't want Amanda to know that he rarely says he can get home, even though his job is no more or less demanding than mine. 'But if one of her parents can be there to meet her from school and put her to bed, they should be, and sometimes . . .' Here I hesitate, but I think *fuck it* and say it anyway. 'I think some of the meetings could wait. Or don't need to happen at all.'

Amanda barks a laugh. 'No need to be so polite, Lily. The amount of time-wasting that goes on is ridiculous. I'm about to implement a standing meeting policy to make everyone want to get them over with and go back to their desks. And believe me, I understand the clock-watching, knowing you're on a tight schedule to get back for the school pick-up, or bedtime. My main anger was reserved for the constantly delayed trains to Esher that meant I ended up late and stewing even when I'd left on time. That was what we got for moving to somewhere where the schools were good. Commuter hell. Do you know where Enid will be going to school?'

'We've just submitted her application so will hear in a couple of months.'

'And the schools are decent?'

'One is. It's quite competitive to get in there, though.' I nibble a bit of the courgette in my pasta. I feel my appetite coming back a little bit. Amanda is one of those people who can draw out your secrets. I just hope I won't regret it later. I can already imagine getting back to my desk, replaying this conversation in my head and cringing.

She nods knowingly. 'I bet. The school catchment wars weren't quite so bad in the eighties, but we still moved to get her into the school we wanted. Of course, house prices weren't what they are now.'

'I'm having to be quite . . . active with the local church,' I admit. 'Although I'm not really doing very well with that either.'

'I've never seen you take a lunch break, and you've never missed a deadline. Some of the team may be staying later but they're no more productive. It *does* get noticed.

From our point of view, you're handling your workload just fine.' The compliment flusters me and I start to thank her, but she holds up a hand and I stop. 'I also wanted to speak to you privately to see if you'll be applying for the Higher Officer job.'

'I was going to,' I stutter. 'I mean, I'm definitely interested, if you think I should.' I look at her to gauge what she's thinking.

'I think you certainly should. You're an asset to the team. But I also want to nurture the talent in our team and make sure you're taking care of yourself if you're running at full capacity.'

'I am.' Total lie, but she doesn't have to know that. 'I try to, anyway.'

'This isn't a trick, I promise. Studies show that workers with balance in their lives are more productive, so there's no value in me testing to see how much stress you can cope with. I want to make sure we're helping you to reduce it, if we can.' She lowers her voice and the professional mask drops for a second. 'I've been there as a mum too. I know how hard it can be.'

I nod silently.

'Do you meditate?' she asks, her voice brisk again. The change of direction takes me by surprise.

'What?'

'Meditate. Use one of those apps. Or do yoga, or take time out to go for a walk?'

I can sometimes be found in the kitchen at about nine o'clock at night staring into space and wondering why I went in there. But I don't think this is what she means.

'Or swim?' she prompts. 'Exercise is good for mental health.' She's down to her last bites of risotto, whereas I've barely touched my pasta.

'I run. Well, not so much any more.'

'Of course. Catching that bolter at the knock has already become the stuff of lore. You'd think you'd chased down Usain Bolt the way John tells it. He's very proud.'

'Usain Bolt is only good over short distances,' I joke to deflect the compliment. 'I've done a couple of marathons. But thank you.'

'I mean it, Lily,' she presses. 'Some separation of work, family and self is imperative. I loathe the phrase "me-time", but it doesn't have to mean a spa day or eating a yoghurt or whatever advertisers currently think "us women" are into. Bring your running kit to work and use twenty minutes of your lunch break to do that – whatever you need to reclaim yourself, and avoid another situation like the one today. And no need to tell me again you're fine. HR would advise leaving the office for some exercise at lunchtime regardless of whether or not an employee had a moment in the staff toilets.'

Amanda puts twenty quid on the table and starts to pull her coat on. 'This is on me. I have to run back. Another pointless meeting, ironically, but you take your time. I've blocked you out until two.' This whole trip has only taken half an hour. I could learn something from her; she's a master of efficiency.

I start to protest about the money, but she waves me away. 'We'll have a team briefing at four and catch up on the case then.'

And then I'm on my own, in Carluccio's at 12.30 on a Monday. I immediately feel guilty that I haven't got anything productive to do in this unexpected pocket of free time. I could have brought a book. I started reading *The Handmaid's Tale* in 2017 when it was on the TV but haven't finished it yet. Instead I pull out my phone. There's a text from Clara.

I know it's short notice, but I'm in quite a bit of pain and Michael wants to take me to get checked out. Is it OK if you collect Jeb today?

It's not my day, but I automatically tap back *Of course*, before remembering the 4 p.m. briefing. Crap. Maybe Imogen can do it. My hand hovers over the screen as I remember what she said at the bonfire and I imagine what she'd think now. Typical Lily, expecting someone else to pick up the childcare slack. She'd be right. This rota was my idea. I told Clara she could count on me. I'll have to make it work. Hopefully Amanda will understand after our talk today. And she definitely thinks I should apply for the job. I could head back now and make a start on it before I have to leave. I flag the waitress down and ask if I can take my food to go while handing her the money and searching my purse for some change for the tip. Does that count as me-time? It's not meditation or yoga and it's not going to help me de-stress. But it's definitely something I want for me.

18

30 January 2019, 1.30 p.m.

Two months until places are announced. The housing market is stagnant. What else can I do? WHAT?

Imogen

New Year, New Beginnings and New Followers!

Hello to all my new readers! I've been honoured to join Earth Mother's team and to work with the women's refuge in east London on the We Are Her campaign. We have much more in the pipeline in aid of this important service, so please do head to Earth Mother's Instagram account (@earthmother) for more details. If you're here, you've reached my personal blog, where I talk about all things mum (all opinions my own, obvs).

And this is me: I'm mum to Winnie. We're past the baby stage, so if you're still in the thick of the non-stop night wake-up and WTF nappy blowout phase, you might need to scroll back to find something that relates to where you are right now. (But believe me, I CAN relate. I can barely remember writing some of the blogs from that time because I was so sleep-deprived, and some of them should come with a trigger warning. Seriously, how did I survive on such little sleep? HOW?)

But that time seems like an age ago now because W's going to start school in September. My current concern is where, because yep, come 2 April I'll be one of those people taking to Facebook to either celebrate or lament what school we've been allocated. (Feel free to mute me, non-parent friends – I would.) All this change makes me actually wish for the simplicity of the baby months. Getting her to eat and sleep: it seems so straightforward – yeah, I know it's not, but maybe I'm rose-tinted because the possibility of me doing it again currently stands at zero per cent, not least because my boyfriend thinks I've turned into some sort of mum-bot and has no interest in having sex with me. I also used to have friends, but because we moved house to get our daughter into a decent school, they're all in south London (they may as well be on Mars in London terms), and despite my best efforts to join the alpha mum gang here, I'm at best a peripheral member. My best efforts also involved sacrificing the one person I might have been able to rekindle a genuine friendship with, before I got seduced by the idea of the alphas. But that's a different story. Oh, and we're probably not going to get into the school anyway because we're still not actually in the catchment area, and working part-time I also don't earn enough money for that to change any time soon . . .

I delete it all, watching the cursor swallow the letters and wishing I could erase how I feel so easily. I look around the tatty kitchen, even gloomier in the flat January light and the unforgiving glare of the buzzing fluorescent strip light. If we owned it, I'd knock the kitchen through to the living room to open up the ground floor and make the most of the bay window at the front. Then a few carefully placed spotlights would warm it up when the weather didn't. I stare at my screen, summoning up the impetus to write something more positive, and flip to Instagram instead. What's the point in slaving over an entire blog post when people only have the attention span for an extended caption anyway? I look at my profile. Five thousand followers isn't bad, and I've had a steady rise thanks to some of Mags's mum-fluencers tagging me. I just need to keep posting content to keep the momentum going now. Except there's no angle to make this configuration of coffee, laptop and kitchen table look good. It looks sepia-tinted, and not in a filter-y way.

The new followers are all ultra-positive. True, most of them want me to check out their own blogs in return for commenting on mine, but if only it was as easy to draw the real mum community into my life as the Insta one.

After school I'm busier than ever, what with tag-teaming playdates with Enid, Ava, Jeb and Arlo, but we're taking it in turns rather than all hanging out together, so I haven't ended up spending time with Lily or Bex. I've actually found myself at a loose end a couple of times a week while the others run them to swimming lessons or give them their tea at their houses. The children are a bit bewildered by us collectively embracing weekday group activities, but they're loving it. And Yasmine seems to have readily accepted that in the interest of her getting some rest herself, she can drop Arlo off and then leave the designated parent to it, to the point where she's even refused to come in for a cup of tea on my last two evenings. She vaguely mentioned having a project to work on but didn't go into it. I'm both offended and relieved she's not trying to draw me into some other random school campaign. Plus, the bigger she gets the more I resent her. I know I'm a bitch, but it's true.

I'll go to a café and work, I decide, gathering up my stuff. That one I saw mentioned on the local Facebook group the other day: they've converted some former workshops into a creative space and a café, and it's meant to be a 'hub' for freelance workers looking for an ad hoc working environment. It's a good fifteen-minute walk, and harder to find than I expect. Sheets of cold wind are pummelling me as I lock the front door, but I pull my parka up around my face. It's still less depressing than sitting on my own in the flat. I take a left down an alleyway that leads to the warehouse buildings but find myself searching a row of workshops, before a man working at the clutch centre directs me to an almost identical building, with no signage on it, next door. I roll the metal sliding door open and warm air, heavy with the smell of coffee and pastries, wafts out. There's a 'living room' area in one corner – two squashy brown leather sofas arranged at right angles to each other with their backs to the rest of the room – and two large communal wooden tables in the centre. It's busy. A quick scan shows the sofas are occupied and there's only one space free at the tables, between two other people working on laptops. I squeeze in and dump my stuff in the gap to reserve it before going to the food counter at the other end of the room.

'A latte and a piece of that vegan chocolate orange cake, please,' I say to the intimidatingly trendy but incredibly smiley girl at the coffee machine. This place will provide a much better photo. I carry back my food and arrange it on the distressed wood table, along with the book I'm reading about how to create a flexible career from multiple streams, and then snap the set-up from a few different angles. It's a bit cramped, but no one bats an eyelid. They probably all took photos of their coffee before they drank it.

Today's office @hub17 in Walthamstow. I found this book so inspiring to help find a system that works for me and my family set-up. Now my office is anywhere that has wi-fi (and cake!). Loads of exciting projects in the pipeline, but first I'm going to work on this coffee.

#workingmama #givemecaffeine #mumlife

The likes tick up almost immediately and the café starts following me within minutes. I open my laptop and reread Mags's latest email. Following the success of the refuge partnership, I'm supposed to be coming up with other ways we can engage with (read: piggyback on) the Instagrammers' built-in audience. I only met Mags in person for the first time last week, and really liked her. She's about the same age as me but has been developing this business as a side hustle for the past three years while working some corporate day job that provides the cash flow. She had the idea for the business when her sister had a baby and they realised how truly horrendous that is for the environment. But being of the Babington House ilk, Mags didn't see why you couldn't produce eco-friendly products for parents and kids that were also on a par with Jo Malone in the luxury stakes. Having now had a face-to-face meeting with her – in Chelsea, at some chia-seed-heavy raw food café – I have no doubt she'll be just as well known in a few years' time. She's already in talks with Selfridges. She was thrilled with the charity angle, and it's already been great for business. She's been profiled in the *Telegraph* and *YOU* magazine off the back of it, so she's instructed me to start working on preliminary ideas for connecting the company to domestic violence awareness week in October that 'don't make her look mercenary'. The last part is the reason I keep putting off doing it and checking my likes instead. People are asking about the book and the café and what sort of cake I'm eating. I tap out a few replies.

Yep, changed my life. No more presenteeism office culture for me!

Vegan choc orange. Dreamy. 😊

Near Blackhorse Road. If you end up in the MOT centre you've gone too far LOL. I'm sure Rich the mechanic makes a great brew though! #e17life

---

I notice a woman standing up from one of the sofas and gather my stuff, readying myself to pounce on the comfier seats before someone else does. She turns and bends down to pick up her coat and I realise that it's Jusna. I haven't seen her properly for ages, but I WhatsApped her the other week to ask if she was doing OK. She told me things were tough, but she was 'getting used to the new normal'.

She's winding a scarf around her neck and pulling on the coat, all the while talking to a person still sitting down on the sofa. It's a man. But I can only see the back of his head from here. Her laugh rings out and she turns and bends down again. This time to meet the man halfway as he leans up for a kiss. I don't know what to do. I'm now half standing, half sitting over my semi-vacated stool, wondering if what I'm witnessing is Jusna's new normal.

'Are you going?' A laptop-toting woman is hovering next to me. She gestures to the table.

My eyes flit back to Jusna. 'Er. Yes.' I make a snap decision. 'Jus!' I call. I see her eyes searching the room for the source of the voice until they land on me. Yeah, not common knowledge then, because there's definitely panic in them.

'Imogen. Hi. How are you?' She takes a *big* stride and walks quickly towards me, intercepting me before I can move more than a couple of steps from my table, and blocks my passage to the sofa. 'I didn't see you there.'

'I've come here to do some work,' I say, brandishing my laptop under her nose as though to prove I wasn't spying on her. 'I was just going to grab that seat.'

A tense smile flickers at Jusna's mouth and she shifts from one foot to the other but doesn't actually let me pass. 'What are you working on?' she asks, looking at the closed laptop with great interest.

'It's a brainstorm for the eco beauty brand I'm consulting for, promotion ideas for the next year.'

'Eco beauty? Tell me more,' she says. A distraction technique if ever I saw one. No wonder she seems so fine about the break-up – she's already got someone else. I play along, though, giving her the top lines about the range and the partnership I brokered via the vicar.

'It sounds amazing. What's it called again? It felt like it was impossible to get lovely stuff like this when we were all pregnant. Maybe we should get a gift basket for Yasmine and the baby?'

While she's prattling on, she keeps her gaze trained on me as though she's fascinated, as if by doing so she can stop me looking anywhere else, but my eyes flit back to the guy on the sofa. He must know he's supposed to be a secret, because who wouldn't turn round to see who their girlfriend was gabbing on to? He has thick black hair, he's medium build and is wearing a blue denim shirt. She definitely has a type, because from the back he looks like Ajay.

Wait.

I strain to look over Jusna's shoulder and get a view of the man's profile. It *is* Ajay.

'Jus,' I interrupt. 'Are you and Ajay back together? That's great news.'

'No, we're not,' she shrieks.

'Then what is —' I point at the settee without finishing the sentence.

'It's complicated,' she says, grabbing my arm. Tight. My coffee spills into the saucer. 'I don't want Mo to get confused. Please don't say anything.' Her look is unblinking, two frown lines etched into her forehead. 'To anyone.'

'Ajay,' she hisses in his direction, and he jumps up. 'We're just trying to work some stuff out,' she says, her voice straining with the effort of trying to sound casual. 'To do with access and money, you know.'

Ajay slinks up next to her, looking sheepish. 'Hi, Imogen,' he says. He moves a bit further away from Jusna, as though realising that a separated couple wouldn't invade each other's personal space like that. There's no trace of tension between them at all. If he's spent more than one night in that bloody flat opposite the school I would be very surprised. The sneaky bastards are just pretending for the second address. I'm guessing their big reunion is due to happen, oh, I don't know, April the second?

'I see,' I reply evenly. What if Mo gets a place and Winnie doesn't? And then: why didn't Danny and I think of this? Especially because we really are barely speaking to each other.

'We — I — better go,' says Jusna. 'You have to get back to work, Ajay. I'm guessing,' she adds quickly. 'Although do what you like, obviously. It's nothing to do with me any more.'

'It's OK, Jus, I won't say anything,' I tell her gently. I'd say that's sixty to seventy per cent true.

'*Thank you,*' she says, gratitude written all over her face. 'I feel so terrible lying, but I didn't know what else to do. And then when I started feeling so rough, I didn't see people as much so it was a lot easier to stay under the radar.'

'Rough?' I say. I suppose she hasn't been on the pick-up scene as much, but Ajay works locally so it's not unusual for him to take a late lunch break and fetch Mo from school. In the last few weeks I assumed he was taking him back to his flat, but now I realise he must have been dropping him at home as usual before going back to work.

'We've just been for the scan, and stopped off for lunch,' she says, thrusting a black-and-white printout under my nose. The impact of it hits me like a punch as I look at the outline of what is unmistakably Mo's brother or sister. 'But what with everything, we're not planning on announcing it for quite a while.'

'Congratulations,' I say, feeling like I'm going to cry or throw up. Or just scream. I mentally adjust the odds of me grassing them up to an even fifty/fifty.

I'm still stewing about it two hours later as I corral Winnie, Enid, Jeb and Arlo onto the bus and take them to the posher of the two soft play centres in Walthamstow. By posher I mean the one with no urban myth following it around about a poo being found at the bottom of the ball pool so old that it had dried out. I wish Lily or Bex were here, so I could share the Jusna revelation with someone. Someone who might agree that it's underhand and that the school should know. There have been loads of stories in the papers about head teachers launching investigations into suspiciously timed break-ups: it probably wouldn't take much to point Mr Brown in the right direction and I wouldn't be implicated at all.

As we board the bus, I force myself to focus. The soft play excursion seemed like a good idea when I suggested it, but the reality of taking four under-fours on a busy bus by myself relieves me of that. The last time I was in charge of more than one child in a public place, I lost Enid. I spend the whole journey barking at them to sit still.

'Want a snack, Mummy,' Winnie announces the second we're safely inside the building, and I sit down at one of the wobbly tables dotted around the big grubby aircraft hangar of a room. There are six different enclosures, decked out with foam animals, tunnels, slides: things to throw yourself down or things to throw yourself into. There are no windows and the whole place smells of stale food and nappy bins that need emptying. Yet it is still the posher of the two.

I reach into my bag and then freeze. Bollocks. In my Jusna haze, I stayed at the café longer than I planned, not doing the work I needed to get done, and then in a rush I grabbed the kids a chocolate brownie each. I completely forgot that no way would Yasmine sanction that as a snack for Arlo. There's a Tesco Express next door – but I can't make them all troop out again now, and there's no one to watch them while I nip there. The only alternative is one bruised pear, which has been in my bag for an indeterminate amount of time.

'Brownies, everyone!' I shout. Fuck it. If Yasmine asks, they were made with dates and ninety-eight per cent pure cacao. I mean, they're vegan. That's the same as sugar-free, right?

The kids swarm around the paper bag and park themselves at the little table with me, their four faces smeared in chocolate the second they tuck in.

Arlo looks like he's just discovered the meaning of life. By which I mean he looks a bit high. God, I wonder if he's ever had any refined sugar before, ever. I probably should only have given them half each.

'This is yummy,' announces Enid, stuffing almost the entire thing into her mouth and jumping up.

'Hands!' I shout, and she runs over, holding them out for me to descale with a wet wipe. The others follow suit, until the table is piled with brown-streaked baby wipes.

'Does anyone need the toilet before you go and play?' I say.

'No,' they chirrup in unison.

'Come back if you do,' I warn them. 'Soft play will still be there when you've had a wee. What did I just say?'

'Come back if we need a wee,' they chorus.

'Good. OK, go.'

They trot off and I watch them for a bit, clambering over foam blocks and hurling themselves down the slides, all while shrieking to each other and running, always running, to the next thing.

My phone buzzes. Yasmine.

Hope you're all having a blast at soft play! Long time no see. Jusna mentioned she saw you today. We should all meet up soon. If you can fit us in between 'business' meetings with the vicar that is 😉

Interesting. Yasmine already knows about Jusna and Ajay. Why am I not surprised? And why has she come out of the woodwork now?

I look at the screen, wondering what to say. What's with the mention of Will? Jusna must have passed on what I told her about Earth Mother, although you'd think Will

235

was the CEO from that text. Why does her message read like a vague threat?

'MUMMY, MUMMY!' Winnie's voice echoes around the room, bouncing from wall to wall. Where is she? 'Arlo wants to go home. He feels SICK.'

I scan the building, Terminator-style, locking on their location just in time to see Arlo throwing up a perfect plume of chocolate brownie into the ball pool.

'I'm coming!'

As I run through the obstacle course enclosure, forcing myself through the various child-sized holes that stand between us, I see the other parents, horrified, shouting for their children to leave the vicinity immediately. It's like that scene from *Jaws* where they're all trying to get their kids into shore, but instead of a shark attack they fear that the ball pool has become a giant gastro-bug Petri dish. Two staff members appear at the entrance to the enclosure the ball pool is housed in and start shouting, 'Everyone out!' before evacuating children via the slide.

'Winnie! Jeb! Enid!' I say, reaching them. 'Go and sit down at the table.' Arlo is sitting silently, dazed, in a puddle of his own sick. I can't remember the last time I upgraded the spare clothes in my mum-bag. If I even have any they will be about two years too small. I carry him out, trying not to retch from the smell, and deposit him at the table with the others.

'I feel poorly,' he says in a sad little voice.

'I know. It's OK, Arlo,' I say, ashamed. I basically just OD'd him. I am the world's worst person. 'You're being very brave. Let's get you home to Mummy.'

'Poor thing,' says one of the other parents in the room, coming over with a wad of kitchen roll she's produced from her rucksack. 'Do you need some help?'

Next a man appears. He hands me an unopened bottle of water for Arlo to sip and I smile at them both gratefully. They both fuss for a minute, and check we're all right, but everyone saw me handing out those chocolate brownies and I can see them both now, judging me with their eyes. Or at the very least thinking: *I really hope they clean the ball pool here more thoroughly than at the other place.*

19

One completely inclusive, everyone's invited birthday party. Surely that's got to carry some God points?

Lily

'IT'S A BIKE!'

Enid starts doing laps of the living room, whooping and pausing only twice, once to ring the shiny silver bell on the handlebars and once to arrange her favourite teddies in the basket at the front.

Joe comes into the living room, looking rumpled in his pyjamas and dressing gown, and hands me a steaming mug of coffee. It's 6 a.m. on a Saturday, because why on earth would Enid wake up at a reasonable time on her birthday? Although it wouldn't be so bad if I'd managed to get to sleep any time before 2 a.m.

He makes an apologetic face. 'It's a bit weak because there wasn't much left, sorry.'

I yawn. 'Yeah, I forgot to get some more.' I take a sip. It's nothing compared to the diesel-strength caffeine I've been mainlining for the past few weeks, but it'll do.

We both sit on the sofa, watching her. 'How does it feel to be four, Enid?' says Joe.

'It's my PARTY today. I'm four, and Arlo is four, and Jeb is four and Winnie is three, and Ava is three but she's four next.'

We both laugh. 'That's right.'

Joe reaches over and squeezes my hand. On top of my now customary five hours' sleep and the churning memories of how overwhelmed and happy I felt at six o'clock in the morning four years ago, when we had a one-hour-old daughter, the gesture brings tears to my eyes. I've joked about Joe's prolonged Christmas spirit a couple of times, but it really does seem to be lasting. It only serves to remind me that this sort of casual affection has been missing for a long time.

'How did you get to be four?' I say, shaking my head slightly. Sometimes it's mad that she can even speak. She told me something was 'outrageous' the other day, and it was the correct word in the correct context.

'Well, I was one, and then I was two, and then I was three, and then I was four,' she informs me.

'It's a good job you did it in order,' says Joe, smiling. 'You could have caused all sorts of confusion otherwise.' He swigs down the rest of his brew. I notice he's had tea, even though he doesn't really like it, because there must only have been enough coffee for one cup. For some reason that makes me well up again. 'I'll shower and then start taking the stuff over to the venue. I told the bouncy castle people to deliver it at nine thirty.'

'Oh. OK.' I pull my dressing gown a bit tighter around myself. It's bloody freezing in here. The heating isn't even set to come on for another half an hour.

'What's wrong? Can't we get into the building until later on?'

'No, we can. They gave me a key. I just . . .' *I just wasn't expecting you to be so on it*, I think. I was half expecting Joe to disappear off to work or the gym and turn up at the party later, once all the food was laid out and the decorations were up and all that needed to be done was for him to be present and in 'fun dad' mode. 'I haven't got all the balloons yet, so I need to pick them up too.'

'I can get them. Normal or helium?'

I snort. 'Normal, unless we want to be ostracised. Again. Haven't you heard? There's a helium shortage.'

He recoils in faux horror. 'In that case, just *one* helium. A giant FOUR.'

'No, honestly, don't.' Things have been ticking over quite well with the school mums. In that I'm on good enough terms with Yasmine for it to be a given that Arlo will come to Enid's birthday party. She even offered to help out. (Ha. As if. Like I don't see through her attempts to control it.)

'Fair enough.' He nudges the pile of boxes sitting next to the front hallway with his foot. They're full of the non-perishable food, biodegradable disposable plates and cutlery, and eye-wateringly expensive party bag toys that can't be classed as landfill fodder. 'I'll take this lot over there in the car and then come back for you two. And then we'll take this bad boy out for you to try out – how about that, E?' He pulls back the living room blinds an inch and sees that it's chucking it down with rain. 'Maybe not. How about we take your bike with us and you can practise riding it in the hall before everyone arrives?'

'Yay! And cake for breakfast?' Her voice quavers and as I burst out laughing it turns into a sob. I'm thinking about a day when her attempts to game me won't be quite so innocent or glaringly obvious.

I pull her in for a cuddle. 'Nice try. No. Cake later. Lots of it.'

Laying out the table of party food a few hours later, I'm nervous on Enid's behalf. Despite the uneasy truce with

Yasmine – a truce that is facilitated almost entirely via group WhatsApp – throwing a birthday party is a different proposition. To accommodate the twenty attending children out of the thirty we invited we've had to hire a party space called The Works, which now, before any of the children and parents arrive, seems massive. Like somewhere you'd have a warehouse all-nighter during your twenties when you invite everyone you've ever met to your birthday drinks – and a good proportion of them actually turn up – rather than a room for some kids' games and a buffet. But it's the only place with the health and safety clearance for a bouncy castle, which Enid has been sleepless with excitement about all week. I hope everyone comes, for her sake. It still makes me feel sick to think of her not making the cut for Arlo's Halloween party.

While I label the different platters – vegetarian, vegan, dairy-free, gluten-free, sugar-free, plus a groaning free-for-all table with all the decent dirty food on there (bloody clean eating, we all know which one will be empty first) – Joe is manning the now-inflated bouncy castle at the far end of the room. Enid is already going berserk on it: 'Come on, Daddy!' she's shrieking, as she bounces higher and higher. I take a few pictures and try to ignore the constant thrumming headache I seem to have at the minute. I've been in court every day for the past three weeks, which has helped in one sense because I *have* to be there. I leant on Joe – although it wasn't even that hard – to take over my rota slots, because an early finish isn't an option, and he's been doing it, without that many complaints. But on the other hand, the pressure of this case is intense, and knowing there's nothing I can do to get home earlier or help more with Clara hasn't made me feel any less guilty about it. I've had to order everything for the party online during recesses, or during the long stretches of night when I still can't sleep. Amanda sent me an encouraging text when I told her I'd submitted my job application, and has forwarded links to 'useful' work/life balance articles, but I think the only thing that's going to help is this case being over, Clara recovering and knowing what's going on with Enid's school place – all things that hopefully will be resolved in the next six weeks. I hate being at the mercy of other people – whether that's a jury, the school governors, or, in Clara's case, the luck of the draw.

'Happy birthday, Enid!' Winnie races in, carrying what looks like a ball of blue fluff as a present, and launches herself in the direction of the bouncy castle.

'Shoes!' Imogen shouts from the doorway, where she's trailing in after her. Joe makes a dive for Winnie as she approaches and sits her down on the front portion of the bouncy castle so she can take her shoes off, with Enid sitting next to her and cooing over the fluff. When they go to stand up Joe starts jumping up and down next to them, meaning they end up bouncing about on their bums.

'Come on, girls, get up,' he says, jumping a bit harder. They giggle hysterically. 'What are you doing down there?' I silently thank Joe for bringing his A-game today.

'The fluffy thing is a bag,' Imogen explains, coming over to the food tables. 'The other bit of her present is inside it. It's slime. Sorry. Winnie insisted.'

'That's OK. All of our soft furnishings are already encrusted with Cheerios and most likely bogeys. What's a bit of slime on the settee when it's already a biohazard?'

'You can get me back by buying Winnie something for her birthday that plays a really annoying theme tune over and over and over again.' She shucks off her coat and throws it onto a chair. 'Do you need any help?'

'I think we're fine. Joe's wittering on about whether we have enough drinks for the adults, but he can deal with that. I've done all this. Thanks for coming so promptly. It's good to see a friendly face.'

'Oh God, Winnie's been ready to come for about three hours.'

I meant it was good to see Imogen, but am too embarrassed to repeat it.

She picks up a pink party ring and bites into it. 'I love these. Eighties-tastic. I feel like I haven't seen you in person for ages. How's the court case, and how are you?' She looks me up and down, giving me a forensic-feeling once-over. 'Have you started running again?'

'I wish.' That's Imogen's shorthand for 'have you lost weight?' Between my coffee dependency, my lack of sleep and the nerves produced by both of those things, my appetite has almost disappeared, so I don't think she means it in a good way. I certainly feel weak rather than lean and I have an almost permanent twitch in my eye. I haven't had another panic attack, but it's there, anxiety bubbling under the surface and a constant pressure.

'I'm a bit stressed out. The weight drops off – you know how I've always been.' She does. When we lived together and I was in a stress cycle, she'd come home with fish and chips and force me to sit down and eat them.

'Make sure you load up a plate with all this,' she says, gesturing to the table, but she doesn't press it. I'm glad. The last time I looked at her blog, which is every time she posts something new because apparently I can't stop reading it, she was going on about all the great quality time she was spending with her daughter and boyfriend and all the adventures they were having. She's also got some amazing consultancy gig and has paired up with our dear church to work on some charity project that the commenters are going wild for. She's managed to ingratiate herself into the community more in four months than I have in six years. Just getting through each week is enough of a challenge for me at the minute.

'No Danny today?' I ask, trying to change the subject.

'He's got something else on,' she says. I feel like her smile flickers, but those two have got the whole parenting balance sussed so I must be imagining it.

Just then Clara arrives, pale but smiling, with Jeb holding her hand and a watchful expression on his face. Poor kid. Worried about Mummy being poorly. He's definitely been subdued during the playdates I've refereed, like he's holding back slightly and not allowing himself to do anything that might get him in trouble, and by extension, upset his mum. Michael immediately takes charge of finding Clara a chair, and she lowers herself into it. Then, aware that he's hovering around Clara and worrying, he says, 'Come on, Jebby, let's give Enid her present and see how high we can bounce,' before racing him over to where the girls are kicking the fluffy bag/ball around the floor.

'I'm fine,' Clara says, raising her palm at me as I open my mouth to ask how she is. 'Michael was all "are you sure you're well enough to come" but I was going insane at home. I wanted to come for a little while at least. I'll let you know if and when I've had enough, and it'll probably be just as the noise and excitement reach their peak, and nothing to do with actually feeling ill. I mean, what's the point of having cancer and not using it to get out of having to deal with tired and hysterical children?'

Imogen and I laugh obediently at her joke and take it as an instruction to talk about other things. 'Well, I hope no one steals the toaster at this party,' Imogen says, steering us out of the moment and telling an anecdote about a house party we once threw, where that happened.

After that, people start arriving in a stream, the low-level hum in the room getting louder and louder as eventually all twenty children, plus at least one of each of their parents, arrive. Being the host of a kids' party is nothing like throwing one for adults. It's basically a concierge job, where I'm constantly expected to direct people to the present table, or the food, or where we're keeping the coats. I never was a great party-thrower, though, so being in charge of tasks means I can flit around without having to engage with anyone for too long.

'Hi Arlo, Thea, Mo.' The kids barely acknowledge me and run past. 'Yasmine, Kim, Jusna.' I follow up with a nod. They're proffering gifts. 'Thank you so much. We're putting them all on that table over there.'

'I didn't really know what to get because you didn't send out a list,' Yasmine says. She always manages to nail the exact inflection guaranteed to make me feel worst. 'So you might already have it. Some people don't like the wish list thing for some reason, but I've always thought it makes everything so much easier.'

I really cannot be arsed to get into this now. 'I'm sure Enid will love it, whatever it is,' I say in my best tolerant tone. 'Do help yourself to snacks. It's all labelled over there.' My voice is more pointed for that part. Maybe I can be arsed to get into it a bit.

'I've actually brought some of my own food for Arlo today.'

'Sure.' I heard about the turbo brownie and the ball pool vom. If even Imogen can't stick to the rules, then I'm not surprised that *I* cannot be trusted to provide the correct configuration of buffet. 'There's drinks over there too. Imogen knows where everything is.'

'And the vicar, I suppose,' says Yasmine with a badly suppressed snigger.

'No, just her.' I'm confused. 'Was I supposed to invite the vicar?' Is this yet another one of those unwritten school things I'm still not doing right?

'No. It's just they're *such* good friends these days, especially when they're behind a bar.' The other two laugh, while I stand there not getting the joke. Whatever it means, I've been on the receiving end of that tone of voice often enough to realise that Imogen is on the outs with the Organics.

'I could do with a drink myself, so I'll come with you,' I decide, accompanying them to where Imogen and Clara are still sitting.

'Hi, Yasmine,' Imogen says.

'Hi,' she replies coolly.

'What would you like?'

'If I say a soda water, will you actually give me a vodka and soda?'

Imogen reddens with embarrassment. 'I'm so sorry again about Arlo. I should have known better.'

'Funny how things always seem to happen to children around you, isn't it?' I shoot Imogen a look to try and tell her to ignore her, but she's looking at the floor, stung. Yasmine pours herself a soda water and then turns, smiling brightly at Clara. 'How *are* you?'

'Yes, OK, thanks,' Clara replies, the fixed smile on her face that she slaps on every time someone asks her that question. I can see the weariness behind her eyes.

'So brave,' Yasmine says, turning to the other two. 'Isn't she?' They beam and nod.

This is horrendous. 'Yasmine!' I jump in brightly. 'When are you due? Can't be long now!'

Thankfully, she bites. 'April. On the one hand I'm so over being pregnant I can't wait to meet her, but on the other I've so much to get done before then that I need all the time I can get.'

I nod politely. Now Arlo's at preschool full-time, I'm not entirely sure what she does all day other than combine almonds and chia seeds into energy balls. 'Yes, getting ready for the next one must be time-consuming.'

'And the new place too,' Jusna chips in.

'You're moving?' I ask. Imogen's head snaps up. I know she's still desperate for a new house.

Yasmine flaps a hand. 'No, we've bought a flat. A buy-to-let around here that we're going to rent out. I know I'll have a lot on with the baby, but I've started thinking about what to do after this one –' she pats her belly '– and it's good for me to have a project.'

'Around here?' Imogen's sheepish tone has evaporated. 'Where is it?'

'Willow Road,' says Yasmine lightly.

There's a loaded pause. I exchange an OMG look with Clara, who instinctively pushes her chair back a bit as though she can sense a grenade is about to go off.

'The one we put an offer in for,' Imogen says slowly. She's standing rigid-backed, a steely look fixed on Yasmine. 'Why did you steal my house?'

For a few moments, Yasmine looks embarrassed, but she quickly rearranges it into her usual self-possessed air and then makes an infuriating flapping gesture with her hand, as though she's waving away the question. 'I didn't *steal* it. It was up for sale. And we've been looking for an investment place for ages, so we put in an offer that was accepted.'

'Funny, because you haven't mentioned that before, and I'd be interested to know the timeline because we'd already *had* an offer accepted. Which you knew about. Because I told you at the Christmas play.'

'Did you?'

'You were sitting right next to me!'

'You were mainly talking to Lily, weren't you,' she says, glancing at me as though for once I have a purpose. 'And Danny didn't seem to want it anyway. I got the impression it was more of an interim place rather than a forever home. So when I got an email from the estate agent telling us that it was ours if we could increase our bid, I didn't think it would be a problem. You'll get something much bigger and nicer and less hassle to do up – it's going to be a total nightmare.' She actually gives a little laugh. She's gaslighting her, I think. It's worse than Yasmine being an out-and-out bitch about the whole thing.

Imogen looks like she's struggling to hold in the tears. 'But why did it have to be *that* flat? You *knew* I needed to get into the catchment area.'

Her response this time isn't so much patronising as reproachful. 'So does everyone, Imogen. What about Jus? She's lived here for years. And what about Bex? She actually *believes* in God. You say it as though you're the only one who needs a school place when you've only just arrived.' She winces a little, putting her hand on her belly as though she's having some sort of twinge. Brilliant. She's going to go into faux labour at Enid's birthday party. God forbid my four-year-old gets to be the centre of attention for one day.

She looks down, releases a little yoga breath, and then smiles as though to say *don't worry, I'm OK, everyone*. I roll my eyes at Clara and she suppresses a laugh.

'Besides,' she says to Imogen, 'you're such good friends with the vicar these days, so I'm sure you'll be fine.'

She leaves the sentence dangling there as Clara, Jusna, Kim and I all look from Imogen to Yasmine and back again. We've all heard the rumours about why Will had to leave his last parish, from affairs with both partners of a lesbian couple to him overseeing a christening attended by the Beckhams and subsequently being employed as the family's spiritual counsel, only to be 'moved on' when his counsel wasn't the only thing Victoria was interested in. But that was all vicar fan-fic, or so I thought.

'Are you accusing me of having an affair with the vicar?' Imogen says eventually. The tearfulness is gone. Instead she looks very pale and *very* angry. I've seen her like this before. It was when she was twenty-five and found out her boyfriend at the time had cheated. She met him at the pub, ordered two pints and then tipped one on his head and one on his limited edition Air Jordan trainers.

'I'm not *accusing* you of anything,' Yasmine says. Another little laugh, which gets echoed by her cronies. 'I just can't help noticing that you've become very . . .' She pauses again, 'Close. And it happened around the time the school applications were due.'

Imogen barks out a bitter laugh. 'So I'm not just having an affair with the vicar, I'm doing it to get Winnie into the school?' She turns away from Yasmine and towards me. 'I have to go for a bit,' she says. 'Can I leave Winnie here and pick her up in a little while? Or I'll send Danny.'

'Yes, of course.' I grab her by the arm and give it a little squeeze. 'But are you *sure* you're OK? Where are you going?'

'To see a friend,' she says, picking up her bag. She fixes Yasmine and then Jusna with a lengthy glare. 'I think it's time I went to confession.'

20

2 p.m.

Imogen

My heart is pounding, pounding, pounding but I'm forcing myself to keep walking because it's the only way I can stop myself from bursting into hot, angry tears. It's just so *brazen*. Why can't Yasmine be happy with her big house, her easy stay-at-home-mum decision and her rich, bad-tempered husband, instead of taking away the *one thing* that would have helped us get into St Peter and Paul's? I'm too angry to feel anything but pure, pulsing rage. She's not the only one who has the power to take things away. I thought Jusna was all right, but she's just another one of Yasmine's cronies. And apparently that makes it OK to game the system. I get to the zebra crossing and am forced to wait as a motorbike screams past without stopping, and it gives me a second's pause to think about what I'm doing. I don't even know what vicars do on Saturday afternoons. Do they get time off? A weekend of sorts? I mean, obviously they have to work Sundays, but do they get the day off in lieu? Does he have to answer the door, or is he allowed to keep the curtains shut and power through a *Queer Eye* marathon if that's what he wants?

And then I think of the way Yasmine spoke to me, as though we don't deserve a school place, and my anger reignites. I half trot the rest of the way to the vicarage, a small, neat, red-brick Victorian building that's only a couple of streets away from the church. Black tiles on the roof surround a restored and working chimney that is puffing out smoke. So he probably is in. I hesitate again, realising it's the first time I've shown up here unannounced, and without a clutch of strategy printouts or a bag of toiletry donations. I'm still simmering with anger, but embarrassment is edging in. Still, I'm here now. My knock is muffled by my thick winter gloves, but I bang hard enough that I'm surprised the whole street doesn't peer out of their windows to have a look. Maybe they're used to unstable people looking for immediate spiritual guidance.

'Hello, Imogen,' says Will when he answers the door a few seconds later. He's in tracksuit bottoms and a hoodie, both grey and plain. Having only ever seen him in uniform, it feels oddly intimate. He looks surprised to see me, but not in a bad way; more concerned. 'Were we supposed to be meeting today?'

'No.' A pause. 'I was just in the area, birthday party at The Works, and I . . .' My voice falters. Why *did* I come here? 'I needed someone to talk to. But if I'm interrupting your afternoon, I can go.' I let the sentence drift off.

'Not at all. Come in.' He steps to one side and lets me pass, through the narrow hallway where a few jackets and a heavy winter coat are hung up, and gestures into the small, cramped living room.

'Would you like a tea or coffee?' he asks.

'I'd love a tea, thank you. Milk but no sugar.' He withdraws to the kitchen, leaving me alone and wondering where to sit. We've never come in here to work. I look around. There's too much furniture in this room. A traditional wood-burning fireplace is on the go, while a fat brown corduroy sofa competes with the dining table and three lots of white Billy bookcases for attention. Together it has the mismatched appearance of furniture that has been inherited or donated, because there are too many opposing styles without any of it looking expensive enough to be antique or stylish enough to be vintage. There's a black holdall in front of the sofa, half packed with sports kit.

I still haven't made up my mind where to sit when he comes back in, a steaming mug of tea in each hand, one with the Chelsea FC logo on it, the other with a Garfield. He knows I like that one.

'Have a seat.' He kicks the holdall out of the way and sits down on the far side of the sofa. I perch next to him and point at the bag.

'Were you on your way out?'

'I'm on a five-a-side football team and I was getting my stuff together, but it's OK, I don't need to leave for a while.'

'Do you play with other vicars?'

He gives me an amused look. 'No. Although other vicars are of course very welcome.' He blows the steam off his tea and takes a sip. 'What can I do for you?'

'It's stupid, really.' I feel myself blushing. This is probably a bad idea, and yet I can't seem to leave. Yasmine. *Winnie*. That's why I'm so mad, because of Winnie. That's the whole reason I'm even *in* Walthamstow. I can't go back to the party – and the woman who's sabotaged my school place – or home to Danny, who isn't talking to me because he thinks I'm stupid for throwing all my energy into trying to get in with the very person who has screwed me over. Working and talking to the vicar is the only place I've been recently where I haven't felt inadequate or judged. 'I was at a birthday party with Winnie,' I say. 'For Enid. Lily's daughter.' He nods, giving me an encouraging smile. 'And I just needed to get away. It's been a hard year, trying to settle into a new area and getting Winnie comfortable with starting preschool, along with trying not to lose myself completely, making some friends and figuring out what to do about getting back to work. It's been overwhelming.'

'It takes time,' he says. His hands are clasped around his mug. 'I definitely know what it's like to be the new kid on the block. This parish feels like a long way from Brixton.'

'Is that where you were before?'

He nods but doesn't tell me any more. Do the Beckhams live near Brixton?

'I've also been doing everything I can to try and get Winnie into a good school.'

He smiles again, but with a slight tightening around the lips this time. 'You're not the only one. It's a *big* preoccupation for the parishioners with young children.'

Emboldened by how understanding he's being, I burst out, 'I'm just so terrified that after all of it, the move, the arguments with Danny – the *effort* – it'll be for nothing, and she won't get in.'

'Would it be the worst thing to happen if she didn't?'

My eyes flick up to meet his. His voice is light, but is that his way of telling me we're *not* in? 'And the other parents seemed so nice at first,' I continue, 'but the longer I'm here, the more I think it's all about appearances to get a school place.'

Will's face is passive, but his look is penetrating. *And you're different, are you*, it seems to say. Or maybe that's the voice of my conscience. He doesn't give me any more reassurance and I realise it's now or never.

'Jusna and Ajay are lying about their break-up,' I say quickly. 'They're pretending so they can register Mo under a second address.' I wasn't exactly expecting to feel purged or as though justice had been served once I said it, but I thought I'd feel like I'd won. Instead I feel like a snitch.

You're no better than they are, I think.

This could get them struck off, and guilt stabs at me. It's not that I want Mo – or anyone – *not* to get in. I just don't want them to get in at Winnie's expense. I look to Will to see what he's going to do with the information. Far from looking outraged by the deception, he just looks gloomy.

'So depressing,' he says, almost to himself, eyes trained on a spot on the wall. He can't bring himself to look at me, I realise. 'Is this what it's all for? For parents and children to learn bits of the Bible by rote so that they can convince a small group of governors that their child is "the right sort" to attend a school? And meanwhile, parents are scheming and lying, building extensions to make their houses a few metres closer to the school or temporarily "moving" while they have "renovations" done so they can register a new address.' He shakes his head slowly. 'And then, a few miles away, there are children in temporary accommodation, who live in one room with their mother and siblings and would be happy with *any* school if it meant a free hot lunch every day.' His mouth curls into a look of distaste and I burn with shame. The anger ebbs away, leaving a nauseous feeling. He thinks I'm like them. It's probably not just Yasmine, *he* probably thinks that this is what the shelter project was all about too.

'You're right. I'm sorry,' I stutter. 'Forget I said anything. I don't know why I did it. I was lashing out because I was mad about what's being said about me, and what I'll do for a place.' I need to prove I'm not the only petty person in the parish, and not here to grass Jusna up. Well, not only here to do that. 'There's a rumour going around that . . .' I take a deep breath and look anywhere except his hazel eyes. 'That there's something going on between us. They're also saying I'm doing it to get Winnie into the school. Which I'm not, obviously. Not that we're more than friends,' I add quickly. 'Or more than vicar and parishioner. Or whatever.'

He whitens, blinking a few times as he sets and unsets his jaw. I can't tell if he's angry or offended. (Charming.)

'I see,' he says eventually.

'It's ridiculous, obviously.' I'm babbling now. 'But if it gets back to Mr Brown, it'll undermine my chances, which I guess is the whole point of fake news.'

He's just sitting very still and looking into his tea, an inscrutable look on his face.

It suddenly occurs to me that I'm not the only one this rumour could affect. 'And of course, even though it's nonsense, you probably don't want everyone gossiping about you either. Maybe we should tell Mr Brown what's been going on.' *Everything*, I think. Not just this stupid rumour.

He finally gives a weak smile. 'I don't think that's a good idea, when it's all tit-for-tat. Mr Brown and I have had our . . . differences for a few weeks now, and I'm not sure rumours or in-fighting between the parishioners is something I should bother him with.' The phrase 'in-fighting between the parishioners' makes me feel like a total dick, but he doesn't sound mad, more that he's tired of it all. When he lays it out like that, I can see why.

'OK, sure. Whatever you think.'

'And it might be better if I step back from the refuge project.'

'What?' Shit. How am I going to explain that to Mags? Everyone thought I was shagging the vicar so we can't be seen together, even for charity work? 'Honestly, I should never have said anything, it's just a stupid rumour. I definitely don't want to stop working with the refuges.'

'Of course not,' he clarifies. 'Your company should definitely continue its work, and I'm pleased I could put you in touch, but it's for the best that you work directly with the charity from now on. You don't need me as a go-between.'

'But why?' I say. 'You've built up such a good relationship with the shelter, and the trust of the women. You can't let gossip stop you from doing your work.'

He sighs, and then takes a long swig of his tea. He looks tired around his eyes. 'It's a bit more complicated than that. Even before this, there have been various clashes with the bishop about some of my ideas.'

'About why you had to leave your last parish?'

He looks taken aback. 'What? No, let's say ideological differences. They think I'm too political.' He says the last word in a mocking tone. 'As though you can avoid being political if you want to engage with the world in any meaningful way.' There's a well-thumbed Bible resting on the arm of the settee next to him and he taps it absent-mindedly with his index finger. 'The church hasn't always been supportive about the groups I want to work with, and it's getting harder and harder for me to accept that. I have to decide if I want to keep trying to fight it from within, but I could really do without gossip undermining the discussions I'm having with the diocese. I'd like to come to a decision about it myself.'

'A decision about what? Are you thinking of leaving the church?'

He winces. 'Not quite. But maybe.' He gives a faint smile. 'I'd appreciate it if you didn't tell anyone.' He sighs. 'You must feel like all you've done today is exchange secrets. I didn't mean to unload that on you and it's not strictly true. Yet. I just need some time to figure some things out. And some space.'

'Yes. Of course.' I'm feeling worse and worse. 'The last thing I wanted was to embroil you in a scandal.'

'It's nothing I can't handle. But I think some distance from all this –' he gestures at the room, but I guess he means church and school rather than his house, although he has just told me he doesn't want to see me for a while '– might be helpful for you too. Focus on your family and your work, and not the external stuff. Winnie has two loving parents, and that's more important than how many streets away she lives from the school with the best Ofsted report. One thing I do know is that a lot of parents forget their own role in their child's education. And I mean spiritual education – whatever your religion – as well as academic.'

His face is serious and it's exactly the sort of earnest lecture I'd expect from a vicar, but that doesn't mean he's not right. It feels like our friendship has finished before it even started. Fucking Yasmine.

Will stands up, which tells me my time is up. 'I ought to finish getting ready for my football match,' he says apologetically.

'Yes, of course.' I get up too, putting my half-drunk tea down on a side table. My hands are shaking as I do it. 'I'll make sure no one sees me leave.'

He frowns. 'Please don't go to any special trouble. It will only look worse if someone does see you. And we don't actually have anything to hide, do we?'

He's being unfailingly polite, but it's pretty clear he's done with this. It's like the end of an internet date when the other person says 'I need to get up early' and you both know it's a lie; they just want to jettison you.

He walks me to the door, and I start to try and say the things I should have said before, about how I've appreciated his friendship and for helping me find my work mojo again, with a project that has helped me professionally and become a passion; that it wasn't all about the school place and I'd hate for him to think it was. But I don't say any of it. Seconds later, the door closes softly behind me, the warmth from the house fading as soon as it shuts. I'm back out in the cold again. No school place, and another bridge burnt.

21

1 March 2019, 5.30 p.m.

Is my attendance at school events still being logged?
Which begs the question: how much school spirit is
enough school spirit?

Lily

Not going to make it to c&w tonight. My raffle tickets are
61–70 – feel free to collect the prize if I win.

Imogen's text arrives the second I get signal when I come
out of the tube station. That's the third time she's dropped
out of a school thing in the last two weeks. Although I
can't exactly blame her this time; the annual cheese and
wine fundraiser isn't exactly on a par with *Hamilton* in terms
of must-have tickets, but I'm sure at one point she was on
the committee for it. As I'm working out what to reply,
another text comes through, and I jab at my messages. It's
not the one I'm waiting for.

No need to go via the childminder on your way home.
I've already picked E up.

I'd half expected to be the one cancelling tonight, having
assumed it would be down to the wire as to whether Joe
would leave work in time for me to go out. But not only
is he home early, he's dealt with the pick-up too, unasked.

I can only assume that, between a non-negotiable court case and a non-negotiable Clara rota, he's experienced a month of what it's like to be on the other side of the childcare divide. Shame it's taken four years. I push the thought away and try to enjoy the moment, slowing my pace now I don't have to go home via Wanda's house. An after-school childminder was something Joe had been initially resistant to. 'Do we really need to add another childcare element into the mix? Especially a stranger,' he'd said in the voice he uses about everything when it comes to Enid's 'welfare', while not coming up with any better ideas as to how one of us (me) would be at the school gate at 3.30 p.m. every weekday and still hold down a job.

Another text. Still not *the* text, but this one brings a moment of elation.

Heads-up. 22 March, 1.30 p.m. Kelsey will email you with the details.

Amanda. I got an interview for the job. Seconds later, Eddie blocks out 12.30–1.30 p.m. on the 22nd in the team calendar, saying he will be OOO. I'm guessing that means he did too, but I have three weeks to prove I'm the better candidate for the job.

My phone vibrates again almost instantly. Another text. This time it's the one I've been waiting for. Two words.

ALL CLEAR!

Oh, thank God. Relief rushes through me. All I've been thinking about this afternoon is Clara's appointment to check the radiotherapy course and surgery have done their job. She's free, for now at least. I pick up my pace and run home, desperate to see Enid.

'Mummy!' Enid shouts from the living room. She's at the dining room table with Joe sitting next to her, surrounded by scraps of material, bits of yellow fluff and plastic goggly eyes.

I put my bag down and appraise the situation. 'Are you doing crafts?' I don't think I've ever done crafts with her. They're always cranking out wobbly pottery and random bits of decorated paper at preschool, so I leave it to them.

'We're making Easter cards!' she calls happily, holding up a piece of card that has some sort of nine-eyed chicken fluff massacre attached to it. 'Me and Daddy bought a set on the way home.'

'Well, aren't you clever.' I say it to both of them, and Joe grins.

'Dinner's in the oven,' he says. 'I thought you might want something before you go to the quiz night thing.'

'Cheese and wine raffle,' I correct him absently. Dinner. Oven. Weird. Has he lost his job and doesn't want to freak me out? Although this Joe-bot is freakier than the idea of him being made redundant.

'Yeah, that one. School thing.'

'Sit down, Mummy.' Enid hands me a piece of card. 'You do one. A rabbit.'

Joe is halfway through fashioning a basket of eggs out of some tin foil, so I dig around in the box and find a template of a rabbit and a square of grey felt. We sit there in silent concentration, cutting and sticking and drawing, and only once does Enid teeter on the verge of a meltdown, when she says 'chocolate egg' and Joe and I tell her *no*.

The room looks like sale day at Tiger by the time we get Enid in bed, and Joe presents me with tray-baked chicken, one of the rotating dishes he would cook when we still used to take it in turns. I shove a load of Easter craft paraphernalia out of the way to make space for us to eat, feeling a bit self-conscious. I've got so accustomed to eating with Enid while Joe's still at work, or grabbing something later, alone, it feels oddly intimate to be having dinner together.

'Clara's in the clear for now,' I tell him as he sits down. 'She found out today.'

'That's good news,' he says. 'Really good news.' He shakes his head slowly, as if he still can't quite believe it. 'She's so young. Our age. It really makes you think.'

My skin prickles with anxiety. 'I've been doing everything I can not to think about it.' Somehow the effort of doing that means I deflect the time I spend awake between 2 a.m. and 5 a.m. onto all the other tiny tasks I need to do, and that also makes me vibrate with nerves in the middle of the night. I wonder if I'll ever not be tired.

'I keep thinking about my parents,' says Joe. 'Especially since Dad's heart attack last year and him being so much frailer. Like, they're getting old and it's horrible, but it's hard enough to cope with in your thirties. Someone Jeb's age shouldn't have to worry about his mum dying. It's so unfair.' I agree. But I won't think about it. I can't. He plays with a potato on his fork, gloomy expression on his face. 'At least if something does happen to one of my parents and there's any decisions to be made, there's my sister to help with it all. Same for you.'

'My sister would be too busy moaning that she'll have to get the kids into after-school club to help decide whether or not we should switch the life support off,' I joke. Clara's cancer is at bay. That's all I want to concentrate on.

'It made me think about Enid, though, and her being an only child at the minute.'

I freeze. *At the minute.* I feel the impact of the words in my stomach. I examine his face to work out if this is a throwaway comment or if he's seriously sounding me out. How can I tell him that my first gut reaction to what he's just said is fear? Fear that he *is* serious. Because every cell of my body is pulsing with *No. Not with you.*

He's still casually eating his dinner. Is that what this is, a meal to seduce me into going for the idea? He thinks he can trade one overcooked chicken breast for the use of my womb for the next nine months? This is a one-pot dish. He hasn't even tried to make, like, beef bourguignon, something that takes time and skill. 'What do you think about the idea?' he asks. I stare at him in undisguised horror.

'Of having another baby?' I say back to him, stalling for time. He must be able to hear the panic in my voice. 'Yes.'

'I don't know,' I say slowly. 'I guess I haven't given it a lot of thought.'

He frowns slightly. 'You could think about it now.'

'I guess . . . I think . . .' I stop, and then start again. 'I'm not sure we're ready to do it all over again.' *Or ever will be*, I add inside my head.

He reaches for my hand. 'Is anyone ever really ready?' he says. It sounds like he's read a wikiHow article on how to do platitudes. 'We weren't even ready for Enid and we tried for so long. And I know it was hard, especially with the miscarriages, but if we want to try for another, we should get on with it. We're both in our mid-thirties now, and with Enid starting school things are getting easier.'

Are they, I think.

'Are they, Joe?' I say out loud. He pauses mid-chew and considers me. Really looks at me.

'Are you OK?'

'Yes! I'm fine,' I say, sounding completely not fine, more borderline hysterical. I take a deep breath. We spend so much time not saying things to each other. I have to be honest now. 'I just don't think I want another baby, and if I do, I don't want one right now. I got offered a job interview today for a promotion at work. I bit their hand off for the opportunity. I didn't even hesitate.' I pause. 'Why are you bringing this up now?'

'These last few weeks, when I've been picking Enid up and bringing her and the others home, I've loved it. It's made me realise what I've been missing when I've been working late or away, and how fun it is when there's a gang of you. It made me think we should do more of it.'

'That's great.' It is. These last few weeks he *has* been different. More involved, more attentive, more hands-on, more *everything*. Is that what it's all been about? Convincing me to have another baby? 'But it's taken you a long time to get here. And remember, that's not actually what having another child means. It would be a baby for a long time before it was a playmate. We'd be starting again from scratch. Night wake-ups, nappies, months before he or she can even focus on us, never mind properly interact.'

'But we'd get through it,' he insists. 'We got through it before.'

'How many night feeds did you do?' I ask bluntly.

He bristles. 'That's unfair. You were breastfeeding.'

'I stopped breastfeeding at six months. Enid didn't sleep through the night until she was a year old.'

'I had to get up for work.'

'You did, yes,' I concede. 'And I was at home and alone for long stretches of time looking after a baby. And I was jealous every day when you got to go to work after a full night's sleep.' I'm still not seriously entertaining this idea, but I decide to test him. 'Say we had another – *if* – would you consider being the one to stay at home, and do the night feeds and the nappies? What if we did shared parental leave? I'd do six months and then you would.'

His grey eyes are wary, and he makes a non-committal noise.

'Is that a yes or a no?' I prompt.

'I can't say that right now, can I? Who knows where I'd be with my clients by the time you were due? I couldn't necessarily drop everything and take six months off.'

I breathe out of my nose. An exhalation that lands somewhere between a sigh and a snort and morphs into a bitter smile. 'Yes. Imagine how taking six months out of your career might look, or what it could do to your promotion prospects and earning potential.'

'You know what I mean. There's just less precedent at my work for this sort of thing,' he snaps. 'No one does it.'

My temper flares. 'You're not exactly selling the baby idea to me. What you're telling me is I'd be the one "dropping everything" – which BY THE WAY already implies that you consider "everything" to be outside the home rather than in it – because you either don't want to have a tricky conversation with your bosses or you just don't want to do it. And then in four or five years' time, when this kid is capable of playing with you, you might muck in for a month or so. That's not going to work for me, Joe.' I can feel my voice shaking as I reach the crescendo; I'm waving my knife and fork around. 'If you want the truth, it's not even working for me now, with one.'

Shock registers on his face. 'I know,' he says quietly. Our food is forgotten now and he puts his cutlery down and clasps his hands in front of him. 'I know I've been shit. And that I've been shit for a long time.'

I feel like the room has been filled with pure oxygen. Or gas and air. I feel light-headed. This is the first time he's acknowledged it. Ever. I'm not sure I trust myself to say anything. Tears press against my eyes.

'Yes. You have.'

'But you let me—' he starts to say. I point my fork at him and he shuts up.

'So far, this week, in addition to my job, I have done the food shopping, five loads of laundry, stocked up on new underwear for Enid, booked her dentist's appointment.' As I start saying tasks, more and more come to me. 'Bought birthday presents for two of her friends' parties, called an electrician about that switch in the hallway that keeps breaking.' I pause for breath. 'Every week is like this week for me. So yes, you have been shit, and I don't think adding a baby into the mix is the way to fix it. But I do think we need to work on us. The you-me us, as well as the family us. Maybe if things were more equal for longer we could revisit the idea.'

'I don't need time, Lil. I know what I want. I want you. I want Enid.' He gestures around the living room, and some stray Easter bunny fluff flies off the table and sticks to his jumper. 'I want this. I want another baby.'

I let the words sink in. 'I have no idea whether I do or not,' I admit. 'And all I can think is: how do you know? The last time we had a baby it drove us apart rather than brought us together.'

'Because I'm different now. I know what I want.' He drops his gaze into his lap. Picks absently at the fluff. And then sets his jaw. 'I wasn't going to tell you this, because it's nothing. It's stupid. But something happened in Detroit, on the last work trip, that drove it home how much you and Enid mean to me.'

'Did you get converted by one of those rabid American evangelical preachers? Don't tell the school.' It's a quip, to match his casual tone, but it's masking a nauseous feeling that's trickling through my system. The last time he was in Detroit was just before Christmas, just before the school play. And around the time he started to be more attentive. I thought the combination of Clara's illness and my workload had finally permeated his field of consciousness, but of course not. It was something external that convinced him to come back to us. Some*one* external.

'Just say it, Joe. Who was it? One of the pitch team?' I imagine him and one of his colleagues sitting in some hipster bar in America, exhausted from the jetlag and the all-nighter they just pulled, as though they're characters in some sexy sitcom, and talking about me as though I'm a problem and a nag. The boring wife who doesn't understand him, while they're far away from the day-to-day reality of mortgages and school runs.

He looks ashamed. Like he might cry. 'No. No one from here. A woman in the Detroit office. We all went for drinks after the meeting and things got out of hand.' He rubs his hand over his chin, muffling what he says next. 'The second it happened I realised what an idiot I was being.'

The nausea crystallises into ice. Some woman in the American office. It gets more and more exotic. 'Do you mean you realised the second it was going to happen, or the second *after* it happened?'

He looks into his lap.

'You were an idiot,' I say. He takes it, nodding his head in silent agreement.

'You don't know how sorry I am,' he whispers, scanning my face for a clue about what I'll do next.

'You don't get to say that and be instantly forgiven. And what exactly are you sorry for? This . . . incident – ' I can't bring myself to say 'woman' ' – or your lack of interest in our family for the last four years?'

'That's unfair,' he snaps.

'*Is it*? I'm not sure you're in a position to tell me what is and isn't fair right now.' I wait. 'You haven't answered the question.'

'I didn't realise you expected one.' His voice is sullen.

'And that's us all over, isn't it?' I shout. 'Even now you expect me to do all the legwork. Fuck's sake.'

'I haven't spoken to her since,' he says desperately. 'Well, I sent her an email saying I couldn't speak to her and that it was all a mistake. You can see it.'

I haven't even asked about that. I don't even care about *her*. I *do* care. But I don't want to care.

I push my chair out, the legs screeching on the wooden floor. I need to get out. Away. From him.

'Where are you going?'

I have no idea. 'You don't get to ask,' is all I say. And then I run to the door, intending to slam it right until the point the door is about to hit the doorjamb. At the last second, I close it quietly to make sure it doesn't wake Enid.

How the hell is the school cheese and wine tasting at the church hall the only place I can think of to go? The first person I see when I walk in is Yasmine. She's handing out tasting notes and trilling to anyone who will listen that it's such a shame she can't join in, but what with pregnancy and soft cheese and wine, what can you do. I almost walk straight back out. There's a pub called the North Star up near the tube. It hasn't been touched by gentrification yet and is rough in the way that all pubs close to train stations seem to be. Its menacing air, born from unconnected strangers being united by their efforts to plough through as much booze as possible before closing time, could be exactly what I need right now. To make things easy, there's also only a wine list of two there: red or white. It's more of a strong lager kind of place. I ferret around in my bag, pulling out three crumpled fivers. If I stick two in the charity bucket, I'll still have enough for at least one of those wines. But as I turn to go, my attention is caught by the sight of Reverend Will perched on the edge of the stage, nursing a glass of red wine. He's got a face on him that I can only describe as brooding. Like Poldark, if he'd just watched his football team lose in the cup final. And the winning goal-scorer was shagging his wife. On closer inspection, I can see the rest of the bottle next to him. He's usually surrounded by a gaggle of adoring fans-slash-parents desperate for a school place, but this time he's on his own, proving that it doesn't matter if you're a man of the cloth: if you have a kami-kaze face on you that communicates *I'll be demolishing all of this booze*, people will give you a wide berth. I wonder what he's got to be pissed off about and then feel mean, remembering how he was my ally during Nativity-gate, and was even kind to me when I got bollocked by Mr Brown at the play. That combination of non-judgemental and on the lash makes him the best person to sit next to in this room, as far as I'm concerned. Maybe we can bring some of that North Star atmosphere to the church hall and ignore each other while getting solidly drunk.

I swipe a plastic glass and an A4 sheet of tasting notes from a nearby table and walk towards the stage, purposefully enough that there's no chance of one of the other parents trying to stop me on the way. Then I hoist myself onto the stage next to him and give him a grim smile. The one he flashes back is wary, nothing like his usual approachable vicar demeanour.

'I'll give the charity all of the money in my purse for a glass of that wine – large, mind – and the opportunity to sit in silence for half, no, three quarters of an hour,' I say.

He picks up the bottle and pours in a generous portion. 'Welcome to pariahs' corner,' he says, his voice tinged with a bitter edge I've never heard before, certainly not during his singsong sermons on a Sunday. He taps his glass against mine. 'Sadly we'll have to pass this bottle on in a minute, but until then, cheers.' He's slightly slurring his words. My stomach is still churning from the conversation I've just had with Joe – if you can even call it that; it was more like a verbal barrage – and I don't really want to get into some heart-to-heart with the vicar, but his tone forces me to direct my attention towards him.

I gulp down half the glass. It's nice, I think, looking at my sheet of paper. It's a Cabernet with a hint of wood, apparently. 'Are you OK?' I ask.

Will shrugs. He looks like a petty teenager. 'I thought you didn't want to talk.'

'Fair enough.' We've got a prime view of the room up here. All the parents are milling about and forming small groups of allies. I use the same loose gaze I do on surveillance jobs, scanning the room without resting it on any one person for too long. It stops people noticing you or attempting eye contact. Occasionally someone looks up to where we're sitting, and I look away. I start to think about my next move. There's only so long I can be antisocial at a school social. I'll finish this and slip off to the pub. After that, who knows. I'm definitely not going home any time soon.

We sit in uncomfortable-ish silence for about fifteen minutes, before Kim's husband scuttles over with a Malbec (this one is described as 'firm') and grabs the half-empty bottle from us. Will silently tops up my wine, tipping the new one directly into my glass with the old one. 'Do you want some cheese?' he asks. There's a whole table of it under the kitchen hatch. Yasmine is near the kitchen hatch.

'No,' I reply.

Will tips his glass into his mouth, and I follow suit.

'Hey . . . hey, er . . .' he says, trying to get Kim's husband's attention again. I smother a laugh as I can't remember his name either. Eventually Kim's husband turns round, fighting to keep a judgy look off his face. Will might be a sloppy drunk but he's still the vicar.

I hold the Malbec out to him. 'This one is too *firm* for us.' The vicar laughs. It sounds like a cackle. 'Can we try another?'

A Rioja is plonked on the stage. 'Velvety,' the vicar says, consulting the notes. His face is very close to the paper.

It's my turn to cackle. 'Why are all the descriptions like something from an erotic novel?'

Erotic novel makes me think of Joe in Detroit. I pour us more wine, sloshing it over the side of Will's glass. I'm starting to feel out of control. It's not an unwelcome sensation.

Kim taps her husband to get his attention and he turns gratefully away. We've started to take sips in a relay, punc-tuating each round by reading out words from the sheet.

'Bold!' I say, drinking some more.

'Medium-bodied!' he says back, touching his glass to mine again. When we run out of words we just sit there glugging whatever wine is placed in our general vicinity.

We're halfway through a 'youthful' red when Yasmine claps her hands and Mr Brown calls, 'Time for the raffle.' I'm sure I hear Will say 'urgh' under his breath but it's not until Mr Brown beckons him over and shakes the bucket of raffle tickets that I can be sure, because Will takes one look at him and turns away, ignoring him. It's as obvious as when Enid doesn't want to go to bed and pretends she can't hear me. I burst out laughing.

Mr Brown is now gesturing at me to get Will's attention.

'Er, I think you're needed.'

'Oh God, I want to get out of here,' he groans quietly into his lap. I make a split-second decision.

'Tell him you're going to the toilet and just don't come back. Do you know the North Star near the tube?'

He nods.

'That's where I'm going. If you want to come, I'll meet you there.' I don't give him a chance to reply, and instead jump off the stage, landing with only a slight stagger.

'Left my tickets in my other bag,' I say, walking past Mr Brown and trying to disguise the slur in my voice. 'I *must* fetch them from the cloakroom.' I walk out of the door and don't look back, powering all the way to the pub.

Five minutes later I'm unscrewing the top of my miniature red at the bar when the vicar walks in, looking as surprised to see me standing there as I do to see him. I didn't *really* expect him to follow me, and can't help but laugh when the barman, clocking the collar, asks if he's going to a fancy-dress party.

'Yes,' he says, and then points at my drink. 'One of those, please.'

The pub is cramped and dim, with the kind of flattened-down, swirly patterned carpet that pre-dates the dawn of the gastro by at least three decades, and fruit machines along the back wall. The other walls are lined with full-to-bursting shelves of knick-knacks and watercolours of dogs in hats. None of it is ironic. There are a few people – all men – sitting alone at tables, and in the end, we head towards a small round table in the knick-knack corner, away from the sporadic chirrups from the Blockbusters game.

I'm starting to feel like I'm in a screwball comedy, but at least this is quite an amusing anecdote from what has been a shitty evening. On the lam with the vicar in the roughest pub in Walthamstow. It's something I might even consider telling Eddie next time we're on a job. When hopefully I will be his boss.

'Exactly how much trouble are you going to be in for bailing on the raffle?' I ask, taking a sip of my drink. I still don't know anything about wine, but this one is definitely not nice in comparison to the ones we were just drinking.

He pulls a face. 'More trouble than I would be had I not already got several black marks against my name.'

I clink my glass against his. 'Welcome to my life. What could *you* have possibly done to upset the church mob? Although admittedly they're a tough crowd.' I realise what I've said. 'Sorry, no offence.'

Will chuckles a bit and tests his drink. 'Wow, that's pretty horrible wine.' He takes a bigger sip. 'And none taken. That's what I like about you, you say what you think.'

It's an off-the-cuff remark, but my entire body goes hot from the top of my head to my feet. It feels like a long time since anyone gave me a compliment.

I snort. 'I don't think anyone in there –' *or my husband*, I think '– would agree that it's a good quality. Isn't "tells it like it is" just a euphemism for "pain in the arse"?'

'Usually,' he concedes. 'But in your case, it's refreshing. I get a lot of people self-editing around me, whereas you don't seem to take any notice of who's there at all.'

I look around the pub, embarrassed. A ceramic beagle with diamanté eyes stares down from a shelf. 'Again, not usually held up as a positive attribute, especially with the other mums at St P and P's, but thank you. I guess that's why you're a vicar, always seeing the positive in people.'

He winces. 'Is there any way we can not talk about me being a vicar this evening?'

Now all I can think about are vicar-related questions.

'Do you want to talk about what's going on with you?'

'What do you mean?' I say, defensive.

'The school fundraiser, alone, can't be your first choice of place to hang out if you have a spare evening to yourself.'

I sigh. 'I was supposed to be coming to the event tonight with Imogen – Winnie's mum – but she ditched me at the last minute.'

He flinches. The rumour about the two of them flashes through my mind. Is it just a rumour? After this evening I can see why she might. 'Sorry, I know you two are friends,' I add quickly. 'I'm not slagging her off. I really like Imogen. I just could have done with someone to talk to tonight, so I'm a bit gutted she's been off the scene. The only reason I came to that stupid cheese and wine thing is because I had to get out of the house. Sorry, no offence again.'

Will doesn't seem to be bothered. He's playing with the lid from his wine, flipping it idly with his forefinger across the table like a tiddlywink.

'I hear you,' he says in the end. 'I've been to enough of those things to last a lifetime.'

'Vicar's fatigue, eh?' I try and lighten the mood.

His face darkens. 'A bit more than that if I'm honest.' He hesitates. 'I wasn't going to talk about this, was I? But I feel like we're both sitting here not talking about the things that have driven us to this pub, together. I'm really not sure the church is the place for me any more – if it ever was. I'm seriously thinking about leaving.'

Whoa. What? Is it because of Imogen? And is that why the vicar seems so unvicar-y? Because he doesn't want to be one? I try and think of something supportive to say that isn't *I've no idea why anyone would want to be a vicar to start off with.* 'Aren't crises of faith to be expected?' I ask slowly. I don't really know what I'm talking about, as I've never had one. You need faith for that.

He gives me a look that makes me think he can see straight through the comment, but nods, conceding the point. 'Yes, but I think the fact that I keep defying the bishop, and ditching raffles, and so on, basically acting out, is me trying to get expelled. I have a bit of a history of it, you see.'

I don't know what to say in response to that, even though I'm dying to know how he's tried to get expelled from God school. But it doesn't matter anyway, because that's when he kisses me.

The kiss is soft and tentative, and then when I sense he realises that not only am I not going to pull away, but that I'm actively, hungrily kissing him back, we start snogging like we're two eighteen-year-olds at 2 a.m. in some student union bar. Is this what he does? Seduce congregants? I should stop him, or at least stop myself, but the impulse has completely overridden my shock. It's been seven years since I kissed anyone except Joe, actually eight, because despite the internet dating I didn't get any action in the year before I met him. And for the past few years it's been nothing like this kind of kissing, as if kissing itself is a worthy activity instead of a perfunctory prelude to sex. All I can think is how good it feels to kiss someone who seems like they *want* to kiss me. And OK, I'm curious. Not just about what it's like to kiss a vicar, but what it's like to kiss someone universally acknowledged to be gorgeous.

Under any other circumstance, would I respond to a hot handsome stranger the way I'm responding to him? I have no idea, but everything about tonight has made me reckless. The booze, the anger, the feeling of unexpectedly finding someone on my side. It feels like a series of urges, rather than any conscious decisions and I want to keep hold of that. Clara's news, Joe's bombshell – make that two bombshells: the baby *and* the . . . whatever that whole thing was or is. I'm sick of juggling plates, of thinking two steps ahead, of having to be responsible. It's so weird, and unexpected, and *subversive*. It's a rush, a very sexy rush. Every time he touches me, there's a delay in my brain receiving the message, but when it does, it arrives in sentences where I can practically *see* the exclamation marks.

OMG the vicar's touching my boob! No, the vicar is caressing my boob!

He pulls away and I catch my breath, my eyes flying open. His are staring back at me, seeming to vibrate. How are we going to talk about what just happened? Then the room seems to tilt when he says, 'Do you want to go back to my place?' I know I shouldn't. Until now it's been a revenge-fuelled experiment and can (maybe) be laughed off. Is this how Joe felt in Detroit? Like he could stop it but didn't want to? Why does he always get to do what he wants and I don't?

'Yes,' I whisper.

We hardly say a word when we leave the pub. The air is sharp and cold on the walk (to the vicarage!), and we keep our hands away from each other, but the forced lack of contact loads every look with fizzing energy. There's a gentle swerve into one another, my fingertip touching his gloved hand, and then his hand pressed gently onto my back as though guiding me over an icy bit of pavement. They're like a tiny trail of mini-thrills, and it's only when we arrive that I remember anyone could have seen us. It barely registers. It's different and new. My heart is pounding, nerves mingling with anticipation, and the second we're through the door, his mouth is on mine again, our hands twining together and snaking down each other's backs, over our coats and then under, before we scrabble for zips and buttons.

The house is in darkness – I'm guessing the whole house belongs to him – and he leads me straight through a hall to his bedroom, where a lamp illuminates a double bed with plain neutral grey bedding on it (thank God there's no monk-like single), white walls and a shelf of books that could belong to any bloke in his forties: a David Bowie biography, Tom Wolfe, a couple of Hemingways. There's a flutter of something in my stomach: not lust this time; doubt. I don't know what I was expecting – chintz chosen by some sort of housekeeper, maybe – but this is minimalism that could be explained by taste, laziness or just lack of interest in decor. I'm glad the lighting is too dim to analyse it all properly. I ignore the niggle and hold on to the way I felt when he kissed me. I plonk myself down on the bed and pull him on top of me, tugging at his clothes. There's no talking, just the noise of his mouth on mine, and the friction of my jumper being pulled over my head before lying back onto the bed.

Underneath his thin black sweater he has on a cotton T-shirt, and underneath that there's a smooth, hard, almost hairless chest. My brain takes me back to that WhatsApp conversation with all the mums, and I suppress a snigger that I now know the answer to the question about what his body is like beneath the cassock. Fit, but not so fit as to seem vain. I can't work out how drunk I am, or how drunk he is, and how much of this is two people being reckless and getting off on the danger. But as I brush my hands over the crotch of his black jeans I can feel he's into it, and as he responds by thumbing his hands underneath my vest top before sliding one of them down to my waist, I'm into it too. Like, blood-pumpingly, knicker-soakingly into it. Right up until the moment it – sex – is going to happen. My underwear is still on and so is his, but we're now breathing hard and heavily. He pushes aside my pants, his fingers swirling outside and then into me. I let out a gasp that progresses into a sigh, and then just like *that* it turns into a moment of clarity. *What am I doing? And with the bloody vicar?* I pull back and away at the same time, sitting bolt upright. This is *not* what people mean by seeing God when they have sex.

'We can't do this,' I whisper.

'We can,' he says back, reaching a hand towards me. He quickly qualifies it with, 'If you want to.' His face in the half-light is stubbly and dishevelled. He's so good-looking. Ridiculously so. This is my chance to get it on with someone ridiculously hot. And I will never need anything from this man, so he can never let me down. I start to lie down again, and he resumes kissing my neck. I want him, but it's there, lurking. Is the urge really for him? Or just to get back at Joe? As soon as that thought crystallises, my body stops responding to his touch. It's instinctively edging away.

'We can't,' I say, more decisively this time. My eyes fly open and the first thing I see is a crucifix above the bed that I hadn't noticed before. 'Oh Christ,' I blurt. 'I mean, shit.' I choke out a guilty laugh. 'We have to stop.'

He pulls his hands away and sits up too, rubbing them over his face and looking like he's trying to regulate his breathing. His body is big where Joe is lean, muscly where Joe is wiry. Smooth where Joe is bristly. Joe Joe Joe. His name won't leave my head. And not from rage now; from guilt. Will isn't saying anything. He looks puzzled rather than angry, as though he's trying to collect himself.

'I'm sorry,' I say, filling the silence and refusing to look at him. It starts to sink in, what we were doing, what I've done. My gaze scatters around the room, searching for my jeans, my thermal vest – if I'd known I was even going to take my jumper off this evening I'd never have worn that. 'I can't be part of whatever . . . this is. I have my own stuff going on. So much stuff. I can't be responsible for you getting thrown out of the church.' I'm prattling. 'I won't tell anyone, I promise. You won't either, will you?'

He just watches me, looking shell-shocked, and only finds his voice as I gather up my things and back out of the room, bumping into some sort of dresser in the hallway. I wrestle my jeans back on out there in the dark, and shove my feet into my boots. 'Getting thrown out of the church isn't what this is about, Lily.'

'Isn't it? Then what? We barely know each other.' I don't want to hear any more. Plus, has he done this before? In his last parish? With *Imogen*? I creep closer to the door, even though my socks are ruched up in my boots, and tear it open. Freezing air blasts in.

He pulls on a T-shirt, and all I can feel is relief that he's got some clothes back on, and that I'm going. 'Please,' he says, his face agonised. 'We can talk about it. Stay.'

'I have to go.'

My only advantage is that I'm dressed and he's not, so I run into the street, quickly taking two turns at random to disguise my route should he decide to follow me. It's so cold my face aches. Good. My head is fuzzy with a half-hangover, and a faint ache behind my eyes. Do I feel sick from booze or guilt? Both. I stop running and walk, slowly, picking backstreets so I can keep circling until I think Joe will be in bed and I can slip home. Flashes of what just happened keep coming back to me, lust mingling with shame. There was penetration. Does it count as sex if it's just hands? Or, like, half-sex? And does half count as not, or is it the opposite? I'm pretty sure the church wouldn't count it in halves. Everything I've read seems pretty black and white on that front. Nausea bubbles in my stomach. Will the vicar have to confess this? What does this mean for Joe and me? What does it mean for Enid's *school place*? Hell. I'm going to hell.

22

Now I'm being ignored by the Organics, will my exist-
ence even register with the school place committee?

Imogen

I'm so sorry to ask this, but would you be able to pick up
E today when you get W? Joe is doing drop-off, but I'm
not well and can't collect her. I'll get the childminder to
return the favour tomorrow.

My mind flashes back to last year when I was regularly
getting these sorts of messages from Lily. This one has come
out of the blue, and her tone is much more conciliatory
than it ever was back then. It crosses my mind that she's
punishing me for bailing on the cheese and wine night.

Of course, no worries.

That probably seems passive-aggressive. She's been
running herself into the ground while Clara's been having
treatment. I've never once heard her complain about needing
to leave work early, even though I know it must have been a
nightmare. And she really didn't look well at Enid's birthday
party. Whippet thin. Stressed out. I fire off a follow-up.

Do you need anything? Feel better soon.

She doesn't reply.

On Wednesday, it's the same story, but she still doesn't say what's wrong with her. 'Your poor mummy isn't well at all, is she?' I say to Enid, as I bundle her and Winnie into their coats in the preschool hallway.

She looks at me, puzzled. 'Is it her tummy?' she asks.

'I don't know. Is it?'

'I heard her and Daddy talking about it when she came in from work yesterday.'

'Oh dear, she must have been feeling sick,' I say. But she *is* at work, I think, so not that ill.

'She said she doesn't want it to rule her life,' Enid says matter-of-factly.

'Her tummy?'

'Yes. It's her body and her choice,' she adds, clearly having no idea what that means.

'I see,' I say, nodding, but the breath has gone out of my lungs. Lily, pregnant? Not her too? Joe has been picking Enid up from ours and he hasn't said anything, although maybe it's early days. We've been getting on better recently, but it shocks me at this second that I hate her with a jealousy that leaves me speechless. Maybe she wasn't ill at Enid's birthday party, she was just early doors pregnant and feeling rancid. *It's not fair, it's not fair, it's not fair.*

'Can we dance to your party mix when we get home?' Winnie asks. They've got obsessed with my university playlist recently. Who knew there were so many songs with dedicated dances in the late nineties and early noughties? And who knew I'd still have perfect recall of Whigfield's 'Saturday Night', Steps's 'Tragedy' and 'Cotton Eye Joe'?

'Yes, yes,' I say, distracted, while tapping out a message to Lily.

Got the girls. Is everything OK?

Yes.

Then:

No

Then:

. . .

The bubbles disappear. Maybe she doesn't want to tell me. She knows I want another baby, and from what Enid said, she's less than thrilled. I don't think I'm the person she'd confide in any more, about this, maybe about anything. I'd got used to Lily being on the scene these past few weeks and now Clara is in remission, which is brilliant, I was hoping the camaraderie might have a lasting effect. Instead it's dissolved as quickly as it started. Bex has started a phased return to work – involving some complicated system of having to go back full-time to then apply for part-time, which she's totally miserable about – and I'm in school-gate Siberia. The few times I've seen the vicar he's barely even looked at me.

As if sensing my thoughts, at that exact second Yasmine and her two henchmen rock up. They practically push past me as though we're in a high school movie and I'm the class nerd, all while saying heartfelt hellos to the two children.

'Ah, ladies, glad I caught you.' Mr Brown follows them in, and Yasmine turns, a winning beauty pageant smile on her face.

'Come on, girls,' I say to my two, pulling a note from behind Winnie's peg.

'You should stay for this, Ms Roberts,' he says to me, and I stop, standing in an awkward semi-circle with the others, but slightly apart. 'Now, I wanted to talk to you all because I've heard some rumours about the St Peter and Paul's mums.'

Jusna's face pales and she looks down at the floor. I look away out of guilt, scanning the line of pegs and dog-eared paintings that circle the hallway walls. As the door closes behind Mr Brown I see Will walking across the playground. He stops as he looks in the door, seeing something going on. Yasmine shoots me the sort of look that tells me she won't hesitate to invoke the vicar if she needs to, while, oblivious, Mr Brown ploughs on. Is he going to expel Mo here and now, or just humiliate all of us for the dirty tricks we've been using? The thought suddenly makes me feel very tired. I wish we'd never moved here. The vicar was right. No school is worth the example I've been setting to Winnie for the past few months.

'I've had someone from BBC News on the phone,' Mr Brown is saying. I can't tell if he looks mad or not. His wrinkly face always looks slightly aggrieved; Lily called it 'resting Brown face'. Jusna gasps. Oh God, we're going to be one of those stories about the lengths parents will go to for a school place, the poster women for the education crisis – as well as moronic parental behaviour.

'I'm not sure what this has got to do with me,' Yasmine says, holding a hand out for Arlo and making to leave. Technically she's right. Who can prove she's had anything to do with it, with her catchment-area house and her God-fearing, churchgoing ways? There's no way she'd admit she knew about Jusna's bogus break-up if she thought she'd be implicated as an accessory.

'Oh, I think it does.'

Yasmine freezes. I see Jusna squeezing her eyes shut.

'The BBC wanted to talk to me about a borough-wide campaign to help women and children in the local refuges.' I let out a breath and see Jusna doing the same thing. We catch each other's eyes and almost smile. Almost. 'She seemed to think that the mothers from St Peter and Paul's have been instrumental in raising quite a lot of money and awareness for several refuges that are on the verge of closure. There's some sort of bubble bath brand involved, from what I can gather —' I hold in a laugh, imagining Mags's face when I tell her that she's running a bubble bath brand '— but it all came about from the community-minded women of Walthamstow. When I heard that I knew exactly who must be behind it.'

As Mr Brown speaks, Jusna, Kim and I seem to diminish as Yasmine's glow strengthens. Anger churns inside me. When has she even asked about the refuge appeal? I oversaw all the additional donations from the church congregation and organised every last battered and unwanted Body Shop Christmas set. Yasmine didn't donate anything.

Jusna throws a quick, guilty look in my direction. She knows. So does Kim, who is silent too. So, Yasmine can't just steal my house; she has to steal my one chance to make a good impression too. What am I doing here, with these people?

'Actually,' I stutter, my voice tailing off halfway through the word. I try again. 'Actually, I've worked quite hard on that campaign.'

Yasmine rests her gaze on me benevolently. Mr Brown notices and follows her look, using it to come to the conclusion that she's letting me bask in her reflected glory.

'The more the merrier, eh, Mrs Swift?' The door behind us opens and Will comes in, looking as worried as we did when Mr Brown first collared us. 'The journalist told me that you are very involved too,' Mr Brown says to Will. The vicar's expression dissolves into confusion. 'The refuge appeal,' Mr Brown prompts, 'that Mrs Swift has been working on.'

'Of course,' Will says. 'The appeal. Well, I just helped a little bit with logistics. The person who has really embraced the community spirit on this one is –' and here he looks at us all in turn '– Imogen. She came up with the original idea of partnering with Earth Mother and has been the driving force behind it. She has it all under control and has helped make a bigger contribution than anything I could have envisaged.'

He's not speaking to me directly but holds my look for a long second afterwards, with just the ghost of a smile on his face. The renewed shame of wondering if Will thinks that this is what the whole appeal partnership was about is interrupted by something else – the warmth of alliance, maybe. Perhaps he doesn't think I'm like them after all. Mr Brown is nodding at me in approval.

Will turns to go, but at the last second turns back towards Yasmine. 'I'm sure you'd have plenty to contribute should you choose to get involved at some point in the future, Mrs Swift, don't you, Imogen?'

As a broad smile stretches across my face I hear Yasmine spluttering about busy schedules and other commitments.

'Absolutely,' I say to her, trying not to look smug. 'The more the merrier.'

23

*The clock is ticking: for my interview, for school places,
for my marr— No, don't think about that now.*

Lily

I check my teeth in the toilet mirror for stray bits of
food and smooth a bit of hair back into my ponytail.
It was so busy in the office this morning that it's only
now that I've started to get nervous about my interview.
I know I'm capable, but so is Eddie. And he wants it
just as much as I do. It still stings that he's my work
superior, but this job is my chance to prove myself. I like
working with him, but I know I deserve to be further
up the hierarchy than I am now. Further up than him.
I've been preparing and preparing, glad of something to
focus on, and not just because of the job itself. My mind
keeps straying back to Will and what happened. I reread
the text I got this morning, from a number I don't have
saved, and try and focus on the breathing techniques I
listened to (albeit at 1.5 speed) on a meditation app that
Amanda recommended.

Can we talk?

It can only be him. I've managed to dodge the school run
for almost two weeks, through a combination of pretending

to be ill to Imogen and Joe being on his best baby campaign behaviour, but now, somehow, he's got my number.

Breathe in for five, Lily.

Joe thinks my resolve is crumbling, but I'm only tolerating his cheating and constant baby 'hints' because, having half sexed the vicar, I'm in no position to take the moral high ground and give him the full force of my anger. Instead I have to listen to him 'muse' about how different a personality Enid's sibling would have, or if his company would let him work from home one day a week to accommodate nursery and school runs. Every time he brings it up I feel sick. I can barely look at him, and just block it out by not listening and nodding, although the other day I exploded at him talking as though a second baby is a given. I don't know if I want one, I told him, and my body is pretty key to the whole project. It hasn't stopped him trying to initiate sex, although invoking 'her' is getting me off the hook for now.

Fuck, what a mess.

I inexpertly apply some mascara to try and perk up my face. How did the vicar get my number? I have no strategy for dealing with this situation, other than to avoid him as well as thinking about it until I figure it out. But if Enid gets a place at the school – which we'll know the week after next – that's not going to be sustainable. Seven more years of seeing him at church every week.

And I'm not sure how much longer I can rely on Imogen. Her last text made it clear she suspects that either I'm not ill at all, or that I'm *really* ill, on a par with Clara. And that's not fair. But I'm avoiding her too, because she and Will are working on some project or other together, and what if she brings it up with him? Or, God forbid, tells Yasmine. If they're even still friends after that blow-up at Enid's birthday.

Focus, Lily. Interview questions.

I have half an hour. I mentally run through our recent cases and how my contribution has directly impacted revenue recovery for the Crown. My phone starts ringing on the sink. St P&P's. That's never a good omen during the working day. I snatch it up, rattled.

'Hello? Is Enid OK?'

'Mrs Walker? Mr Brown's secretary Nicola here. I'm calling because there's been an incident. Would you be able to come into the school?'

'Is Enid OK?' My heart is hammering in my chest. 'An accident? What's happened?'

'She's fine.' Her voice is crisp. 'It's an incident rather than an accident. Mr Brown would rather discuss it face to face. Can you come?'

'What does that mean? She's not hurt or ill, is she?'

'No.'

'When do you need me to come in?'

'As soon as possible.'

Annoyance briefly displaces the worry. The same kind of frustration at being locked out – again – of an online account you can never remember the password for. Because it's always me they call, isn't it? Never Joe.

'I have a meeting in half an hour,' I say. 'I could ask my husb—' As I say it, my brain snags on the word 'incident' again. Shit. I'd definitely say that semi-shagging the vicar counts as an incident, and of course they're not going to discuss that over the phone. Fuck, I'm being called in to explain what happened to the head teacher. Who told him – Will? Was that 'can we talk?' to try and forewarn me about this? Maybe what we did is a conflict of interests when it comes to school place applications, and in a fit of vicarly scruples he decided it had to be declared. All I know is I need Joe as far away from the school as possible.

I realise I'm holding my breath and exhale loudly. The heart-hammering is back. 'Let me move the meeting. I'll be there as soon as I can.'

I've never actually been into the main school before and getting anywhere near Mr Brown's office is a two-step process. One door into the holding pen outside the secretary's window, and then another to get into the waiting room itself, both only accessible when Nicola presses the release button. I walk in nervously, expecting to see Will, but I'm the only one in here. Maybe we're going to be questioned separately, or maybe it's just me that's going to be punished for it. Blaming the woman would be very on-brand for St P&P's moral code. The room's painted in rainbow colours, with the school motto ('Do unto thy neighbour') scrawled in wavy script around the border at the ceiling. It's meant to be sunny and bright, but still has all the allure of the waiting room at the clap clinic, and much like that it comes with the ominous feeling of being in trouble, but not knowing exactly how, or how badly. I check my phone for the eight millionth time. Amanda hasn't responded to my email pleading to rearrange the job interview. I'm not surprised. She's been so kind to me over these last few weeks, both professionally and personally. Cancelling a job interview she recommended me for, by email, with less than twenty minutes' notice, is not just bad form, it's really rude.

I looked for her before I left, but the interviews were back-to-back today. Eddie disappeared from his desk before I got the call to come here: he's the last one before my no-show. Not getting the job at all is devastating but to lose out to Eddie is somehow even worse. He'd be good, I know that, but I know I'm better. I won't have the chance to prove that now.

The door from the reception window clicks and then rattles but doesn't open. A knot of dread works its way from my stomach into my throat. It clicks again, and the same thing happens, and then I hear the muffled sound of Nicola shouting, 'Push it after it buzzes, no *after*,' with increasing levels of irritation in her voice. I can barely sit still at the thought of us both being trapped in here, waiting to find out our punishment. Maybe I should have just responded to his text. The panto with the door goes on for two minutes before it finally releases, but instead of the vicar Imogen falls into the room, red-faced after putting too much effort behind her final push.

'Imogen! What are you doing here?'

'I got a call that I had to come in. What are *you* doing here?' She pauses and looks me over. 'You look . . . well?' It's an accusation dressed up as a question. I can't really blame her, seeing as I'm sitting here in my best suit with a full face of make-up on despite feigning illness for over a week.

'I was at work when they rang.' I flap a hand at my front in vague explanation. 'I got the same phone call.'

What has Imogen got to do with me and the vicar? Oh God, has the vicar really had a thing with me *and* Imogen? I search her face for signs of guilt. She just looks worried. But about Winnie or herself? I shift uncomfortably in my seat.

'Ms Roberts? Mrs Walker? Please go through,' Nicola interrupts, coming out from behind her window and ushering us into a large airy office where neat binders line shelves behind a large uncluttered desk. The only things that stand on it are a little collection of potted succulents, an Apple laptop and a fancy fountain pen, with Mr Brown sitting behind it in an expensive-looking ergonomic chair. The window behind him has wooden blinds – not the usual horrible metal ones – and a few pictures are dotted around the walls, done by children by the looks of them, but they're in tasteful wooden frames, so the effect is less ramshackle than the waiting area. So this is Mr Brown's domain. It's all very Marie Kondo considering he's the head teacher of a primary school.

Mr Brown stands up, a manoeuvre that takes no small bit of effort considering his age and doddery frame. I stand there wondering whether I should help him or if that would be considered patronising. As soon as he's upright, he says, 'Sit down, sit down,' and without looking at each other we slide into the square armchairs that face his desk. Mr Brown sits back down, painfully slowly, as the ominous feeling burrows further into my stomach. I look around to see if the vicar is going to make an appearance, and resist the urge to blurt out what a terrible mistake it all was and please not to take it out on Enid.

'Thank you both for coming in,' he says, closing his laptop. 'It's quite a delicate matter, which is why I wanted to see you both in person.'

Sick, I feel sick. Why would he bring us here together? I can't even look at Imogen. Have we both got off with the same bloke? It would be nauseating if we were still in our twenties, but now it's humiliating too.

'Yes, Mr Brown,' we chorus. We've regressed into the schoolgirl version of ourselves, sitting up straight and looking earnestly in his direction.

'Your daughters, er, Enid and Winnie – is that right?' We nod. 'Are both at our preschool.'

'Yes,' we chirrup.

'I was told Enid was fine, though,' I add. 'She's not hurt.'

'Me too. About Winnie, that is.'

'Right, right.' He pauses, and we wait for him to get to the point. It's agonising. Is this where he brings up the rule I've contravened about parents fraternising with the vicar? I mean, aside from the Bible rule, that is. 'I've had a report from Charlotte in Gabriel room that the girls have been seen making –' his voice lowers to a whisper '– an *obscene* gesture in the playground.'

'WHAT?' I burst out in relieved laughter, and look across at Imogen, who is staring at Mr Brown incredulously. She turns to look at me and laughs nervously too. 'What?' I repeat. 'What does that even mean?'

Mr Brown shoots a stern look at me in reprimand. 'I don't think it's funny, Mrs Walker. This is a serious allegation. We need to investigate.'

I press my lips together to smother a grin. Imogen has her hand in front of her mouth, trying to hide her muffled sniggers with a cough, and hearing it sets my giggles off again. He doesn't know. *Thank God*.

'Mrs Walker, Ms Roberts,' Mr Brown says sharply. 'A report about a sexual gesture is serious. It can result in social services getting involved.'

The shock makes me gasp out loud. Imogen is also silent, her hand frozen in front of her mouth, but her eyes look frightened. 'You're not serious. What sort of gesture –' I can't bring myself to say 'obscene' '– was it? She hasn't taken her clothes off in public since she was two.'

'Her clothes were on,' is all Mr Brown says.

'So, what then? I obviously don't need you to demonstrate, but could you describe it?'

Mr Brown shuts me down. 'It was inappropriate.'

I look at Imogen, trying with my eyes to urge her to say something, but she just looks terrified. 'Social services?' she whispers in the end.

'Mr Brown.' My voice is jagged. 'You cannot threaten us with social services if you're not prepared to tell us what our children are supposed to have done. How are we meant to judge whether it's inappropriate if we don't know what it is?'

'I don't know what you consider appropriate at home, but *I* will be the judge of what is appropriate in my school, and this most certainly wasn't.'

'She's never shown any signs of doing anything remotely "obscene" at home,' I snap. 'And I want to know what it is. *Now.*'

'From what I can gather, Mrs Walker, you'd hardly know if that was the case. I understand you habitually work long hours that take you away from the home.' His tone is pitying, but I know exactly where he's going with this. The implication of blame is right there in his ancient, saggy eyes. 'It can be so difficult to keep track of what your child is being exposed to when you're not around to supervise.'

'WHAT?' I explode. Next to me, I hear Imogen gasp. Blood pounds through my body and before I know it I'm out of my seat and pacing the room. 'So not only are you saying that Enid is displaying sexual behaviour, but you're also saying that the reason she's doing it is because I have a *job*?' Mr Brown is staring at me silently, as though my reaction only proves what he's just said. I run a hand over my hair and mutter to myself. 'I knew this school had some backward attitudes, but are you having an actual laugh? Yes, I work long hours, Mr Brown, but so do a lot of women. So do a lot of men! And when I'm not at home, do you know who is? Her father. Who probably would have mentioned it if she was displaying the behaviour you're accusing her of.'

Imogen stands up and puts a hand on my arm. I flinch, expecting her to try and calm me down, but instead she gives it a squeeze and shouts, 'YES!'

Her face is flushed with anger and she's glowering in Mr Brown's direction. 'What's your theory behind Winnie, Mr Brown? I only work part-time, but apparently she's also a deviant.'

'I didn't say deviant,' Mr Brown starts to stutter, terrified by two women shouting at him and knowing he's lost control of the situation. 'Winnie has had a lot of upheaval what with moving to a new area, so that may be why she has acted out. But we also find in these situations that one child is a natural leader and others are followers.'

Red spots. There are big red spots in front of my eyes, but I fight to keep my tone neutral, despite the fury pulsing through me. 'I see. And you have Enid down as a ringleader, do you? Everything you've said today has consolidated what I've been wrestling with for some time now. St Peter and Paul's is not the right place for my daughter to receive an education. I know school places aren't announced until the beginning of April but if we *have* been allocated a place, it's safe to say we'll be turning it down.'

'Look here, Mrs Walker,' Mr Brown starts to say, but I don't hang around to listen to any more. I tear at the office door handle and throw it open.

'And by the way, the Nativity most definitely *is* a made-up story,' I spit over my shoulder. It's the perfect exit. Right up until I get caught in the same door click loop that Imogen did on the way in.

24

After all this, are we about to be expelled anyway?

Imogen

I watch Lily leave and stand stock-still in Mr Brown's office. Part of me wants to go full Thelma and Louise, tell him to go fuck himself and that Winnie's out too, but the other part – the *much* bigger part – is terrified he's going to lump Winnie in with Enid and say that we're all expelled. He never actually said what the outcome of this was before Lily stormed out.

'I'm so sorry about all this,' I say in a toadying voice that makes me hate myself.

Mr Brown frowns, as though I am an irritating distraction. 'I think Mrs Walker's behaviour has demonstrated where Enid gets her impetuous streak from.'

Enid is a four-year-old child, I want to say, but I don't. 'What you said . . .' I start. I can barely bring myself to remind him of it. 'About social services. That won't be necessary, will it?'

He gives me a gruff but somewhat sympathetic smile. 'I'll check in with Charlotte. I'd say it's unlikely. That was more to try and get to the bottom of it all, but I think we've got our answer, don't you?'

The fact that it was a threat doesn't stop my hands

296

shaking. 'Unlikely' isn't a definite no. 'OK. So, Winnie isn't expelled then?'

He peers at me, surprised. 'No.'

'And Enid?'

'Neither of the girls will have to leave the preschool. But I must say, Mrs Walker withdrawing her application for the next academic year has prevented me from having to make a difficult decision.'

'Oh. OK,' I hear myself say. 'I hope this doesn't affect our application to the school.'

All Mr Brown says is, 'After all the good work you've been doing for the school this year, you'd do well to keep your child away from unchristian influences, Ms Roberts.'

I just nod. Letting my silence betray Lily, as though that's any better.

'I think that's all,' he says. And I am dismissed.

I catch up with Lily outside the school gates. She's leaning on the wall with her head back, breathing heavily. Her eyes fly open as I approach.

'What have I done?' she groans, worry etched all over her face. Then her jaw sets in a grim line. 'How dare he.'

'I know,' I say. 'I'm still no clearer on what they're supposed to have done.'

She gives me a thin smile. 'I'll have to ask Enid to demonstrate. I hope we haven't ruined your chances of getting into the school.'

I keep quiet for a moment, and then I blurt, 'I ended up apologising to him. I'm a terrible person. I feel like a traitor.'

Lily smiles, more broadly this time. 'You *are* a traitor,' she says, but I can tell she's joking. 'Don't be daft. You moved here to get Winnie into a good school. And this *is* a good school. The best school.' Her eyes are shining, but I can't work out if she's upset or they're tears of annoyance. 'I can't send her here, though, Imogen. Although I'm sure we wouldn't have got a place anyway, even before this happened, but I can't pretend to be their type of Christian. The people you have to keep in with – sorry, I don't mean you – it's so two-faced. He's right, we're not the right sort. I'm not, anyway.'

'You say that like it's a bad thing,' I tell her. 'It's not, believe me. The moral code is all upside down here. I should know, I'm as bad as all of them.'

'The hypocrisy was making me physically ill,' she says. She looks completely desolate.

'I thought it was being pregnant that was making you ill,' I quip, trying to lighten the mood.

From the stunned expression on her face, I'm guessing I'm wrong about that. 'You're joking, aren't you?' she says quietly. 'I'm definitely not pregnant. And have no intention of being.' She lets out a deep breath. 'It's a long story. God, I have no idea what to do now. Do I pick Enid up early? Is she expelled? What time is it?'

'Two. And they're not expelled. It's business as usual.'

She looks up and down the street as though the answer will emerge from one direction or another.

'Do you need to go back to work?' I ask.

Her face, if it's possible, looks even more downcast. 'No,' she sighs. 'I don't think so, anyway. It's another long story.'

'In that case, do you want to go and get a coffee?' I think about stopping there, but we've just been threatened with social services. 'I could do with someone to talk to.'

'So what you're telling me is, I've been excommunicated even though I *haven't* slept with the vicar, while you've had a torrid fling with him that no one knows about?'

'SHHH.' Lily looks around the café, a greasy spoon that does giant slabs of Victoria sponge, not a red velvet in sight, and chosen for the very reason that it's not the kind of place any of the other parents come to. We're surrounded by the builders who are working on the new apartment blocks, as they sit around the Formica tables and fuel up on tea. Lily rests her head in her hands. 'It's not a torrid fling. It was an almost-thing. Half a thing.' She pauses. 'I told you, I don't belong in a Christian school. I'm a bad person.'

'Without getting all biblical about it, isn't it part of being a Christian to err? Besides, you just told me that Joe – who, by the way, has been a douche for about four years now – shagged someone in America. How are you the bad guy?'

'That doesn't mean I'm blameless,' she says gloomily. She pours a sachet of sugar into her tea. 'Just that we're both the bad guy. What a mess.'

'Have you spoken to him?'

'Joe? We speak all the time. Well, he speaks, and I say words back occasionally. He wants me to get over it and have another baby.'

'No, sorry, I meant Will. The vicar.'

Lily rarely blushes. But she does now. 'No.' Her body language seems to tighten. She's clammed up. 'But I got this message.' She swipes through her phone and shows me. 'I think it's his number.'

I get my own phone out and have a look through the short message chain we exchanged before I started keeping my distance. 'Yep.'

'I've been avoiding him. Which will be easier now there's no need to go to church on a Sunday. I don't know what to say. Or even whether to reply.'

'Do you like him? I mean, if you weren't married with a kid, and he wasn't the vicar. Or even if he was the vicar and you weren't with Joe?'

'I barely know him,' she reminds me. 'And it's irrelevant. It was a really stupid thing to do, a childish reaction against all the stuff with Joe.'

'And what about another baby?'

She snorts. 'Because in the history of the world, having a baby has been proven to be the best way to patch up a failing relationship. The thought of it makes me want to run away from my life. But while Joe thinks it's on the table, and while he thinks he's "making it up to me", he's being the hands-on father I've desperately wanted him to be. I know what he's like when he doesn't get what he wants.'

'Petulant.'

Lily looks at me in surprise.

'I lived in that flat too, remember? I saw what he was like when he went for that job interview and didn't get it.'

'God, he still has a vendetta against that agency. We're not allowed to buy any products by the people they represent. I need to deal with it. All of it. Somehow.' She looks off into the middle distance for a moment and then seems to snap back into the room. 'But what about you? Everything's going well – well, aside from this – right?'

The urge to agree is so strong. But I don't have the energy to keep up the front any more. Not with Lily. 'You're joking, aren't you?'

'But I thought . . .' She stops. 'I've been so jealous of the way you and Danny parent together. I mean, you both seemed a bit weird at Christmas, but I thought that was about the flat sale.'

'It was about the flat. But then it turned out it wasn't just about the flat. It turns out that he thinks I had a lobotomy when I had Winnie, and all I care about is mum stuff. We might be all right parents but we're currently a shitty couple.' I try to laugh, but it comes out as a sob. 'At the moment we barely talk to each other when it's not about Winnie.'

'But . . . so what?' She gestures a bit too wildly with her mug and tea sloshes out. She grabs a handful of napkins from the metal dispenser on the table. 'Danny adores you. It's obvious. Have you talked to him about it?'

Another laugh, more bitter this time. 'I'm not sure he even likes me right now. We've just got good at keeping up appearances. I'm too scared to have a proper conversation with him about it in case he tells me that it's over. The whole time I thought Jusna's marriage was falling apart I kept thinking how awful it would be if Danny left us. Left me.' I stir my drink to give me something to concentrate on. It looks all misty as tears flood my eyes. 'Of course not only are Jusna and Ajay fine, she's pregnant too. Some people get everything they want, don't they?'

'Wait.' Now she looks confused. 'Jusna and Ajay are back together?'

'They were never broken up.' I raise an eyebrow. 'They faked it so they could register a second address.'

'Cheeky bastards!' Lily smiles. 'Is it bad that I'm quite impressed? So, I'm guessing that's all wrapped up in your beef with Yasmine?'

'The bit where I snitched on Jusna to get back at Yasmine for nicking my flat probably sealed the deal. I feel bad about that. Well, bad about snitching. Not about getting back at Yasmine. You were right about her.' Lily laughs, nodding in a knowing way and forking a bit of the giant cake into her mouth. I resist the compulsion to tell her to tuck in. She's far too thin.

'She used me for some school campaign thing, stole my

flat, then she spread the rumour that I was shagging the vicar, presumably to keep Jusna's chances up. And now I have no friends at St P and P's. Not even you.'

'We can still be friends, even though Enid won't be at the school. And with a bit of luck Bex will get in, and Clara too.' She swigs her tea thoughtfully. 'I forgot about this café. I used to come here with Enid when I was on maternity leave rather than the new hipster ones where all the mums seemed to be mates with each other and I felt like a loser. Everyone here used to make a fuss of her and I'd get to read the paper for twenty minutes.'

On the table, her phone rings. Lily jumps and then looks at it as though it's a grenade about to explode. The name Amanda is on the screen.

'Who's Amanda?'

'She's the boss I was supposed to have a job interview with today before I had to cancel and come to the school. It's not just my personal life that's a mess, Im.'

'Answer it,' I urge.

She sits up straighter and picks it up, taking a big breath in before accepting the call. 'Hi, Amanda. Before you say anything, I can't apologise enough for today. It was completely wrong of me to leave at such short—' She purses her lips as she's cut off. Her face reminds me of that night she told me she was worried she'd never meet anyone. 'Oh,' she says next, before relief spreads across her face. 'Yes.' I'm dying to know what this 'Amanda' is saying. 'That would be wonderful, thank you. Yes, see you then. Bye.' She pulls the phone away from her ear and checks she's hung up, staring at it a bit disbelievingly.

'She says they can still see me. Tomorrow. First thing.' The colour has come back to her face. 'I'm still in with a chance.'

25

School places available – to us? Minus infinity. Shit,
shit, shit.

Lily

I give Yasmine a cheery wave, to the point where she looks
over her shoulder to see who I'm directing it at, because no
way can it be her. There's no one there. She looks back,
shooting us both the filthiest of filthy looks. 'I feel so free,
Imogen!' I say, which is obviously bollocks, but I push
away thoughts of all the other things that I am currently
shackled by. Rubbish marriage, vicar who could blow my
life apart with one email to Joe, the problem of where to
send my daughter to school in September. 'I mean, my
daughter will probably end up being the sort of character
I arrest in a tax evasion raid in fifteen years' time while
your child is applying to Oxbridge, but at least I won't
have to see Yasmine every day for the next seven years.'

'Don't. You're actually making me jealous. Not the
criminal daughter bit. Although isn't my daughter supposed
to be so easily led that Enid will probably draw her into
her web anyway? The difference is that she'll just be a
lackey, rather than the mastermind.'

'What can I say, some people are sheep.' It doesn't feel
comfortable joking about it, but I don't know what else to
do. Maybe if I get this promotion we can send her private?

I try not to get ahead of myself and jinx it. Amanda's phone call has been the only decent thing to come out of these shitty few weeks. I look across at where Imogen is standing next to me by the school gate, as we wait for our daughters. Well, maybe there have been two decent things.

The gate opens, and we move as a wave into the playground towards the nursery entrance.

'Mummy, Mummy!' Enid runs towards me, a clutch of blobby paint-drenched bits of card in her hand. She's so happy to see me when I come and pick her up. If only I could do my job and make it here every day to fetch her.

I notice Will in my peripheral vision, plus there's that ripple of mum-giggling that seems to follow him around. He's laden down with bags-for-life that are overflowing with Easter eggs. We lock eyes before I quickly turn away. Imogen busies herself with zipping up Winnie's coat, deliberately not looking in his direction.

'Shall I meet you back at mine with the girls?' she says, standing back up and communicating via the medium of unsubtle eye gestures that I should go and talk to him.

'Mummy, yes!' shouts Enid. 'Let's have tea at Winnie's. Her mummy makes nicer pasta than you.'

Charming. 'Er, I'm not sure we were being invited to eat there, Enid—'

'Yes, good, that's sorted then,' says Imogen briskly. She grabs each of their hands. 'Let's go. Your mummy just has to talk to the vicar about . . .' Her eyes widen as she gets to the end of the sentence without having thought through the lie. I watch her face as she mentally contorts what to say next.

'Hymnbooks!' I shout.

All three of them look at me like I'm mad, including Imogen, who is supposed to be helping me. Hymnbooks, FFS.

'Errr, yes, hymnbooks for the twin school in Africa. He wanted to ask me about export duties for sending them over.' Enid's eyes glaze over as they always do when I talk about my job. The only time she was vaguely impressed was when I passed my advanced driving course and took her in a car with the sirens on. 'I'll catch you up.'

Before I can talk myself out of it, I shout 'Will!' to get his attention. It comes out all shaky. I feel like all the other parents are looking at me as I approach him, even though now we're so close to school place announcements no one is taking the slightest bit of notice.

He stops, giving me a nervous smile. There's about ten metres still between us. 'Let me help you with those bags,' I offer, for something to say, as well as something to do with my hands.

'Sure. I'm taking them to the church hall,' he says, his voice even. 'We're making a stockpile to give to the food bank.' If I wasn't so jumpy, this would seem like a perfectly normal conversation. I take one of the bags and follow him out of the school gate and down the road to the hall next door, keeping my eyes to the ground the whole way. He unlocks the double doors and I follow him in. 'This way,' he says cheerfully. 'There's a larder in the kitchen we can lock them into.' It crosses my mind that we're now alone in the church hall and what that might mean. What would I want it to mean? He's wearing a black jacket so I can only see his hands carrying the bags, but I know – God, do I know – what his taut arms look like underneath. But he's giving me no indication that we've shared anything other than communion wine. I'm starting to doubt he even sent that text. There's a skittish feeling barrelling around in my stomach.

He pushes open the kitchen door with his hip, staying close to it to hold it open for me, and then snaps on the light, a dim bare bulb. I go in and put my bag down on the counter. I wonder, after this year, if I'll ever enter this hall again. Will Enid still get invited to the other kids' parties when she's at some other primary school? Will she want to go, or will she make other friends and forget the ones from nursery? Please let her make other friends easily.

'So,' says Will, coming up next to me and putting his bags down. 'You got my text.'

'Yes. Sorry for not replying. I didn't know what to say. I still don't.'

'I wanted to put the other night behind us, in person.'

'Oh, right.' Even though this is probably exactly the right thing to say, my feelings are scorched. Putting it behind us means it was a mistake. Which it was. But hearing him say it seems harsh. 'Yes. Put it behind us. That's the best thing to do. I don't want things to be awkward.'

'And I also wanted to tell you that I've decided to leave the church.'

'What?' I actually take a step back from him. There's no way I can deal with the responsibility of this right now. 'Because of –' how would I even describe it? '– the thing with us?'

He crinkles up his face as though it's neither a yes nor a no. 'Because of a lot of things. I'm telling Mr Brown at the end of the term.'

'ABOUT US?' I might actually vomit in the kitchen of the church hall.

'No, sorry, that didn't come out right. I'm telling him about my decision to leave at the end of term, but I wanted to let you know that, as of next year, you won't have to worry about any awkwardness at church or school events, because

I won't be here. I know you think I only made a move on you out of some self-destructive reflex, which is probably not totally untrue –' he smiles, and it gives me a flash of the sexy cheeky man he must have been in his twenties '– but in all honesty, I'm not sure seeing the married parishioner I like as more than a congregant would be wise.'

A dizziness sweeps through me. The room seems too bright, even though the bulb is too low a wattage for it. I like the fact that he said it too much.

'You won't need to worry about that. I – we,' I correct, 'aren't going to be in church either,' I say. 'Enid's not coming to this school next year.'

He fixes me with a look. 'There's no need to hedge your bets. I've seen the list. She has a place.'

I ignore the punched-stomach feeling of knowing how badly I've fucked this up. She *was* in. 'No. No, she doesn't.' I force myself to be cheerful. 'Mr Brown and I parted ways earlier today. It's fine. This isn't the right place for us. Just like it isn't for you.'

He nods as though he understands.

'What are you going to do?' I ask him.

He pulls a big bunch of keys out of his pocket and unlocks the larder door. 'I'm going abroad for a while, I think. My friend runs an NGO in Cambodia and I'm going to volunteer there for a while in the legal aid field – I have a law degree and have used it over the years when assisting parishioners with domestic situations. I think that's what I'll be aiming for eventually.' He picks up one of the bags from the counter and deposits it on a shelf, giving me a wry smile as he does. 'But who knows? It's a relief to have made a decision.'

'It sounds like you're doing the right thing.' I'm jealous. Not of Cambodia, but of taking control of the things making him unhappy. For the first time, I allow myself to think it: *I want to separate from my husband.*

I pass him another bag, and our hands touch briefly as he takes the handles from me. I pull them quickly away. 'What about you?' he says. 'Enid will be absolutely fine, by the way. There are other good schools around here.'

'I know. I'll work it out. There are a lot of things I need to work out. But I'm glad we had this chat. Good luck with your next step.'

He nods again, shutting the larder door and locking it. I feel like I need to get out of here, so I start walking out of the kitchen without waiting for him.

'For what it's worth,' he says from behind me, 'if you ever need someone to talk to, you have my number.'

I let out a whoosh of air and turn to give him a grateful smile. 'I'm not sure that's a good idea, but thanks.' I turn to go again, and then pause. It's worth a try. 'If you have any sway over that list and she's not already on there – which, by the way, I don't want the responsibility of knowing – can you give Imogen's daughter Enid's place?'

I feel like all I've done today is leave places, but as I walk out of the church door, maybe for the last time, it feels like I've actually cleared up one of my messes rather than blown something else up.

A glass of red wine is waiting for me when I get to Imogen's. 'How did it go?' she murmurs into the cooker, while stirring some sort of sausage pasta sauce.

The ten-minute walk hasn't done anything to stop my heart banging as hard as it was when I caught that crim, but I say, 'OK. I'll explain later.' Imogen gives me a little close-mouthed smile.

'Things will work out. I can help you look into the other schools. I've got a binder with all my research in it about the other primaries in the area.'

I chuckle. Classic Im. This is what this year should have been about. Imogen and me, Enid and Winnie. Hanging out with our daughters and sharing the load. 'Thank you,' I say quietly. 'For everything, Imogen. I know I'm really bad at showing it, but I really do appreciate how you've helped me out.'

'Oh, shush,' she says back. 'I just wish we'd spent more time together and I hadn't wasted it with the wrong people.'

'Why are you whispering?' Enid interrupts.

'Because we're talking about Winnie's birthday in the summer,' Imogen fires back.

'Am I having a face-painting party?' Winnie asks.

'I don't know, are you? Maybe that's why we need to whisper.'

The two girls start giggling. 'In the meantime, why don't we have a kitchen party while I finish making your dinner?'

'Mummy's party mix, please!' shouts Winnie.

Imogen presses a button and the 'Grease Megamix' booms out of some speakers on the kitchen counter. The girls start jumping up and down.

'You always had super-cool taste in music,' I tell her.

She laughs. 'It's a classic. It's been on every party playlist I've made since 1997. Besides, they bloody love it.'

Enid and Winnie are screeching along, and Imogen goes back to stirring while singing both the girls' and boys' parts in the voices of the respective *Grease* characters, occasionally throwing in a Rizzo- or Danny-style gesticulation. I watch them absently and sip my wine. Joe's going back to Detroit early tomorrow. He went on and on assuring me that he wouldn't see 'her' while he's there and that I could trust him. My nausea at the prospect he might is still less than my relief that he'll be out of the way for a few days. Just Enid and me. It's harder, but in a lot of ways simpler at the same time.

'Wait for it, wait for it,' Imogen says as the song builds up. As they all shout 'wella wella wella, huh', the girls explode into a round of joyful T-Bird-style pelvic thrusts and I burst out laughing. Until Imogen stops dead and claps a hand over her mouth. 'Oh my God, Lil,' she says, completely mortified. 'It was me. *I* taught them the obscene gesture.'

26

Imogen

The front door bangs, shocking me from where I'm sitting on the sofa, guilt humming through me. Lily left with Enid twenty minutes ago, insisting that it didn't matter where the girls picked the obscene gesture up from, and that Enid would never have got a school place anyway. But she might have, and it's my fault that she hasn't. She wouldn't talk about it over tea, although the girls sitting there made anything but coded messages impossible anyway. Is there anything I can do to make it up to her?

'Oh,' is all Danny says as he walks in and sees me there.

After talking to Lily earlier I was all set to try and speak to him, properly. Especially after hearing how bad things are with Joe. I don't want that to be Danny and me, with nothing left between us but our child. But his flat 'oh' is even more insulting than our now default withdrawn-yet-respectful routine, and my hackles instantly rise. I've had enough of being ignored by him. I'm sick of not knowing the rules of who I can speak to, and how.

'What, Danny?' I say in a tense voice. 'Is it annoying you that I'm sitting here in my own living room, just *mumming* around the place?'

I don't know what sort of greeting he was expecting, but it wasn't that. He hasn't even taken his coat off yet.

It's clear I'm picking a fight, though, and his participatory reflex kicks right in.

'I didn't realise you'd be here,' he says tightly. 'I thought it was one of your playdate days, or if not, I thought you'd be blogging about your last playdate.' The word 'playdate' here could easily be substituted for 'drink with Kim Jong-un' and the tone of the sentence would remain exactly the same.

'The playdate has happened, and Winnie is now putting her Sylvanians to bed,' I reply, mirroring his tone. My anger is simmering, feeding on itself. 'But spending time with our kid is what, contemptible now?'

'No,' he says with a sigh that says 'I can't be arsed to get into this'. But then he moves a step closer from the hallway, and away from Winnie's room. His eyes are pure steel. 'It is if you're doing it to exploit it online.'

'WHAT?' What the fuck is he talking about?

'I've been reading your blog, Im, and I've been trying to keep quiet about it, but the way you talk about Winnie, the way you talk about it all, it's as though you're using us to fabricate some fantasy version of a mummy-blogger life that I don't even recognise.'

'The blog. I didn't know you read my blog.'

He takes off his jacket and flings it over the back of a chair. Said chair is dangerously close to toppling over due to all the other coats hanging off it, but I force myself not to reprimand him about it. 'I haven't for ages. I used to, when Winnie was a baby and I was at work. It gave me an insight into what you were doing at home, and what the challenges were. You often talked about things I hadn't even thought of and it gave me a different perspective. I've been trying to work out what's been going on in your head recently, and thought it might help. But I don't recognise the people in the posts. And I don't recognise the person writing them.'

I think about my last few blogs. All the #mumcrew hashtags, fabricated days out with Danny and interiors #inspo for a house we don't even own. I knew he looked at it now and again but didn't think he *read* it.

'It's just stuff I write, to keep posting, and to keep my followers up,' I say sullenly. Guiltily.

He walks over to the sofa and drops onto it. It makes a whoomphing sound as he does. 'I feel like since we moved here, I don't know where you've gone,' he says. My barriers are up but his voice is gentler than I was expecting. He sounds uncertain, but he sounds more like himself than he has for weeks. 'It feels like this — us — isn't enough for you.'

'*Me*?' I burst out. 'It's *you* that doesn't want to be here. You don't want to get married, you don't want to live around here, you don't want to have another baby.' I tick them off on my fingers as tears start leaking from my eyes.

'Wait. Who says I don't want to get married? I *did* want to get married. But not to get into a school or to create content for a Pinterest board or something.' He fixes his blue eyes on me, his face as hurt as I've been feeling since that stupid row at the school play. 'How many times have I proposed to you, Im?'

I shrug, but my heart is leaping. 'A few.'

He pulls a face. 'And then I proposed a few more times. *You* never wanted to. Until the school thing. I do want to marry you, but only *if* it's because you actually want to get married. Otherwise I'm quite happy to be your permanent boyfriend. *Do* you want to get married?'

'Is that your proposal?'

He sighs in mock annoyance. 'No. It's a question. An adult conversation about what you actually want, which I will use as the basis for any future proposals.'

I think about it. Winnie would like it, especially if we have a party. But could I even get my parents in the same room, never mind at the same table, without killing each other or ruining the day? Do I want to wear a white dress? Do I want to spend a lot of money on a generic party?

'No,' I say automatically.

'OK then,' Danny says with a smile. 'As for a baby . . .' He rubs a hand over his face, blinking a bit. 'We've never even talked about it. You seemed out of sorts coming here, and so focused on moving house and getting into the school that it wasn't something on my radar.' He drops his voice. 'Plus, we haven't had sex for a *really* long time.'

'Because you haven't wanted to.' Shame pulses through me as I remember the aborted sex attempt, but there, I've said it. We might as well get to the bottom of it. Something squeezes inside as I realise this is the moment he could tell me he doesn't love me any more. Doesn't fancy me either. This could be the end. 'I tried, and you knocked me back.'

'That day I was working?' He looks bewildered. 'Im, it had been over a year and I was waiting for a call from my boss. I was hoping our first time this year could be slightly more of an event.' He gives me a weak smile. 'After that it felt like you weren't that interested in me. I was just a name on a webpage that I didn't even recognise.' He's scratching the skin between his thumb and his forefinger, like he does when he's nervous. He was doing it in the hospital when we were there waiting for me to be induced with Winnie. One of those little gestures I stopped noticing ages ago. 'Do you know what I heard one of the parents say the other day? They obviously didn't realise I was in the park with Winnie or didn't know who I was. She said that the redhead mum is having a thing with the vicar.'

'I will fucking kill Yasmine!' I explode.

'Mummy!' Winnie shouts from her room. She's using her stern voice. 'The jar.'

'A pound in the swear jar. Sorry.' I grab my purse and make a big show of rattling the money. 'Fucking Yasmine,' I hiss, dropping some more coins in Winnie's jar. Luckily she's never got as far as counting it and doesn't realise I also use it to get change when I haven't got any cash. 'You know it's bollocks, right? It's a stupid rumour she's spreading because I told the vicar that Jusna and Ajay are only pretending to get divorced, so they can get a school place. That was Yasmine's way of trying to block our application.'

Danny looks completely lost. Now I've said all that out loud I realise how ridiculous it is. 'It's not true,' I reiterate.

'I know,' he says, although he doesn't look entirely convinced. He shakes his head slowly. 'Who would spread that kind of rumour? *Why*?'

'It's my fault,' I blurt. 'They were my friends – kind of. I attached myself to them to try and get her into the school. And then clung to them a bit when you told me I was pathetic for not wanting to work full-time.'

Danny looks horrified. 'I didn't do that.'

'You did. You said I should go back to work full-time.'

'I said you needed to work full-time *if* you wanted to buy a house around here, yes, but not because I'd think any less of you if you didn't. You were so determined to get a new place, but I couldn't make the numbers work on just my salary. It felt like it was my fault. And that you were sick of us and what we already had. I don't care if you work full-time, part-time or ad hoc as long as you're happy – and if you can accept that we can't buy a three-bedroom house in Walthamstow on one full-time and one part-time salary. I'd happily move further out of London—'

'No way,' I interrupt.

He gives me a rueful smile. 'Well then. I'm glad we didn't end up getting that money pit shithole—'

'DADDY!'

'All right, bat ears!' Danny pulls out all the change in his pocket and jangles it, before dumping it in the jar.

'Why don't you put some music on and dance?' I shout back to her.

'I want Mummy's party songs!' she squeals.

'Nope,' I shout back, mentally searching through all the music we have for something that definitely doesn't contain any sexy lyrics or provocative dance moves.

I Alexa her up with Ed Sheeran and turn my focus back to Danny.

'I was trying to go along with the place you found before Christmas, but you still didn't seem happy, and I admit I was glad when it fell through. It would have cost us at least another hundred grand just to extend the lease.'

My stomach is flipping, but in a way that for the first time in a long time doesn't feel like it's churning with anxiety. It feels like we're actually talking to each other, rather than just speaking. I think about that flat. It *was* crap. 'That's Yasmine's problem now.' Danny's about a foot away from me on the settee and I scooch over, bridging the gap. When I'm about halfway there he pulls me the rest of the way over onto his lap. He buries his head in my hair.

'For the record, I would like to have another baby with you. But the real you, not the blogger-bot on the internet.'

316

My heart explodes a little. If only Winnie weren't here, we could get started right now.

'But,' he says, tracing a line down my arm with his finger, 'can we please work on having some sex just for the fun of it, before we start trying?'

'Yes!' I say, kissing him. That's a bit annoying, but it'll do for now. The room explodes with the sound of Ed warbling on about something and we both jump. 'Turn it down, Winnie! ALEXA, VOLUME DOWN!' It drops to a less eardrum-destroying level. I wrap my arms around Danny. How long since we did this? Too long.

'You're not really having an affair with the vicar, are you?' he asks in a small voice. I consider telling him about Lily, but it's probably better he doesn't know about the vicar's antics regardless of who they're with.

'Oh, Dan.' I stroke his face kindly. 'I only wish I was conniving enough to have thought of that as a way to get into the school.'

27

9 August 2019

30 places available for the 2020 intake

Lily

The scan is unmistakable. 'Winnie's having a baby brother then?' I say, raising an eyebrow in Imogen's direction.

She laughs. Despite the fact that she says everything except the constant consumption of breadsticks – which she always carries about her person – makes her throw up, she's been beaming ever since she arrived with the printout from the hospital. 'We weren't going to find out, and this is only the twelve-week scan so it's too early anyway, but the ultrasound technician had such a clear shot there was no hiding it.'

'I'm so pleased for you.'

'Me too,' says Bex, sniffing through her hay fever and pulling Grey back onto the patchwork of picnic blankets, from where he's making a break for the spiky grass to pull into his mouth. 'Plus I can offload all of Grey's old stuff onto you, because I am *done*.'

'Are you sure? I'll look after them in case you go in for a third,' says Imogen.

'No way,' she fires back. 'I'm closed for baby business but open for *actual* business. I've got an interview for that job I went for.' Less than six months after she went back to her old job, Bex realised the office culture there was never going to change and has been on the hunt for a part-time position ever since. This one actually mentioned their flexible working ethos in the advert and she's desperate to get it.

'Oh, well done! Fingers crossed.'

'If I get it, it'll mean I end up starting just as school begins, but I'll cross that bridge when I come to it. Speaking of which, Imogen, have you already bought the trousers and jumper, because I've found a place online that's much cheaper than the uniform shop the school recommended.' She pulls up a webpage on her phone, showing the grey trousers and green jumpers that Ava and Winnie will need when they start at St P&P's in September, and hands it over to her to see.

Wispy clouds are floating through the blue sky above Walthamstow Marshes, and the temperature is hot and dead enough for one of us to jump up at fifteen-minute intervals and frantically apply suntan lotion to every child they can lay hands on. The children are in the playground ahead of us, ensconced in a complicated game that involves them racing each other up the climbing frame before having to buy imaginary ice creams from a random child who has set up his 'stall' at the top. When they need real sustenance, they run back over to us for juice and snacks before racing off again. It's the kind of scene I hope sticks in Enid's long-term memory, rather than the one this morning where she dropped a pair of scissors blade-down millimetres from my naked foot and I shouted at her.

'That's a *lot* cheaper, isn't it?' Imogen leans in, shielding her eyes from the sun as she takes a closer look. 'I bet there's no affordable version for you, is there?' she says to Clara.

'Nope,' Clara says with a laugh. 'You pay through the nose for *everything* at Morris School. But that's what you get for sending your kid private.' She shrugs. 'We can afford it.' She glances at me, embarrassed. 'Sorry, Lily, I didn't mean that to be as smug as it sounded. You know I'd rather have tried to keep them together. It's just such a good school and with everything this year . . .' She tails off.

'Clara, it's OK, honestly.' Even though Jeb was allocated a place at St P&P's, after a load of back and forth on it, she turned it down. Like me, she was never comfortable with having to adhere to a religion she didn't believe in, and she's had enough roulette in her life recently without playing the grammar school lottery when, like she says, she can afford to send Jeb to private primary *and* secondary school if she needs to. Her mother-in-law was desperate for her to give up work and stay at home – apparently, she read an article online about stress causing cancer – but as Clara finds being at home more stressful than the job she loves, she's back at work part-time, with a view to going back full-time once she feels up to it. Her mother-in-law has now taken to posting every article she reads about miracle cancer cures on her Facebook timeline. Clara is very close to blocking her.

'Now I've been promoted, we could probably afford to send Enid private too,' I say. 'If I wasn't desperately saving to make sure I have enough money for if Joe and I do get divorced.' It still feels like a failure every time I say the D-word out loud, but the impact has diluted into a dull feeling rather than a sharp pain.

'Is the counselling helping at all?' Imogen asks, giving me a sympathetic look.

I fiddle with one of the Tupperware boxes on the blanket. 'Sort of. She told us at the beginning that it won't help us stay together if we're not committed to it, which I found less depressing than it sounds. It hammered home that we have to do the work, as well as really think about it.' I open and shut the Tupperware lid a few times. 'Joe's already cancelled one session.'

'He hasn't?' Imogen is outraged on my behalf, but I can't muster up the same rage. I think back to the conversation I had with Amanda when she told me I'd been promoted.

'Can I offer you some unsolicited advice, Lily?' she'd said. 'My career flourished when I split up with my husband and the access arrangement meant he legally had to pick up the childcare slack.' She apologised for overstepping, but I wasn't offended at all. I'd thought about the same thing. Which shows that both of us have half a foot out of the marriage, I'd say. And that's before my regular Instagram stalking of where non-vicar Will has got to on his travels (Phnom Penh as of last week).

The other thing we've been trialling is the scope for me doing compressed hours Monday to Thursday, so on Fridays I can make it to both the school drop-off and pick-up. My 'allowances' are the only thing Eddie's been snarky about since he was told I'm now his boss, but as I'm now his boss I don't have to put up with his snark. Regular lunches with Amanda are making me feel more and more that I deserve the job, and that I don't have to pretend my family doesn't exist in order to make a success of it.

I lift up my sunglasses to check where the kids are. Enid's walking up the slide and blocking it for all the other children trying to come down.

'Enid! Off! No, *now*, please.' Jeb hurtles down the slide, narrowly missing taking her legs out from under her as she jumps out of the way. 'See,' I say. 'Someone will get hurt.' I watch them run en masse to the roundabout and start some similarly hazardous-seeming game that has me wondering if I should let them get on with it or let my overwhelming helicopter instinct to win.

'Ava! STOP. Everyone in the sandpit.' Bex makes the decision for me and buys us all five seconds before someone gets sand in their eye or mouth. 'At least you got your second-choice place,' Bex says. It's true. I rang Blake Primary the week the results came out and explained what had happened. We were lucky and they still had places.

'You know they got Ofsteded in the last two weeks of term – the poor gits – but have gone up to Outstanding,' Imogen chips in. Imogen's school research never stops, even now Winnie's a confirmed St P&Per and she's flat out working for Earth Mother. They can barely keep up with orders at the moment. Im's trying to spin the fact that they keep running out of products as a deliberate limited edition set-up, and it's turned them into a must-have cult beauty brand.

'Yes, I do know that,' I say. 'And also that the *Walthamstow News* gave them a front page because a record number of their pupils got a place at the grammar school this year.'

I see Bex and Imogen exchange a look: a moment of wondering if they put their eggs in the right basket. 'It's not too late to try and come with us,' I say jokingly, but not really. 'But if not, please don't ditch me and Enid next year when your lives are being controlled by the Organics.'

'Typical that they all got a place,' mutters Clara, rooting through another Tupperware for mini-sausages.

'Of course we won't,' Imogen says. 'Not now I've finally found my mum-crew up here. Besides, Arlo likes Enid so much, I think you'll be on the St P&P's birthday party circuit for quite some time.'

'We're going to start doing drop-off parties soon, though, right?' Surely the point where we can dump them and retire to a café – just us lot – has got to be approaching. 'Enid gets to hang out with Arlo, I get to not hang out with Yasmine – it's win-win.'

'God, I hope so,' she grins. 'Although it's all been quiet on the Yasmine front recently. I think she's got her hands full with the new baby. I ran into Kim and she said Tom hasn't taken any parental leave at all, not even during the six-week holiday to help with Arlo.' She rolls her eyes. 'But he *has* managed to squeeze in a golf weekend with his mates.' The baby is only three months old. Tom's crapness is enough to almost make me feel sorry for Yasmine.

Almost.

A big group of women with buggies and backpacks start spreading blankets out a few metres away from us. Babies are brought out of prams and laid down, while the mums put up parasols to shade them from the sun. The babies are all pretty similar in age; they can't be much more than six months old.

'That'll be you next year, Im,' I say, and she looks over, getting a dreamy look on her face. From everything she's said, she loved the early mat leave days. Rather her than me.

'They look like an NCT group,' she says. 'Do people do that with their second?'

'No,' says Bex, 'who has time for picnics in the park when you're beholden to the school run? Besides, right now sleep schedules, feeding and the contents of their babies' nappies are the eye of the storm, and the last thing they need is some second-timer making them panic about all the stuff they haven't even considered yet.'

'You're right,' I say. And then: 'Do you dare me to go over and say that I have a family house in the St Peter and Paul's catchment area that might be up for sale in the next few months?'

'Don't start turning them against each other just yet,' Imogen says, laughing. 'Besides, whatever happens, you'll be able to keep the house. We worked out the numbers.'

We did. Imogen sat me down one evening and we worked out my exit strategy, should I need it. It made me feel more in control, and I was grateful to have her there, offering me practical advice and a place to go when I needed to cry about it. But that doesn't stop the churny feeling I get when I think about what might happen.

I look back at the sandpit, where miraculously the kids are still all playing nicely. Enid and Winnie are scooping sand into a Gherkin-like structure and singing a song they made up about going to the toilet. Who knows whether Joe and I will be together in six months' time, or how Enid will find the transition to primary school in September, but I'll try and make sure her biggest concern is working out what best rhymes with poo.

I'll do whatever it takes. We all will.

We hope you enjoyed
The School Run!

If you're navigating the politics of the playground or battling for a school place, the last thing you want to do is spend hours in the kitchen.

That's where *My Fussy Eater* by Ciara Attwell comes in!

Jam-packed with easy, practical and delicious meals that the whole family will enjoy, we're delighted to be able to share two exclusive recipes from the book here.

My Fussy Eater by Ciara Attwell is available to buy now in all good bookshops.

Recipe Key:
GF – Gluten Free (or where you can easily make it gluten free with a substitute)
DF – Dairy Free (or where you can easily make it dairy free with a substitute)
FR – Freezer-friendly Recipe
BC – Batch-cook recipe
KM – Recipes that kids can help to make

Beans on Toast

GF, DF, BC, FR

Serves: 4 | Prep time: 3 minutes
Cook time: 10 minutes

Making your own baked beans at home is easier than you think.
Use a tin or carton of cooked cannellini beans and in less than
15 minutes you will have a healthy beans-on-toast breakfast with
a lot less sugar and salt than shop-bought baked beans.

Ingredients

1 tsp olive oil
1 shallot, finely chopped
1 garlic clove, crushed
300g passata
1 tbsp tomato purée
1 tsp Worcestershire sauce
1 tsp honey
½ tsp smoked paprika
¼ tsp dried mixed herbs
350g cooked cannellini beans
   from a tin or carton, drained
salt and pepper, to taste
4 slices of sourdough bread,
   to serve

Method

1. Heat the oil in a saucepan over a medium heat and add the
   chopped shallot. Fry for about 2 minutes until the onion has
   softened, then add the crushed garlic and fry for a further
   minute.

2. Add the passata, tomato purée, Worcestershire sauce, honey,
   smoked paprika and dried herbs and bring to the boil. Reduce
   the heat and simmer for 5 minutes.

3. Add the drained cannellini beans and cook for a further 2–3
   minutes until the beans are warmed through.

4. Season to taste with salt and pepper and serve on toasted
   sourdough bread.

Finn's Sweet Potato Chocolate Cake

GF, KM
Serves: 6 | Prep time: 10 minutes
Cook time: 20–25 minutes

This is my son's favourite homemade cake. In fact, the first time I made it I left it to cool on a wire rack in the kitchen. I went outside into the garden and came back to find him and the cake on the floor, and most of it eaten!

Ingredients

200g cooked and mashed sweet potato

100g apple sauce (see page 186 for my homemade apple sauce)

80g coconut oil or unsalted butter, melted, plus extra for greasing

1 tsp vanilla extract

60g plain flour

60g wholemeal flour

30g soft light brown sugar or coconut sugar

25g cocoa powder

1 tsp baking powder

1 tsp bicarbonate of soda

50g milk or dark chocolate chips

plain Greek yoghurt, raspberries and blueberries, to serve

Method

1. Preheat the oven to 200°C/180°C Fan/Gas Mark 6. Grease a 22cm round cake tin and line it with baking parchment.

2. Put the mashed sweet potato, apple sauce, melted coconut oil or butter and vanilla extract into a bowl and mix together.

3. Put the plain and wholemeal flours, light brown or coconut sugar, cocoa powder, baking powder and bicarbonate of soda into a second, larger bowl and mix well, then stir in the chocolate chips.

4. Add the wet ingredients to the dry ingredients and stir until all the ingredients have combined.
5. Pour the cake mixture into the prepared tin and bake in the oven for 20–25 minutes until a skewer inserted into the middle of the cake comes out clean.
6. Remove from the oven, leave to cool in the tin for 10 minutes, then transfer to a wire rack to cool completely.
7. Serve with Greek yoghurt and berries.

Acknowledgements

I wrote a book! It's a lifelong dream to have a book published and I still can't quite believe I am writing the acknowledgements page. Thank you so much to my super-agent Sarah Hornsley (am I the first one to use your married name?!) who has coached and championed me since she took me on in 2017, and to Sam Eades, editor extraordinaire, whose feedback (and also gossip) is always spot on. Without you both I wouldn't have got to write this book and it definitely wouldn't be as good.

I'd also like to thank the many women who have supported me, listened to me and vented to me – some mums, some not, all the heroines of their lives. This means you Al, Claire, Vickie, Ros, Natasha, Carrie, Grace, Zee, Amy, Emma, NCTers Becky, Lorna and Tasha, and the Chezzies – Liz, Anna, Nic, Charl V, Jess – and with particular thanks to Charl C who let me bombard her with questions about her job and who really *can* drag a suspect out of a car window. Any errors and/or embellishments to the world of HMRC are mine.

To my mum and dad and John, THANK YOU for basically everything. Having a voracious reader for a mum who took me to the library every Saturday morning definitely shaped my author aspirations, and having parents who have always encouraged and supported me (and in dad's case, picked me up from gig venues in various northern cities at 1 o'clock in the morning) is something I only now as an adult fully appreciate, but I really do.

There's a lot of talk about whether writing and parenthood (well, motherhood mainly, let's face it) are compatible, but for me, there's no way this book would exist without Isaac and everything he's taught me about mumming and myself (errr, maybe not all of it good in the case of the latter). I love you my hilarious, kind and smart boy.

And to Ian, who I am so glad I met and even gladder I married. The best husband and support system, not just for writing but for life. There's no one I'd rather muddle through it all with.

PS, I made it past chapter one!